still
breathing

a novel

E. A. FOURNIER

Also by E. A. Fournier

Now & Again

To Jane, my beautiful and long-suffering wife.
To Diana, my lovely Ugandan daughter-in-law.

A new broom sweeps better,
but the old one knows all the corners.

a saying claimed by many countries

ONE

Leaving Hospice

The dying room was cheerful. Long ribbons of morning light poured through the east facing windows and painted a glowing pattern of blinds across the floor. Lizzie eyed the dust motes slowly turning in the sunbeams. That hopeful, inquisitive sun was sniffing around again, and this time Lizzie felt as if it mocked her. She liked it, anyway. For her, the sun could do no wrong. She had loved its feel on her skin all her life, but her husband liked the seasons and the shade and the snow. So here in the Midwest was where they'd ended up, and here they'd stayed. Nothing to be done about it now.

Lizzie stretched and drew in a breath. Her back ached from the extra weight it supported, and no chair ever felt comfortable for long. Her eyes slid across the pastel walls where numerous photos of smiling adults and children topped kids' drawings and get-well cards. The effect proved to be a friendly visual chaos of good wishes and bright lives, all within easy eyesight of the occupied hospital bed. Turning her attention there, she studied the bed sheet and followed its steady rhythm as it rose and fell. Inhale, exhale. Inhale, exhale.

Jonathan Warton reclined on his back, his head propped up by pillows. Pale and gaunt, his lined face looked as if it needed glasses to complete it. Small indents at the top of his narrow nose told the same story, but his lids remained closed and even the eyes beneath them seemed still. His arms lay slack atop the sheet. If he was awake, she saw no sign of it except for the tuneless humming that came from behind his lips. It started months ago without pre-amble, seldom ceasing since. It varied in pitch and timing. Not a tune exactly, at least not one she recognized. His lips played no part in it. It was just an internal humming.

What did it mean? Why did he do it? Did he even know he was doing it? No one had an answer, the doctors as puzzled as anyone else. There was so much in all of this that no one seemed to know. Jon used to like to hum when he was busy, or happy, or both, she thought, but not like this, never like this.

Outside the room, spring was very busy about itself. The lively repetitive songs of cardinals and chickadees followed one another through an arbor. April was a lovely month in Eden Prairie, a time when the snow was finally gone and the ravenous mosquitoes still slept in their sanctuaries. That's what Jonathan used to say, and she remembered it. She remembered a lot of things – silly things, sad things, unforgettable moments that only the two of them were there for, but he didn't. He didn't remember any of it, not any longer.

Elizabeth Warton kept her quiet vigil seated beside her husband. She watched and waited. He breathed and hummed. She suddenly pictured the two of them side-by-side on a counter, an impaired set of salt and pepper shakers. She snorted, wondering which was which and if she, too, was losing her mind. Not a cheerful thought.

"Everything okay?"

Lizzie looked up at the kind face of a hospice nurse, who had just peeked in the open door to check the room. Lizzie nodded, smiling wearily back to her.

The nurse stepped into the room and gazed quietly at the bed. She listened to Jon's humming, tipping her head slightly as if about to offer a translation, and then reconsidered. She folded her arms in a companionable way beneath her draped sweater and looked back at Lizzie once again.

"Can I get you anything? Tea? Juice?"

"No. We're fine. Thanks."

"You're sure? It's no trouble." Her face was open, her voice soft. Lizzie shook her head.

The nurse looked around, puzzled. "Where'd the kids go? I thought they were still here."

"Out for breakfast. The little ones were hungry. They'll be back soon. They needed to let off some steam."

The nurse smiled and nodded. "If you change your mind, just let me know. Any of us. Whatever you need. Okay?"

"Okay."

The nurse left. Lizzie watched her go until the doorway was empty again. She blinked and let her mind settle on the vacancy of the hall. She ran her fingers through her hair, then yawned while rotating her neck slightly left and then right to relieve the pressure that so often perched at the top of her spine. Jonathan once helped with that. His strong fingers knew just where to push and how hard to squeeze to force out the tightness. She never needed to ask. He just knew – and soon she would be without him. What would she do? His care had occupied all her space for a long time. She would soon get all of it back again. What then? What would she do then? Who would she be without him?

It was hard enough that the disease had robbed her of his mind, cell by cell, but now it would claim his body and his soul, as well. She'd thought herself prepared. She'd had years to get ready, she told herself, and so what was new? She shrugged. Nothing. It would just be the end, and endings always felt new.

She abruptly noticed a change in the room. The humming had stopped. She realized she didn't know when it had stopped or how long the room had been silent.

Jonathan calmly sat straight up in bed, supporting himself without the pillows. He squinted at the walls and the photos, and then he slowly tracked the sunlight across the floor, up to his wife's familiar face.

"Lizzie?" His question seemed to come from far away.

"Here," she said, her voice more a breath than a sound. She cleared her throat and tried again. "I'm right here."

He blinked and focused harder. "Where am I? Is this home?" He swallowed as he peered deeper into the room. "This isn't home."

"Do you know me?"

"What?" His forehead furrowed for a moment. "Yes...of course. But Lizzie I...I don't know where I am."

Lizzie pushed up cautiously from the chair and moved closer to the bed. She found herself stepping on tiptoes, as if to avoid shattering a spell. "You're in a hospice center."

"Hospice?" He looked suddenly reflective. He repeated the word carefully, tasting the meaning. "Hospice."

Lizzie stood awkwardly beside the bed. "Yes."

Jonathan gently rotated his hands and studied them. He moved his legs under the covers, watching the interplay of sunlight and shadows across the sheets. Smiling to himself, he canted his head to look at her. "You're kidding?"

"No."

He rubbed briskly at his eyes and sniffed. "Why?"

"Because the doctor says you're...dying."

Jonathan looked suddenly forlorn, his hands settling on his cheeks. "Am I?"

"Yes. Jon, you *are* dying. Really." She sighed, "You have been for a while."

He blinked slowly, watching her face for more clues. "What from?"

"Alzheimer's."

"Oh..." Recognition rose in his face. His hands sank back to his lap. "That's why..."

"Why?"

"…the pieces are all messed up." He smiled sadly. "And there's so much missing." He took a little breath and let the air hiss back out. "I remember why now. I remember why I don't remember."

They shared an ironic smile as Lizzie wrapped his hand around one of hers.

Jonathan slowly scanned the lovely room. "How'd we end up here?"

"Long story. Are you back?"

He thought about that; he stared inside for an extended moment before replying. "I guess. For now."

She sat on the edge of the bed and held his hand. She was afraid to do anything sudden. This felt like a moment outside time's normal flow. They were together again – salt and pepper, good to go. No need for words. They just rested together until Jonathan showed signs of reawakened fretfulness.

She studied him. "Do you need anything?"

He shook his head and then frowned. "Sorry."

Liz smiled. "For what?"

His words came slowly. "For being such a…drag. On you."

"How do you feel?"

"You're changing the subject." He smirked, "I know your tricks."

She waved a hand toward the other end of the room. "The kids were just here. They'll be back. Some were here all night." She patted his hand. "Can you stay?"

A feather of panic brushed his face. "Don't know." His eyes turned inward as he struggled to hold onto his thoughts. He licked his lips with the effort. His knees rose as his legs pulled tighter to his body. "Coming apart. The faces are…sliding. Everything is sliding…"

Lizzie captured his other hand and held firmly to both of them. She leaned in close to his face. "Stay with me!"

"Trying…but – Lizzie, do something."

"I can't make it stop. I…"

"Not what I mean." His hands trembled.

Lizzie was distraught. "What, then? Do what?"

"I mean...I'm dying. I know that...that's all back." His voice sounded rushed, frantic, his disjointed thoughts tumbling together. "Not talkin' about me, talkin' about you! Something that matters to you. Do it!"

The muscles in his neck stood out in cords; he raced to stay a step ahead of the disease. "You did what I wanted. Never what you wanted. Sorry." His voice turned shrill and pleading. "I was always in your way. Always... Only thing clear in..."

Lizzie felt shaken by his outburst. "Shhh! Jon, it's okay..."

"Don't shush!" He leaned closer, desperate, his forehead shining. "Do something big..." An incongruous grin tickled the edges of his lips. "Without worrying about...anyone else."

She stroked his cheek now, trying to soothe him. "Stop it. You're working yourself up for no reason. Calm down. The kids should be back any time, Jon. Stay with us?"

He squeezed her hand and pulled it tightly against his face. His eyes filled with alarm. "For once, Liz. Just for this once..."

"Jon..."

He lost her hand as his grip relaxed and his shoulders betrayed him back into the pillows. His face sagged. The little hills in the sheets sank as his legs slid flat. He'd run his race; he'd won the moment, but he'd sacrificed all of his reserves. Nothing left. His drained voice held no colors anymore. "One by one and...one..."

Jonathan's arms dropped to his sides and his eyes closed.

"Jon, are you still..." The tuneless hum without the words returned. Lizzie let her question trail off unfinished. Her eyes brimmed with angry tears. "It's not fair! It's just not. None of it!" She brushed the hair off his forehead and let her tears go. "You dear, dear man."

Jonathan's face remained blank as he continued his tuneless humming.

Lizzie sat back down in her chair. Her spine ached. The muscles in her neck were tight. She dug out a crumpled Kleenex from a hidden pocket and wiped at her eyes and nose. "I'm so sorry the kids weren't here. Oh, Jonathan…"

Suddenly, boisterous from breakfast, the rest of the Warton family could be heard in the distance trooping down the hospice hall. Adult voices shushed the children to keep the laughter and noise suppressed as they neared the door.

Joanie, the eldest daughter at thirty-three, paused at the threshold and peered in, catching her mother's eye with a question. Lizzie sniffed quickly, stuffing the tissue away, and rolled her shoulders, as if to confirm that nothing had changed. Joanie's husband appeared beside her in the doorway. He smiled gently at Lizzie. The bright faces of their two elementary schoolers appeared on either side of Joanie as they squeezed by their parents and waved brightly at Grandma.

The rest of the family poured through the door, sweeping Joanie and her husband in along with them. Twenty-eight-year-old David, Lizzie and Jon's only son, entered with his dark haired wife and their giggling preschooler. Just behind them came twenty-six-year-old Cecelia, the Warton's youngest daughter. She made buzzing noises as her fingers swarmed over David's young son, causing the boy to hop and howl in high-pitched glee. Cecelia's wiggling hands pursued him, relentless in their attack.

David glared at his sister. "For God's sake, Celia, leave off, will ya? I'm about to lose my mind."

Cecelia stopped and glanced up, grinning at her big brother. "Okay, okay. Just havin' a little fun. Ya know it's fine with Ma. And Dad sure doesn't care."

David never wavered. "Well, it's not fine with me. Alright? So, cut it out!"

Cecelia swept the little boy up into her arms and patted him on the rump. "No more for now, buddy. Daddy says he's going craaaazy." She rolled her big eyes at David.

David tossed her a sour look, but he bit back any reply. His wife gave him a soft but solid nudge with her hip.

Joanie settled her kids onto a small couch by the windows and then looked back with concern at her mother. Lizzie still hadn't moved from her chair beside the bed.

"You okay, Mom?"

"I'm fine, dear." She took a breath, stood and bustled about the room, patting heads and smoothing collars. "So, how was the big breakfast?"

Joanie wrinkled her brow. "No. You don't look okay. You look different, somehow. What's up?"

Alerted, David moved to the foot of the bed and stared with concern at his dad. "Did something happen to him, Mom?"

He glanced accusingly at Joanie. "I knew one of us shoulda stayed. Didn't I say that? Didn't I?"

He moved closer to his mother. "Is Dad okay? Should we call the nurse?"

Lizzie deftly patted David's back. "Now, now. Relax, will you?"

She stepped to the bed to smooth Jon's covers near the railing, then sat back down. She faced her family and placed her hands firmly in her lap, one over the other. "No. Nothing happened. I was just thinking about the past, that's all."

She paused to let the apparent truth of her words sink in. "Just memories, lots of memories." Her voice grew ever firmer as she talked. "I'm glad you went to breakfast. All of you together. Don't worry about me. And stop imagining things. Everything is the same. It's just – just the same."

She patted her hands firmly against her knees and smiled widely. "Now, Will and Sandy, and Tomlin, I want to hear all about your breakfast. Come over here and tell Grandma everything that happened. Okay?"

The children eagerly gathered around her and began to pour out their food stories, each interrupting the other, and all of them trying to be first.

Lizzie sipped coffee from a Styrofoam cup in the church gathering hall. She watched the long lines of friends and family working their way through the post-funeral buffet. She smiled to herself and thought again of her friend Ruth, who loved any church gathering that involved food. Ruth would stand next to her in line, her plate filled with samples of everything offered, and shake her head. "One of these days, it's gonna be macaroni salad and red jello over us, you know." Then she'd laugh and smile indulgently down at her plate. "But not today!"

Lizzie heard a familiar voice call her name. She glanced into the dining area. George, her youngest brother, stood up from a folding chair and waved her over to a table full of relatives. Balding on top, shining with perspiration, and also in his sixties, he shared her size but didn't carry it as well. In fact, he seemed to be limping.

"Lizzie, Lizzie, I'm so damn sorry about all this." He gave her a side hug and tapped her shoulder as he spoke. "Poor old Jon. It's been such a long haul for him, but that's just the way it is." He smiled sadly at Lizzie. "Lose this, forget that, and pretty soon... know what I mean? You and me, we're at the wrong end of the hill, and that's for sure."

George dropped back into his chair with a thump and a heavy wheeze. Lizzie smiled tolerantly down at him and planted a motherly kiss on his forehead. "Speak for yourself, George."

"Yeah, yeah, okay. Just wanted to tell you that you and the kids did a great job." He squeezed her hand. "Really. Strictly first class."

He looked around the table at the familiar faces. "Didn't we all say that? We were just sittin' here talkin' about that." Everyone nodded and agreed. George looked back at his sister. "Jon woulda been so proud."

Lizzie nodded. "I hope so."

Jon's funeral had been crowded and touching, with plenty of flowers and a eulogy filled with humor and good words. Oh, there had been plenty of tears, and difficult moments, too, but plenty more of laughter and grins. The kids had pulled together and stayed up very late to help Lizzie sort and choose the photos. The grandkids fell asleep on couches in the living room, or with their little legs spread wide across cushions laid out on the rug. Joanie, David and Cecelia ate sandwiches and cookies at 3 a.m. at the dining room table. Lizzie had gently pushed aside the piles of pictures to make room for the food.

There was so much to recall and cherish, so much forgotten and now remembered, and each memory linked to other memories and other times. How could they leave any photo out? In the end, eight large display boards held all of the images. At the crowded wake the family groups would clump in front of certain memorable photos. The old tales would be retold and friends would join, attracted by the noise, to add their versions, and the old stories would change and expand with fresh bits and new pieces, and suddenly, for a moment, Lizzie sensed Jon standing among them, chiming in. She actually turned once, half expecting to see him. The irony wasn't lost on her: the fact that these shared memories, so healing and so powerful for a grieving family, represented the very things denied Jon by the plaques and tangles of that hideous disease.

Through it all, Lizzie made sure everything went the way Jon would have wanted. "I don't want people checking me out and saying stupid things." His casket stayed closed. There was a violin duet in the middle of the funeral service called "Ashokan Farewell," because it was his favorite. As the draped casket was smoothly pushed down the aisle towards the hearse, the choir sang "On Eagles' Wings," because Jon had maintained that it was "the best damn hymn ever written."

In short, it was a good goodbye, in exactly the style he said he wanted, but in the end, Jon remained gone and Lizzie alone.

Nothing unusual about that, she consoled herself. Most women outlived their men, so what else was new?

She didn't miss the *Jon of the disease*, and she felt thankful to see him released. However, she bitterly missed the *Jon of before the disease*, but that agony had transitioned into a familiar ache many years before he took his last breath. She didn't feel like a new widow now. Instead, she felt like a seasoned widow wearing someone else's black dress.

Still, funerals celebrated the past, and while Lizzie valued the memories, she felt as if she had lived on the fumes of their history for the last decade. She didn't want to live there any longer. Somewhere during Pastor Anderson's eulogy she gave herself permission to recall Jon's surprising outburst in the hospice room, and to consider her present and her future. She felt a twinge of guilt to be doing this now, during his service, but the present was the present, she reasoned, and she might as well get used to living in it again. So, Lizzie sat with quiet eyes in the front pew, surrounded by family and friends, properly somber, dressed in black, but with a mind brightly straining against the harness that had long been fastened around her shoulders. An oddly delicious struggle, to be sure, and not one she could have easily explained. She cautiously banished all signs of it from her face while she appeared to attend to her kind pastor's labored words meant to honor Jon and to comfort her.

TWO

Back to Normal

The center of Lizzie's Cherrywood dining room table usually contained a delicate Havilland soup tureen with pink and blue floral patterns, and flanked by a pair of brass colonial candlesticks, but not this morning. This morning they were shoved aside, the premium spaces occupied by stacks of investment reports, social security letters, medical insurance documents, filed tax statements, life insurance papers, trust documents and mortgage records, along with all the other typical monthly invoices. Lizzie herself perched on one of the dining room chairs at the mid-point on the long side of the table. She busily jotted notations onto a legal pad and occasionally keyed numbers into a sleek digital calculator. The sounds of Cecelia upstairs pulling her wheeled suitcase across the second floor hallway caused Lizzie to leave her work in a rush.

When she reached the main floor landing, she watched her youngest daughter muscle her hefty suitcase down the stairs. Cecelia grunted on each step, her oversized carry-on bag slapping against her other side.

Lizzie frowned up at her. "Let me help. You're gonna hurt yourself."

"I'm fine, Ma. Really," she gasped. "Just stay where you are. I've got bigger triceps than you think."

"You're just like your brother. You always have to do everything in one trip."

Cecelia reached the main floor and worked her way around her mother. Still refusing help, she proceeded down the additional steps to the foyer, finally parking the suitcase next to the door. She huffed out a breath with a smile and shook her head. "If there's one thing I certainly am not, and never will be, it's *like my brother*."

Lizzie frowned. "When will you two stop picking at each other? He's the only brother you have, and here he is kind enough to leave work and take you to the airport."

"Yeah, what a guy." Cecelia shed the carry-on bag and dropped it next to her suitcase. "Any coffee still hot?"

"Always." Lizzie went back through the dining room to the kitchen and began to pull out a mug. Her voice carried some chiding. "I thought we were having breakfast together?"

Cecelia's response drifted in from the front of the house as she moved toward the kitchen. "Um, we were but, I just...I just got behind with the packing and I...okay, I overslept but...look, I just need some coffee's all. Nothin' special." The voice seemed to pause in the dining room. "Mom, what's all this?"

Lizzie poured the coffee. "What?"

"This on the table."

Lizzie brought the mug to the entry way into the dining room. Cecelia was studying the paperwork stacks and lifting a few of the pieces to read the headings.

"These aren't just bills; I mean, there are bills, but a lot of these look like investments, assessments, insurance...taxes. Mom, why are you looking at all this now?"

"Here's your coffee. Are you still pretending to like it black?"

"What's goin' on?"

Lizzie handed her the steaming mug and smiled with just her lips.

Cecelia stared at her, waiting. "Mom?" She took a tiny sip from the hot coffee and nodded at her. "C'mon."

Lizzie retreated back into her kitchen. "I don't exactly know yet. Maybe nothing."

Cecelia followed right behind her. "Is there something you're not telling us?"

Lizzie busied herself at the sink. "Oh, stop it. It's nothing like that."

"What is it like then?"

David suddenly called from the front door. "Hello? Airport taxi anyone?"

Lizzie stepped around Cecelia to answer him. "Hello, David! We're here in the kitchen. Bags are by the door." She bustled to the foyer to greet David, relieved for his interruption. "Let's go, Cece. Bring your coffee."

In the foyer, Lizzie kissed her son on the cheek. "I told you, you didn't need to do this – leaving work and everything. It's silly. I'm perfectly capable of running people to the airport. Done it for years."

David grabbed all the luggage at once and backed out the door. "Don't worry about it. This's what sons are for." He disappeared outside, his voice carrying back from the driveway. "Dad would have expected me to help."

Cecelia stepped into the foyer, still sipping her coffee but now rolling her eyes.

Lizzie caught the look. "Behave! He's just being kind – in his own klutzy way." She rewarded her daughter with a tiny eye roll of her own.

Cecelia nodded, took a breath and slowly let it out. Her mother slipped into a light jacket and pulled it straight. "Do you have your phone?"

Cecelia patted her purse and scowled.

Lizzie gathered her own purse. "Ticket?"

Cecelia slapped her purse again and curled her lip. "In the phone!"

"License?"

"You know, we don't have to go through all this."

"Wallet?"

"Mom. I'm not eighteen!"

"Just making sure."

"Thanks. Now, stop."

"What about…?"

Cecelia growled in annoyance. "Mom!"

Lizzie grinned and pinched her cheek, "Oh, you've always been such an easy tease!" She breezed by her daughter, still chuckling. "And now get ready for David to ask you the same questions once you're in the car. Be nice!"

Cecelia snorted and steeled herself for the ride to the airport.

David merged from Highway 5 onto east 494 and settled into the middle lane as he headed for the Minneapolis-St. Paul International Airport. He looked over at his sister in the front passenger seat. "Which airline?"

Cecelia paused to think.

Lizzie immediately chimed in from the back seat. "It's Delta. Her plane doesn't have a gate assigned yet but her flight number is 2214. It's a non-stop to LaGuardia."

David nodded. "Okay. Delta."

He glanced at Cece. "Still not buying your own tickets, huh?"

Cece glowered. "What's your problem?"

"What? I'm just trying to figure out which terminal I need to head to. Delta leaves from Terminal 1, so that's Lindbergh."

"Yeah, right. What's it to you who's payin' for my flight?"

"Doesn't matter." David calmly checked his driver's side mirror. "Just an observation."

Cecelia jammed her coffee mug into the holder. "Well, next time how about not observing out loud, okay?"

Lizzie calmly inserted herself. "Cece, I'm sorry I spouted off from back here, but let it go. And David, if I choose to pay for something, I don't need you to second guess me."

David clamped his mouth shut. Cecelia sat quietly looking forward. The car tires hummed.

Cecelia turned in her seat to look back at her mother. "You gonna be okay?"

"I'll be fine, dear. Don't worry about it."

David perked up. He flicked his eyes at his sister. "What's up? Why wouldn't she be fine?"

"Financially. Mom was…I mean – back at the house – I don't know, she was looking at finances. It was spread all over the table."

"Cece, please…" Lizzie's voice sounded tired.

David scrunched up his face. "Are you kidding? You're worried about Mom? She's got the house, Dad's life insurance, his social security, his pension – she's on easy street! You're the one we're all worried about."

"David!" Lizzie's voice flared from the back.

Cecelia glared at him. "Me? I'm okay. I'm busy."

"Right. Busy. I'm sure. More gigs for charity? Easy to stay busy when you're giving it away."

Lizzie tapped on David's headrest. "Stop it. Now."

Cecelia snapped back at her brother, "Maybe *my* life's not about money."

"Oh, and mine is?"

"Didn't say that."

Lizzie tried again. "Can we move on now, you two?"

"But maybe that's what I shoulda said."

Lizzie was shocked. "Cecelia!"

David angrily changed lanes. "You're so busy! I'm surprised you could tear yourself away long enough to come home for Dad." He checked his mirrors again and then glared at his sister. "You haven't exactly been a regular show-up."

Cecelia's anger suddenly turned inside out, then gave way to guilt. "That's not fair! I wanted to come more…but…well, I—"

"Oh yeah. The struggling artist, right? But what do I know? I'm just another workin' stiff puttin' in my time."

Lizzie slapped both front seats with her hands. "Stop it! Both of you! I don't need this on top of everything else. We've just buried your father! Show some respect."

The inside of the car became abruptly quiet. Everyone became painfully aware of the swish of air rushing over the windshield. Seams in the pavement clicked loudly as the tires passed over them.

Lizzie stared at the back of David's head, sensing his growing discomfort. She knew what was coming next and felt the same ham-fisted awkwardness creep over her that had plagued her while raising him. He was the only son and like the first pancake on the griddle, she knew he hadn't come out perfect.

David exhaled loudly. "Sorry! Okay? I'm sorry." He waggled his head back and forth. "Same old, same old. Me and my big mouth. Stupid! I'm an idiot. What can I say? Okay?"

No one replied. Ahead, the freeway sign for Airport Terminal 1 appeared and flowed by the car. David signaled for a lane change and prepared for the upcoming exit.

"So, Cece, I know you're leaving, but I was thinking, why not consider moving back home? The way things are now, sounds like Mom can sure use the help to keep organized and to get around, and then you could find a real job and—"

Both women cut him off, talking on top of each other.

Lizzie was livid. "Get around? What do you think I am, an invalid?"

Cecelia erupted, "I have a real job where I am! I have lots of real jobs. They're just not *real* jobs to you."

Lizzie continued, on the heels of her daughter, "Don't you get it? It's easier now, without your Dad. It's a hell of a lot easier than it's ever been for the last ten years with him!" Lizzie's face flushed in shame. The sudden silence in the car took on a new and bleaker tone. Her voice fell to a whisper. "That didn't come out right."

David dutifully pulled into an opening near the Delta drop-off area and popped the trunk. Lizzie and Cecelia slid quickly out on the curbside of the car. David brought the luggage around and set it on the sidewalk beside his sister.

She nodded brightly at him, her face a study in *pleasant*, but when he made as if to help carry her suitcase farther, she held up a hand and firmly shook her head. "No, no, really, I've got it from here."

David stood stiffly with his hands dangling until she squeezed his shoulders and pecked his cheek. He wanted to say something but couldn't seem to find a start. "Have a...do you have your phone?"

Cecelia barked at him. "I'm warnin' you, do not even start that litany!"

"Ah...okay. Sorry. Bye." David awkwardly returned to the car.

Cecelia looked at her mother and growled. Lizzie made a tired face and wriggled her eyebrows. Cecelia finally slid an arm through one of Lizzie's, and linked together, they took a few steps away from the car.

"Sorry about your brother, dear."

"Yeah, I know." Cecelia tipped her head until it touched her mother's. "And if I had a dime for every time you've said that over the years, I wouldn't need one of David's *real* jobs."

Lizzie's face softened. "He does have a good heart. Just not always a...a good head." Despite herself, Lizzie giggled at the whole pathetic moment. She brought a quick hand to her lips to muzzle anything further but soon realized that she was powerless. "Oh, dear!"

Once the laughter escaped Lizzie's mouth, there was no stopping it. Cecelia was quickly overwhelmed as well. Like a surprise flash flood in the desert, all their departure decorum was instantly swept away. Soon both of them were sniggering and coughing, sputtering and trying to talk, stamping their feet, holding onto each other, and all the while dabbing helplessly at streaming eyes. If David saw them, they didn't know. Neither of them dared to even look his way.

Cecelia was the first to compose herself enough to talk. "Next time, I'm takin' a taxi, and I don't care what you or anyone else says."

Lizzie fought off a few last hiccups and caught her breath. She produced a tiny Kleenex pack and jerked out a few tissues for each of them. "Okay, but you're paying for your own taxi."

Cecelia nodded as she blew her nose. "I insist on it."

Her mother smiled back, content again.

Wrapping her in a tight hug, Cecelia spoke into her ear. "Love you so much. Thanks for everything. Promise you'll talk to me before you let that cat out of the bag."

"And what cat might that be?"

Cecelia broke the hug and gave her a mocking smile filled with intrigue. "I don't know yet. You refused to tell me, remember?"

Lizzie smiled coyly back. "Meeeooow! Okay. When I know, I'll let you know."

Holding hands they strolled back to the waiting baggage. After a final kiss to her mother's cheek, Cecelia lifted her carry-on, shouldered her purse, pulled up the handle from her suitcase and marched into the airport.

~§

Back on the highway again, David's car was as quiet as a tomb. He parted his lips a few times, as if about to say something, but he never did. Sighing, he casually leaned forward to push the button for the radio.

Lizzie's eyes darted his way. "Don't."

His finger jerked back as if she had said, "*Hot!*"

Lizzie stared firmly forward, but she was aware that he kept stealing glances at her. When she heard him clear his throat, she stiffened even more.

"Look, Mom, I'm sorry about how things went. I'm just not good with words."

Lizzie considered for a moment before replying. "You don't say. But I'm not the only one who you need to apologize to."

David nodded. "Yeah."

He watched the road for a time. "Why were you looking at all the assets and stuff? Did you lose something?"

Lizzie closed her eyes. Her head felt stuffed with wads of cotton. "Will you leave it alone? It's nothing. I just wanted to check where I stood, so I could decide what I want to do next."

David scoffed. "Do? You can do anything you want. Must be nice! Eat, drink and be merry – it's not rocket science. Dad set it all up for you."

Lizzie felt her fury race up the scales like the propelled weight at a carnival after the mallet struck. She was in a desperate struggle to avoid dinging the bell. "That's it! Cece's right. You need a license for that mouth!"

David looked shocked. He started to reply, but Lizzie cut him off. "Shut it! And keep it shut."

He closed his mouth.

Lizzie stared coldly out the side window. "And turn on that damn radio!"

THREE

A Guest Speaker

Late by choice, Lizzie swung her car into a familiar open spot in the last row of the upper church lot. It would mean a bit of a walk to the front door, something she seldom minded, but the unspoken reason she preferred to park there was due to the proximity of twin maple trees. Cheerful survivors of two church expansions, these tall trees pleased her. They stood green and graceful in the summer with their pointy, hand-shaped leaves. In the fall, their boughs filled with sudden flames of red and orange, often the first leaves to turn. And in the winter, despite their desolate branches, they displayed their strong black lines, elegantly edged in snow. She had spent many minutes every Sunday over the decade of Jon's illness fortifying herself through the patient ministry of these stolid trees. Now, standing quietly beside her car, seeing the hopeful buds at the end of each branch, she found it hard to turn and trudge toward her church, but she knew she was already late, and she didn't want people to talk.

Entering the vestibule, she took a bulletin and smiled at the greeter inside the door. A handsome young man and the son of a friend, his face shone with the open hopefulness of untried youth.

She liked that look. She liked it a lot, and hated to watch life grind it down. She wondered what people read in her face. She hastily shushed that thought as she slid through the twin doors into the chapel, a hymn already in progress.

Lizzie slipped into an aisle chair near the back. Since the congregation was already on their feet singing, her entrance caused barely a ripple of notice. She liked that, too. She stood facing forward, joining in the familiar song as she carefully inspected the sanctuary. She wanted to get the lay of the land, but didn't want to be seen doing it. She enjoyed being prepared, preferred surprises she knew about, and relished making lists. Lizzie noted that the usual people stood in their usual places – Ruth on the right, near the front, Todd and his wife midway back beside the main aisle, Ron at his post near the exit. She also observed that there were more people here than usual, many unknown to her. She glanced down at the bulletin, saw that this was missions' week, and understood.

The hymn rolled into its second verse. Lizzie looked up to read the projected words at the front of the sanctuary. She noticed a new figure on the platform, standing next to Pastor Anderson.

The guest speaker, a tall man with a bald head, wore a pale, three-piece suit, accented by a silk pocket square of bright orange. Clearly at home with the words of the song, his mellow voice added a deep, male warmth to the predominantly female voices on the stage. His large hands seemed to float in the air, adding their own syncopation, while the rest of his body wove itself into the rhythms flowing around him.

Lizzie studied his skin: a shade of black unfamiliar to her, so rich and deep as to almost approach blue when he moved. Even from her seat at the back of the room, she could feel such a contained intensity radiating from him, she felt tempted to slip back out the door before he uttered a single syllable from the pulpit.

She learned from Pastor Anderson's introduction that his name was Agaba-Benjamin Kajumba. He had founded fifteen churches in Uganda, in addition to the one he pastored there, and he had started a Christian primary and secondary school in Kampala. There were ten children in his immediate family that he was raising – four of his own, and six more from two male cousins who had died from AIDS.

When the missionary first stepped up to the clear acrylic podium to speak, holding his worn Bible in his hands, his head bowed, and his lips moving in a silent prayer, Lizzie found herself unaccountably dry-mouthed and short of breath. She glanced around the congregation as they all sat down; she wasn't sure what she expected to see, but whatever indication she was searching for wasn't there. Everyone else appeared to be unaware: she caught a few smiles exchanged; she heard the predictable rustle of bulletins and bibles, the clack of repositioned chairs, and the thin hiss of cushions squishing. Nothing unusual. Nothing to betray the sense of a visitation she felt ringing inside herself. Lizzie belatedly settled into her chair and busied her fingers with meaningless arrangements in her lap while her mind scolded her. Nothing portentous here; he was just another missionary with a good story and a need for money. For goodness' sake, get a grip!

And then he began to speak.

"Do you know, I travelled across England before coming here?" Pastor Kajumba's voice effortlessly filled the chapel, all the way to the back corners. His accent mixed British and Ugandan tendencies as clipped and precise consonants commingled with broad vowels.

"Have any of you been to England? Her churches are empty. Perfectly empty. Oh, they are beautiful, so beautiful, but they are empty." He wore a sad smile as he recalled the experience. "They are – what is your word? Not *churches* anymore but…museums."

He looked at them all, moving his head from left to right, holding that same sad smile. His rich voice suddenly crackled with power. "I discovered that you cannot call out to God in England! Not anymore! It is like yelling into an iron wall. Your voice booms and bounces back. Nothing gets through. At least, that is the way it felt to me."

Agaba-Benjamin deftly fished out a snowy handkerchief from an inside pocket and wiped his shining forehead. He let the silence draw out as he meticulously refolded the cloth and positioned it on the pulpit. "But here in America," he continued in a softer tone, "you can still call out and break through into the heavens. You are blessed! Do you appreciate that?"

He took a few steps to one side of the platform and moved closer to the congregation, letting his voice rise again. "You are still alive! Here in America, you still have time! Your clock has not run out yet. You can still afford to dream."

The tall missionary slipped back behind the pulpit. He took a sip of water and checked his notes. His wonderful voice dropped into a conversational sing-song. "But what do you think this American Dream is? Do you think it means that you can make a bunch of money and then sit back and relax?" He wrinkled his brow. "What is that?" He changed his inflection and asked again, stronger. "What is that?"

Agaba-Benjamin looked across the faces and caught eyes here and there. He held them briefly before moving on. Lizzie was sure she could feel his eyes pause on her. She jumped as he suddenly thundered, "Don't abuse God's time!"

Pastor Kajumba strode across the platform, his body in rhythm with the cadence of his words. "You breathe! You wake up in the morning, and you are still breathing! You don't know why. Every four seconds, you breathe again. You thank God that you are breathing, but you don't know why." He paused and then raised his voice. "You are still breathing because you have life to give! That is the reason! You are supposed to bring life to someone who does not yet have life!"

Lizzie abruptly realized that she herself had stopped breathing. She sucked in a quick, needy breath and looked around. No one noticed.

a delectable shade of golden brown as she placed them on the stove top to firm up. Lizzie's mouth opened in shock.

Ruth stopped chewing. "What?"

"I forgot to flatten these."

"Oh. Probably because we were talking and—"

"No. I never forget that." Lizzie seemed distraught. "What's wrong with me?"

"Easy, girl. I'm sure they'll go down fine and head straight for my waist, like the rest."

Lizzie didn't laugh. "Did I leave anything else out? Do they taste right?"

"They taste perfect." Ruth grew concerned. "Relax. I forget stuff all the time. It's our age, dear."

Lizzie scanned the unblemished skin of the cookie tops. "How'd I make a mistake like that?"

"Lizzie. It's just cookies."

Lizzie snorted and tipped her head. "You're right. It's just cookies." She took a slow breath. "It doesn't mean anything." Lifting the new sheet of flattened cookie dough she slid them into the oven and closed the door. "Sorry."

Ruth waved it off.

Lizzie transferred the cookie mounds to the cooling rack. "Well, so much for my plan to sway your opinion."

Ruth brightened. "About the Africa thing? Forget it. I think you need your head examined." Ruth caught the quick look from Lizzie. "Oops. Poor choice of words. But, anyway, pick another continent. Or, if you're so hung up on the *doing good* part, send money. That's what I'd do." She raised a fresh cookie and studied it thoughtfully. "If you still need to go somewhere, book a tour to Ireland, or Italy, or at least someplace with nice toilets."

Lizzie paused in her rolling of more dough balls. "Ruthie, people go to Africa every day."

"Yeah, if they work for National Geographic."

"I'm not on safari. I'd be helping at a school. Why don't *I* get to try new things?"

"You're supposed to try stupid things when you're younger, not at our age."

"Says who?"

"Says everybody."

"I was busy then." She placed the dough ball on the sheet and started another. "And maybe I wasn't ready yet."

Ruth rolled her eyes. "And what makes you think you're ready to be stupid now?"

"I have time now." She placed the last balls on the sheet and carefully flattened them with a fork.

"Time and sixty extra pounds." Lizzie glared, but Ruth plowed right on. "I just don't get you. Where is this coming from?"

"What? I'm the same person I've always been. I'm just released. I feel like I'm supposed to go there. Why is this such a nutty idea?"

"Because these are your twilight years, and you're expected to enjoy them. Haven't you ever heard that?"

"Of course, I've heard that. I just never bought it."

"And besides, you deserve some TLC. C'mon, Lizzie, you've more than paid your dues."

Lizzie slapped down the fork. "Is that what you think I was doing?" Her mouth tightened and her eyes suddenly glistened.

"Oh, Lizzie, I'm sorry." Ruth's face filled with contrition. "No, no, it's just a figure of speech. You know me, tongue ahead of my mind – that isn't what I meant at all. You were being the good wife, I know, I know."

"You're not helping me right now." Lizzie snapped open a cabinet and grabbed a glass. She crossed the kitchen to the refrigerator and yanked out a plastic milk container. "I can't eat cookies without milk." She flashed a look at Ruth. "And if you need some too, well you can just get it yourself! If you can remember how!"

"I – look, I just meant you're allowed to kick back and enjoy life again. That's all."

"That's not me!" Lizzie slapped a glass on the counter and filled it with milk. "You know I don't 'kick back' well." She snatched a cookie and gave it a ragged bite.

"Well, I think you should give leisure a few more tries. It's workin' for me, since Harry died. I think I'm really gettin' the hang of it."

"I'm not wired like you."

"Maybe not, but I bet it's what Jon would have wanted for you."

Lizzie leaned on the kitchen island and fixed Ruth with a sarcastic look over the brim of her milk glass. "Really, Ruthie? And how do *you* know what Jon would have wanted for me?"

"I…that was a…of course, I don't know. I…"

Lizzie straightened back up and shook her head, all of her sarcasm evaporating. "Forget it. Maybe I didn't know him as well as I thought, either."

"What does that mean?"

Lizzie stood still. "Never mind."

Ruth studied her friend for a moment, then carefully phrased her next question. "And this is about that black preacher, isn't it? That – what's his name? Something Jumbo?"

"Kajumba, Pastor Kajumba; and no, it's not about him. I was looking for something before he came along; he just made things clearer."

"We've been friends for twenty years, Lizzie. This is the first I've heard about you wanting to go to Africa."

"It's not even Africa, I just want to be useful. For the last ten years with Jon, even though I felt on the shelf, I knew what I was supposed to do. Now, I'm not so sure."

"Okay. I guess I…maybe you're not *totally* nuts. Is there a group? Is Kajumba sponsoring a tour? Is that it?"

"No, nothing like that."

"So, what's the plan?"

"I don't know. I'm meeting with him tomorrow."

"You won't go overseas by yourself, though, right?"

"Why not?"

"People just don't do that."

"They used to."

"Who?"

"Just people."

"You mean bratty college students with backpacks?"

"No. Normal people. No muss, no fuss, it used to be simple. People who felt they were called to go somewhere, just went. No tour group. No big deal."

"And they were never heard from again. Get serious, Lizzie," she scoffed. "Who're you talkin' about? Saints?"

"I'm not a saint, but I'm serious. And I can afford to do it."

Ruth sat quite still, her third cookie forgotten. "But you're sixty-nine years old. You're not allowed to do crazy things like go alone to Africa."

"I'll be sixty-nine whether I'm in Africa or not. And don't be so dramatic – I'm sure I won't be working alone."

"And what about the *being called* part? What does that even mean? Did God send you a text, or a tweet, or…"

Lizzie's nose wrinkled. Oh, no! She suddenly whirled around in horror, sweeping up a hot pad. "I never reset the timer!"

Rushing to open the oven, she jerked out the sheet of burnt cookies. In her haste, her thumb slipped off the hot pad. Screeching, she dropped everything onto the stove top. Dark crisscrossed cookies bounced off and rolled over the counter. Whipping her thumb into her mouth, Lizzie mumbled, "I can't believe this!" She used her other hand and a hot pad to dump the remaining cookies along with the sheet into the sink. When the clatter subsided, she turned to stare at an equally stunned Ruth. "Okay, forget all this. Let me tell you the truth."

Lizzie moved around the island to Ruth's side and leaned on the butcher block top, their faces level. She analyzed her thumb's rising blister and then put it aside. "We're friends, right?"

Ruth pulled back slightly. "Right."

Lizzie held her eyes. "We've been through some heavy things together."

"Uh-huh."

"And I let you say a lot of outrageous things because we understand each other?"

"Okay..."

"Here's what I know, Ruthie, and you're not allowed to make fun of it, not even a little bit. You hear me?"

Ruth nodded silently.

Lizzie licked her lips with a tiny flicker of her tongue and then continued. "When Pastor Kajumba was speaking, I could just feel that I should go there. No. That's not right. It wasn't really a feeling; I don't even know how to describe it, a *sureness*. Is that even a word? It was like something solid dropped into me. I mean, inside me. I know how this sounds, but I don't even care. I saw my own feet standing on a red dirt path and when I looked up, there were walls of grass swaying around me and a hot sky over my head. I was there. For an instant, I was actually there. I'm telling you, I could smell the dust and feel the heat of the sun. I heard insects buzzing. Nothing like that has ever happened to me before. I think it might be a *call*. I don't know if I've ever had one before. But if it's not a call, what else do you really think it could be?"

For once, Ruth didn't have a comeback, or a wisecrack, or a tease. She just watched with wide eyes and then replied in a small voice, "Oh, Lizzie. You scare me. You really do."

⤚

He listened carefully to her speak. He didn't interrupt or try to control the talk. Sitting straight in the stiff wooden chair, with his tie loosened and his coat hanging nearby, Pastor Kajumba simply paid close attention. Lizzie found that his surprisingly bright, brown eyes held hers with a firm expectancy that was at once disarming and yet conveyed the uncomfortable suspicion he could hear far more than her words.

The Ugandan's large scarred hands remained casually folded together on the scratched surface of the tiny desk. The room, cramped and drab, projected a faint musty smell. They sat across from each other. Their size differential alone was laughable, as if a giant sat before her. Lizzie briefly broke her gaze from his eyes to glance behind him at the discolored walls of the church office. She couldn't help noticing that the walls needed fresh paint or, at the very least, a good scrubbing. She continued to talk even while her inner mind helplessly proceeded down that housekeeping rabbit hole, dutifully and thoroughly ticking off the cleaning products, rags, brushes, buckets and tools she would need to do the job right.

Lizzie seldom visited the traditional red brick neighborhood churches of North Minneapolis, but she had learned that Kajumba was a moving target. If she intended to talk with him, she would need to discover where he was preaching. That proved easier said than done. His idea of itinerant ministry was to simply go wherever he was welcomed. He left the planning up to God. The one certainty: the energetic pastor would soon leave the state. His appearance at Lizzie's suburban church, it turned out, was the simple confluence of fortunate events – her church's annual missions' week, the last minute cancellation of their scheduled speaker, and the timeliness of a simple e-mail request.

"Mrs. Warton?"

His voice shook her, triggering the awareness that she wasn't sure exactly what she had just been saying.

"I cannot make decisions for you. No one can. I don't know what God is telling you. He is big but He deals with us one at a time. I don't understand how He does, but I know that He does."

He slid his chair back and stood. "I am a simple minister. My approach is to ask the Lord what He wants me to do next, and then I listen very carefully. What I can understand of what He tells me to do, I do. And then I go from there."

He picked up his suit coat and began to slide his long arms into the sleeves. "I'm sorry, I will need to go soon for the afternoon service here."

Lizzie nodded but looked disappointed. "I just thought that you, of all people, might know whether this was a call from the Almighty or just a few silly squeaks from my own mind."

Kajumba laughed deeply. He stretched his arms wide. "Me, of all people! How funny that is. Perhaps you and I will have time someday for me to explain."

He tightened his tie and tidied his shirt collar and then leaned on the desk to look at her with kind eyes. "For now, let me tell you this. I have learned a few things about working with God. The first is, He is in charge, not you. But He never forces anyone to do what He says, and that's the second thing – you are free to ignore His voice."

"I don't want to ignore it." Lizzie sounded exasperated. "But I don't want to be stupid, either!" She stood and gathered her purse. "Look at me. I'm overweight. I can order off the seniors' menu. The farthest I've ever travelled anywhere is Hawaii. Okay? There's gotta be better people available, don't you think? Why would God call *me*? Especially now?"

Pastor Kajumba wasn't the least bit put off by her outburst. In fact, he seemed amused, as if the answer was obvious. "Because of your obedience. You took care of your husband. You obeyed. So, since you were found worthy in the one thing, God may be offering you another."

Lizzie repositioned her hold on her purse and blinked a few times as she considered his words. Finally, she looked up. "Oh, that's just great. So, let's say, hypothetically, that this is all God, all the time here, okay? And He picked me out of the blue to head to Uganda, a country I couldn't have found on a map, to work for an African pastor whose name sounds like a sneeze, and who I had never even heard of before last week. What on earth would I even be doing there? Can you at least tell me that?"

Kajumba grinned, enjoying her rant. "How should I know, Elizabeth? What are your skills?"

Lizzie rolled her eyes. "Current skills? Well, besides being a mother and grandmother…and former wife – in good times and in bad – before all that, probably before you were born, I was an Information Specialist at a public school."

"What is that?"

"Something seriously out of date, I'm afraid. I actually thought I was quite good at it, at the time. I don't know what they call us now, maybe a digital archive person or a cyber something, but we used to be simply librarians. Probably the last thing you need in Africa, huh?"

Kajumba's face changed abruptly. He looked at Lizzie with wide eyes and shook his head in awe. "My, my, my." He sat back down and folded his hands on the desk. "Of all the things for you to be! Surely, God has a sense of humor."

"Now wait, you wouldn't have come all the way from Africa just to find an old, out-of-practice school librarian!"

Kajumba smiled. "No. Not me. But maybe God would. Sit. I have a few minutes before I have to go. We need to talk."

Still clutching her purse, Lizzie sank slowly into her chair.

FIVE

Getting Ready

That's fine, ma'am. Right there. No, don't smile. No teeth. They just want a neutral look with your lips closed. There we go."

Lizzie winced when the flash went off. "Sorry, I think I blinked." The strobe went off again while she was still talking. "Oh, no. That's not...can we try again? Sorry."

An irritated look briefly crossed the face of the young Walgreens photo technician as she stepped over to her computer. "It'll just be a minute." She methodically used her mouse to delete the shots and then reset the camera. "Where you travelin', anyway?"

Lizzie was looking down, focused on feeling stupid, and didn't hear the question. "I'm sorry, what?"

"Goin' anyplace interesting?" The tech was back at the camera again. "I mean, since you're gettin' a passport and all."

"Africa."

The tech paused. "Where that dentist was killin' lions?"

Lizzie's mind hiccupped and then recovered. "Yes." She nodded. "Well, no." She shook her head. "It's a big place. I – I won't be...I'm not going anywhere near where that happened. Really."

The young worker cocked her head, trying to recall something else. "Isn't that where they have Ebola? I think we talked about it in health. Why'd you wanna go there?"

Lizzie frowned at her. "Excuse me? Can we get back to taking passport photos?"

"Oh, yeah, okay."

The tech studied the camera's preview image on her monitor. Lizzie's face carried a decidedly aggressive look. "Lookin' good. Ready? Here we go, that's perfect. Don't blink."

The flash went off.

⌾

Lizzie sat in the well-appointed waiting room of the Travel Health International clinic. One entire wall was dedicated to an updated world map with individual countries highlighted by contrasting colors. Lizzie recognized the trivial grey hunk of Uganda sandwiched among the larger wedges of neighboring countries: pink Sudan to the north, red Kenya to the east, green Tanzania to the south and the fat taupe region to the west that was the Democratic Republic of Congo. Little Uganda appeared to be hopelessly squeezed by its neighbors and about to be gobbled up. She reminded herself that it was only a map.

The black faux leather waiting room chairs matched the upbeat décor of the clinic, but they utterly failed at being comfortable. Lizzie tried another position and rearranged the manila envelope she balanced on her lap under her purse. She idly fiddled with the flap on the envelope's open end as she evaluated the prospective travelers sitting around her. Nearby, an old man sat slumped over, a worn beret in his hand. Beside him, a patient young woman held an antsy toddler who kept grabbing her necklace. Was this an unlikely threesome heading for a reunion? Or something more complex? Where were they going? France? Or maybe Spain? Across the room, she observed a young man filling a cardboard cup with coffee from a Keurig machine. He seemed relaxed with the intricate process – perhaps he had one at home, she thought.

In the chair behind her, she heard the sudden rattle and scrunch of newspaper pages as a man settled into his seat to read an article. When he started humming to himself, sudden memories of Jon rushed upon her with such an intensity, she actually groaned out loud. Embarrassed, she quickly rearranged herself in the chair and noisily cleared her throat. It was these unplanned lulls between being busy, she told herself, that gave her the most difficulties. Little triggers could catch her then: a slant of light, a walking man seen from behind, a certain scent, a particular cough, or a voice. And when the switch flipped, the unbidden tapes would roll and familiar images and conversations would inexorably tumble through her. She brushed at her eyes and sniffed, sensing her uncertainties slinking back in. What would Jon say about her flying off to the small land of lions and Ebola? Of course, if he were still here, she wouldn't be in this waiting room anyway, would she?

"Warton? Elizabeth Warton?"

Lizzie startled. She looked up and saw a stylish young black woman in a white lab coat, propping a door open with her foot. Her lips were full, her hair in braids, and she held a sheet of paper while examining the room expectantly.

Lizzie gathered her purse and the folder and stepped forward.

The woman smiled brightly at her. "Elizabeth?"

"Yes."

"Welcome. My name is Doreen. I'll be your travel health advisor. Come this way."

Doreen motioned her into a small office that contained a glass topped desk and chairs. Lizzie took the nearest seat and set aside her envelope and purse. Peering down through the transparent desktop, she glimpsed horizontal cubbies just beneath the surface, which held stacks of colorful handouts: *Typhoid Fever: Know Before you Go; Trip Insurance: Why and Why Not; A Complete Guide to Traveler's Diarrhea.*

"So, you're taking a trip? Lucky you!"

Doreen's warm voice brought Lizzie's face back up. She smiled self-consciously at the pretty woman seated on the other side of the desk. "Yes, I hope so."

Doreen spread out some printed sheets in an open folder. Lizzie noticed the woman's long, manicured nails were elegant and painted a dark shade of gold, except for her fourth fingers, which were pink with delicate white lace overlays. Lizzie couldn't remember the last time she had pampered her own nails. Of course, she told herself, everything looks beautiful when you have that color skin. She realized, belatedly, that the nurse was talking.

"You said Kampala, Uganda in your online application, right?"

"Yes."

"Business or pleasure?" Doreen's voice was smooth, professional.

"I...well, it's not business, but..." Lizzie felt tongue-tied.

The nurse scrunched her nose and glanced out the door, lowering her voice. "Don't sweat it. Sometimes these questions don't fit. What'll you be doing in Uganda?"

Lizzie relaxed. "I hope to work at a school there. I'm supposed to help set up a new library."

"Sounds interesting. Would you say it's a mission trip?"

"Well, I guess."

Doreen jotted a note. She pushed aside one of her thick braids. "Do you think you'll be out into the countryside at any time, say as a part of a medical outreach?"

"Not that I know of...but...I suppose anything can happen."

Doreen chuckled and nodded. "How long will you stay in Uganda?"

"Not sure. I have an open return on the plane and...it depends on...things."

"Best guess? Three weeks or three months?"

"At least three weeks." Lizzie blinked a few times. "Unless I hate everything."

Doreen lifted an eyebrow. "Fair enough. We'll revisit that in a bit. Let's check your medical info now, shall we?"

Lizzie nodded.

Doreen waited and then finally pointed with one of her golden nails. "I'm guessing that's what's in your big envelope?"

Lizzie flushed. She'd already forgotten. "Oh. Yes." Yanking the envelope from under her purse, she handed it over. A transitory worry flitted through her mind, wondering if this was just forgetfulness in a new situation or the beginning of something worse.

Some minutes later Doreen set aside the medical records. "Well, you're up to date on most of your vaccinations, including your flu shot. That's great. And it appears you already have immunity to Varicella from childhood."

"From what?"

"Chicken Pox. And you look to be okay for measles-mumps-rubella, too."

"Okay."

"Now, let's talk about malaria. Uganda carries a high risk of contact with malaria."

"You mean mosquitoes, right?"

"Yes, that's the transmission route. And it can happen all year round, everywhere in the country. But these aren't the big, hungry ladies we have here." She held up her graceful thumb and first finger and squinted. "These little girls are itsy-bitsy, and you may not even feel their bite."

"I didn't know that."

"No worries. There's preventative medications for it. We recommend Doxycycline."

"Is that a pill?"

The health advisor nodded. "Or a capsule. They typically come in 100mg doses."

"How often do I have to take them?"

"Every day. And you'll need to start at least two days before you leave, then every day you're there, and for twenty-eight days after you're back."

"Really?"

"Really."

"That's a lotta pills. What if I need more? Can I buy some there?"

Doreen clicked her tongue and leaned forward. "To be honest, it's tricky. Forty percent of pharmaceuticals over there are counterfeit. That's why we want you to bring a full supply with you. That said, if you need more, find a doctor in-country, preferably from the west, and ask how to safely buy more."

"Now you're making me nervous."

The black woman touched Lizzie's hand. "Don't worry, lots of people go to and from Africa and have zero problems."

"Unless they're illegally shooting famous lions, I suppose."

Caught off guard, Doreen snorted out loud, betraying some of the real woman behind her polished exterior. "But that's not you, right?"

"Not this time."

"Elizabeth, I like you. You really got me there."

"I have my moments. Call me Lizzie, *Elizabeth* sounds like the queen of England."

"Okay...Lizzie, just a few last things on malaria. Use mosquito repellant on your clothing every day and, if you can, always sleep under netting."

Lizzie sighed. "Look, should I be taking notes?"

"No. It's all in the packet we've prepared."

"That's good, I'm starting to feel overwhelmed."

Doreen laughed. "Well, you better take a big breath then, because we've only just begun." She flipped through the pages of the bound booklet on her desk. "We still have to talk about Hepatitis A & B, pneumococcal disease, poliomyelitis, meningitis, typhoid fever, AIDS, yellow fever, cholera, diarrhea and the importance of bottled water, among a few other important things."

"I can hardly wait."

"It won't be so bad. I promise."

"Will I be getting shots today too? And pills?"

"Yep. Most of what you need I can take care of today. Entirely up to you. Should we continue?"

Lizzie ignored the question and looked closely at Doreen. "Where're you from?"

"Right here in Eden Prairie. Born in Detroit. But if you mean my ethnicity, my dad was born in Nigeria." Doreen grinned as she took a handful of her hair. "And if you're wondering about this big braided look, that's not tribal, it's just me."

"Ever been to Nigeria?"

"Nope."

"Africa?"

"Nope."

"Wanna go someday?"

"Doubt it. I'm a drinks-with-a-little-umbrella kind of girl myself." She smirked. "Never been a big fan of third world beaches."

"I see." Lizzie looked uneasy. "Do you secretly think I'm foolish to take this trip? At my age?"

Doreen's face softened with concern. "No, no. Lizzie, I was just kiddin' around. I wasn't implying anything. No, I don't think you're foolish, and I don't think age has anything to do with it. We're gonna make sure you're safe." Doreen gently stroked her hand. "No, you go, girl, and have your adventure! Really! And who knows, when I'm your age, maybe I'll go to Africa."

Lizzie winked at her. "Trust me, you never know."

Doreen sat still for a moment, then turned over one of the booklet's pages. "Now, ready to talk about hepatitis?"

Lizzie drew in a breath and sat up straighter. "Absolutely. I was hopin' you were gonna ask me that."

ॐ

Wearing her shabby garden gloves, Lizzie bent a thick hosta plant and clipped the stems close to the ground. It took the beefy clippers a number of squeezes to work through the clustered stalks and slice them from their roots. She finally pulled the severed plant free of the ground, admired its size, almost regretfully, and then shoved it into a bulging yard bag. Moving on, Lizzie repositioned her rubberized kneeling pad at the next hosta. Puffing out a breath, she began the process again.

These got way too big, she thought, as she clipped the plant. I should have divided them last spring and spread them out. Jonathan always said my eyes were bigger than my hands. When did he say that? She paused in her cutting and reminded herself why she had found so little time last spring to deal with gardens, or much of anything else. She sighed. Maybe next spring.

She made it through the next plant and rocked back onto her heels to let the wind play with her gray hair. She'd never colored it – never saw the point. She felt that the seasons of life, like nature's seasons, should be accepted, and not lied about. Still, her pragmatism didn't extend to the extra weight she carried, nor the teeth that she whitened.

Looking up at the trees overhead, she noticed a few curled clusters of obstinate leaves still clinging to the branches. Even as she watched, wind gusts shook a few more free. She wondered what new insights she would have about herself by next spring, where she'd be then, and what she'd be doing. She knew a day would come in the future when she would remember this moment in the garden from the vantage point of the other side of her journey. What would she think then?

The trip was set, the passport done, shots, medicine, travel insurance. She even bought new suitcases – orange, her favorite color. Jonathan would never have allowed it, but the bags had good reviews on Amazon and were delivered in two days. In any case, Jonathan's taste held sway no more.

She'd notified Pastor Kajumba of her flights and times. They'd e-mailed back and forth, but the process frustrated her and his response times felt haphazard. He was occupied and travelling, he explained. Besides, he admitted that his country's electrical power was undependable and would often disappear partway through the day, or for days at a time. So, she shouldn't worry about his tardiness.

Really? She wasn't sure if his clarification was just an excuse or the actual truth, and she questioned which was worse.

In the last few weeks before leaving, Lizzie had better luck communicating with Nankunda Birungi, the school administrator and a member of Kajumba's local church. Mrs. Birungi assured her that they would all gather at the Entebbe airport to meet her. She cautioned Lizzie to beware the many vendors trying to get her attention as she exited the airport. She told her to ignore them all and keep walking until she got outside, near the taxi stands. No worries, they would be there.

Lizzie had worked out her expenses with the help of her Edward Jones agent and wire transfers to her local bank. She had even taken a big step, for her, and arranged online for most of her monthly bills to be paid automatically from her account. The post office had been notified to hold her mail, and she asked Ruth to periodically check on the house. In fact, she took care of nearly every important detail except the one she knew she should have done first: tell her family.

She couldn't put her finger on exactly why she felt so reluctant – even afraid – to tell them. She told herself that it wasn't easy to explain her trip without sounding somehow critical of Jonathan or too *goody-two-shoes* religious about herself. She worried her kids would decide she was being self-indulgent, or worse, peculiar. She imagined the guarded looks in their eyes or the tiny shakes of their heads as they sent silent signals to each other – this was how it started with dad. Just the thought of that would cause something to rise up in her and stiffen. She would feel a heat in her chest that proclaimed she had every right to do what she decided to do, whether she explained it to everyone or not! And that reaction inevitably left her feeling guilty about the whole thing.

She knew her internal struggles were all a part of the new world Jonathan's death had forced her to live in, but she chided herself for not doing a better job of adapting. In the end, while she kept churning the situation over and over in her mind, she dawdled. Admittedly, there was much to do for the trip, and she had stayed busy doing it; but always quietly, under the wire. Somehow, she had tricked her own mind by picturing her future self smugly shutting down the garden in the fall, with that pesky family announcement all done, delivered, and safely behind her.

Well, now here she knelt, putting the damn gardens to sleep for the winter and her departure announcement remained unvoiced. None of her children knew. And now, when she finally told them she planned to leave for Africa in November, she would also have to explain why she had dawdled.

I'm going to Africa. Why is that so hard? They need a librarian in Africa. I'm available, so I'm going there for a while. Would it kill me to just say that? I think I'm supposed to go to Africa. It's not that big a deal, okay? I just want to do it, and it's only for a short time. Really. She could hear the words and sentences in her head, but they simply refused to flow out of her mouth. Why? Grunting in frustration, she viciously jammed the clippers into the next hosta and tried to chew her way through the stalks. Because I'm an idiot and a coward, that's why!

The blades twisted and stuck. She couldn't get them free no matter how she growled and pulled on the clippers. Angry at herself, she pawed through her gardening bucket and latched onto an old butcher knife. Since the edge was dull, she tried stabbing the stubborn plant. The knife made a fresh popping noise with each downward thrust. It somehow felt good – terribly good! She kept stabbing the plant with a growing fervor until the hapless hosta started to come apart.

"Mom? Are you outside?" Joanie's voice floated from the side of the house.

Lizzie looked up in shock. Was she hearing things?

"Mom?"

"I'm in the garden," she called back, hurriedly tossing the knife into the bucket and retrieving the now liberated clippers.

Joanie came around the house. She wore jeans and a sweat shirt. "I called the house but no answer. Tried your cell, too."

"Sorry." Lizzie patted her pocket but came up empty. Her hands trembled. "I guess I left it in the house." She smiled apologetically. "It's probably on silent, anyway. You know me."

Joanie pulled a pair of work gloves from a back pocket as she walked over to where her mom knelt. "Figured you'd be doing outside jobs today. Thought I'd give you a hand."

"Sweet of you."

"That's true," she said as she smiled, "but I admit that I may have an ulterior motive."

Lizzie shook her head. "Can't wait to hear this. Before you explain, can you drag over that rake and grab another yard bag?"

Joanie found the stack of biodegradable bags beside a long row of filled bags. As she shook open the new bag, she withdrew a rake from the garden shed and headed back to her mother. "Wow! You've filled a lot of bags already."

"Two days of outdoor work'll do that for you."

Joanie switched out Lizzie's full bag with the new one and crouched down beside her. "Well, I'm impressed. What do you want me to do?"

Lizzie finished cutting through the shredded hosta and hurriedly stuffed it in the bag. "You can do what I'm doing but on the other side of the birdbath. Here's my other hand clipper. You just cut the plant off right at the ground."

Joanie took the extra shears and crossed to the other side of the small circle of plants that surrounded the dry birdbath. She knelt down, facing her mother. "How careful do I have to be?"

"Not at all. You can't kill a hosta."

"Okay. Here goes." Joanie gamely started in on one of the sturdy plants.

"How are Will and Sandy?"

"They're great. They love school – especially Will. He's just blossoming."

"I remember those days. When do you have to meet the bus?"

"Don't worry. Not for a few hours yet."

They both worked for a while without saying anything further. Mother and daughter clipping plants and filling bags. Finally, Lizzie said, "So, what's this other motive of yours? Not that I'm complaining about the help, mind you."

Joanie's eyes danced. She grinned. "I'm dyin' to tell somebody. It's almost official." The words gushed out, as if they'd been under pressure. "You know, Mike's had a great sales year. I mean, it's been tough and he's been under a bunch of pressure, but things just broke his way this time. It's unreal!"

Lizzie stopped cutting. "Mike's always been a hard worker. I'm excited for you."

"Thanks. It's just that Mike says this almost never happens. It's like all the stars have to align, that sort of thing." Her words ran together. "It's amazing! His commissions have been great, but on top of that he's gonna get a big bonus." Her body made tiny bounces and her voice went up a pitch. "Oh, Mom, Mike's been selected salesman of the year for his region! He's won an award and a trip!"

Lizzie smiled and patted Joanie's hand. "Congratulations! That's terrific."

"It's the first time anything like this's happened for us. All the winners and their spouses get to go to Cancun. Really! Four days at a fancy resort with all expenses paid! I looked online. It's dreamy: infinity pools, perfect beaches, prepaid activities, even cash for shopping." Joanie finally took a breath. "I'm so pumped! There's no way we could afford somethin' like this."

Lizzie kept smiling but a second sense within her niggled a warning, "When is it?"

"Oh, that's the other fun part. It's in November, so we get to escape the snow and cold here for a glorious tropical week. Can you imagine?"

"What about Sandy and Will? Don't they have school?"

"Well, yes. That's where you come in. They adore you so much, I just know they won't be a problem. It'll be a special Grandma time. That's how I look at it. I figure you can stay at our house for the week to make it easier. They'll be in school most days, anyway, and…"

Lizzie's face fell. "But. Wait a minute. Let me think about this."

Joanie looked momentarily confused but quickly rallied. "I guess I didn't mean to spring it on you. But it shouldn't be a problem, should it? I mean they're good kids and you can do things together, you know?

"No. It's not that. I'm sure the kids would love it. So would I. I just…"

"I mean if you think you'll need some help, I bet I could arrange to have—"

"No. It would be fun…but…"

"What then?" Joanie cocked her head. "Mom, this's the trip of a lifetime. I – I want to make sure the kids are covered." She sounded hurt. "Surely, you have the time now…" Joanie's face grew brittle. "Look, I just need you to help us out a little bit."

"Oh, honey, you don't understand." Lizzie stared down at her half cut hosta and lowered her clippers. "I won't be here."

"What?"

"I won't be…here…in the country."

Joanie's expression went slack. Her eyes squinted and then cleared. "Wait. What? Where will you be?"

Lizzie cringed. "In Africa."

Joanie shook her head trying to clear the cobwebs. "Africa? *The* Africa? The country of Africa?"

Lizzie looked at her and sheepishly nodded. "Kampala, actually. That's in Uganda."

"Uganda?"

"Yes."

Joanie carefully set her clippers on the ground as if to distance herself from sharp objects. "Mother, have you completely lost your mind?"

"I hope not."

"You are serious? Uganda?"

"Yes."

"What on earth for?"

"I'm helping a school with a library."

"A school? For how long?"

"I don't know exactly."

"Why?"

Lizzie furrowed her brow. "Why, what? Why don't I know how long? Or why am I going?"

Joanie looked stupefied. "Either. I don't know."

Lizzie tried to organize her thoughts. "I…I—"

Joanie suddenly waved her hands as if erasing her previous questions. "Forget that. When do you leave?"

"The first week in November."

Joanie digested this for a moment and then narrowed her eyes. "Mother, am I the last to know, like usual?"

"No. Nobody…none of the family knows yet. I wanted to tell them, but I—"

"No one knows?"

"No."

"Why not? What is wrong with you?"

"I'm sorry. I just couldn't think of a proper way to explain it. I was worried that—"

"What are we supposed to do? How will Mike and I go on our trip now? For God's sake, Mom! How did you let this happen?"

Lizzie felt trapped and shamed. Tears rose in her eyes. "I didn't mean to make a problem. I just...your father told me on that day in hospice when I said—"

Joanie looked horrified, quickly moved to her mother, and knelt beside her to give her a hug. "Stupid! Listen to me! I can't believe myself. I'm so sorry! I sound like such a spoiled brat! Mom, I didn't mean it the way it came out. Africa! Why didn't you tell us?"

"I didn't know how. I still don't."

Joanie's eyes started to fill with tears, too. She dug out some crumpled Kleenex from a pocket and shared the pieces with Lizzie. "Look, Mom, can we forget about this fall cleanup crap and go inside and talk?"

Lizzie nodded while she dabbed her eyes. "I'd like that. I would really like that."

They stood and abandoned the garden. They left behind the bags and the tools without a second thought, heading across the deck to the back door. On the way, Joanie glanced at her Mom with an odd expression. "Am I *really* the first one in the family to know about this?"

"Yes."

"Cool. 'Cause usually you tell everything to Cece first and then David or me are last. I always hated that."

Lizzie smiled tiredly. "For the record, I promised Cece I'd tell her first, but I never did."

Joanie's eyes shone and a little grin twisted her lips. "Even cooler."

Lizzie shook her head at the comment. "But what about Mike's trip of a lifetime?"

"Ah, forget it. I was just being a jerk. We'll work somethin' else out."

SIX

Setting Out

It was early in the afternoon at the crowded Minneapolis/St. Paul International Airport. Will and Sandy could barely contain themselves with the commotion. Lizzie watched her grandchildren's bright faces. They seemed to drink in the energy from the turmoil of travelers flowing by them. She crouched down to get their attention and wrapped them in a group hug. "Thanks for coming to see me off." She gave them both a solid kiss on the cheek. "You be good while I'm away, okay?"

Both children nodded with serious eyes, then became distracted by the appearance of a skycap pushing a cart of checked bags. They poked each other with squeals of delight and raced away to follow the cart. This brought sharp cautionary calls from Joanie and Mike.

Still crouched, Lizzie held a hand out to her other grandchild, Tomlin, who leaned against his mother's leg nearby. The young boy's eyes carried a dazed look. He had one small arm wrapped around his mother's thigh, the other cradled a stuffed chipmunk. Sharon, David's wife, nudged him gently with her knee. "Go on, give Gramma a hug. She's going bye-bye." Tomlin snuggled tighter to her leg and buried his face.

Lizzie softly tousled the boy's hair as she stood up. "That's fine."

She stretched and looked out at the busy departure area, letting her eyes rove over the rushing people. Most moved with a deliberative pace, wrapped in their own worlds, but a few frenzied souls weaved through the lines, roller bags wobbling in their wake. Not for the first time, Lizzie wondered how God actually kept track of all these people, and all their choices and plans, or if He even did. Is He guiding all of us, or none of us? The answer seemed so clear when she was thinning carrots in her backyard garden, but right now, as a nameless member of a crowd, the concept felt highly suspect.

David watched her. "Having second thoughts, Mom?"

Lizzie smiled. "No. Not really. A little nervous maybe."

Their small group had gathered against a wall, near the currency exchange window, and was shielded from the passing people. She had her new orange carry-on parked beside her and a bulky zippered bag over her shoulder. She felt just a bit conspicuous in her Safari vest and Cargo pants. But the practicality of multiple pockets and an elasticized waistband had won her over. Her carry-on contained a light jacket, perfect for the fluctuations in African temperature. Her calm face masked the rising panic and wild anticipation that warred inside her. This goodbye was her last step, she thought, before her next first step. She was all checked in, stamped and approved, had her passport secured, carried her money in more than one place, had extra glasses along, knew her seat number, knew her gate, had her phone safely stored, had her liquids and pills in Ziplocs, and now simply had to pass through the TSA screening.

She smiled at her family and nodded with what she hoped was finality. "Okay. Thanks for all this. And now, you have your own lives to go back to, and I guess I have a plane to catch. One last hug, then I'm off."

David was first. He murmured into her ear, "You're sure you have everything?"

"Yes. And please don't go through your list."

Sharon was next. "Take care of yourself."

"Don't worry. I'm sure I'll be fine."

Joanie kissed her and held her tight. "You certainly caught us by surprise, but the more I think about it, the prouder I am of you."

"Really?" Lizzie moved her back so she could look her in the eyes. "Thanks. That means a lot. Sorry about messing up your trip."

Joanie shook her head. "Didn't I tell you? Cecelia's comin' to watch the kids. Mike used some frequent flyer miles. You didn't mess anything up. Everything just worked out a different way."

"I'm so relieved."

Mike was last. "Remember that you're on an adventure."

"I'll do my best."

"And surprises may happen. But if at any time you don't know what to do, here's my secret." He glanced around and lowered his voice. "Once, when I was lost driving in Portugal, I kept coming up to these roundabouts and going round and around, not knowing which turn to take. I started to panic. But then I found a way to stop it. I just asked myself what Jason Bourne would do." He nodded. "You know? I just stepped on the gas and became him. It really works."

Lizzie patiently waited for Mike to say something more. When it was obvious that he had nothing further to add, she asked, "Who's Jason Bourne?"

Mike smiled wryly and shook his head. "Ah…never mind."

Everyone waved, even Tomlin, as Lizzie headed off, primly pulling her new carry-on behind her. She followed the path created by stanchions and retractable straps until she joined the other people in line, shuffling toward the TSA checkpoint. She glanced back at her family. They seemed unsure of what to do next, so she waved to them again and then shooed them away, motioning with both her hands. Reluctantly, they left. Lizzie felt a sudden urge to swallow back a lump in her throat, and then returned to her current job of waiting.

⤚

The KLM Airbus rose in a soft updraft and then sank again, causing Lizzie to weave as she walked forward in the long left aisle of the plane. Her seat was in the high numbers, well back in the aircraft, and her ankles were swelling. She remembered that same problem when she and Jonathan had taken their infrequent road trips, and the rare flights to Maui to visit his brother. Walking the aisles was a traveler's trick she had belatedly read about after her first long flight. This time she had the foresight to reserve an aisle seat, which made it a snap to get up when she wanted and trudge the narrow walkways. She had switched from her practical shoes to the KLM booties almost as soon as she settled into her seat. As she walked, they provided a pleasingly tactile feeling against the carpet, especially when she swiveled her wide hips to avoid bumping the shoulders of sleeping passengers. Timing her sojourns to avoid beverage carts and meal services, she often had the aisles nearly to herself. She would hike to the front of the aircraft, take a right just before the first-class cabin, cut through the food prep and toilet areas, and then return down the right aisle, back to the tail, round and round, as if she were marching to Amsterdam.

At one of the large exit doors between sections, where there was open space to stand, she often paused to glance out the door's inset rectangular window. There was seldom anything to view except the gray slate of a remote ocean.

On one of her stops, a round faced businessman in a wrinkled shirt joined her near the door. "Feels good to walk, huh?"

Lizzie nodded and stretched her stiff back. "Do you know how much longer?"

The businessman thought for a bit. "A few more hours to Amsterdam. Is that your final destination?"

Lizzie shook her head. "Uganda."

The man gave her a surprised look. "No kidding? I've been to lots of places but never there. I'm headed to Dusseldorf this trip. Business meeting."

"You travel much?"

He nodded tiredly. "Too much. Ask my wife."

They stood together in the unrelenting rumble of the jet engines and the hiss of the air handlers until the man looked puzzled. "What's that airport in Uganda?"

"Entebbe."

"Oh, that's right, *Entebbe*. Yeah, that's where the Israelis rescued that plane of hostages. Entebbe."

"What?"

"Yeah, they tricked old what's-his-name? You don't remember that?" He appraised her. "You're old enough."

"I don't think so."

"Well, it was…a long time ago, I guess." His multiple chins sank into his chest as he thought. "Amin! Idi Amin! That's the guy. He's dead now. Well, he was nuts. He killed a lotta people. They made a movie – a couple of movies, in fact."

"Oh. A long time ago."

"Yeah, quite a while. I'm sure it's all different now, huh?"

"Yeah."

"Why're you going there?"

Lizzie considered the many paths the conversation could take from here and suddenly heard her cramped but quiet seat at the other end of the plane calling to her. "Business," she replied as she walked off.

⌁

After more than eight hours of flight time, Lizzie's plane arrived in the morning at the Netherlands' busy Schiphol Airport. The deplaning process went smoothly, if slowly, and she soon found herself walking through the central hub of the bright, spacious welcome hall. It felt like an upscale mall with its multi-stories of shops and wildly colorful advertising. Amsterdam was seven hours ahead of Minneapolis time and Lizzie's body felt floaty as she wandered around. She knew her head and her stomach didn't agree on the time of day or the need for food, but she was desperately thirsty. "Stay hydrated," everyone had told her. "Keep drinking water even if you're not thirsty," she remembered her friend Ruthie warning her. So she grabbed a large bottle of water from a nearby shelf. As she approached a cashier, she recalled that she had no euros. Fumbling with the zippers on her over the shoulder bag, she pulled out a ten-dollar-bill and flashed a smile at the young woman behind the counter. "I'm sorry. I feel so stupid, but can you take U.S. dollars?"

The cashier tipped her head cheerfully. "Of course, madam. We take most major currencies, but your change will still be in euros, if that is acceptable." Her voice sounded smooth, her lightly accented English flawless.

Lizzie nodded, relieved. "Yes, that's fine. I'll spend them on the way back. Promise. Sorry, I'm not used to all this; it's my first trip."

The cashier made the exchange and handed her back some euro bills and a few coins. She leaned a little closer to Lizzie and lowered her voice. "Enjoy your visit. Some advice: stay calm, and remember that no one can tell from the outside who you are. Just pretend you're someone else, and let your worries go."

Lizzie nodded, surprised by the clerk's kindness. "Thank you."

As she walked away, Lizzie fingered the odd-sized paper money and unfamiliar coins. She shoved them into a pocket in her vest and zipped it shut. Straightening up, she squared her shoulders and took a long look around. "Jason Bourne," she whispered to herself like a magic spell. Oddly enough, she actually felt a small surge of confidence. Smiling shyly, she took a firm step forward, pulling her bright orange carry-on, and began the search for her departure gate.

Around her, clumps of travelers, some in groups and many in couples and a few singles, moved briskly by, preoccupied with their own destinations and time tables.

Lizzie had no way of appreciating the many changes the Schiphol administrators had enacted to make life smoother for transit passengers from *clean* flights, like herself. Indeed, further physical alterations to airport gates and control areas were still underway. She passed yards of yellow caution tape blocking off certain areas and heard construction clatter from behind the temporary canvas walls. Lizzie didn't know that the recent upsurge in terrorist activities in Europe had thrown even the newest procedures and personnel back into flux again. In the view of the Netherland airport security services, passengers arriving from a country that had a screening level approved by the EU were deemed *clean* and did not have to re-clear security when transferring. On the other hand, those making connections through Schiphol but who had arrived from a non-cleared, or *dirty*, country exited their plane on the new upper floor. There they were required to go through a thorough security check and scan before being allowed to move to their connecting gate, or have access to the rest of the airport.

Due to the practical nature of the Dutch mind, the signage and directions at the airport were easy to see, clear in their wording and plentiful. With few problems, Lizzie was soon approaching the correct gate for her KLM flight to Entebbe. During her walk, she noticed with apprehension how prevalent the Dutch Military Police presence was in the hallways and at the gate lounge areas. She furtively moved her eyes to observe the three stern-faced young men standing stiffly against different walls near her flight's gate. They wore dark uniforms and berets, and held identical stocky weapons in two handed grips, the barrels slanted toward the floor. Their heads and eyes often moved, and their belts bristled with radios and other gear she couldn't identify. The words from an old movie floated through her mind and she realized anew that she was a long way from home.

For international flights, Schiphol provided two waiting areas at each gate: an outer, more spacious area with easy access to the rest of the airport facilities; and behind glass walls, a more restrictive waiting area, designed for final boarding. Since Lizzie was early for her flight, she entered the outer lounge and felt quite satisfied with herself. She made herself comfortable in a surprisingly soft chair in a row of stylish chairs. Sitting one seat down from her was a mustached man in a tweed suit jacket. She glanced at a narrow briefcase at his feet and observed that *De Telegraaf*, a daily Amsterdam newspaper, was opened in his hands. He had a kindly face. She assumed he must be a local businessman.

Lizzie adjusted herself in her chair and then activated her iPhone. She composed a group text to her family to let them know she was fine, had arrived in Amsterdam, and was safely at the gate for Entebbe. *No worries, love you all*, she thumb-typed at the end and pushed *send*. The phone chirped its hopeful *delivered* notification and Lizzie sighed with an unexpected flash of homesickness. She was deciding whether to text Mrs. Birungi and Pastor Kajumba in Kampala when she looked up and caught the eyes of the man in the tweed jacket watching her.

He smiled apologetically. "I'm sorry, but I just admire how flexible you Americans are. Even *you* text." His voice carried the warm open accents of the Dutch.

"Even an *old* American grandma, like me, you mean?"

"No. I would never say that." He laughed. "Here, we prefer to say, *seasoned*."

"And how can you be so sure I'm an American?"

He wore a curious look. "Let's just say, I'm a good observer. My mother noticed that about me when I was still a boy."

"Oh? And does *she* text? Your mother?"

He laughed again. "No, no, not at all. That's my point. I can't get her to try anything new. She says the old ways are better."

"Looking at these soldiers around us, I would say she's probably right."

The man's eyes moved swiftly across the area, noting the

locations of each soldier, and then came back to rest on her face. "Point taken, madam, but we all do what we must."

"Yes, so we say. Are you going to Uganda on business?"

"Me?" He looked at her with surprise. "Oh, no, I am not going anywhere near Entebbe. My flight doesn't leave for hours yet. I'm heading to…Milan. How about you?" His eyes briefly darted toward the glassed-in final boarding area for Lizzie's flight, where uniformed agents questioned a young man in a dark green jacket.

Lizzie didn't notice. "My final destination is Kampala."

His gaze shifted back to her. "Really? How unusual. What will you do there?" The man's left hand unobtrusively touched a small device in his ear.

Lizzie wondered if the poor man needed to adjust a hearing aid and felt self-conscious about it. Just in case, she spoke a little louder. "It's a long story. I'm just helping a private school. Nothing special."

"All the way to Uganda?" he replied. "That seems special to me. You must be an old hand at this. I suppose you travel often?"

Behind them, the interrogation in the next room escalated. The man in the green jacket was arguing with two blue-shirted security agents. A third agent spoke to another passenger, an olive-skinned man with a shiny Halliburton briefcase. The briefcase man angrily snapped out his passport and handed it to the agent. A female KLM attendant joined the group with a printout in hand. She compared the man's passport to something on her paper and asked him a question.

Lizzie, unaware of the drama behind her, glowed with satisfaction. "That just shows you may not be as observant as you think. This is actually my first real trip anywhere! But I was told if I pretended to be confident on the outside, no one could tell I was terrified on the inside."

The man in the tweed jacket carefully set aside his newspaper. His eyes looked past Lizzie even as he answered her. "Good advice for another time. Today, I'm afraid, nothing is what it appears to be."

His voice abruptly jumped in intensity. "Stay very still, madam!"

Loud shouts and scuffling broke out in the final boarding area. Lizzie, and most nearby passengers, turned at the racket. The olive-skinned man suddenly slapped his metallic case across the attendant's face. She screamed and collapsed. A nearby agent jumped at the man to restrain him, only to be yanked backwards by the other man in the green jacket. The agent was thrown viciously into a row of chairs, his arms flailing as he went down. Other officials struggled to grab the two men, but their efforts were too late. The desperate suspects were already running. They leaped a low barricade and forced their way back out into the lounge area.

Lizzie watched frozen, her phone still in her hand. The black-clad soldiers around the gate area came instantly to life, swinging up their deadly weapons.

The two fleeing men bolted in different directions. One dashed away, toward distant stairs. The other sprinted directly at Lizzie and leaped over her row of seats. Lizzie's body instinctively ducked without ever consulting her conscious mind. The man's foot clipped the phone from her hand and sent it tumbling. The momentum carried her out of her seat and face down onto the floor.

Lizzie had trouble processing her reactions. Nothing like this had ever happened to her before. Her body felt suddenly strange. She was aware that her perception of the sounds around her had an oddly hollow and ringing quality. It was not that she couldn't hear, it was as if her hearing, on its own, had selected what it wanted her to pay attention to. Stuck in the half world of shock, she lifted her head from the cool tile and observed a number of unexpected things. The fleeing man managed to keep his footing – she clearly heard the sharp squeaks of his rubber soles on the floor. A few travelers stumbled, trying to get out of his way. Why was he running?

Suddenly, the man in the tweed jacket was there, sweeping the young man's feet out from under him. What? Lizzie's mind had trouble sorting out the blur of images and sounds presented to it. Her ears clearly heard the solid smack of the young man's head hitting the floor, but her eyes had trouble following the motions of the man in the tweed jacket. All she knew was that he suddenly ended up on top of the other man. His knee ground into the young man's spine. Somehow, like a rabbit out of a hat, a gun appeared.

Lizzie's mind stuttered. A gun? Shoved against the back of the young man's head. A gun! Where had that come from?

Her internal questions were shattered by the powerful voice of the man in the tweed jacket. "Stay down! Now! That's a gun on your head! Don't move! Now!"

Lizzie's ears and eyes abruptly caught up with each other. All the sounds in the airport came crashing back into full sync and clarity. She was suddenly aware of people's voices around her, rapid voices, many in foreign languages, some in panic, others sharp, and a few angry. She shook her head, bewildered by the cacophony of sounds. In the distance, she heard an incongruous final boarding announcement for a flight to Brussels.

She noticed groans and abrasive sounds nearer at hand and was startled to see two of the armed soldiers fall upon the dazed young man. They wrenched his arms behind his back.

The man in the tweed jacket stood now, his gun still at the ready. He barked orders in rapid-fire Dutch.

The soldiers nodded in quick obedience. One tightly handcuffed the man's wrists. The other took a quick step back, rotated his weapon, and aimed it at the young man. The first soldier yanked the suspect to his feet and gripped him by the collar.

The man in the tweed jacket turned away and stood still, listening, one hand cupping his earpiece, the other hanging slack beside his leg, idly fingering his gun. He nodded curtly and made his weapon vanish behind his back, beneath his coat.

Lizzie slowly climbed to her feet and found him immediately beside her, supporting her arm. "Let me help you, madam. I am so sorry. Are you hurt?"

"No. I don't think so."

He guided her back to her seat and knelt in front of her, still grasping her arm. "Look in my eyes. Nice and wide. There. Yes. Let me see your – what do you say? The small round parts of the eyes…"

Lizzie stared into his concerned face and smiled. "Pupils?"

"Yes, I want to see your *pupils*. The sizes." He put his face close to hers and carefully checked her eyes, rapidly looking from one to the other. "Did you hit your head?"

"No. I think I ducked."

"Good for you. You were fast. I saw you."

"No, I wasn't."

He winked. "Fast enough." He patted her knee. "Your pupils look okay. Okay?"

She nodded. "Who are they – the two men?"

Before answering, he stood and fired a sharp question in Dutch to someone behind her. Lizzie turned to see the other fugitive approaching. He was bleeding from his nose, handcuffed and bracketed by scowling soldiers, and limping as they hustled him along. One of the young soldiers held up the metal briefcase and replied with a gruff, "Ja!" and a fleeting smirk.

In the busy airport areas beyond the soldiers, Lizzie noticed groups of security people, some with blue shirts and ties, and others with bright yellow vests and helmets, moving intently through gawking travelers, all swiftly converging on her gate.

The man in the tweed jacket knelt back down in front of her. "Who are they? Terrorists. They were both on your flight."

Lizzie felt surprised at how calm she felt. "That's what I thought. Is there a bomb?"

"Doubtful," he shrugged. "They were on their way to someplace else to do their mischief. Not here."

Lizzie felt a little queasy, as if her mind was still a half-step behind her body. "What happens now?"

"Your plane will be searched. The flight is cancelled, I'm afraid."

"Oh, my!"

He made a face. "Rules are rules. Everyone must be interviewed, even you. I apologize. Much delays."

She looked thoughtful. "Wait. How did you know about them?"

He looked away, considering whether to explain, and then looked directly into her face. "Security spotted one upstairs, during the screen. He is on a list. We watched him here until he gave the other away. Two birds, one stone." He winked as he stood up. "Now, I must go before the paperwork begins."

She touched his arm. "Thank you, for what you do."

He leaned over her. "No, madam. Thank you for what *you* do."

Lizzie looked at him oddly. "What do you mean?"

"You are doing something good. Not business. Not pleasure. You are more important than all the rest of this." He picked up his briefcase. "Goodbye, madam. Safe travels."

He walked away and she called after him. "Give my regards to your mother."

He grinned, executed a gracious nod in reply, and then he was off, effortlessly blending into the crowd.

SEVEN

Change of Plan

Lizzie let her face hover over her steaming cup of Dutch tea and breathed in the tantalizing orange pekoe fragrance. Exhausted, she could feel a headache growing. She needed sleep but she no longer needed more food. The KLM gate agents were doing their best to soften the stressful experience for their passengers. The airline kept a wide table supplied with raw vegetables, tiny sandwiches and tea treats. Lizzie had sampled too many of one particular local delicacy, a tempting crispy waffle cookie with syrup in the middle, called *stroopwafel*.

But a delay remained a delay, despite the heady feeling of catastrophe averted. Their old departure gate had been taped off and all the passengers had been trooped together to a new gate nearby. Lengthy interviews followed, along with bag checks, dog sniffing, passport scrutiny, and on and on – now into the fourth hour. They watched out the tall terminal windows as their former plane was emptied of every piece of checked luggage. The multitude of bags ended up spread out on the tarmac, no bag allowed to touch another, and thoroughly searched. Meanwhile, other agents clambered inside the dark holds with flashlights and bomb dogs.

Finally, an announcement was made in multiple languages that a replacement aircraft had been secured and prepared and would soon be taxied to their current gate. A fresh flight crew had been assigned and were on their way. New tickets would be issued and seat assignments made within the hour.

The flight to Entebbe was tentatively scheduled to depart at 4:55 pm local time, which would put them on the ground in Uganda around 2 am in East Africa time tomorrow. Sighs and grumbling swept through the gate area at the news, but Lizzie's heart sharply skipped a beat. She had failed to notify Pastor Kajumba or Mrs. Birungi about her situation! It had never entered her mind! What was wrong with her? Her last text to her family had said that all was well and she was sitting at the gate waiting to board. That felt like a lifetime ago.

She grabbed her personal bag and unzipped it on her lap, checking every pocket and pouch. She dug around inside vainly searching for the cell phone. Stunned, she felt a sudden weight drop into her stomach. Of course it wasn't in her bag! She vividly recalled where that iPhone had to be.

≼

A stocky Dutch policeman with a bright yellow vest over his uniform held up a tagged iPhone from the cluttered evidence tables. Lizzie stood nervously outside the security-taped boundary of their former departure gate and nodded her head.

"Yes, that's it! Can I see it, please?"

The policeman brought it over to her in his latex-gloved hands and carefully held it up, just out of reach, for her visual inspection.

"Yes, that's definitely mine. I dropped it when that terrorist knocked me down."

"Is broken," he said simply.

Lizzie cringed at the phone's shattered face and the chipped corner. "Can I have it back?"

The policeman paused. "Is evidence. Can you prove you own?"

"Sure. If you turn it on, I can enter my passcode."

"Does not turn on. Is broken."

Lizzie was stymied. "Wait. No. For Pete's sake, look, the face has my fingerprints all over it. Here you can check." She wiggled her fingers at him. "They'll match. Clearly, it's mine."

The policeman slumped his shoulders. "Madam, it is logged as evidence and cannot be released. I am sorry. You can leave contact information and we will— "

"No. This is crazy! Look, sir, officer, I have to text people. I mean, the ones who are supposed to meet me. My plane has changed. They don't know. Please. Their numbers are in that phone!"

The policeman held the phone and gave her a blank look.

Her exhaustion forgotten, Lizzie struggled to keep her panic suppressed. She swallowed her fear and kept her voice level. "Can you just try pushing the *on* button for me so I can see it really doesn't work?"

The officer pushed the large *start* button at the bottom center of the face. He watched and then held the phone out for her to see the result. Nothing happened on the broken screen. Not a flicker.

Lizzie paced. The policeman started to walk away. "Wait, wait! Try that button on the top edge." She demonstrated with her hands. "Top right edge. See...see it there?"

The policeman looked at the phone and nodded.

"That worked for me once," she said. "Hold that down a few seconds and then let go. It should...restart. Honest. A young man showed me once. I had to do it one other time."

"Madam, we already checked this..."

"Please. Just try it." She mustered a weak smile. "Humor an old woman, will you?"

The policeman sighed. He awkwardly rotated the iPhone, depressed the *wake/sleep* button on the right top edge, and held it for a few seconds before releasing it. He again dutifully extended the phone for her to verify. Nothing changed. The shattered screen remained utterly lifeless.

"Is broken," he repeated gently.

⌇

Back at the new gate area, Lizzie knelt beside her orange carry-on spread open on the carpet. She anxiously flipped through folders and notebooks, searching for her Kampala phone numbers. Behind her, at the gate desk, fellow passengers exchanged their old tickets for new boarding passes with updated seat assignments. The rebooking announcements had been repeated a number of times. Lizzie knew she needed to get in that line, but she felt she had to solve this dilemma first. At last, she turned over another folded page and there was her backup list of important phone numbers!

She ran a finger down her choices. Pastor Kajumba: he was hard to reach and slow to get back. Not him. The general school number was no good. She glanced over at a local clock: 4:30 pm. Kampala was an hour ahead – 5:30 pm. Too late. No one would be there. She decided her best chance was Mrs. Birungi, but Lizzie wasn't sure if the listed number was her personal cell or a shared phone. They communicated mainly by e-mail and only recently by text. It didn't matter. It was all she had.

She flipped closed her messy suitcase and knelt on it to get it zipped. She gathered everything together, threw her zippered bag over her shoulder, and rushed into the wider lounge area. Moving at a quick walk, her eyes scoured the walls for a public phone. Nothing. She remembered seeing one somewhere, but couldn't recall where. She had thought it funny, at the time, since the wall phone had been colored a bright green.

Lizzie hurried down a hallway, reading every public sign, hoping for some direction. Failing to spot anything useful, she urgently waved at a pair of female airport agents who happened by. "Excuse me? Is there a public phone nearby?"

The pair stopped and looked at her. One was older and shorter than the other. They briefly consulted with each other in Dutch before answering.

The younger one scratched her head. "*Ja*, public phones." She nibbled on her little finger, thinking. "Not so many, these days."

The older agent pointed farther down the hallway. "Think there is still one near news shop. *Ja*, think so."

The younger one nodded, unsure. "Maybe. By news shop. Okay. Follow hall and then go left."

Lizzie looked where she pointed. "How far?"

"Not far."

"Thanks." Lizzie started off.

The older woman asked, "You have phone card?"

Lizzie stopped. "No."

"You need phone card."

"Will cash work?" She fingered her vest pocket. "I have some euro coins and paper money."

The woman shook her head. "Not that phone. No cash. Not anymore. Phone card is best."

Lizzie was frustrated. "I have a…what about a credit card?"

The Dutch pair looked at each other.

Lizzie's mind was racing. "Visa? Will it take Visa? I'm running out of time."

The younger agent nodded while the older one shook her head. The younger one said, "Yes, it take Visa, and…other cards."

"But no, don't use credit cards!" The older one immediately chimed in. "Big scam! When you see bill, you will be not happy!"

The younger one belatedly agreed. "*Ja*, rip off! Charge hundreds of euros. No. Buy phone card at news shop. Much cheaper."

Confused, but resigned, Lizzie nodded and hurried off.

Inside the news shop, Lizzie threaded through spinner displays of European magazines and newspapers, trying to find a clerk. At the other end of the store, she spotted a middle-aged Indian lady in a dark pink veil who turned and smiled at her. "May I be of help?" She wore a nose-to-ear-chain dangling tiny jewels and seemed the picture of serenity.

Lizzie fought to catch her breath. "Can you sell me a phone card?"

"Of course." The clerk's head softly rocked back and forth in the Indian way of agreement. "Do you mean a KPN card? That's the most accepted."

"I don't know what I mean. I'm gonna use that green phone right outside. I have to call Uganda."

"Then the KPN card is best." The Indian clerk moved gracefully to racks of phone cards and indicated a row of KPN cards with *5*, *10* and *20* euro values printed on them. "How much do you need?"

"Who knows? I've never used one." Lizzie brushed at the beads of sweat glistening above her eyebrows. "How much do you think? I'm calling Kampala."

The woman rocked her head back and forth. "Kampala? I know not. I have zero friends in Africa. Will you be making more than one call?"

"Beats me. Depends if they answer."

"More calls, more fees." The clerk held a single manicured and jeweled finger up. "You only will get the best rate if you only make one phone call."

Lizzie looked at her with an empty expression.

The clerk assessed the situation and reluctantly nodded. "Okay. The safest path for you is the twenty-euro card. Whatever minutes are left over you can use later. It will expire not for three months."

"Alright." Lizzie sounded relieved. "The twenty-euro card. So, how much?"

The clerk stared quietly at her. "The twenty-euro card is… twenty euros, plus a small fee for activation."

"Of course." Lizzie felt so stupid. "Of course, twenty is twenty. I knew that. I'm a little rattled. I meant, how much in U.S. money?"

"Oh, I see. In U.S.? Yes. I will need to check. Please allow me a moment?" Lizzie nodded. The clerk glided back behind the cash register and lifted out a formidable calculator.

Lizzie leaned against the wall next to the bright green public phone. She had the receiver scrunched against her shoulder while she used her fingernail to scratch off the coating over the phone card's PIN. In the same hand, she clutched the paper with Mrs. Birungi's phone number. Her orange carry-on and bulky zippered bag were huddled about her feet.

Flipping over the phone card, she squinted at the printed instructions. I can do this, she told herself. It's just a phone call. I'm a grown woman. She held up the card and voiced herself through the first step. "Okay, to begin, dial the toll free number." She dialed a *1* followed by the ten digit 800 number printed on the card, being careful to get every number right. She was immediately confronted by a loud warbling tone. A robotic voice declared that the call could not be completed as dialed.

"What? That's crazy!"

She flipped the card over and back, checking both sides. "I'm sure I dialed it right."

She felt the rising pressure to return to her gate and get a boarding pass. It wouldn't help if she missed the flight! Out of ideas, she hung up the receiver and then noticed prominent printing across the front surface of the base unit, just above the handset. *If making an international call, or toll-free call, please include the Netherlands international calling prefix, 00.*

Lizzie shut her eyes in a brief fury. She took a breath and held it, until she felt back in control. Opening her eyes again, she slowly exhaled. Note to self, she thought. You're no longer in the United States – you idiot!

She lifted the receiver again and dialed *00* followed by her toll free access number. This time, she heard a few *pings* and *clicks* and a *chime,* followed by an accented female recorded voice. "Thank you for using KPN cards, your best value in the Netherlands. Please enter your…six-digit PIN…now."

Lizzie brought the phone card close to her glasses in order to read the PIN. She cautiously pushed each digit. A new series of *clicks* sounded, and then a relaxed male digitized voice said, "Welcome! This account has a balance of…twenty-euros…remaining. Please enter the phone number you wish to call, including the country code."

Lizzie breathed a quick prayer as she dialed the Uganda country code, *256,* followed by the number for Mrs. Birungi. The male voice was back. "Funds in this account are sufficient for…thirty minutes…of air time to this number."

A distant and muffled ringing began. It was nearly drowned out by loud *clacks* and persistent pounding, almost like a hailstorm. She heard the connection open and a remote female voice, "Hello. *Ono ani?*"

Lizzie wasn't sure what the other words meant, or even if the voice belonged to Mrs. Birungi. The interference on the line was now roaring in and out, like an angry tide. Lizzie spoke slowly and clearly into the phone. "I am trying to reach Nankunda Birungi. Is this Mrs. Birungi?"

The voice on the other end was hard to hear. "*Sikuwulira.*"

Lizzie shouted into the phone. "What? Can you hear me?"

"*Wangi?*"

"This is Elizabeth Warton. I am trying to reach Nankunda Birungi. Can you help me?"

"*Wangi? Sikutegede, nnyabo.*"

The interference on the line altered again. This time every sound echoed and popped, but at least it was easier to hear words. Lizzie tried again. "Birungi! Mrs. Birungi! I need to talk to Mrs. Birungi!"

"*Birungi, Birungi taliwo. Damu okube edako.*"

Lizzie felt a sliver of hope. "Yes, Birungi! Mrs. Birungi! Can you talk English?"

"*Nsonyiwa, nnyabo. Byoyegera sibiwulira.*"

The woman's voice sounded irritated, to Lizzie. She could sense her desire to end the call. "Don't hang up. Okay? Please!"

"Call back, *nnyabo.*"

Lizzie was startled. "Wait! You *do* speak English." There was a long gap. The hisses on the line were growing worse. "Are you still there? Hello?"

The woman's voice finally came again. "Call back."

"You don't understand. I'm at an airport."

"*Weeraba.*"

"No!"

The woman ended the connection.

Lizzie stood in shock, the handset still against her ear. The male voice said, "There are *twelve-euros* left on this card."

She hung up and leaned her forehead against the phone. Maybe that wasn't Birungi; or maybe it was, but the noise made it impossible for her to understand the situation. Lizzie had never actually talked to Mrs. Birungi, so she wasn't sure how fluent her spoken English was. She only knew she needed to try again. The woman had said to *call back*. Lizzie knew that really meant *call back later*. But she didn't have *later*. She only had *now*.

The heavy plastic of the phone unit felt cool against her forehead. What would she do if no one was at Entebbe to meet her? What then? At 2 in the morning! She hissed like a teakettle to stop her dark thoughts. She wouldn't allow herself to face those fears yet. First things first. And first, in this case, meant that she needed to redial all those numbers again.

On her next adventure with calling, Lizzie noted that the male voice claimed there were now only *nine-euros* remaining in her account. Wait! Hadn't he just told her she had *twelve*?

After she successfully dialed Mrs. Birungi's number, he assured her she had sufficient funds for *eight minutes* of air time. What?

How did this work? Hadn't he said she had *thirty minutes* before the last call? So far she could swear she'd barely talked even a minute!

Her questions stopped when she heard the phone ringing. The line was clear and clean this time around. The phone kept ringing. Lizzie waited. She had time to reflect upon the fact that Uganda used double rings before their pauses, instead of the single rings as in the U.S. Why didn't someone answer? The double rings kept going and going. Suddenly, there was an abrupt *clack*, an extended *clunk*, and then the dial tone.

In Lizzie's next try, after the obnoxious *chime*, the male voice declared that she had *two-euros* left and that was only worth *three minutes* of air time. Lizzie had given up trying to understand. She just plodded ahead, pushed the buttons and waited for the ringing to start. The noisy line was back. She heard a remote double ring in a sea of static. She thought she heard a connection made but it just as quickly vanished into the noise. The male voice calmly affirmed that there were *zero euros* left on her card.

❧

A tired KLM gate agent studied Lizzie's original boarding pass and frowned. "I'm sorry you didn't get here sooner, ma'am."

Lizzie sighed, "You and me both."

The agent looked up. "What?"

"Nothing."

The agent nodded, typed a few keys and stared. "I'm afraid I no longer have any aisle seats available. This is a smaller plane."

Lizzie leaned heavily against the ticket counter and didn't say anything.

The agent glumly pecked keys. "The best I can do is put you in a window seat one row up from the back. Sorry."

"It's not your fault."

"At least, the seat still reclines," she smiled apologetically.

"And I'm close to the toilets, I guess," Lizzie added, trying to sound upbeat.

"Yes, there is that." The agent struggled to preserve a neutral face. "You are...quite close to the toilets." She made a few final keystrokes and a printer spat out the new boarding pass. She handed it to Lizzie. "And at least you can see outside."

"Right. Thank you."

"Have a good flight."

❦

Lizzie's head rattled against the small round window as the plane rode out another period of turbulence. In her vain efforts to sleep she had learned that every minor bump the aircraft encountered was exaggerated by the time it reached her seat in the tail. She recalled playing crack-the-whip with high school friends on an outdoor skating rink. Not a good memory. She loosened her seatbelt and shut her eyes. Her tired mind tried to cope by conjuring dreams of fat dolphins lurching up and down the heaving waves in a troubled sea. Her aching body was wrapped in a thin KLM blanket that never seemed to reach both her arms and ankles at the same time. Her skin alternated between shivering and sweating. The air was a miasma of airline food prep, human bodies and chemical odors. An hour earlier, the bony man beside her had let his head collapse onto his long arms, which were crisscrossed over his fold-down tray. The man's labored breathing and frequent snorts confirmed that he still lived.

A sudden *whoosh* from one of the ever-busy toilets just a row behind her seat put an end to Lizzie's dreams of sea creatures. Painfully aware that she was now wide awake, she refused to open her eyes. She wiggled her numb toes, certain her lower legs were swollen. When she shifted her body, trying to get comfortable, she felt the first pressure of an awakening bladder. She wondered how much longer the trip would take. The last time she had attempted to use the touch screen on the back of the seat in front of her, their little plane icon was pinned above a huge orange desert. The counter indicated that there were more than five hours left to go. She had little sense of how long ago that was. Her journey had taken on a never-ending quality, but every time she thought of her night arrival at this alien airport, with no one to meet her, she shuddered.

EIGHT

First Impressions

The smell was the first thing to hit her. She felt a breeze coming off Lake Victoria, which was close beside the airport, but instead of freshening the air, it carried the disturbing sweetness of wet, rotting vegetation. When mingled with jet fuel exhaust and the heavy smells of unwashed bodies, the result was memorable.

From the top of the passenger stairway ramp Lizzie saw little of the nighttime countryside, just the barest hint of sparse trees. The humidity settled on her like a damp sweater. The bland three-story terminal building was poorly lighted and displayed a blue horizontal sign with white English lettering: *Welcome to the Pearl of Africa.* She brushed at her nose and descended the worn metal steps. Once at the bottom, she yanked up the handle on her bag and followed the other passengers as they crossed the cracked tarmac ahead of her.

There were two lines for immigration. One was for Ugandans returning home – that line, short to begin with, had held no one for an hour. The other line was for everyone else on the plane. It snaked out the door and down the outer entry hallway. Two unflappable immigration officials, in wrinkled ties and ragged royal blue coats, sluggishly processed the travelers.

Lizzie felt dazed. She was pleased to put off making decisions for the time being, and oddly content to slowly shuffle forward, with baby steps, toward the next hurdle.

She had anxiously watched out her window when the plane was on final approach, wanting to see something – anything. Not that she had high expectations. After all, it was the middle of the night. She had thought maybe there would be a few scattered lights, an illuminated roadway, perhaps, the twinkling jewelry of a town or two, even the lonely headlights of a car on the road. What she saw instead was unrelenting darkness, no matter where she looked. Her impression was that there was nothing out there at all, as if the pilots were lowering their landing gears over an immense hole in the earth. It had frightened her. The only thing she had seen in her window, even when she cupped her hands around her head, was her own reflection, staring.

"Good morning, lady." The immigration officer had a wide face and a shining, hairless scalp. He was a big man with large hands. His skin glowed in the fluorescents, and the whites of his eyes carried yellow tinges in the corners. "Papers, please."

Lizzie slid her passport, her yellow-fever immunization card and arrival papers across the narrow marble counter.

The officer quickly fanned the documents out in front of him with a practiced flourish. He looked closely at her passport photo and then swiveled his chair to look intensely at her face. Satisfied, he thumbed noisily through her passport booklet to the visa page. He made a repeated popping sound with his thick lips. Concluding his study, he sniffed officiously and gave her a sideways glance. "Missionary?"

Lizzie paused, then said, "No. A librarian."

"Librarian?" He slowly rolled the unfamiliar syllables on his tongue, "*Li-bay-lee-an.*" He flipped one of his hands palm up, as if to say, *Huh?*

"Books. I take care of books. I'm helping a Christian school with their books." She hesitated, thinking. "We're making a library."

The officer propped his chin onto his thick fist and leaned closer. "A library? Where?"

Lizzie felt the beginnings of unease. "In Kampala. At the school. It's in the Makindye District."

"No libraries in U.S., lady?"

"Many libraries," she said carefully.

"How long you stay?"

"I don't know yet."

The officer cocked his head at her and waited for a better answer. One thick brown finger tapped the countertop.

Lizzie tried again. "Well, at least three weeks. I've never been here before."

"Visa good for much longer."

"I know."

He shook his head. "Why you come here, lady?"

"To help." She didn't know what he wanted. "They asked for my help."

The officer bobbed his head a few times and squinted in thought. His free hand reached for his stamper. Clearly, he had made up his mind and expected no further interaction.

"Three months! Missionary!" He swiftly banged his stamper down on her visa page and onto the other arrival papers. Sorting everything into a neat pile, he shoved it back at Lizzie. "Enjoy your time in Uganda, okay, lady?"

Still a little anxious, she took the papers in one hand and her carry-on handle in the other. "Thank you," she said.

But the big man had already turned away, waving forward the next person in line.

In the cramped baggage hall behind immigration, Lizzie saw her checked bag sitting on a stalled carousel. Its orange color looked ghastly under the harsh overhead lights. The ceiling seemed low to her. When she looked up, she realized a number of the fluorescent tubes were out, while others buzzed ominously. She was surprised by the sudden appearance of a baggage handler who crawled through the cramped bag doors on what should have been a mechanized conveyor belt, dragging more luggage. The short man dropped the new luggage on the carousel next to her bag, and then exited out the same little doors, presumably to get more.

Nearby, a pair of black soldiers in camos, with loosely strapped weapons, watched Lizzie pull her bag off the conveyor. She self-consciously stacked her luggage into a single unit, sliding the cloth strap of the carry-on over the handle of the larger, checked bag, just as she had seen demonstrated on the Amazon video when she bought the set. Now, what?

She observed a few fellow passengers exit the hall through large, frosted glass doors on the far side of the room. In front of these doors were multiple stations for customs agents. No one currently occupied them. Sets of empty tables stood near the walls, clearly meant to be used for searching luggage. Signs around the room warned against smuggling and threatened import fines and incarceration for those caught making false declarations. Swallowing nervously, Lizzie pulled her bags behind her and moved in that direction. Keeping her head down, she expected to be stopped or questioned by someone at any moment. Instead, she passed between the vacant customs stations and out the frosted doors into Uganda, without a single word being uttered.

Exiting the terminal doors, Lizzie was immediately confronted by smiling and waving Ugandans. They called out in English, or Luganda, or one of their other dialects, and there was much pointing and hugging as they greeted their arriving friends and relatives.

Despite the early hour, many members of the crowd were dressed up in their cultural finery. Older women wore their *Gomesi*, floor-length, brightly colored dresses with a square neckline and short, puffed sleeves. The dresses were tied with wide sashes placed below the waist and over the hips. Lizzie felt pleasantly surprised by the generous size of most of those hips, and immediately more confident about her own appearance. Some of the men wore suit coats over long flowing garments. The rest of the members of the excited crowd appeared clad in a hodge-podge of clothing types and levels of quality. American T-shirts seemed to be one of the staples with the boys, along with jeans and flip-flops. Many of the young women wore stylish European outfits and braids with vividly colorful accents. The public lighting outdoors proved sparse, but the locals came prepared with flashlights and kerosene lanterns. Obviously, by the size of the turnout, Lizzie's fellow passengers had been able to communicate the flight arrival change to their contacts.

Lizzie's eyes swept futilely over the noisy crowd. She prayed for the tall presence of Pastor Kajumba. Deep down, she didn't really expect to see him, but his confirmed absence rattled her anew. Many of the Ugandans held signs with hand-written names, and they continually waved their lights across them. She checked each one just to be sure, but her name remained missing. Lizzie's exhaustion rapidly shifted into panic. Jason Bourne didn't help in the least. What should she do?

Eventually, she cleared the crowd of greeters and now faced a collection of Ugandan cab drivers, hawking their services. The taxis consisted of two types: white vans with a row of blue squares painted around their middles, suitable for taking multiple people to various destinations; and small private cars, mostly white, which were called *special hires* and took one person to one destination. Some of the vans did a brisk business, loading up newly arrived Ugandans and their hosts. Fat suitcases and boxes were muscled onto the worn cargo racks on top. Full vehicles pulled out in a blare of horns, the happy crowd rapidly thinning. The arrival of Lizzie, however, with her bags in tow, and a lost look painted across her face, brought new hope to the collection of disgruntled drivers still waiting for a fare.

Calls of "*Muzungu! Muzungu!*" could be heard as they rushed toward her, jockeying with each other for her attention. Since all the taxis faced the terminal and most of their headlights were on, Lizzie only saw silhouettes of the men calling and gesturing at her. The headlights glared in and out of her eyes as the men passed back and forth in front of them.

"*Muzungu,* over here!"

"Cheap taxi, lady!"

"*Mumerika,* over here! Look!"

One suddenly blocked her way. "Hey *muzungu,* where to? Let's go!"

She turned and angled around him.

Another pulled on the handle of her bag. "Best taxi, yes?"

"*Ogenda wa, nnyabo?*" shouted another as he grabbed the other side of her bag and tugged against his rival.

Lizzie jerked back control of her luggage with an audible grunt. She turned away from them all, but the drivers pursued her.

"Where you need ride to, lady?"

"We help. Come with us."

"No problems, lady."

Lizzie finally glared at them and shouted. "Stop it! Stop talking and listen!"

Shocked at the outburst, the drivers stood still.

"I need to go to Kampala. Wobulezi School. Do you hear?"

There was a lull. At first, no one responded. Then a few called out, "Kampala, okay!"

Lizzie persisted. "No! Not just Kampala. I said the Wobulezi School in Kampala. Who knows?"

A few voices echoed back, sounding puzzled. "Wobulezi? Wobulezi?"

A nearby driver stepped up. "No problem, get in, we ask." He pointed to his van and bowed lavishly like a hotel doorman.

A few of the others started up again, not to be outdone. "No! *We* can ask. Lady! Over here!"

Soon they were all once again shouting and struggling to regain Lizzie's attention.

One of the men from the *special hire* cars pushed through the noisy van drivers and placed himself in front of them. He was middle-aged, his hair cut high and tight. His eyes were large and he was better dressed than the rest of the men. He wore a grey baseball cap and doffed it before addressing her in a polite tone. "Madam, did you say Wobulezi School? The one in Makindye District?"

Lizzie looked at him with unabashed relief. His English pronunciation was excellent. "Yes, that's right." Her voice was failing and her throat was dry. "Do you know it?"

"Of course. I have a young nephew who went there."

Lizzie brightened with sudden hope. "Really? Do you know Pastor Kajumba or Mrs. Birungi?"

The man shook his head gently. "No. I am sorry."

Lizzie let out a frustrated breath. "But you could take me to the school?"

"Of course."

"How far is it?"

"About forty-five minutes."

Lizzie was momentarily shocked but shook it off. She had no idea that the school was that distant.

The other drivers saw their fare slipping away and made some last appeals. "This is *special hire* driver – not taxi!"

"Too expensive, lady."

"Don't believe him."

The *special hire* driver's eyes flared, and he took a threatening step toward the van drivers. "*Vva mu kino! Osise ekira! Genda!*"

Shocked at the anger, Lizzie looked confused. "What are they saying? Aren't you a taxi?"

"Yes, lady. I am for hire, same as them." The other drivers backed off, but their expressions looked foul. "They have van taxis and they pile in riders, each one paying part of the fare. That's why they say they're cheaper. But it's crowded and makes many stops. I am a *special hire* car. You are my only passenger, and I take you directly to your destination. I am more expensive but also safer, more private and faster."

"I see. How much will you cost?"

"From the airport to the school…maybe, 100,000 shillings."

One of the nearby drivers called out, "Too much, lady. We do for 70,000."

Another shouted, "No trust him, lady."

The *special hire* driver glared back at them. "*Kitte, Mbwamwe! Wange! Zikira bwoba omanyi kyoyagala!*" The muscles in his jaw pulsed in anger and then relaxed.

He turned back to Lizzie and calmly motioned for her to walk with him away from the other taxis. "Perhaps we could go to a quieter place to talk. You look so tired."

Lizzie fretted over the verbal exchange, but she nodded. She was fed up with the pushy cabbies. The sound of their language grated on her ears. Her weariness threatened to overtake her. She remembered again just how thirsty she was and figured that she must look a fright. Pushing a few wayward clumps of hair out of her eyes, she followed along behind the driver. He smoothly took control of her bags and guided her to his car.

When he opened the back door for her, Lizzie balked. "Wait. I haven't decided that I'm going with you yet."

"I understand, madam," he replied smoothly. "I'm just offering you a place to sit and some quiet, as I said. Nothing else, yet. Trust me."

She sank into the soft seat and sighed. "Okay. Thank you. Just so you know, I don't have any shillings. So, how much is 100,000 in U.S. money?"

"About 30 of your dollars. And you won't have to convert it, I can take American cash."

Lizzie thought for a short time. It didn't seem that expensive compared to taxis at home, even Uber. If she rode for 45 minutes in any city in the U.S., she'd expect to pay a lot more than that.

"Are there any other charges? Or extras I don't know about?"

The driver smiled serenely as he leaned an arm on the roof of the cab. "No, lady. Of course, not. No hidden fees. Not like those other taxis."

Lizzie closed her eyes and took a deep breath, even more aware of the comfort of the seat and the pleasant receding of her earlier panic. She opened her eyes and looked up at the patient driver. "I'm sorry I'm so slow to decide what to do."

The driver gently tapped the top of his car and stepped back to give her space. "Take your time. Rest. I am in no hurry."

Lizzie felt awkward and defensive. "You understand that my flight was unexpectedly changed. I mean, my people would have met me here, for sure, but I was unable to call them."

The driver nodded slowly.

Much to her embarrassment, Lizzie began to cry. "That's the only reason I'm in this situation!"

The driver came back close enough to softly squeeze the top cushion on her seat. "You will be fine. If you wish, you can stay at the airport until the sun comes back. Their chairs are uncomfortable, but you will be safe. Your friends should find you by then, yes?"

Lizzie nodded and turned away to rub at her stupid tears. She faced him again and put on a brave front. "The Wobulezi School has boarding students, so I'm sure someone will be there to help me."

"It is up to you, lady. I can walk you back to the airport or just put your bags in the trunk and be on our way? What do you want?"

Lizzie slumped back into the plush seat and held a breath. She let the air out and glanced at the driver. "Let's go."

He gave her a quick smile, stowed the luggage, and carefully shut her door. As he walked around the cab, he snapped his hat back on. It was grey with a black Nike *swoosh* logo on the front panel. Lizzie saw him scowl over at the other drivers and tip his chin up in a dismissive taunt before climbing in. She felt an odd twinge of apprehension, but it faded as the car lurched into motion.

They departed for Kampala, following the Airport Road north through the town of Entebbe.

Lizzie rolled down her window and let the moving air cool her face. The humidity made her blouse stick to her skin under the Safari vest. She told herself she'd be losing that layer as soon as practical. She imagined how nice it would be to take a long shower – whenever that might happen here, if ever.

As the taxi continued down the divided highway from the airport, Lizzie understood why everything felt so peculiar. The driver sat on what to her was the passenger side of the car. Her senses kept warning her that they were on the wrong side of the road. She, of course, knew about this ahead of time but, like so many other things, actually living it was much different from imagining it. She kept reassuring herself that everything would be fine.

She looked outside. Silhouettes of unfamiliar trees clicked by the window. She watched a moon path reflection in the nearby lake race along beside the car. The surface of the water was unruffled, she realized, because the wind on her face was artificial, caused totally by the forward motion of the car. Lizzie studied the black water, wondering what hid beneath it. She was reminded of her thirst. When she first got off the plane, she had meant to check the airport for shops, but one thing had led to another, and she'd forgotten. It irritated her. But now she recalled that it had been the middle of the night, so it didn't matter, nothing would have been open, anyway. Her mind felt sluggish. She loudly cleared her throat in frustration.

The driver looked back. "Everything okay, lady?"

"Yes. I'm just tired and thirsty. I'm not used to the heat."

"Where are you from in the U.S.?"

"Minnesota."

The driver smiled and played with the name. "*Minn-ee-sow-da.*"

"It's a state...an area of the country. I'm near the city of Minneapolis."

"*Minny-apples-sus?*"

"Close enough," she said as she sighed. "It's cold there now. Not like here. It's so hot."

The driver laughed. "This is not hot. Just wait."

"Well, it's hot to me."

"Sorry, lady. Do you have drink?"

"No. I thought I could get some at the airport, but...I couldn't."

They rode together quietly for a time and then the driver spoke again. "I can get water for you. There is petrol station ahead. They sell water, too."

"Is it safe?" She thought of that black travel nurse from Detroit, and her warnings about water.

"Yes. Bottled water. I know which to buy. You must be careful here, lady. Many bottled water companies and many fakes. Very dangerous. Many people get sick."

"Yes. I was told to be careful."

"But no problem. Don't worry. I will get the right bottles, right company, still sealed and not fake. I buy all the time. Aqua Pure. Okay?"

She wasn't so sure about this. "Okay."

Lizzie looked ahead to the left side of the multi-lane road and saw the lights of a KPI Petrol Station come into view. As they pulled in to the brashly painted but shabby store beside two sets of rusty gas pumps, she heard the chugging grumble of a generator supplying the electricity. The driver parked and killed the engine.

Lizzie unzipped one of her vest pockets and leaned forward. "You'll need some money."

The driver held up a hand. "My treat, lady. A thank-you for riding in my taxi."

Lizzie smiled. "That's very kind."

"Don't mention it. Besides," he grinned, "water is not very expensive."

He shuffled smoothly toward the station with a kind of joint-less leg motion, as if his knees were incidental to his feet. But then at the corner of the shop, he looked back. "Oh, and lock the doors, lady. Okay? To be safe."

Lizzie immediately locked her door and then stretched over to lock the other doors. She nodded at the driver.

He gave her a *thumbs-up* before disappearing around the corner and into the decrepit store.

Sitting back, she found she couldn't relax. Her eyes kept jumping around, first checking the cracked concrete slabs near the car, and then searching for movement in the distant blackness of the trees. Her ears strained for any odd sounds. A distant chorus of frogs filled the empty corners of the night. She sat up, startled. Her window was still down! Feeling exposed, she hurriedly rolled it up while inwardly shouting at herself for not noticing something so obvious.

A few minutes later, Lizzie was relieved to see the driver round the corner of the store carrying liter-sized water bottles held together with plastic rings. So happy to see him, she paid little heed to the subtle metallic gleam of something slim that glistened briefly in his hand before he slipped it back inside his pocket.

Smiling now, the driver approached her door and motioned for her to lower the glass. As she did, he peeled one of the sweating bottles free of its ring and handed it to her. "See, still sealed. All perfect. You can open it yourself."

Lizzie nodded and twisted the cap off the bottle of Aqua Pure water, hearing the reassuring click of the seal breaking. She paused to read the crisp blue label and stare at the clear water within before taking a long drink. It was heavenly.

Back in the front seat, the driver peeled off a bottle of his own and unscrewed the cap. He turned around and toasted her. "Drink! Here is to your stay in Uganda."

They both drank large draughts. "Good, huh?" asked the driver.

Lizzie giggled, enjoying the feel of the cool liquid caressing her scratchy throat. "Good!"

Sitting back, she cuddled the bottle. Things would work out. She felt hopeful again, and safe. Her fatigue seemed to lift, and she experienced a momentary rush of euphoria that tingled through her limbs. She tipped the bottle and swallowed some more. Had she ever tasted anything so good? The car backed up. She reveled in its motion, feeling invincible. It switched gears and headed back onto the dark public highway, continuing towards Kampala.

A short time later, an unexpected heaviness settled over her. Gradually, the repetitive drumming of the tires on the pavement captured her rapt attention. She caught the eyes of the driver in the mirror watching her. The whine of the treads drew her helpless mind, until her head lolled against the door. When she tried to sit back up, the commands from her brain failed to reach her muscles. The water bottle hit the floor, the sound peculiar and far away. Her hands were insensitive to letting it go. Her ears picked up the liquid gurgle as it emptied out by her feet. Her eyelids drooped. She squinted and blinked to keep them open.

Sudden tendrils of fear spawned in her mind. She needed to stay awake! Something wasn't right! She squirmed in her seat. She pinched her leg. She tried to recite the alphabet backwards. She only made it to the letter *W* before a fading epiphany dawned and died within her; she was only dreaming that she was fighting to stay awake. Her eyes and her mind had already closed.

NINE

A New World

Air tickled her nose. Soft. Warm. What was it? Was it the wind? Her sluggish mind complained at the questions and tried to fade away, but her will forced it to stay on task. There, the air came again! Moist and warm. This time she heard a ragged sigh along with it. So, it can't be the wind, she thought. It must be…a breath? What? She suddenly felt claustrophobic. Is someone breathing on me? Where am I? Her body shuddered. She sensed something cool and solid pressing against the front of her. She heard a groan and realized, belatedly, that it came from her. Her eyes flickered open. She hadn't, until then, been aware that they were closed. Nothing was in focus. She huffed in frustration and felt her own breath tickle her nose. Her face rested flat against a filthy concrete slab – that's the reason nothing was clear; everything in her view was only inches away.

Her fingers scrabbled for her glasses but came up empty. Grit and damp pebbles stuck to her hands. Summoning all the strength she could find, she rolled her head to the side and squinted. It was still night. She was outside. There was no taxi.

Her eyes were drawn to the leaping flames of a fire in a nearby trash barrel. A ring of black figures danced around it and pushed each other. She heard high-pitched laughter. Without warning, behind her, there were a few quick flaps followed by a slide. She felt a bump against her feet and then a quick yank. Small hands were trying to take off her shoes! She attempted to kick back against her assailant, but her legs barely stirred. Desperate, her mind screamed for help while her lips emitted only a paltry moan. Then she heard a different series of flaps from another direction, growing swiftly louder, like someone running. A voice shouted words that sounded short and harsh. Her shoe robber dropped her feet and fled, his flapping sandals receding into the distance.

Lizzie blinked and slid a numb arm under her head. A shadowy figure moved near her face and was rim lit by the distant flames. As her eyes brought him into as sharp a focus as they could, she saw a black boy looking down at her with wide, curious, dark eyes. His lips were full, almost puffy, his nose broad. Tiny, tight curls covered his head in rows like a finely knitted black cap, except for an empty row just above his forehead. His over-sized sweatshirt hung off to the side so that one round shoulder peeked through. He wore old jeans rolled up at the ankles. With one leg tucked under himself and the other one up, he gave the impression of being completely relaxed. A grimy hand was casually draped over his up knee and held an opened plastic bottle. He calmly sat on the dirty pavement beside her, almost as if on guard duty. He leaned over to take a quick sniff from his bottle, and Lizzie noticed a collection of old scars and bumps across his brow.

When he saw that she was watching him, he said, "Wake up, lady. Now. Not safe here."

Lizzie breathed and continued to look at him. Her grip on her consciousness was still a tentative thing. She focused on his young face and found it to be lovely, scars and all. Their eyes held each other's for a moment and something passed between them. Lizzie felt her body coming back to life. The lethargy that had held her prisoner was leaving. Her arms and face began to sting from small scratches that had gone unnoticed until now. Unfortunately, her sense of smell was back as well. She scrunched her face up and looked around at the piles of picked-over garbage. What was this place? It appeared to be a twisting, narrow alleyway running between tall walls. In most places, the walls were constructed of brown mud that bulged around a cross-hatching of horizontal sticks lashed to vertical poles. In a few places, handmade red bricks of varying sizes replaced the mud. The unsteady illumination from the barrel fire lent a flickering unreality to every-thing. She saw broken concrete paths that sank into hard-packed soil. Hidden somewhere close by, a stream trickled.

Clearing her throat, Lizzie croaked out a question to the boy, but her voice was too weak for him to hear. As he leaned closer, her nose picked up the puzzling smell of gasoline from his bottle. She tried to speak again, louder. "Who are you?"

"My name is Dembe," he replied.

She cocked her head and concentrated. "Dem-bee?"

He nodded.

"Dembe, where am I?"

The boy glanced around himself. "This is where we sleep – sometimes."

Sliding her elbows in beside her, she ignored the pain as she leveraged her torso up a bit. "No. I mean…where…the place? Is this Kampala?"

His face clouded and then cleared. "Yes. Kampala." A fleeting smile passed by. "A small part of Kampala."

Another question sluggishly occurred to Lizzie, but before she could ask it, debris was tossed into the trash barrel and the flames roared up. Someone yelled in anger. A shoving fight erupted between two of the boys. The rest quickly gathered in a loose circle to laugh and taunt the fighters.

Dembe's head snapped toward them. He snarled something Lizzie didn't understand.

Angry words flew back from the group, but the fighting stopped. The fire was already dying back down.

Dembe's face wore a calculating look. "Can you get up, lady?"

"I don't know." She managed to work into a sitting position. "I think so. Give me a minute." Pausing to let a sudden bout of dizziness pass, she spotted her feet and was pleased to find that she still wore both shoes. A glimmer next to her foot caught her eye. She retrieved a pair of mangled glasses. Reshaping the nose bridge, she carefully put them on, bending the temples over her ears to make them somewhat level. While the look was comical, being able to see again gave her an emotional boost. Lizzie looked closely at the boy, this time seeing him clearly. "How did I get here, Dembe?"

His face was unreadable. "You were already here when I found you."

She felt so confused. "You didn't see a car or a driver?"

Dembe stood and offered his hands. "We need to go. You can't stay here."

With his help, she made it to her feet and stood still for a long moment, testing her balance. She finally nodded at him. "I'm okay. I'm not dizzy anymore."

Dembe stepped back and pointed down the alley. "This way." After capping his bottle, he slowly started off, keeping a cautious eye on her.

Lizzie stepped delicately after him, upright but a little wobbly. She noticed many boys asleep in the shadows, stretched out on burlap sacks or cardboard, some with odd layers of shirts, most wearing old flip-flops, some barefoot. "Where are we going?"

"I know a place."

"Wait." She stopped and rested a hand against the wall. "What am I doing?" Feeling a sudden sharp pain in her finger, she jerked it back and examined it. The knuckle on her ring finger was raw. Tiny drops of blood seeped out between the wrinkles. Her wedding ring was still intact, but someone had tried to force it off. "What?" Her eyes frantically looked around. "Where are my bags?"

Taking a half step back, she hesitated, unsure what to do. She turned in an unsteady circle. Her hands jumped to her loose Safari vest. Her fingers found that every pocket had been unzipped and emptied. "No, no, no, no…"

Panic descended on her like a weight. She slumped back against the dry mud wall. "My pills, my passport, my money, all my clothes…"

Dembe came back and stood by her. "We need to go."

Lizzie didn't budge. "No. Did you see any of my things?"

"No, lady. Just you."

"Just me," she whispered. "Just me."

She weakly pushed off from the wall, methodically placing one foot in front of the other as Dembe led off again. The immensity of her losses staggered her. What should she do now? She stopped. "Wait. We can't just leave the scene of a crime. We need help. Shouldn't we…shouldn't we call the police?"

Dembe fixed her with a dark look. "No police!"

"But I need help. I – I was robbed! I've lost everything. You don't understand."

"I am taking you to a place with help." Dembe led off down the alley and motioned for her to follow. "There is an American lady there."

Still frustrated, Lizzie started walking. "Fine! But don't you think we should first—"

Dembe abruptly hissed her to silence. He crouched against a crumbling wall. They were near the end of the alley where it spilled out onto a shabby cross street. Lizzie groaned as she knelt beside him, her swollen joints screaming in protest. Looking over Dembe's shoulder, she saw broken bits of concrete and large potholes across the outer road. Far in the distance, a display of tantalizing lights twinkled in white, yellow and orange colors from tall buildings in a downtown area. Then, her gaze shifted back to the opposite edge of the roadway across from them, where shuttered shops and wooden shacks leaned against each other in the darkness. She thought she spotted movement. Yes. There it was again. Maybe a man in a hat… and another. More over there. One crossed the street, angling their way. Others followed. A collection of similar figures crept toward the mouth of their alley.

Dembe yanked her up. He pulled her behind him as he rushed back up the alley. Sweeping his hands along the wall, he found a break. He squeezed the two of them into a slim opening between the mud brick walls. It was a constricted passage that led to a closed wooden door. Clearly, it was an alley exit from one of the nearby dwellings. They crouched together in single file in front of the door. Lizzie's calves threatened to cramp. She didn't dare make a noise. Dembe's fingers found a cast-off piece of thin bamboo fencing and used it to shield them from view. The bamboo was broken, parts of it had decayed away. Anyone could easily see right through it, but the darkness might allow it to mask their shapes.

Lizzie felt her heart clench. Who were they hiding from? She instinctively trusted Dembe's decision, but she felt utterly terrified. Her eyes stared intently through the bamboo fencing and into their narrow view of the alley. Figures moved swiftly by. Some wore hats, some wore helmets. All carried batons.

Suddenly, a piercing whistle blew from the other end of the alley. An answering whistle sounded from the closer group. Lizzie gasped and held her breath. She heard yelling from the surprised boys, then the deeper sounds of men's voices shouting commands. Light beams flared and waved. More whistles, this time from many sources. Sounds of struggle and running floated to them. Batons striking flesh. Bodies falling. Shrieks of pain. Through it all, Dembe remained stationary. His arm held up their pathetic covering, his other hand at his mouth, finger poised before his lips – *stay silent*. Lizzie heard the rising noise of feet and voices as the group returned to their end of the alley. She only caught glimpses as they passed by their hiding place: swinging flashlight beams, bound hands, frightened eyes, bleeding heads, and uniformed men with laughing faces.

When everyone had gone by, Lizzie sighed in strained relief. She turned to Dembe, about to speak, but he shook his head. A new noise came from the alley! She caught her breath again and watched a bright flashlight beam paint a narrow path across the walls. A final figure slowly passed their opening, casually sending his light slithering across their bamboo fence, searching for stragglers, and then continued on without stopping, his boot heels clunking on the hard ground.

Lizzie carefully breathed out. Dembe gently put down the bamboo. Out in the roadway, a couple of pickup trucks started their engines. A few voices shouted something. Someone laughed. Trucks pulled away, gears whining. Their engines slowly faded into the ordinary night sounds of crickets and frogs.

Dembe looked at her with a grim smile. "Those were the police."

❧

They moved quickly along the edge of a hard-packed, dirt path. It meandered between tightly squeezed shacks on one side and a deep concrete flood channel on the other. The night was dark and there were no lights, but Dembe kept their shoulders nearly brushing against the walls to make sure they stayed in the deepest shadows. Every time they came to a tree, or a broken box, or some abandoned item he would signal a halt and silently sink to his knees to listen. He called it *staying invisible*, but Lizzie suspected it was to help her catch her breath.

They moved steadily for an hour. Each time she tried to learn how much farther they needed to go, he waved her off with the whispered words, "Still a little ways, lady."

Now they crouched next to a shattered clay oven, their way forward blocked. Up ahead, a narrow shop pumped out distorted Ugandan pop music over cheap speakers. *Club Rowiz*, a local bar, had its metal shutters wide open. It was busy despite the hour. Lizzie saw

Nile Beer signs propped up atop the heavily rusted metal roof. The façade was a crazy quilt of boards, tin sheeting and wood panels attached in every direction. Inside the tight interior, a noisy crowd of men and a few women shouted for service or danced. Others milled around outside where plenty of paraffin lanterns and fat candles provided wavering pools of light. Harsh laughter and raucous singing spilled into the night. A few drunks had already passed out on the path, others huddled near a crooked retaining wall. Lizzie saw a large woman with a red head scarf slumped against a street sign. She appeared unconscious but she moved her round shoulders to the beat of the music and her lips still synced to the words of the song.

Dembe watched and waited. Lizzie shut her eyes, trying to focus on happier times. For whatever reason, the image of her friend Ruth, eating peanut-butter cookies in Lizzie's sun-dappled kitchen filled her mind.

Suddenly, a big noise came from the bar. Something had fallen over. Angry voices erupted. Glass broke. Lizzie's eyes jumped opened. Figures streamed from the bar to the path, two loud men clutched each other awkwardly. A drunken fight ensued that was more pushing and falling down than punching.

Dembe whispered to her, "Bad. We go around." He pointed in the direction of the flood channel and moved off, cautioning her over his shoulder, "Quiet!"

Lizzie climbed back to her feet, staying painfully bent over to make herself small, and trailed after him. She whispered, "How do we get across?"

Dembe didn't respond.

Lizzie soon saw her own answer. They came to a loose set of old planks that had been stretched over the six foot wide channel as a footbridge. Coated with mud and festooned with weeds and wet newspapers, the cracked wood looked treacherous. She could hear and smell the water churning below her.

Dembe was already across, moving nimbly, like a monkey in the trees. He turned to check on the bar fight. The crowd sang and danced. The former opponents now stood arm-in-arm, heads together and giggling at each other. Another man, perhaps the owner, angrily shoved them away and yelled something before going back inside. The two staggered off, keeping each other on their feet, heading down the path toward Lizzie.

Dembe anxiously motioned for her to hurry up.

Lizzie sucked in some air and stepped out onto the slick wood. She took a second step, but when she felt the planks sink down under her weight, she froze. Her arms spontaneously snapped up on either side of her like heavy wings. She teetered in place. Unable to advance or retreat, she just squeezed her eyes shut. Why did I ever leave home? What would Ruthie say now? God are You there?

Luckily, the oblivious drunks paused in their crooked trip down the path to say a few words to the large woman at the street sign.

Dembe understood that the *muzungu* was stuck. With the drunks occupied, he scampered out onto the planks. Grabbing ahold of Lizzie's Safari vest, he drew her toward his side of the channel.

Lizzie squawked and stumbled forward, her legs maintaining just enough balance so she didn't fall while crossing. Once on solid ground again, they both rolled onto the wet earth. Dembe scrambled on hands and knees to hide behind a low pile of metal siding. He gestured at Lizzie to join him. She forced herself to crawl forward and then let him drag her the rest of the way.

The drunks looked up at the sounds and wandered over to the bridge to investigate. With nothing in sight and no further noise, they easily lost interest. Continuing down the path, they started to sing to each other.

Behind the siding, Dembe pushed up to his feet and wiped his hands on his jeans. He spoke low, "Lady, you okay?"

She scowled. "Oh, yeah! I'm just great!" She pawed at the new mud caking her vest, "Just great."

Dembe noticed her glasses were missing. A quick search found them close by, nestled among broken bricks. Ever so gently, he retrieved them but the nose bridge was now severed. The frames split into two parts in his hands.

Still sitting in the mud, Lizzie frowned. "Give 'em here."

He reluctantly handed them over. "Lady, maybe I can fix them."

She shook her head, "Don't worry about it." Stuffing them carelessly into one of her empty vest pockets, she zipped it shut. "Well, that's that." She flopped her hands listlessly against her wide thighs before looking up. "What's next?"

Dembe offered to help her up.

She shook off the last of the mud from her fingers and then took his hands. Struggling to her feet, she looked him in the eyes. "I'm not crossing any more bridges. You got that?"

Dembe nodded. "Sorry. This is better place, now."

Lizzie slowly looked around, straining to see without her glasses. She noted piles of trash, abandoned bricks and a narrow path leading between high walls that were topped by razor wire. "If you say so."

"This way, lady." The boy led off, his flip-flops making soft sounds. "We are near a big road. Safer."

She followed behind him. "Dembe, can I ask you something?"

"What?"

"How old are you?"

"Maybe fifteen years. I think."

"You're not sure?"

"No." He glanced briefly back while still walking. "How old are you?"

Lizzie frowned. "Old enough."

Dembe smiled to himself. "Are you sure?"

Lizzie stumbled on a bump in the uneven path but quickly righted herself. "How come you speak English so well?"

He flashed a grin back at her. "Because I am so smart, lady."

TEN

Finding Safe Haven

The big road that Dembe had talked about was bigger than the path but it was still just packed earth, barely enough room for two vehicles to pass side-by-side. Shops and stands cluttered both sides of the roadway, all shuttered, padlocked and sealed up for the night. Without warning, a nearby dog erupted with a volley of vicious barks, causing Lizzie to rapidly close the distance between herself and Dembe. As they passed a vacant lot overgrown with vegetation, their steps startled something that squealed and blundered off through the undergrowth. Lizzie put a hand over her mouth to stifle a shriek and bumped into Dembe. She hadn't realized he'd already stopped. He stood still, his head lifted as he listened intently.

Lizzie snorted an apology.

Dembe frowned. "Shhh!"

She watched him, outlined against the grey horizon, straining on tiptoes, and looking back down the road. That was when Lizzie first noticed the night was becoming marginally brighter, and that she was about to experience her first day in Uganda.

Dembe ducked down and scurried into the brush near the road. "Trucks are coming. Get down!"

Lizzie's mouth opened with an unspoken question, but the boy disappeared from sight. She hurried reluctantly after him. The narrow leaves from the dense bushes slid unpleasantly across her face, like tapered fingers. Her shoes made soft squishing noises beneath her. She heard buzzings at her ears and a flutter of wings. Who knew what was in here with her?

She felt a hand pull her down. She nearly squealed, but it was Dembe. Soon they hid among the slim grey trunks of new trees, their eyes almost level with the road. Lizzie knew she could feel the rapid tickle of many little legs crawling on her, and she kept swiping at her arms, her neck, her hair.

The grind of downshifting truck gears and the strain of the engines soon became audible. Heavy vehicles lumbered up the empty road toward them. Lizzie squinted when the bright bouncing headlights from the two-truck convoy revealed a brief kaleidoscope of colors from the garishly painted shops. The truck beds were open at the top with shoulder-high sides. Helmeted heads, with the black shafts of rifles beside them, were jostled and rattled with every pothole as the packed transports snaked along the rutted road. A few soldiers perched precariously outside the rails, at the back, no room left for them inside. Their camouflage uniforms billowed around them, untucked and unbuttoned.

A short time later, Dembe and Lizzie climbed back onto the road. Lizzie could still hear the trucks toiling in the distance. "Whose soldiers were they?"

Dembe was already walking again. "The government."

Lizzie rolled her eyes. "Wait. What? You mean *our* troops? I mean, *your* government troops?"

"Yes."

"So, why did we hide?"

"You never know."

"Know what?"

"What they are doing."

"But…"

Dembe glanced back and raised a hand to stop further questions. "We are close now." He pointed. "Left here."

Ahead, the road sprouted a smaller branch that split off to the left and uphill. Dembe followed a footpath next to the road. It curled in a shortcut around a low area filled with man-high elephant grass and fat shrubs. Lizzie smiled at the spirited serenade of a multitude of frogs and toads. Their croaks and chirps, throat thumps and warbles, which she had heard sung in the background for the entire night, now swelled to an almost unbelievable volume.

The grey of the coming dawn softened shadows on both sides of the road. They soon walked beside high walls, mostly made of bricks or coated in stucco, but all crowned with embedded pieces of broken glass and thick coils of razor wire.

Lizzie observed that each of these perimeter walls boasted a locked metal car gate built into it across the driveway. The gates were as tall as the walls. Constructed of metal rods with sharp points at the top or entirely of sheet metal, they were formidable structures, hinged on each side and separated in the middle. In addition, most gates featured a lockable pedestrian door inset into one of the sides. This smaller entry had a closeable slot cut into it, designed for seeing and questioning whoever stood before the gate.

Dembe motioned to the other side of the road at a white stucco wall with an orange brick top ledge. "That is the place. They will help you."

As they walked across the road, Lizzie evaluated what she could see of the house beyond the wall. She decided that it didn't look all that promising. "What is it?"

"Safe Haven."

"Safe Haven? What's that?"

"A boys' home – for street boys."

"An orphanage?"

"No, lady. We are not all orphans. We just don't have homes."

"Do you live here, Dembe?"

"Not here. There is another house for the boys."

"Do you live there?"

"Not anymore."

"What happened?"

"Many things."

"What is *this* house then?"

"This is where Uncle Jed and Auntie Meg live."

They arrived at the pedestrian door in the solid metal car gate. Dembe stepped to the side of the door and hid his plastic bottle in the weeds. He scraped across the dirt and uncovered a small rock. Picking it up, he moved back to the gate and rapped loudly against the metal. The knocking sounded sharp and it echoed, causing a brief lull in the songs of the frogs and toads.

A high-pitched single syllable erupted from inside the compound.

Dembe tapped his stone again, this time more insistently.

A young crabby voice called out a rapid series of questions in Luganda.

Dembe immediately rattled back a quick response, ending in an upward tone.

The other voice spit out more terse remarks and then stopped.

To Lizzie's ears, whoever it was sounded angry, but when she looked at Dembe he wore a small smile. "He asked if we know what a clock is, or if our eyes noticed that the sun is not up yet. And then he said a few *other* things. I told him it was an emergency."

From inside, they heard the soft shuffle of bare feet coming closer and a sullen voice muttering to itself. The metal door slot slid open with a screech. A puzzled black face appeared, angling and twisting in the narrow opening, trying to get a good look at them both. Lizzie couldn't help but think of *The Wizard of Oz* movie when Dorothy and her friends were stuck outside the gate to the Emerald City. As tired as she was, she nearly lost it and started to giggle. She managed to control herself, figuring such an outburst wouldn't do much to enhance her already awkward situation.

The boy's face in the door slot blossomed into wide eyes and a toothy grin. His excitement carried through his lively Luganda language. *"Dembe? Dembe! Is that really you?"*

Dembe grinned right back. *"Musaazi! I thought that might be your voice. What are you doing answering doors?"*

Musaazi's pliable face instantly changed to an expression of mock horror. *"Me! What are you talking about? I still live at the home. We do jobs here! Not like you street boys! You do nothing! Except steal."*

Dembe laughed, enjoying himself. He broadly waved at Lizzie with both hands. *"Does this look like nothing to you? Look at me! I'm saving a lost muzungu VIP lady!"*

Musaazi made a loud fluctuating sound in his throat as he studied Lizzie through his slot.

Dembe continued. *"C'mon, speak English, if you can still remember how, so I don't have to waste time playing your translator."*

Dembe angled his body to face both of them. "Lady, this is my good friend, Musaazi. We used to live on the street together. In those days he was my brave warrior, but today he is just a gate boy."

Musaazi groaned at the snub and fired back in English. "Hmm! Gate boy! What do you mean, gate boy?" He snorted. "I am the defender of the doorway! Gate boy!"

Dembe ignored the interruption with a smirk. "I told him to speak English, lady, so you can understand us. I am already sorry for you, because his English is so terrible."

Musaazi's eyes grew large and he was about to protest when another voice speaking in Luganda floated down from an interior room. *"Musaazi? Who are you talking to?"* It was a man's voice – a strong, commanding man's voice.

Musaazi's face promptly sobered. *"It's Dembe."*

"Dembe?"

"Yes, Uncle, Dembe."

"At this time in the morning? Why is he here? Tell him to go away. We haven't changed our minds – rules are still rules."

Musaazi's eyes flitted back and forth between the two figures outside the gate and the unseen presence above him. He switched to English so everyone would understand. "But…but Uncle, he has an old *muzungu* lady with him, and she is covered in mud. He says it is an emergency."

"What? Am I still asleep or is this real? Meg? Wake up."

Lizzie heard other voices then, calling out inside the house, too low to understand the words, but clear enough in tone to recognize the turmoil. Soon, doors opened and closed, clothes hangers rattled on the floor, sandals slapped on concrete, and then hurried foot-steps approached the gate. Lizzie felt a startling ache when she heard a woman's voice speaking with the familiar inflections of Midwest America. "Musaazi, for goodness' sakes, open the door. Y'know I hate talkin' to people through that silly hole. Now, let 'em in."

A door bolt loudly slid home, and the pedestrian door swung open on rusty hinges. Musaazi peeked out and sheepishly waved for them to enter. Dembe stepped through first, ducking automatically at the low head jamb, and Lizzie followed, imitating him. They both stopped just inside the gate.

Lizzie took in the compound at a glance. She saw a simple tan colored stucco and brick house with white accents, security bars on the windows, and a wide, inviting porch. A brown rooster with a red face, drawn by the commotion, cautiously stepped around the edge of a beat up compact car.

Lizzie scrutinized the people watching her. Musaazi, who was closing and re-bolting the gate entry, was taller than Dembe and skinnier. He was swimming in a large T-shirt and had bare feet. She caught him sending an eyebrow twitch to Dembe, who answered back with the ghost of a smile. To her left, Uncle Jed was a thick-shouldered Ugandan about Lizzie's height with a goatee and full lips. He wore a patterned shirt that hung far over his khaki shorts.

At the moment, he had his arms folded and his head tipped slightly to one side. To her right, Auntie Meg regarded her with such a look of sorrow and compassion in her round white face, Lizzie felt it almost as a physical pressure against her chest. Meg was quite short, maybe five feet, and stout, but the power of her presence made her seem to be the tallest of the group.

Tears of relief and repressed panic began to make their way down Lizzie's dirty cheeks and she was utterly powerless to stop them. "I'm so sorry. I don't mean to impose," her voice quavered. "This was never my plan."

Meg rushed to her and took one of her hands. "Your voice sounds American."

Lizzie nodded, her tears unabated.

"Oh, you poor dear. Have you just arrived? What happened?"

"I don't exactly know." Lizzie's words began to tumble out, unplanned, much like her tears. "My plane was...delayed in Amsterdam. I landed here in the dark and no one met me. I tried to call but..." She used the somewhat clean backs of her hands to rub away tears. "I didn't know what to do. I...I took a taxi. I tried to be careful but...and I was so thirsty..."

Meg pulled her into a hug and softly patted her back. "I know. I know. We've heard about things like this. He tricked you and drugged the water, didn't he? There's no way you could have known." She shot an upset look in Jed's direction. He in turn said something low and quick to Dembe. The boy simply rolled his shoulders, his face a blank.

Lizzie straightened up and sniffed back her emotions. "I've lost everything. He took my passport, my medicine, my money, my suitcases, everything."

"I am so sorry. But you're gonna be okay now. Don't worry. What's your name, dear? Mine is Meg."

"Lizzie." She swallowed and calmed herself. "Well, Elizabeth Warton, but most of the time I'm just Lizzie."

"Okay, Lizzie. I'm Margaret Mayombwe, but most people use Meg. A few call me M&M, but the boys say Auntie Meg." She motioned with her head. "That quiet, good looking guy over there is my husband, Jedediah. I usually call him *sweetie* or *handsome* or some such thing, but I'm sure you can stick to Jed. And you've already met Musaazi at the gate. He's one of our Safe Haven boys. And then Dembe…" A sad look briefly passed across her face and then vanished. "Well, you know him."

Lizzie nodded at each during their introductions. "If it wasn't for Dembe I don't know what would have happened. I woke up in some horrible alley. He saved me from thieves, from police gangs, from drunks and…a lot more. And then he brought me here." She looked over at Dembe still standing near the door. "I owe him…" Her voice faltered. She stopped for a moment until she could handle the feelings. "I think I owe him my life. That's what I think."

Dembe looked down and brushed at the dirt with a foot, uncomfortable at being singled out.

Jed kept his wary eyes on the boy, but he turned briefly toward Lizzie. "Police gangs? What do you mean?"

"I don't know. They wore uniforms and blew whistles. There were two groups, one at each end of the alley where the street boys sleep. Dembe helped me hide, so we could only hear the terrible things they did. But I saw the boys taken away in pickup trucks. Dembe said it was the police."

Jed nodded once, his jaw tight, his eyes smoldering.

Meg tried to defuse the rising tension. "Dembe is a very smart boy…and good in a pinch." Her eyes held Dembe's for a moment before he looked away. "You're lucky he found you." She took a breath, gently shook her head, and changed tones. "But never mind about all that now. We'll talk more in a bit."

Meg folded her strong arm around one of Lizzie's and walked her off toward the house. "Come with me. I'm sure you want to get cleaned up. And we'll find you some clothes. Are you hungry? You walked all night! Hid from the police! You must be so exhausted. I can't imagine it!"

Behind them, Lizzie heard Jed fire questions in Luganda at Dembe and the boy answer back. The exchange didn't sound very friendly. But, then again, Lizzie really had no idea what was being said.

ELEVEN

Nothing as It Seems

Lizzie carried a towel, some rags, a folded robe, a big bar of deep blue soap, and a pair of flip-flops. Meg walked just ahead of her, lugging a large plastic bucket of warm water in one hand and tapping the ground ahead of them with a long stick.

"We rent this house," Meg said, "and the owner keeps talking about upgrading to indoor plumbing. That'd be nice but we're afraid if he does, we won't be able to afford the rent. So far, it's just talk."

They passed long sets of clothes lines near the back perimeter wall and approached a painted enclosure with two wooden doors. Meg pulled open the left side door and stepped inside the closet-sized room, setting her bucket down on the slightly canted cement floor. "As a result, you will have the pleasure of a more traditional clean-up experience." She grinned at Lizzie. "I know, it's not exactly the Ritz, but bucket baths have their own rustic charms."

She repositioned the two small benches in the room, pushing one against a wall and sliding the other into the center of the space. Turning back to Lizzie, still standing at the door, Meg set down the stick and held out her hands. "Here, gimme those, and I'll set things up."

Lizzie handed everything to Meg who efficiently arranged the items in a practiced order, using the outer bench and some convenient wooden pegs set into the walls.

"Okay. Let me show you the basics." Meg crouched over the bucket and pretended to cup handfuls of water and toss them onto one shoulder and then onto the other. "You just kind of get the water going where you need it to go. Then you lather up. Rinse off. Repeat. It's not complicated."

She snickered and patted Lizzie's shoulder as she exited. "Wait'll you have to do it with cold water. I'll remind Musaazi to leave another bucket outside the door for an extra rinse." She winked. "I'm sure you'll need it after all you've been through."

Lizzie peeked inside the stark, white painted room and her eyes grew wider – there wasn't any roof! She heard Meg outside explaining the next room in the enclosure, so she ducked back out to catch up.

"This is the bathroom side," Meg explained. "I know it feels primitive but it's clean. Just pretend you're camping in the woods and you'll be fine. Most women carry TP with them. You'll get used to it. Here, the boys do a good job of keeping ours stocked." She smiled as she stepped out so Lizzie could get a look. "And they no longer steal it, so that helps."

Lizzie stepped into the bathroom, reassured to see a corrugated roof above her. There were a few pegs in the walls and a hole in the cement floor with room for feet on either side. A generous roll of toilet paper was within easy reach, and a small shelf nearby held two more rolls. She heard Meg's voice continuing so she stepped back out.

"I know this is a lot to deal with, but you'll be fine. Now, I'm sure you're anxious to get started. I'm gonna go pull together some breakfast." She stepped off toward the house, then stopped. "Oh, and just drape your dirty clothes over the bath wall. Musaazi'll gather 'em up, and I'll get 'em washed. Okay?"

Lizzie felt dazed, but not unpleasantly so. "Okay."

Meg studied her for a moment, unsure whether to leave. "You'll get your feet under you soon. I promise."

Lizzie cocked her head, uncertain.

Meg grinned. "You're made for this place, Lizzie. I can feel it."

"Am I?"

"Yep. Despite this beginning, you're gonna love Uganda."

Lizzie slowly shook her head. "Meg, tell me the truth. Why did those police beat the street boys and take them away?"

Meg's face changed and her eyes glistened. "Okay. They call it *street sweeping.*" She took a few steps back to Lizzie and lowered her voice. "It always happens during the elections, but other times too, before big events. Jed says there's a state visit from Japan in a few days. Homeless kids on the street are an embarrassment to the government, so they have the police round them up. The ones they catch are jailed and abused and then thrown back on the street when the event's over."

Lizzie stared at her, bathrooms and bucket baths forgotten. "I had no idea."

Meg's face looked fragile. "And the truth? It's what AIDS and corruption can do to a country." She paused for a moment as if wondering if she should continue. She took a breath and then went on. "In a way, it's how Safe Haven got started. Back then, Jed and I were newlyweds and wannabe missionaries. We thought it'd be fun to reach out to homeless kids by holding a few sports days in empty lots. Sort of soccer and soft drink events, you know, and share the gospel. Simple. Safe. Limited. We didn't think about the fact that elections were near. After one of our sports days, fifty street boys followed us home and begged us to hide them from the police. Once we understood, how could we say no? When the elections were over, I had fifty lost boys saying, 'Please, Auntie Meg, don't send us back.' I felt like *Wendy* from *Peter Pan*, except these boys *wanted* to go to school. They wanted to have real lives again."

She glanced over at the house and then back. "Jed says God tricked us into this ministry. He's kidding, but it's kinda true. It's not that we regret it for a minute, mind you, but our marriage and our life took a big surprise turn in the road, that's for sure."

Lizzie stood quietly by the door to the outside bathroom and couldn't think of anything to say. Behind her, unseen, the first colors from the rising sun painted the bottoms of the soft clouds along the pale blue horizon. Meg motioned for Lizzie to come to her. Once she did, Meg gently turned her around so she wouldn't miss her first sunrise in Africa.

They both stood still and silently drank in the glory until Meg squeezed her arms and softly said, "Now, you go get cleaned up while I get movin' on some food."

ৎ৯

With her hair still slightly damp, Lizzie entered the small eating area next to Meg's tiny kitchen and breathed in the heady fragrance of fresh bread and fried eggs. The room had been filled with the happy babble of Luganda and English and the universal language of laughter, but it all tapered off when Lizzie was noticed. Everyone she expected to see was crowded around the metal table in mismatched chairs. In addition, she spotted some new little black faces among the others.

Meg set filled plates in front of the three children, who looked to be four or five years old, and smiled at Lizzie. "Feel better?"

Lizzie nodded.

"I bet you do." She touched one of the children. "These are Safe Haven's youngest members. They're staying with us for a while until they're ready to move to the boys' house." Meg looked directly at the young boys until their eyes stayed fixed on hers and they stopped fidgeting. "Boys, I want you meet our very special guest, Aunt Lizzie."

The children kept staring at her until Jed's deep voice repeated the words in Luganda. The boys' eyes went to him until he finished and then back to Meg when she continued.

"Lizzie, I would like to present Gwandoya, Mukiibi, and Waloga."

Jed translated and the boys' eyes did their group swing back and forth again, but this time they ended up expectantly focused on Lizzie.

She smiled and nodded at them. "I'm happy to meet you."

Jed translated but the boys never wavered in their stare at the new *muzungu*.

Lizzie continued, "Now, let me try. Uh…Gwandoya?"

The little boy nearest to her squirmed and ducked his head.

"Mukiibi?"

The next one grinned and rolled his eyes.

"And Wa…Waloga?"

The last one scrunched his face, but was clearly pleased at the attention.

Lizzie grinned. "You have such wonderful names."

Jed translated the last bit. Meg beamed. "Lizzie, please, sit down." She indicated a chair that had arms and occupied the place of honor at the head of the table.

Lizzie sat while checking out the food choices. She saw a stack of flat, pan-grilled bread, a serving bowl with scrambled eggs, some sliced tomatoes, avocados and a few yellow bananas. There was also a large, steaming kettle in the center of the table that gave off a spicy scent of ginger and cinnamon mingled with tea.

Meg laughed at her. "Nothing too dangerous here, dear. At least not this time. Really." She pointed out the plate of warm bread. "This is *cha'pati* – it's an African version of flat bread, except much better! Otherwise, I think you recognize everything else. Take what you want. There's plenty."

Lizzie picked up her plate and started to select food. She noticed that the older boys and the adults waited for her, quietly sitting before their filled plates. Self-conscious now, she speeded up her food choices and settled back in her chair.

Meg filled Lizzie's cup with a rich, mahogany liquid from the tea kettle. "This is chai. You'll be drinking a lot of this from here on out, so I hope you like it. It's a mix of black tea, milk, and *tea masala*, which means spices – mainly ginger, cinnamon and nutmeg. You can add sugar yourself, as you like. Okay?"

Lizzie nodded and looked around the table, catching Dembe's eyes for a moment before settling on Jed's calm, kind face.

Jed nodded to Meg and bowed his head. "Father God, you gave us breath, you keep us breathing, and when we breathe our last, we go to you. We thank you for this food. We ask you to bless the hands that prepared it. And we ask you to guide us in your ways. Let us be about your work while we are still breathing."

Lizzie sipped the chai tentatively at first and then with more gusto. "Meg, this is wonderful!"

Meg nodded. "We think so."

Lizzie tucked into the eggs and tore off a piece of *cha'pati*. "I didn't realize how hungry I was."

Dembe stole a glance at her as she devoured the breakfast, then winked at Musaazi as they both quickly finished their own plates.

Meg folded her hands on the table. "So, Lizzie, I'm just wondering. If everything had worked out the way you expected, who was supposed to meet you and what were you planning to do here… in our fair city?"

Lizzie swallowed hurriedly and dabbed her lips with a paper napkin. "Oh, I'm so sorry. I just make one mistake after another, don't I? That should have been the first thing out of my mouth."

Meg waved her hand. "You had a few other things on your mind."

"Pastor Kajumba and Nankunda Birungi – she's the school administrator – they were supposed to meet me. I'm helping to set up a new library for their school – Wobulezi Primary and Secondary school in Makindye. I'm not even sure where that is, but..." Lizzie saw Jed and Meg shoot each other troubled looks. "Do you and Jed know them?"

Meg's face smoothed quickly. "Yes. We know Pastor Kajumba and Mrs. Birungi. A few of our boys used to attend his school." She glanced over at Jed for help.

Jed jumped in. "Yes, we have talked with them before. We have a lot in common. I'll call. I'm sure they are concerned. But it is only 7 now." He glanced back at Meg. "So I may let them sleep a little longer before I tell them the...ah, good news."

Meg looked back at Lizzie, shaking her head. "I guess I still don't understand how you missed each other."

"It wasn't their fault," Lizzie replied. "My first flight was cancelled because of two terrorists who tried to board."

"What?"

"Yes. Can you believe it? My first international trip, and I run into terrorists! Anyway, in the fight to capture one of them, my cell phone was broken and—"

"A terrorist broke your phone while you captured them?" Meg sounded skeptical.

Lizzie laughed. "No, not *me*! That's a lot more exciting than it was. I was trying to get out of the way. And, well, to make a long story short, I wasn't able to reach Mrs. Birungi with the new flight info, so..."

Meg nodded. "So, you landed alone at Entebbe. No one to help you. And everything went to...went from bad to worse."

"Pretty much, until I met Dembe. But I wasn't sure about him either, at first." She looked up and noticed that Dembe was on his feet, standing next to Jed, who remained seated. Dembe's plate was clean. Musaazi had already left. Jed was in a quiet conversation in Luganda with Dembe. The boy nodded sadly and replied with something short and sharp. Jed shook his head. Dembe turned away, heading out.

Lizzie was confused. "Wait! Dembe?" She stood up. "What's going on? You can't be leaving."

Jed looked at her, his face impassive. Nearby, Dembe stopped and looked back.

Lizzie's voice grew stronger. "Jed, you can't let him leave. The police are still out there sweeping the streets, aren't they?"

Jed opened his mouth to reply, but Meg's voice jumped in ahead of him. "Lizzie, you don't understand."

Lizzie knew she should sit down and be quiet, but she couldn't help herself. She had been through too much. She was tired of putting up with things. Sick of not speaking her mind. "Of course, I don't understand! I just got here! But I already know a few things. I know something happened between you people and Dembe. And I know this boy just saved my life. That has to count for something!"

Meg's face was a study in turmoil. "Lizzie, please…"

Jed stayed seated. "Yes, it counts for something." His voice remained calm, but the restrained authority within it compelled Lizzie to listen. "But nothing in Uganda is as it seems, Mrs. Warton. Not the police, not the street boys, not anything."

Lizzie's mouth set in a firm line. She moved purposefully around the table and stood behind Dembe, her hands squeezing both of his arms. "I just don't want him in danger. Surely you can shelter him for a few days. That won't hurt. That can't be too much to ask."

Dembe's face remained unreadable, almost serene.

Jed breathed in and breathed out before he spoke. "He'll be fine. He's a street boy. He knows how to hide in plain sight. He had his chances here. I am not *letting* him leave. I am *telling* him to leave. Street boys are wild creatures. They must be broken before they can be trusted. He betrayed that trust – more than once. He knows."

Lizzie was flushed. "But what about mercy? What about other chances? Isn't this a ministry?"

Jed stared into Dembe's eyes. The boy never blinked. "Dembe is a thief," Jed said. "A trickster. He bites the hand that feeds him. He is smart and a leader, but not for anything good. And he has not changed, yet."

Jed looked away from Dembe to focus on Lizzie. "So, please, *nnyabo*, open your hands. Let him go back to the street, where he belongs."

Feeling stung by his words, Lizzie released her hands and let her arms drop to her sides. Dembe turned his head and pushed his face briefly against her side. He breathed in her clean scent, and softly rubbed his ebony cheek against her pale arm. Then he was gone from the room, without a sound.

Lizzie felt the eyes of the little boys on her before she looked down and saw them. They had turned in their chairs, and they stared up at her with open faces. The wear of the past days and nights, that she had somehow held at bay, came due all at once. Lizzie swayed, nearly asleep on her feet. She heard the scrape of Meg's chair sliding back, but her fatigued mind failed to comprehend what it meant, until Meg stood next to her. Lizzie rallied one more time, knowing she needed to apologize. Her eyes caught Jed's, and she felt Meg's hand warm against her back.

"I'm sorry – both of you. I'm a nobody. I shouldn't have put you on the spot."

Jed rose and helped to guide the young boys to pick up their dishes. "Don't worry about it." His eyes twinkled ever so faintly. "Uganda isn't anything like the brochures, is it?"

Lizzie was slow to respond, but when she understood he meant his question as a joke, she replied in a low voice, "No."

Jed shepherded the boys toward the kitchen, helping them balance the silverware on their plates, encouraging them in Luganda. They headed outside, where the dishes were washed.

Meg gently prodded Lizzie in the opposite direction, toward a doorway that led deeper into the house. "We've cleared a room for you. What you really need is sleep. We all know you aren't yourself right now. Who would be?"

Lizzie allowed her body to drift along with Meg to a guest room at the front of the house. The first thing she noticed was the cement floor. It was painted red and shone in the morning sunlight. There were two open windows without screens on the long side of the simple room. Thin, undecorated cloths were pinned to a wooden rod and gathered near the windows – designed for light control and privacy, not aesthetics. A metal framed bunk bed stood against an inside wall, and a single bed was in the middle of the room. Green translucent mosquito netting hung rolled up like pale hammocks above each narrow mattress.

Meg went to the single bed and began to unfurl the netting. "I'll get this ready if you'd spread that fabric over the windows. We'll have you snoring in no time."

Lizzie slowly pulled one of the cloths over the left window and moved to the right one. As she drew the material over the right window, she noticed that it overlooked a part of the car gate. She saw Dembe and Musaazi talking beside the open pedestrian door. She might have been mistaken, but she thought Musaazi handed something to Dembe. The two said a few more words and then poked each other goodbye. Dembe ducked his head to leave but stopped and turned around. Almost reluctantly, he fished into a hidden pocket and slipped Musaazi a couple of flat items. With a final word and an airy wave, he disappeared from sight. Musaazi closed and bolted the door. He glanced nervously around. Lizzie pressed herself against the wall, fearing his eyes might pass across the window.

Behind her, Meg finished prepping the bed and tucking the netting under the mattress. "C'mon, Lizzie, hop in and I'll zip it. You look like you're falling asleep against the wall."

Lizzie crossed to the bed and crawled inside the netting. Her mind was so distracted by what she had seen, she barely noticed

Meg zipping the netting closed. As her head sank into the pillow, she thought Meg said something about waking and Pastor Kajumba. Her mind disengaged, and she never put the words together to make a complete thought before she fell asleep.

Something woke her, something scraping against the outside wall. Her sticky eyelids resisted the demand to open. It was still bright day and the sun made the thin curtains glow. Squinting and blinking, she sat up and stared at the windows. The green netting altered all the colors in the room and made her feel as if she were wrapped in a diaphanous cocoon. There were sudden moving shapes at the bottom of the right window. The shapes resolved into fingers and then hands. They scrabbled at the security bars and shoved something over the window sill and into the room. She was about to call out for help when the item was dropped. It hit the floor with a small slap and separated into two pieces. Immediately, the hands released their hold on the bars and vanished from sight. She heard feet rapidly walking away.

Lizzie stared at the items lying beneath the window. Without her glasses, she couldn't see clearly. More curious than fearful, she unzipped the netting and carefully stepped over to the wall in her bare feet. On the floor, lying face down, was a blue booklet. Next to it, tightly folded paper, perhaps money. When she turned over the booklet, she saw a familiar golden eagle clutching arrows in one claw and an olive branch in the other. Flipping it open to the photo page, she confronted her own unsmiling face. It can't be! Her heart leaped and her mind clinched, all in the same instant. She opened the money, unsurprised to see an American twenty-dollar bill.

TWELVE

Something Missing

Lizzie was dreaming, and she knew it. She had had this dream, or something like it, over and over again since she was a girl. In it she was always late, terribly late, and lost. The dream never revealed what she was late for, and she never knew where she was going, but her mind always felt the weight of high expectations and the drive to keep moving forward. This time, she slogged through unending mud. Her legs felt heavy and unresponsive, like sacks of sand. The mud sucked wetly at her feet with every step. A voice floated from somewhere nearby, the meaning of the words barely registering. She kept pushing forward, step after step after step. Her frustration built until it grew so large, she just gave up the struggle and stopped. She felt her feet encased in soft mud up to her ankles. She looked down. The surface of the mud hunched up and undulated until it all became utterly smooth and undisturbed around her legs. She looked out to the horizon. The slick skin of the mud extended unbroken for as far as she could see, no footprints, no marks of any kind to show that she had passed this way. You're dreaming, she reminded herself. Why don't you wake up?

Her eyes opened to a green room. No. Mosquito netting. She

remembered she was inside the netting, inside a bed. One of her legs had tangled in the netting. She slid it free and drew her bare foot back towards herself. A sudden thought struck her. She pushed an inquisitive hand under her pillow and sighed in relief when her fingers closed around her passport. So, that part had not been a dream! She turned her head at a sound to find Meg leaning toward her, holding a folded set of clothes.

"Lizzie, it's time to wake up. I have your clothes. Pastor Kajumba and Mrs. Birungi are here."

Lizzie considered her appearance in Meg's small wardrobe mirror. She was pleased that her face was clean, although it displayed more than a few pink cuts and scratches. Not much else in the reflection encouraged her. Naturally wavy, her grey hair coiled and curled mischievously in the humidity. She ran her fingers through it, scrunching here and there, but resigned herself to the fact that it was basically out of control. She studied her head from various angles, deciding that it was hardly her most captivating look. The Cargo pants seemed passable, not that she had much choice, and the long-sleeved blouse had fared surprisingly well, she thought, except for the muted stains on the elbows.

Meg appeared in the mirror behind her with the Safari vest. "Don't know if you want to wear this right now, but at least it's clean."

Lizzie took it from her. "I'll just carry it. Thanks."

Meg gazed thoughtfully at Lizzie's hair. "I'd offer you my blow dryer, but the power's out again, like usual."

Lizzie did a *thanks anyway* shrug while checking the vest, front and back. Something poked at a memory. "Say, Meg, did you find a broken pair of glasses in one of these pockets?"

Meg was furling up the netting over the bed. "No. But Musaazi did most of the heavy scrubbing on that. I'll ask him."

Lizzie posed for Meg. "Well, whaddya think? There's not much more I can do. Will I scare them?"

Meg laughed. "You look fine. They'll be so relieved to see you're okay, they won't notice anything else. You should have seen their faces when they arrived."

"Really?"

"Oh, my, yes. All of them are ashamed."

Lizzie looked horrified.

Meg continued, "You have to understand your position in this culture. You're an elder as well as an honored foreign guest. They failed you inexcusably."

"But it wasn't their fault."

"I know that. They know it, too. Jed and I told them what you said happened. And they heard it from the airline when they checked. But they still failed you, Lizzie, and they can't get over it unless you help."

"The culture didn't seem to affect that taxi driver."

"That's a different story."

"What should I do, Meg? What should I say? I'm tired of messing everything up."

Meg thought for a moment. "Okay. Smile a lot. Let them apologize to you. Make sure you actually forgive them. Say the words, okay? And keep insisting that it was nothing – a little inconvenience, like dust in your soup or a lumpy mattress, that's all. They know exactly what happened, and they know how serious it was, believe me, but make sure and minimize it so they can move on. Alright?"

Lizzie nodded nervously. "I'll do my best."

Meg patted her arm. "I'm sure you will."

They turned to leave the bedroom, but Meg paused at the door and lowered her voice. "And just so you know, some of our *big* problems with Dembe happened at Pastor Kajumba's school. That's why none of our boys are welcome there any longer. This is the first time we've met Pastor since then, and never at our own house."

With that, she swung open the door to prevent any questions, letting Lizzie precede her into the hall.

The living room was sparsely furnished. Lizzie noticed a cheap couch on one side, assorted wooden chairs arranged around a scratched coffee table, and a few end tables supporting electric lamps and paraffin lanterns. The remains of teacups and saucers, along with some biscuits, gave evidence of time spent waiting for her to wake up.

As she entered the room, wearing as big a smile as she could summon, Lizzie saw tall Pastor Kajumba rise and hurry over to her with his large hands out.

"Elizabeth! Dear, dear Elizabeth!" He enveloped her hands in his and peered openly into her face with immense kindness evident in his eyes. "How sorry we are for what happened. It was unforgivable."

Lizzie focused on continuing to smile. "No, Pastor, it *is* forgivable. You did nothing wrong and, besides, it could have been a lot worse." She noticed a solid shaped woman in a long skirt rise and step forward behind him as she continued. "Look, here I am. I'm fine. No big deal."

Kajumba grinned. "*No big deal!* You Americans and your words." He bowed his head. "Thank you for your graciousness."

He stepped back and lightly touched the sturdy woman's shoulder. "Elizabeth, allow me to introduce my wife, Sophia. Dear, this is Elizabeth Warton."

Lizzie felt the woman's strong, cool hands close over hers. "Elizabeth, I apologize for your treatment. We have no excuse."

"Please." Lizzie kept up her smile. "It's in the past now. Really."

"But we heard you have lost everything. I hope we can make it up to you."

Pastor Kajumba nodded and took back the floor. "Yes. With Mrs. Birungi's help, we will do our best to help you replace what we can."

"Thank you. I guess I do need some assistance there."

Kajumba stared at her kindly and shook his head. "I am just so glad to see you again."

Mrs. Birungi, a large-hipped, round faced woman of forty, sweating in a pretty blue and white *Gomesi*, nervously stood. She clutched her white leather purse like a life ring.

Kajumba waved her forward. "Elizabeth, I know you've e-mailed each other many times but please, finally meet my associate, Mrs. Nankunda Birungi. Mrs. Birungi, I present our librarian, Mrs. Elizabeth Warton."

Lizzie smiled and took her extended hand, while struck by the fearful look in Mrs. Birungi's eyes. Was this really just a cultural moment, as Meg had said, or was there something else at stake? Tiny gender alarm bells were dinging in the back of Lizzie's head.

Mrs. Birungi looked straight at her and smiled unhappily. "I wish we could have met under better times, Mrs. Warton."

"Me, too," Lizzie jumped in. "But just call me Lizzie, please. And I'm sure we will have better times ahead of us."

Mrs. Birungi refused to be deterred from her task, "You are too kind, Lizzie. I utterly failed you. It was all my fault. I feel so terrible!" Her eyes took on a pleading appearance. They anxiously flicked towards Kajumba and then back again, as if trying to signal Lizzie a message. "I wish you could have called me on my cell. I would have done anything to help you if you had called."

Lizzie felt the woman squeeze her hand a little more tightly as she waited for a response. The woman's face shone with perspiration and hope. It dawned on Lizzie that this deep, well-practiced voice was *not* the one she had heard on the airport pay phone – not the one who had hung up on her. What was going on? She glanced furtively at Kajumba. He still stood in the same place, his demeanor nothing but supportive. Her mind nimbly gathered the available data pieces and clicked them into a few conclusions. He doesn't know, she decided. Birungi never told him what *really* happened! And she doesn't want him to know now. Lizzie may not have been adept at African culture, but she was well acquainted with a feminine dilemma when she sensed one; and she knew how to duck and cover.

"Mrs. Birungi, please understand, it was my own fault. I dialed wrong. I've never used a phone card before in my life, and the lines just never connected – not even once. I'm the one who should apologize. It had nothing whatever to do with you."

The relief in Mrs. Birungi's face was unmistakable. Her lungs released a delayed breath. "Your words are so kind. You have no idea how they help me to feel better." Smiling, she pulled Lizzie into a warm, polite hug. "I would be happy to teach you all about phone cards, Lizzie."

Lizzie patted her soft shoulder. "And I'd like to learn. I'm sure you have a lot to teach me, Mrs. Birungi."

Mrs. Birungi straightened up again, her face now untroubled. "We will talk much more later. But please, use my short name, *Nana*. That is what friends call me."

"I would be honored. I hope to deserve your friendship, Nana."

Mrs. Birungi filled the shabby sitting room with a rich, sunny laugh. "Oh, you already have, my dear. Believe me. We are friends already."

⌘

Lizzie stood beside Kajumba's small car with her vest folded over her arm. Mrs. Birungi had already climbed into the back seat and was on her phone. Musaazi swung the car gate fully open and stood with his back against one of the sides to keep it open. Kajumba and Jed spoke in Luganda a few steps away. Their tone seemed cordial, if not actually friendly.

Meg gave Lizzie a hug. "This isn't really goodbye, you know. We'll visit again. We have to have you over to the boys' house."

"I'd like that. Thanks again for saving me from the street."

Meg winked. "It's what we do here." She nodded toward her

husband and lowered her volume. "FYI, things are much better with Pastor Kajumba now. Thanks to you."

"And Dembe."

Meg's lips scrunched, "Yes, that's true, but since he caused the problem to begin with…"

Lizzie looked at her with her lips closed and waited.

Meg surrendered. "…Okay. And Dembe."

Lizzie rewarded her with a little pat. "Thanks for that. Every little bit helps."

"You be careful with that one. He's a charmer."

"I know. But I'm a grandma, so I wasn't born yesterday."

Meg laughed. "*Jjajja.*"

"What's that?"

"Grandma in Luganda. *Jjajja.*"

"*Jjajja.* I like that."

Kajumba and Jed wrapped up their talk and walked back to the car. Lizzie thanked Jed and said goodbye. She turned to climb in the front passenger side and only realized her mistake when she opened the door to see the steering wheel. "Oh, my! I'm still not used to this, am I? Sorry."

Kajumba laughed. "Elizabeth, if you want to drive here in this crazy country, we can teach you, but you first must forget everything you know about driving in Minnesota."

"No, thanks," she said. Embarrassed, she hurriedly crossed to the left side, got in smoothly, and shut the door.

As the car pulled out, Lizzie squinted ahead to see Musaazi waiting at the gate on her side. "Pastor, just a minute please."

The car stopped beside Musaazi.

Lizzie lowered her glass. "Musaazi?"

"Yes, lady."

"Did Auntie Meg ask you about finding some eyeglasses when you washed my vest?"

"Yes, lady."

"And did you find them?"

"No, lady." His face remained calm and still.

"And you looked everywhere?"

"Yes, lady. I even checked wash buckets and weeds where we dump the water."

She watched him steadily, hoping to see a tic or a flutter. Nothing.

"You're sure?"

"Yes, lady."

"Thank you for looking, Musaazi."

"You're welcome."

The car carefully descended the driveway lip and onto the street. It turned right and headed for the Makindye District. Lizzie turned back and watched Musaazi close the car gates to Safe Haven behind them.

THIRTEEN

Starting Over

Pastor Kajumba took long strides across the uneven courtyard of his school. Clearly delighting in the moment, his long arms swung wide to make his points to Lizzie and Birungi. "Education! That's the key for these children. True education, with God at the center."

The two women lagged in his wake. His lovely voice carried in the still afternoon air. "I'm convinced that this can unlock their futures. This can change a nation!"

The whirlwind tour of the pastor's nearby church buildings and his litany of the ministries and projects he oversaw had already left Lizzie feeling insignificant. She'd barely kept pace with his feet, let alone the exhaustive scope of his work.

The tireless, though sweating, Birungi had doggedly stayed ever at her shoulder, her face tranquil, nodding and smiling at Lizzie, as if to ease her mind. During one rare lull, as Lizzie puffed, Birungi leaned close to her ear and, between breaths, said, "Do not worry. We will talk."

Lizzie learned that Kajumba looked after some 150 churches in the country, and was constantly on the road. If he wasn't pastoring or counselling, he was preaching somewhere and raising money. He had also initiated numerous projects that partnered foreign churches with local community members to encourage self-sufficiency. There were farm projects, bike projects, goat and poultry projects, and the ever popular pig projects. In addition, he used his vacant classrooms at night – electricity permitting – to teach sewing and small engine repair, side-by-side with biblical topics. Kajumba, clearly a dynamo, seemed to have few *off* buttons, but the obvious apple-of-his-eye was his primary and secondary schools.

The Wobulezi school buildings were long and two stories high. They faced each other across an open expanse of red dirt and stubborn grass. The result of sustained efforts and prayers over many years, the simple structures had clean lines with large barred windows for each classroom. The red metal roofs gleamed in the late sun. They contrasted well with the pale yellow painted stucco that covered the rest of the buildings' exteriors. On one side of the quad stood the primary school, and on the other side, the secondary school. Kajumba proudly pointed out a third structure at one end: a dormitory for boarding students.

Kajumba paused near the center of the field to catch his breath. He smiled apologetically at the two perspiring women. "I am sorry to get so carried away. I want to show you the library, Elizabeth, but first…" He hesitated. "Mrs. Birungi, do we have time to pop in on some of the classes?"

She checked her cell and looked startled at the time. "No, Pastor, you forget that we started late. Classes are about to be dismissed. In fact, the bell is on its way."

Lizzie noticed two sets of ladies with large hand bells heading for the same end of each of the buildings, one woman on the ground level, the other directly above on the second floor balcony. At a signal from one of the ladies, they all began ringing their bells as they quickly walked the length of both buildings. Behind them, black children of all sizes, dressed in nearly identical school uniforms and dragging or wearing backpacks, poured from the classroom doors and onto the quad. The uniforms on the primary side were yellow blouses or shirts and blue jumpers or shorts. On the secondary side, the tops were white with red ties and the bottoms were dark grey skirts or trousers.

Kajumba smiled in delight. "It is later than I thought. You will have to take her to see classrooms on another day, Mrs. Birungi."

"Yes, Pastor."

The primary students were the first to spot them, and many shrill voices cried out, "Pastor! Pastor!"

Kajumba's face crinkled in pleasure. He put his arms around the shoulders of the first students who reached him, leaning down to listen and laugh with them. More and more yellow and blue clad children circled happily around him, all talking at once. Kajumba looked over at Mrs. Birungi and called out something in rapid Luganda.

She nodded as she replied, then pulled gently on Lizzie's arm. "Come. He wants to greet his students while I show you the library. He will join us when he can."

Lizzie was amused at the scene of the tall Ugandan pastor bobbing in the colorful waves of grinning students. She was surprised to find that she had difficulty distinguishing genders. Except for the telltale jumpers vs. shorts, or skirts vs. trousers, most of the gender cues were missing. The young girls had their hair shaved close to their heads, just like the boys. Even the high schoolers were difficult to classify.

As she followed Birungi, she glanced back to see the calmer group of older, white and grey uniformed students walk toward Kajumba to shake his hand, or smile a greeting, or receive a wave. A few teachers observed from the balconies, shaking their heads knowingly and smiling to each other. Below them, Pastor Kajumba moved unhurriedly through the milling students, his hands and arms busy weaving his magic, every bit as effective as the Pied Piper, cheerfully stealing the children away.

❧

Lizzie wore a perplexed look as she stared out of a bank of ground floor windows that illuminated the library. The sun sat low in the sky. She squinted, her eyes taking in the messy heaps of construction debris outside. She let her gaze trace longingly over the lush trees in the distance.

"I guess I'm more than a little confused, Nana."

Mrs. Birungi joined her at the dirty windows and nodded with understanding. "Pastor Kajumba is a man of great vision, Lizzie. But sometimes, even though the center of what he sees is clear, the edges can stay a little...frazzled."

Lizzie snorted in surprise and turned to face the vacant room. "*Frazzled*? That's a very special English word!"

"Is it?" She did a slow stroll along the bank of unfinished windows. The other side of the room had no windows but the floor was marked out for rows and rows of future bookcases. "Well, I think I have had to learn many *special* English words while working for him."

"I can imagine."

Lizzie tipped back her head and studied the array of skinny trusses that supported the uncompleted metal roof panels. Rickety scaffolding remained in place in the center of the room, and a pile of rivets littered the scuffed cement floor beneath it. "I don't mean to sound critical, but I expected things to be a little farther along than this."

"I know. Believe me, I know." She bent over and used her finger to trace a gouge in the floor. "It is not for lack of trying. But there is a problem."

"I can see that." Lizzie stepped back toward Mrs. Birungi.

"No, you cannot."

"What do you mean? I can see that the library's not finished. You don't have shelves. No tables. No chairs. No files. No lights. What can't I see?"

Mrs. Birungi slumped back against a window frame. "Those are just the normal impossible needs that we fix for Pastor all the time." She smiled tiredly. "No. It is the books. We have no books."

Lizzie wrinkled her brow. "But I thought the donation had already happened. That's what Pastor told me months ago. Did the donor back out?"

"No. The Austin Independent School District in your Texas did what they promised. They shipped us their old books." The heavy lady sighed and closed her eyes. "How wonderful it must be for a school to have unlimited money for new things."

Lizzie smirked. "That's not how it works, Nana. I'm sure the Texas voters would have a different story about the school district's spending bill. So, what happened?"

"How they picked us as the target of their charity we do not know, but we accepted. Pastor Kajumba accepted. He saw it as the hand of God. And that was why he began to build this. He was so excited. We all were."

"And?" Lizzie rotated her fingers in a tight circle trying to speed up the story. "Did the books come, or not?"

Mrs. Birungi would not be hurried. "Yes, eventually. They kept us up to date. The Austin schools formed teams to pack the boxes. UPS donated their services to move them to your east coast. The district hired a shipping company there to do the rest. The books filled an entire container and were sent by ship from your Boston to Port Mombasa in Kenya. All shipping costs were prepaid. It took three months to arrive."

"Kenya? Why Kenya?"

"Kenya has seaports. Uganda has none. Then it moved by truck to Kampala. So, it is here, but it is not here. It is locked in a customs bonded warehouse in the city. We cannot get it out."

"Why not? Paperwork?"

"Yes, but more than that. URA says we owe taxes. Other agents say we must pay handling fees, inspection fees, storage costs, highway user charges and now, the shipper claims rental fees for the stalled container. Everyone claims we are missing something or must pay something."

"What's URA?"

"Uganda Revenue Authority."

"Of course." Lizzie's lips curled. "The tax man."

"Here in Uganda, taxes on import items are based on their value and their quantity. Since the shipment is books, URA says it must assess each one."

"But it's a donated pile of used books! You didn't buy them! You're not selling them! That's not right!"

"Exactly. But Lizzie..." Nana looked uncomfortable. "...we are a poor country. And poor countries pay their agents poorly. It is the way things are. Every shipment is seen as an *opportunity* – even if nothing is wrong. Each official is quite *hesitant* to release it for free. Do you understand?"

"I get it, Nana. Trust me, I get it. But there must be a way. It's just one container, right? How much can that cost?"

Birungi looked at her strangely. "Do you know how big an ocean container is?"

Lizzie felt sheepish. "I guess I don't. Not really. How big?"

The Ugandan looked out the window and gave it a thought before refocusing on Lizzie. "Do you know the large trucks you sing about in some of your country western songs?"

Lizzie blinked. She could not, for a moment, think of a single thing to say. When was the last time she had listened to country western? "Umm...you mean like...18 wheelers?"

Birungi cocked her head. "What is 18 wheels?"

"It's the number of wheels on the trailer and then the...ahh..." She tried to picture it in her mind but lost count. "Forget it. You mean it's the same size as one of our over-the-road trucks?"

"Yes."

Lizzie nodded, her face registering awe. "I get it. It's a container ship container."

"Yes. A person can climb it and walk around on top. We have tried to free it many times, but with no luck." She lowered her voice before continuing. "We are limited in how we can solve this situation and still keep Pastor's blessing."

Lizzie considered the tortured wording of Nana's last statement. "Okay…"

"Do you know what I mean?"

"I think so. You're caught between a rock and a hard place."

Birungi considered that. "But a rock is a…" She blinked, then she nodded with a broad smile. "Oh. Yes. Exactly."

"And so far," Lizzie continued, "I'll assume prayer hasn't worked." She made a face. "So, if you're not allowed to grease a few palms, you're never gonna get the books out."

"Grease palms?"

Lizzie winced. "It means to put money in hands. You know, like grease on a sticky wheel makes it turn better, so cash in the right palms over at customs could…make their wheels turn."

Birungi scowled. "Right. And we cannot do that. So, we felt discouraged. Work on the library stopped. But when Pastor returned from his last trip, he had his confidence back. He got the contractor moving again. Construction restarted. He has no doubt now that we will get the books released."

"What?" Lizzie frowned, nervously. "Why?"

Birungi's face brightened. "Because you are here to help us."

"Me?" Lizzie was shocked. "What do I have to do with it?"

Mrs. Birungi wore a knowing smile. "You are God's librarian from the United States."

Lizzie suddenly barked out a derisive laugh. She leaned against an unpainted wall, insides churning, legs feeling weak. "That's silly! What do I know about shipping fees or bonded warehouses?" She kept shaking her head. "You've gotta be kidding!"

Behind Lizzie, a secondary school girl peeked nervously in through the doorless entryway. Lizzie noticed her. The student's forehead was smooth and shiny and appeared more prominent because of her lack of hair.

She said something in Luganda.

Nana turned with a warm welcome in her face. "Afiya, come in! I'm so glad you found us."

Afiya replied in Luganda, but Birungi waved it off. "No, speak in English, dear. I want you to meet my new friend, Elizabeth."

Lizzie stood straight, pasted a pleasant smile on her troubled face, and looked closer at the girl. The teen seemed quite cute in her white blouse with the red tie and grey skirt, but she appeared to be painfully shy. Her lips were very full and made for smiling, like her mother's, but she wasn't smiling now.

Afiya momentarily glanced at Lizzie, her eyes widening in alarm, before lowering her face again to stare at her shoes. She muttered, "They told me, Mother, you are here in library."

Lizzie's ears tingled at the sound of the girl's voice as she spoke English.

Nana approached her daughter and folded her into a hug. "Afiya, I want to present to you Mrs. Elizabeth Warton, our new librarian. Lizzie, this is Afiya, my youngest daughter."

"Afiya, what a lovely name." Lizzie smiled at them both, her busy mind quite pleased with itself as it pressed the final puzzle piece into place. "You have no idea how glad I am to finally meet you."

The girl barely lifted her eyes. Nana released her from the hug and let her stand on her own beside her. "Go ahead. Show Lizzie that you know how to be polite."

Afiya took a breath and then replied by rote, "I am pleased to meet you, too, Mrs. Warton."

Lizzie continued to smile at her. She enjoyed the obvious similarities in eyes and facial structure from mother to daughter. A little irritated with herself, Lizzie found that she just couldn't resist making sure she was right. Stepping closer, she offered her hand to Afiya. "Now, I wonder if you can do something for me."

Afiya looked curiously at her as they lightly shook each other's hands.

Lizzie continued, "Can you say for me the words, 'Call back'?"

Afiya's response was nearly instantaneous. She dropped Lizzie's hand and buried her young face in her mother's ample chest.

Nana rolled her eyes at Lizzie and grinned with her wide white teeth. "What can I say? You found us out!" She chuckled and cooed as she stroked her daughter's head. "She took my phone when I was asleep to chatter secretly with her friends. And, yes, that is when you called. She panicked. Poor child! She even hid my phone when it kept ringing. If Pastor knew, he would be so terribly disappointed in her, and Afiya could never bear it."

Lizzie at first felt guilty at putting the teen through further turmoil, but then, as she thought about it, she didn't actually feel *that* guilty. After all, her needless *stroll* through the slums could have turned out even worse. Still, after a short while, she placed a gentle hand on the girl's shoulder and softened her voice. "No one will ever know, Afiya. And I forgive you. Everything worked out. I'm fine. Okay?"

Afiya's eyes opened slightly and Lizzie discerned the barest of nods from the girl's head.

Nana smiled and wiped at her daughter's tears with one of the puffy sleeves of her *Gomesi*. "It is all done now, child. Life goes on. No more tears. Save some for other things."

The chastened student stood again on her own two legs and nodded. Suddenly, her wet eyes widened at a noise behind Lizzie.

"So, there you all are!" Pastor Kajumba's rich voice echoed in the empty room as he entered through the same doorway Afiya had used.

Mrs. Birungi hurriedly cleared her throat and smiled. "Yes. Here we are, Pastor. We have taken the tour and..."

"Good, good. I'm glad. Now, I am embarrassed, but I must leave right away. I am already late for a meeting with the primary teachers. And tomorrow morning, as you know..." He eyed Mrs. Birungi. "I leave for the conference in Nairobi."

He paused, his expression serious. "I am so sorry, Elizabeth, I wanted to talk to you in detail about the books."

"Yes, I heard about the problem, but…"

"Ah, Mrs. Birungi explained? That's good. Good! She is much better at it than I am. So you see what we are up against?"

Lizzie tried again. "Yes, but I don't think you understand that—"

"And I apologize for the way your building looks. But do not worry, I have talked to the workers. Things will go faster in the morning."

He looked up at the ceiling, slowly rotating his head, as if checking out the roof panels. "I am sure, God willing, that everything will be done in time for the arrival of your books."

He turned to leave.

Lizzie felt desperate now, and her voice carried a shrill edge to it. "*My* books? They're not my books! But, but that's just the point, Pastor, I don't think it will be—"

Kajumba turned back toward the women. "The point is, I will leave it in your capable hands. It is settled. Mrs. Birungi, you have my permission to do whatever Elizabeth feels is necessary. She is the expert. God has sent her for just such a time as this. Bless you both."

Then, he walked off briskly to his next meeting.

Birungi and Lizzie eyed each other in stunned silence. Lizzie's cheeks showed blotches of color here and there as she struggled not to screech. Mrs. Birungi's face gave away nothing.

Lizzie spoke through tight lips, her words strained. "I have met people of great vision before. They usually ended up causing a lot of thankless work for *other* people."

Nana snorted in loud agreement. "True. Too true!"

Unable to stop herself, Lizzie started to giggle. "What have I gotten myself into?"

Nana patted her shoulder. "Oh, Lizzie, we are going to be such friends!"

Lizzie nodded. "I hope so, Nana. I need friends. I'm feeling pretty shaky at the moment."

"Do not worry. Here is what our first step should be. We need to replace the clothes that you lost. A woman needs to look smart if she is going to fight a war."

Lizzie took a bleak look around the unfinished library and humped her shoulders. "A war? Really?"

"Yes. Tomorrow we will go to Owino Market and see what we can find for you. They have everything there."

Standing between them, Afiya's glum face perked up considerably at the magical word, *Owino*. "Can I come, too?"

Nana quickly shook her head. "No, child. You have school. Did you forget?"

"No. But you know I am a good little shopper."

Lizzie felt a rebellious tug. "Let her come."

Nana looked up sharply, surprised at being countermanded.

"Pastor just said you have permission to do whatever I feel is necessary," Lizzie explained. "And right now, I feel I need this *good shopper's* help."

Birungi pouted. "Oh, Lizzie! You cannot do this to me."

"Oh, Nana. Yes, I can!" Lizzie's firm expression said it all. "In fact, as God's own librarian, I insist."

Afiya looked at the old *muzungu* with new eyes. Her mother relented, giving her begrudging assent. Afiya did a little hop of adolescent glee, then looked earnestly at Lizzie. "*Jjajja*, we must make a list."

⁓

The fat sun had set two hours earlier into a thick nest of dark clouds. Mrs. Birungi's house, where Lizzie had been provided a small room, remained still and dark. The darkness was partly due to the electricity being out, which no one seemed to expect would return any time soon. The stillness was because Nana and Afiya had gone to bed early. Exhausted from compiling their lists of what Lizzie would need, they were determined to get an early morning start to the market. Making the lists had been fun at first, more for them than for her. But after a while, Lizzie had found herself withdrawing more and more, until she had stopped participating at all. Mother and daughter hadn't noticed, since they were fully engaged in creating a workable wardrobe from scratch for their personal *muzungu*. In her heart, what Lizzie really wanted was all of her own things back again.

Outside her window, the amphibians and crickets, who never seemed to sleep, chanted their ceaseless choruses to the moon. Unfortunately, Lizzie's body was unswervingly convinced that it was morning. She sat in a wooden chair facing the window, aware of her own breathing – how each breath was uniquely hers, and hers alone. She recalled the distinctive sound of her husband's throat-clearing. It, too, had been unique. Even now, if she heard it in a crowd, she'd recognize it instantly. She'd probably identify him in heaven by that sound. Tears filled her eyes and slid silently down along her nose. She missed Jon. There was nothing specific this time, just him no longer beside her, just him no longer on the earth with her. It was pure loss, by itself. For a moment, she pictured Jesus at the tomb of his friend, Lazarus. He wept at his loss, too, even knowing that he would bring him back to life. She had always wondered about that.

Lizzie counted her breaths. It was something she had learned in childhood as a way to calm herself. She'd had a lot of practice over the years, and she found herself doing it now without thinking. Outside, the evening rain advanced like a wet curtain, swishing heavily across the rooftops, drawing ever nearer. Soon large drops began to drum on the metal roof above her head. She instinctively looked up, realizing her tears didn't feel so out of place anymore.

FOURTEEN

Owino Market

The diesel exhaust from the rusty produce truck beside them billowed through the taxi van's window. The payload end of the truck was piled high with stacked bunches of what looked like small green bananas. *Matoke,* Nana had told her. Lizzie anxiously fanned her hand in front of her face to clear the air. Her eyes stung. To Lizzie, it seemed incredibly early in the morning, but Birungi insisted an early start was critical to getting the best clothing selections. They had coached her about what it would be like in the market. How crowded and confusing it would be. How vendors would touch your arm or take your hand, and lead you toward their stalls. How there were no prices on anything and the sellers expected you to bargain. How everyone would notice her because she was white, and few white people visited Owino. She wondered now if they would ever arrive. The massive traffic jam they had crawled through for the past hour, which was beyond anything Lizzie had ever seen, underscored the fact that apparently everyone else in the city had had the same idea about starting early.

Afiya slept soundly against her mother. Lizzie thought she'd like nothing better than to curl up next to Mrs. Birungi and do the same thing, except for the noise and smells, and the ten other chatty passengers pressed into the bench seats around her. The whole situation struck her as ironic. She'd had the entire night to sleep but couldn't. Now, when she wanted to be awake, her body was shutting down. She stared outside to distract herself. She had plenty of time to sightsee along the side of the road since their taxi, and the hundreds of honking vehicles on every side of them, were all going nowhere at a snail's pace.

The broken streets carried few road markings, not that anyone paid any attention to lanes. Lizzie saw no traffic lights, so when the troubled seas of taxis, cars, trucks, motorbikes and buses encountered each other at road junctions, there was a chaotic mingling that followed no discernible rules. Lizzie would have called it gridlock, but it wasn't; people somehow still found ways to pass through, go around and keep moving.

Most shocking to her were the numbers of weaving motorbikes, many with multiple passengers swaying on the back. Women in fashionable garments and men in suits calmly balanced on the rear cushions of the snarling two-wheelers. She observed that women perched in a demure side-saddle pose, purse or packages on their laps, knees together and usually facing left. She watched in awe as the bikes snaked through plodding traffic, threaded openings between taxis and trucks, and pushed through waves of crossing pedestrians, all while beeping their shrill horns.

Birungi called them *boda-bodas*, and Lizzie learned they were a staple part of Kampala's human transport, not to mention a significant contributor to its traffic accidents. For just a moment, Lizzie's mind jumped to car insurance, and she wondered if there was a law here about the need for it. She instantly chuckled to herself at the absurdity of the thought and the odd way that her mind worked. Mrs. Birungi gave her a questioning look, which Lizzie promptly ignored.

Lizzie noticed a steady stream of young people walking beside the road, struggling to tote heavy plastic jerry cans – of a size she would not attempt to lift. Nana explained that they contained drinking water from a nearby public water site. She said everyone would return again in the afternoon to refill. Eventually, they passed the distribution site itself: two pipes jutting out side-by-side from a concrete wall. Women and children took turns sliding their jerry cans under the spigots. There seemed to be much laughing and talking while they waited beneath the pitiful trees. Lizzie figured that for them it was the place to learn the latest news and share gossip, like the mythical water coolers of the west or the ancient wells of the east.

As they neared the Owino Market, Lizzie became aware of multi-storied buildings on both sides of the street. They featured large, modern-looking shops on the ground level and expansive balconies on the upper floors. She saw a four story structure wreathed in green, semi-transparent construction cloth with a forest of lashed poles sticking out every which way. Workers crawled over it like termites preparing to fly.

"Is this what Owino is like?" she asked Nana.

After examining the buildings beyond the taxi, she shook her head. "No. Not at all. This is all recent. The city tries to look modern, like the west. If they could, politicians would do away with Owino. The new shops are pricy. Owino is the old way – the African way. It is said, if you shop Owino, no matter how poor, you can afford something."

Lizzie's eyes caught a sparkle of reflected sunlight in the distance. She saw a shining mosque with slender minarets and a tall chanting tower rising above rusty roofs. An exterior staircase coiled around the central spire. An array of loudspeakers crowned its top.

The taxi swung through a large roundabout and actually began to pick up speed. The congestion loosened as other vehicles exited off in new directions. Lizzie caught a glimpse of a street policeman in snow-white pants and long-sleeved shirt, wearing a black beret. He stood near the center island, vigorously pointing at some cars while waving his hand at others. As her taxi passed by, Lizzie noticed that his spotless pants were neatly tucked into ink-black boots. How on earth does he stay so clean? She pointed him out to Nana.

"I didn't know the police had white uniforms, too."

"Those are just for traffic police," she explained. "Each department has its own uniform. Regular police wear khaki or olive green."

Lizzie's eyes hardened. "The ones I saw in the alley with Dembe were dressed in blue and white camouflage."

"Those are also police, but a special unit." Nana sadly nodded. "Lizzie, I know what they did was bad, but not all of our police are that way. My younger brother is a patrolman near Owino. There is a large police station close by there."

Lizzie sighed as she thought of Dembe living in danger on the streets. Where was he right now? What was he doing? She looked away.

The taxi moved at a reasonable clip now. They passed a massive Hindu temple. It squatted on the corner of two streets like a resting elephant. Swastikas decorated its black metal gates, and a sign in English welcomed visitors. Lizzie admired the alternating blocks of coffee and cream colored marble that climbed in a cascade of terraces and colonnades to reach an impressive height.

Nana grunted as she shook Afiya awake and nudged Lizzie. "This is the old taxi park. We walk from here."

Lizzie looked out at the lines and lines of empty white taxi vans parked tightly, nose-to-tail and side-by-side across a giant red-dirt lot. It seemed as if a person could march from one side of the lot to the other on the roofs of the taxis, and never touch the ground. She wondered how they got the vans in and how they would ever get them out again.

Her thoughts were interrupted by Nana hunching up in her

seat and calling out in Luganda. The young taxi conductor nodded and hailed the driver. The van pulled over with a grinding of old brakes, and the conductor rattled the side door open for them.

Nana led the way with firm strides. Afiya stayed beside Lizzie to make sure she kept up. The packed dirt sidewalks were uneven and dotted with treacherous puddles. People of all sizes and ages filled the lane, bumping against each other. Luckily, most were fellow shoppers and going in the same direction. Their little band stayed with the crowd as it swept across a busy street, temporarily blocking the frustrated drivers and the peeved *boda-bodas*. Finally, they crossed a concrete bridge that spanned a roaring storm channel. Ducking under sagging banners and wide, tattered umbrellas, they suddenly arrived at Owino.

Nana guided them off the path to catch their breath and to admire the view. Behind them, the river of shoppers continued to sweep by. The three stood for a moment on the slight promontory, looking down.

Lizzie struggled to take it all in. Below her, there were long narrow roofs here and there, outlining the boundaries of the market. They looked like tall pole barns but without walls. In the middle area, she saw faded bouquets of umbrellas and fluttering blue tarps above the colorful masses of milling people. Buried beneath the moving shoppers, only the barest hint of a network of passageways could be discerned threading between the crowded stalls. Her mind couldn't relate the complexity of what she saw to anything in her experience. She thought it most resembled a sporting event, because of the staggering numbers of attendees. But here there were no players to watch or stands to sit in, and the spectators ruled the fields. Lizzie felt the distant roar of many voices wash over her, an insistent din beating against her ears. The smell of the market crept up the hill and wrapped her body in a potpourri of dust, gasoline, pungent smoke, sewage and roast chicken.

Even while she stood watching, Lizzie noticed the numbers of shoppers passing by hadn't slackened. There were teens in T-shirts and old men with canes, clusters of Muslim women in full robes and young men with dreadlocks, heavy-hipped mothers with knotted headscarves and lean business women with stylish briefcases. A modern African parade on its way to market, and Lizzie observed it all from a front row seat.

When she turned to check on Nana and her daughter, she saw that they glowed with an itching anticipation. They conversed intensely, their heads together. Lizzie saw their eyes mapping out the best pathways from one area to another. She admitted to a quickening of her own shopper's heart, anxious to wade into the mix, despite the language barrier and the daunting view below. This should be an interesting day, she assured herself.

Afiya leaned close to Lizzie and raised her voice, shyness forgotten. "*Jjajja*, here is food market." She pointed below them. "Clothes and goods are over there." She waved her arm to the right, towards another section of the extensive market, partly hidden from view by old buildings. "We pass through this part to get to that part. Looking only here. No buying until we get over there." She flashed her teeth and caught Lizzie's eyes with an upbeat, aggressive stare. "Ready?"

Trying to match the girl's excitement, Lizzie put on a devil-may-care expression, checked her vest to make sure the zippered pockets were shut, and squeezed her hand. "I'm ready if you are, little Miss."

Afiya chuckled and nodded to her mother. Mrs. Birungi quickly led them off at a good pace. The three fell into step with each other as they joined the crowd and descended into the market.

"Hey, *muzungu*! Over here!"

"Lady, best prices in Owino!"

"I have jeans. You want jeans? New styles from America!"

"Hey! Pretty white lady! Over here!"

"Best quality! Best prices! Today, only for you, *muzungu*!"

"A new shipment! Come and see!"

"*Muzungu*! Lady, what you need?"

Lizzie soon tired of the accented voices shouting at her. She saw no other white women in the claustrophobic market. In fact, she saw no white faces at all. Warned in advance, she ignored the hands on her arms, the fingers trailing across her fingers, even the nudges to move her toward their shops, but she was fed up with the vendors' constant calls aimed at her. Still, she doggedly maintained her wooden smile, even though she gritted her teeth behind it.

At one point, a vendor called out a question in Luganda. Someone else answered. Lizzie felt sure it had something to do with her. Laughter broke out. Other voices chimed in with more quips. Grinning faces nodded at her as she walked away.

Lizzie shot a questioning look at Nana, who frowned, even though a smile tugged at her mouth. "It is nothing. Just vendor talk. Ignore it. We need to go over that way." Nana pointed to a split in the congested path ahead, and steered them to the right.

Afiya pulled abreast of Lizzie a little later as they bobbed through a brief opening in the moving crowd. "They said they not sure you are white or Ugandan."

"What?"

"It was joke. Our people always make jokes."

"How was it a joke?"

"Somebody said you half Ugandan." The girl suppressed a grin.

"I don't get it."

"They said you have white top but Ugandan bottom." Afiya smiled broadly as she said the line.

Lizzie looked back, puzzled.

"This kind bottom." Afiya patted her own rump. "Word means both things. They admired your...bottom." Afiya couldn't help but giggle as she repeated the word.

Lizzie understood and sighed. "Well, I guess that's not the worst thing I've ever heard." In her mind, a little appreciative thought blossomed at still being noticed in that way, at all. She hastily chided herself and kept walking, but her hips now swayed a tiny bit more, nevertheless.

The mud pathways between the shops were constricted by the merchandise and littered with twine and packaging debris. The little stalls were crammed together side-by-side and extended as far as the eye could see in every direction. No actual roofing covered the market; everything was open to the sky. However, the tarps and plastic panels that spanned the tops of the stalls often overlapped each other, and made the shopping world beneath them feel dark and enclosed. Getting lost inside the market wasn't a fear, it was a given.

Lizzie's respect for Nana deepened as she watched her work Owino. The ever proper and polite school administrator revealed herself as a combative and creative negotiator. Lizzie relished the give-and-take she witnessed, the jibes that were flung and returned, Birungi's threats of walking away and the vendors' pursuits. Afiya translated the blow-by-blow for her and provided explanations when needed. Lizzie would have been sorely tempted to try her own hand at bargaining, except for the language.

So far, they had secured some towels, a sun hat, two bottles of mosquito repellent, various toiletries, and three pairs of socks. Nana proudly carried their purchases in the vendor-supplied black plastic bags – Afiya called them *buveres*. Mrs. Birungi guided them toward a different group of shops. She claimed this seller was well known locally and owned large shops that specialized in quality second-hand American women's clothes, handbags, belts and shoes. She and Afiya had had good luck there in the past. They were determined to visit him again. Lizzie followed dutifully behind.

Most of the stalls were simple wooden platforms with makeshift crosspieces nailed to the sides. Clothing and accessories dangled at eye-level and above, sometimes in staggering quantities. In addition, on the platforms themselves, towels, T-shirts, pants, shorts, shirts and shoes were stacked in precarious piles right up to the edges of the paths. Shoppers cruised in both directions, constantly scanning and handling the displayed products and loudly bickering over prices. All the while their fingers clutched their purses or their hands sealed their billfold pockets, on guard for thieves. Vendors sat in chairs or leaned against their stalls, trolling the shoppers with their hands and their voices, grabbing and coaxing the passersby to stop, look, haggle and buy their wares.

By the time Nana declared their arrival at one of her preferred shops, Lizzie was worn out. She was relieved to see that this seller's space was considerably wider and deeper than the others. In fact, the shop was longer than three or four of the usual stalls and deep enough to actually step inside. It even had small aisles around the neatly stacked and hangered clothes. The layout of the store made sense: there were purses and belts in their own areas, dresses and skirts in theirs, sunglasses and hats in theirs, and so on. It was a welcome change from the rest of the day's experiences, and Lizzie actually felt her tired inner shopper begin to stir.

Plenty of other buyers filled up the narrow interior aisles, but Lizzie's white skin drew the shopkeeper to her side as surely as metal to a magnet. He smiled in a friendly greeting that showed off rows of white teeth and gold fillings.

"My shop sells the finest clothes in Owino, madam. How can I be of help?"

Middle-aged and bald, the vendor had a thick neck. He may have been muscular at one time, but he wasn't any longer. Taller than Lizzie, his bulky body was clothed in an expensive short-sleeved shirt and fashionable slacks. His large hands moved continually as he talked, rings gleaming from multiple fingers.

Lizzie let her eyes rove the store in a pretense of disinterest, trying to mimic Nana. "I'm not sure. I need to look around and get a feel for what you have."

Nana and Afiya stepped up beside her.

The vendor nodded and smiled at them all, instantly recognizing that they were a team. "If you have any questions, ladies, please wave at me or call my name. I am Wasswa. Hoping to be of service." Still smiling, Wasswa glided away to greet other customers.

Birungi evaluated the racks and piles of merchandise with a practiced eye. "This is a good shop. We should divide up. I will look at purses and belts. Lizzie, you look at blouses and skirts. Afiya..." She couldn't spot her daughter. "Afiya?"

Lizzie didn't see her either.

When a nearby clump of shoppers shifted, Afiya reappeared an aisle over, trying on a pair of aviator-style, mirrored sunglasses. She noticed their gaze and struck a celebrity pose. "What you think?"

Lizzie laughed. "Not exactly my style. Or are you shopping for yourself now?"

Nana shot a dark look at her daughter.

Afiya deftly put down the glasses. "Just pretending." She sent a sunny smile back at her mother. "But I can keep looking, yes?"

Her mother nodded resignedly, then headed off to check on purses.

Lizzie paused next to Afiya. "I'm going to look at the skirts and blouses, okay?"

The girl looked up from burrowing in piles of sunglasses. "Yes. Shall I find glasses for you? Not sunglasses. Real glasses?"

"No," Lizzie scoffed. "There's nothing in there for me. Cheaters won't help."

"What are...*cheaters?*"

"Reading glasses. They just make things bigger. My friends at home carry lots of them. That's not my only eye problem."

"Oh."

"I have...complicated glasses. I need to see an eye doctor and get a new prescription and..." A wistful expression passed across her face. "I don't even know if you can make them here."

Afiya looked as if she didn't follow all of that explanation. "We don't do eye doctors."

"What do you mean?"

"If our eyes need help, we try old glasses. Cheaper. Keep looking. Something will work."

Lizzie shook her head. "That's crazy. Afiya, I need sunglasses, so do that. Okay?" Lizzie headed off. "But if you really feel like digging through other people's glasses, knock yourself out."

Afiya seemed pleased as she spread out the cardboard boxes of sunglasses and cast off prescription glasses, and began sorting them into styles she thought looked good. "Knock yourself out," she mumbled with a grin.

Lizzie chuckled over Afiya as she picked through some skirt styles she thought might be workable. The sizing was mixed, so she needed to dig to find several that could fit her. She struggled with her eyes to correctly read the sizes on the tiny tags. Unfortunately, her busy presence inevitably brought other customers hurrying over to paw through the same racks, right beside her. It was like one squirrel finding a nut and drawing all the other squirrels over, worried that they might miss a treat.

Surprisingly, Lizzie found two skirts whose styles she liked and that were in her size. The quality seemed good. There were no obvious stains or rips.

Like a ghost, Wasswa appeared beside her. "A popular style, madam. I sell many of those."

Lizzie managed to remain calm even though he had startled her. "Hmm. Do you have more in this size?" She flashed him the tag inside the seam and let him read it for himself.

"Yes, I am sure we do. This is a good size – a large size. Large sizes are also quite popular here."

Lizzie gave him a dirty look, but he didn't see it as he guided her to another part of the small shop. With a flourish, he uncovered additional stacks of skirts in various colors and designs. "I import many clothes every week from your United States." He ran his hand across the skirts and rubbed an edge of one between his thumb and first finger. "Feel the craftsmanship. Lovely, yes? America, not China."

"Yes, of course." Lizzie's eyes had jumped when he said the word *import*. She dutifully began to rummage in the pile, but her mind was already working on her other problem. "These are too small. Oh, wait, maybe this one will fit." She slid one of the skirts free, considered it, and flipped it front to back. "This might work for me." She held it up against her generous waist. "Not bad. What do you think, Wasswa?" She batted her eyes at him and smiled just a little as she used his name.

"Lovely," Wasswa beamed. "It is a wonderful choice, madam."

"Thank you. And if you don't mind my asking, do your import shipments have any problems with the customs people?"

Wasswa was momentarily caught off-guard by the sudden change of topic, but he quickly recovered. "Not anymore. None that I cannot handle." He smiled proudly. "I am one of their favorites. We call each other by name. I see them every week." His face clouded slightly. "Why?"

"Oh, nothing. Americans are curious people. Are all your clothes imported?"

"No, not all. I have buyers here in Owino, too. They pick the best from the bulk shipments." He warmed to the topic. "And, sometimes, I have good luck with *local* sources. This is a tricky business, lady, but I have learned that there are many ways to skin kittens, as you say. Right?"

"To skin a cat."

"Skin the cat. Yes. Sorry. Many ways to skin a cat."

"Good for you." Lizzie continued to sort through the pile and discovered another skirt in her size, but this one puzzled her. It looked so familiar – in color and style. She held it up against herself and knew instantly that it would fit, knew even how she would look in it. Gazing down at the skirt, she experienced a wave of *deja-vu*, as if she had already worn it. Goosebumps pebbled the backs of her arms.

Wasswa was very pleased at the four skirts she had chosen. Lizzie scowled to herself, recognizing the dollar signs in his eyes. She feared she'd overplayed her interest, and now even Nana would have a tough time driving the prices down. Oh, well! She gathered the skirts together and looked around. "Maybe I should hunt for blouses now. Something that would go well with these."

Wasswa's face brightened. "Of course, madam, but now that I see your taste, I have some new items from a special supplier that might interest you." He lowered his voice and moved closer, adding an air of mystery to his words. "There are skirts and blouses, and other things. We are still sorting it out for display. The quality is very high and, I believe, in your size."

With his glittering hands weaving a path, he led Lizzie effortlessly through the other shoppers. As they passed near the sunglasses area, Lizzie saw Afiya frantically beckoning to her with an alarmed look in her eyes. Wasswa also noticed the odd behavior. Lizzie stopped him.

"Would you give me a moment, please?"

He nodded. "Of course, I will wait here."

Lizzie hurried to Afiya. The girl gasped and swallowed nervously, looking around as if afraid of being seen.

"Afiya, what's wrong?" Lizzie put down the skirts and placed a hand on the girl's forehead. "Are you sick?"

Afiya's big eyes stared into hers. "No," she whispered loudly. "Turn, so we look away from him."

"Who?"

"Him!" She made a tiny movement of her head and eyebrows to indicate the shopkeeper.

"You mean, Wasswa?"

"Yes," she hissed.

Lizzie stole a glimpse at the vendor. He benignly stood among the shoppers, patiently waiting.

Afiya gripped Lizzie's arm. "Turn!"

They both rotated together and faced away from Wasswa. Afiya handed Lizzie a pair of prescription glasses. "Try these."

Lizzie curled her lips. "Not this again! Don't be silly. I told you sunglasses were—"

Afiya's voice grew firm. "No! Try them!"

Lizzie took the glasses in her fingers and stopped. The weight and feel was strangely comforting – familiar. She carefully slipped them onto her face and watched the entire shop immediately snap into focus. Her eyes automatically looked up and looked down, the progressive bifocals keeping everything sharp no matter where her eyes wandered. It was such a stunning visual feast after the days of eyestrain, Lizzie caught her breath in a rush. She marveled anew at everything around her. She turned up her palms and held them at a reading distance from her nose. The lines in her hands showed fine detail and shadow. She remained still for a time with her eyes open and her hands motionless, but she no longer saw them. Instead, her mind was fully occupied, roaring through the possible implications of this startling development. Goosebumps returned with a vengeance.

Lizzie forced herself to calmly remove the glasses and hand them back to Afiya. Her voice was low and precise. "Is my name imprinted on the inside edge of the frame?"

Afiya didn't need to look. "Yes, *Jjajja*, that's how I knew."

"How many did you find?"

"Two."

"Good. You have found them all."

"What does it mean?"

Lizzie suddenly hugged her. "It means you are the most surprising young girl I have ever met! And I am so glad we got to know each other."

Afiya glowed, even though she didn't completely understand.

Lizzie turned them both back to face Wasswa again. He was still waiting in the same place. She caught his eyes, smiled, and held up a finger as if to say, *just one more moment.*

"Now, my dear," Lizzie kissed Afiya lightly on the forehead. "Let me think." She slowly breathed in through her nose and out through her mouth, like a cleansing breath. "Okay. Give me one pair of glasses and you take the other. Show your mother what you found, and ask her to call her brother, the policeman. She must get him here as fast as she can. Okay?"

Afiya looked nervously around the shop. "But, what if—"

Lizzie shushed her. "Uh-uhh! No *what ifs*. Trust me."

"What are you going to do?"

"Talk to Wasswa, of course."

"Is this a crime?" Her eyes widened. "Are we in danger?"

"Not yet. Now go!"

The girl hurried off, pushing through the shoppers. Lizzie watched her go and shook her head, now playing a part. She casually returned to Wasswa, smiling. "Sorry. Children are so easily upset over the smallest things. Do you have children, Wasswa?"

"Yes, lady. Twin boys."

"How nice. You'll have to tell me about them later."

Wasswa smiled in pleasure.

Lizzie continued, "Now, you were about to show me some... special clothes."

"Oh, yes. This way."

FIFTEEN

The *Muyaye*

Wasswa tried to maintain a neutral face but Lizzie saw he was thrilled by the impending sale. The two of them stood around a small uneven table at the back of his shop, away from the shoppers. The tabletop held a number of skirts and blouses, scarfs and slacks. Lizzie cooed and gushed over each new item as Wasswa presented it to her. The excited shopkeeper got his younger brother, Rokani, a partner in the business, involved as well. Tall and thin, Rokani would duck into a curtained-off area and then return with something new from their special cache.

Lizzie made a show of raving about everything – as well she might, since all of these *special clothes*, every single piece, were her very own clothes from her stolen suitcases!

When she could, she furtively checked the shop for any sign of the young patrolman. Nothing yet! Lizzie was painfully aware that she was running out of time, because she knew she had recovered nearly all of her goods. She gave one last glance back and sighed in relief. There was Afiya, grinning ear-to-ear, and with both thumbs up.

Wasswa noticed the exchange as well. He tipped his head, mildly perplexed.

Lizzie took a deep breath and placed both of her hands on the table. "Well, Wasswa, I am most impressed."

"Thank you, lady. We aim to please."

"You really outdid yourself. I have never seen a shop like this. Do you have a business card? My friends may be interested in visiting you."

"Of course." Wasswa smoothly brought out a leather card holder and pulled a business card from it to present to her. He nudged his brother to do the same. Rokani awkwardly dug in his dirty pockets, finally fishing out his own ragged card.

She studied the information. "I see. Wasswa Salongo, or do I say it the other way around, Salongo Wasswa?"

He smiled. "Either way is proper in our country, madam."

"Okay. So, we should negotiate. Isn't that the custom? That's what we do next?"

Wasswa rubbed his hands together and gave a perfunctory bow. "As you say. Now, there are many items here so there are many paths we can take to arrive at a final price." Clearly pleased with himself, he glanced out into the shop. "Should your friends join us?"

Lizzie rolled her shoulders, seemingly unconcerned. "Oh, they will soon. One more question?"

"Yes."

She handed him the glasses Afiya had found. "Wasswa, I also want to include these, but I wonder if…"

He turned them over in his hands, confused. "Used prescription glasses?"

"Yes."

"Fine. Why not?" He started to hand them back but Lizzie shook her head. She began her question again.

"But I wonder if you can tell me what the name printed inside the left temple means?"

Wasswa brought the glasses to his eyes, turned them, squinted a bit, and read aloud, "Elizabeth Warton?"

"That's right. Why is it there?"

The shopkeeper was at a loss. This all seemed odd to him. He showed the glasses to his brother, who also shook his head.

Wasswa waved a hand in the air. "We sell many glasses. Maybe these are a designer style and that is the maker's name – you know, like Versace or Prada. Someone important."

"Maybe you're right." Lizzie unzipped a vest pocket and took out her passport. She opened it to the photo page and displayed it to Wasswa. "And whose important name is here?"

He leaned closer to stare at the name beside the photo and then looked Lizzie directly in the eyes. An understanding of the true situation, spread out on the table, was finally clear to him. Wasswa's eyes grew larger as his attention was drawn to something else behind Lizzie. She turned and saw Mrs. Birungi standing in the shop flanked by two men in olive green uniforms. Afiya grinned and waved hello.

Wasswa straightened up and cleared his throat. His voice remained admirably steady, considering everything. "Mrs. Warton," he said, enunciating her name carefully. "What is it that you want from me?"

Lizzie returned her passport to her pocket and took back her glasses. "Mr. Salongo, I still intend to negotiate a deal, but not for my own clothes."

Wasswa furrowed his brow. "But what about the police?"

Lizzie put on her glasses and just enjoyed the act of seeing for a moment. "Oh, them?" Her eyes found Wasswa's. "They're my leverage."

For a short time, Wasswa studied Lizzie's face with open respect. Then his eyes grew suddenly hard, and he put his big hands on the table, leaning toward her. "Well played. But we are not in your country now." His voice carried a menacing edge. "And here, lady, in my city, there are always ways for certain people to get out of certain problems."

Lizzie looked steadily back at him. "I'm depending on that, Mr. Salongo. Believe me, I have no great love for your police. Yes, I do expect all my clothes and goods to be returned to me *at no charge*, but I also want something more from you. Think of it as the cost for buying stolen goods, or the price for me to tell the police this was all a misunderstanding."

The shopkeeper's steady stare broke. He blinked nervously, but his face showed curiosity. "What else do I have that you could want?"

Lizzie lowered her voice so that only he could hear. "Your friendship."

Wasswa was speechless. His face went through a number of expressions as he tried to make sense of this. "I don't understand."

"I need an ally. I'm desperate. I need someone to help me free an import shipment stuck in the customs warehouse."

Wasswa's shoulders began to relax. His face smoothed. "Customs...I see. What kind of shipment?"

"Books. Donated books. Lots of them."

Wasswa rolled his eyes upward. His face blossomed with comprehension. "Let me guess. They locked them up, right? And they have made up all kinds of fines and charges, and extra extras, right?"

"Yes."

"Of course, they did! That pack of thieves!" His hands flew in the air. His eyes gleamed. "It is how they make their money! I despise them! What you need is a *muyaye* to help you."

"*Muyaye?*"

"Yes, in my country we call him *muyaye*. In your country, I don't know. The one who makes things happen, the strongman, the fixer, the smart guy in the street, the one with...as you say, pull."

"Do you know a *muyaye* here who can help?"

"Yes. Absolutely." Wasswa laughed loudly and slapped his brother on the back. "Me! *Muyaye*! Huh, Rokani! We are the two best *bayaye* in Owino." Rokani laughed and tossed a comment back in Luganda at his brother. They poked each other. They shot quips back and forth. Wasswa finally smiled at Lizzie. "Madam, can I call you *Elizabeth*?"

"No. It's just Lizzie. But you can't call me *Lizzie* unless we have a deal. Do we?"

"Yes, yes, certainly we have a deal! You will say it was all a mix-up. I will give everything back. And together we will battle the customs." He made a vigorous nod. "Deal! And may I say that you, Lizzie, are not at all what you appear to be." He graced her with a broad smile and linked his hands together. "You should be proud. No one, in my life, has ever taken more advantage of me!"

Lizzie politely bowed at the acknowledgement. "In the United States, when we have a deal, we shake hands. I don't know your customs. What do you do here?"

Wasswa extended his glittering hand. "We shake hands here in Uganda, too."

Lizzie grasped it and they solemnly shook.

❧

Three figures slowly trudged up the path from Owino market, heading back to the old taxi park. Tireless Mrs. Birungi led their trio, towing a large orange suitcase and leaving twin wheel tracks in the packed dirt. Lizzie and Afiya walked side-by-side, Lizzie pulling her carry-on and Afiya swinging a black plastic bag. The young girl wore mirrored sunglasses and hummed a pop song as she walked.

Birungi looked back at Lizzie. "Did I not say you could find everything in Owino?"

Lizzie nodded. "Yes, you did – *almost* everything."

Birungi lowered her head. "Okay. Too bad about your mosquito medicine."

"True. Not to mention my cash, but I got the suitcases back and, thank goodness, they even returned my unmentionables."

Afiya scrunched her nose, confused. "What do you mean, *un—men-shun-ables?*"

Lizzie sniggered. "Unmentionables. You know, bras and underwear, and other things we don't talk about."

Afiya suddenly giggled. "But we *do* talk about them."

"I mean in public, dear, when everybody is listening."

"Oh."

They walked on, Afiya watching Lizzie. "I like your face better with glasses."

Lizzie winked at her. "Me, too. It's like I had my eyes returned, thanks to you. How do you like your sunglasses?"

She strutted for a few steps. "I love, love, love them!"

Nana scowled without turning. "A waste of shillings! I thought Wasswa could have given them as a gift."

Lizzie made an exaggerated sigh. "Sorry, Nana. I guess we can't expect him to lose money on everything. Even a thief has to pay bills."

Nana huffed in loud annoyance. "Do you really think that dishonest shopkeeper will help us free the books?"

Lizzie's voice sounded firm. "He must. We shook hands. We made a deal."

Nana suddenly rattled off a spate of lively phrases in Luganda to her daughter. Afiya made an odd sound in her throat and rolled back a reply. Nana again lapsed into silence, plodding on. Lizzie thought she had heard the word, *muyaye*, in there somewhere, maybe more than once, but she wasn't sure. To her ears, the sounds all ran together.

As they crossed the concrete bridge over the now sedate storm channel, Lizzie caught Afiya's eye and quietly asked, "What did your Mom say?"

Afiya's smile was enigmatic. "She said, maybe you are real *muyaye*."

SIXTEEN

Learning to Cook

The sun sat low in the cloudy sky, and Lizzie heard the late chorus of amphibians warming up their throats. She swatted a mosquito against the side of her neck and worried about finding more malaria pills – that would be tomorrow's task. Tonight was their Owino celebration dinner, and she'd demanded to help.

Mrs. Birungi grunted as she lifted the large steaming pot of *matoke* off one of her charcoal stoves. This allowed Afiya space to toss in a few more handfuls of the lumpy charcoal. Clay lined the inside of the open-top metal stove and an array of holes across its surface provided air to the glowing bed of briquettes. Nana set the pot back on top, sliding it onto the stove's three metal lips to suspend it above the heat. She poured some additional water over the tied banana leaf sack which held the peeled *matoke*, and then she wedged an inverted pot over the top to make a steam dome. Waving her hand at swirling flies, she wiped an arm across the sweat droplets beading her forehead. "Another hour to go. How's the soup?"

Lizzie stirred the thick stew in the pot on the second charcoal stove. She poked at the diced pieces of chicken. "Another hour would be just fine and dandy."

Afiya, standing near Lizzie, casually observed the sky and played with the new phrase. "Fine and dandy. Just fine and dandy. So fine and dandy."

Nana glanced with some concern at Afiya. "Child, what happened to the chai you were making?"

Afiya's face fell. "*Aiyeee! Nsonyiwa!*" She immediately sprinted away, flying through the side door into the kitchen, still wailing.

Nana shook her head as she stepped up the small curb and onto the narrow concrete veranda. "I am sure the water and milk boiled over onto my clean counter. It happens every time I let her make chai." She sighed loudly as she lowered her heavy body into a white plastic chair. "Come, Lizzie, and sit down. If we are lucky, we may have some chai soon."

Lizzie joined her. "With an escort?"

Nana nodded contentedly. "Yes, with an escort – or two."

Lizzie learned that most cooking and clean up in Ugandan homes took place outside. The indoor *kitchen* was simply a storeroom with counters where they kept the pans, dishes, bags of charcoal, and staples like rice, beans, oil, tea and sugar, along with the ubiquitous jerry cans of safe water. Nearly every meal required fresh food purchases, which meant a walk to the local outdoor market.

Lizzie tagged along so she could experience the real thing. Strolling to the market had been fine, with towering, flat-bottomed clouds floating majestically overhead, across the pale blue sky. The busy marketplace itself, squeezed between permanent buildings and tiny shops, was a haphazard arrangement of stands and tables in an open lot. Lizzie marveled again at Nana's skills to drive a bargain. It wasn't what the woman bought that mattered as much as the way she coaxed and wheedled and teased the grinning vendors. Shopping in a live market wasn't just buying and selling, it was the subtle dance of words and gestures offered by one side and answered by the other. The investment of time and effort elevated simple commerce into something higher. After half-an-hour of haggling, Birungi had secured a clump of small green bananas, some huge banana leaves, a handful of Irish potatoes, a few onions and some ripe tomatoes.

They stopped at a different table, and Afiya took on a far livelier role in weighing options. Her decision-making processes included licking her lips, squinting seriously and making various throat noises. As far as Lizzie could determine, the young girl had narrowed her choices down to banana pancakes, *cha 'pati*, or *samosas*. In the end, the *samosas* won the day. She selected nine of the small, triangular shaped, deep-fried, dough pillows. The burly female vendor showed off her quick fingers to the *muzungu* as she wrapped the delicacies, first in waxed paper and then newspaper. Maintaining a restrained smile, she carefully placed the neat package in Afiya's hands with a little bow.

Afiya waved the package at Lizzie. "These are *samosas*. You will love them!"

Lizzie mimicked her pronunciation. "*Sam-boo '-sah*? What's in them?"

"Good things." The young girl twirled in place. "So good! These are beef. It is an escort."

"Escort?"

"Yes. With chai. You know?"

"Oh." Lizzie finally understood. "You mean it has to come out with the tea? It shares the plate with the tea cup?"

"Yes. If you have one, you must have other. We say, *escort*."

"An escort."

"Yes."

Lizzie turned to look for Mrs. Birungi. She spied her on the opposite edge of the market, paying a vendor for a fat, brown-feathered, squawking chicken. She watched in shock as Birungi casually grabbed the bird by its tied legs and swung it, head down, next to her side like another bag. The chicken instantly ceased its noise and hung contentedly. Birungi moved easily through the loose crowd walking toward them, swinging the clump of *matoke* and banana leaves in one hand and the semi-comatose chicken in the other.

Afiya clapped in glee at the night's culinary prospects. Lizzie looked from one to the other. "A live chicken? For tonight? You must be kidding!"

Birungi gave her an innocent look. "You said you wanted to help, Lizzie."

"I know, but I never thought…"

Mother and daughter chuckled together as they ambled up the red dirt path between the buildings, heading home.

Lizzie stopped talking and fell in line behind them, feeling utterly useless. "Can you, at least, let me carry something?"

Without looking back, Nana lifted up the fluttering chicken and waggled it at her.

"Okay. I mean, besides the chicken?"

They peeled the *matoke* outside, near the stoves, using very sharp knives. Lizzie sat on an old stool while Nana and Afiya crouched on the hard-packed dirt on either side of her. The cream-colored inner banana was firm, almost like soft wood. Once peeled, it was temporarily dropped into a pan of clean water. When the peeling was complete, Birungi used a large banana leaf to create an outer wrapper for the *matoke,* which she piled inside. Gathering the leaf together at the top, she used a tough strand of fiber pulled from the banana leaf stem to tie it off. It made a kind of green sack. Then, she placed the sack in a pot and added some water. Finally, she set the pot on top of her hot charcoal stove and inverted another pot over the top of it.

Pleased with her handiwork, Nana curled her hands on her hips and waited for Lizzie to look at her. "People will tell you there are many ways to prepare *matoke.*"

"*Mah-tow'-kay?*" Lizzie repeated.

"Yes, *matoke.* They make it every place in Africa, and they all have their own ways. But we make the best *matoke*, my tribe, the *Buganda*, right here in Kampala."

She sounded so formal, Lizzie couldn't help but grin. "Of course, you do."

Nana tried to maintain her composure, but her face gave her away. "Why are you laughing? I am serious."

"I'm laughing, because I know you're serious."

Nana laughed long and deep. "Just wait."

Slicing the head off the chicken wasn't as funny to Lizzie. Afiya held the legs while her mother stretched out the unlucky bird's neck on a plank, making sure to spread the feathers apart so she could target a clean neck. The knife slice, when it came, was surgical and efficient. Birungi held the bird tightly against her until its body stopped shuddering, all the while aiming the neck down, so its bright blood would flow into the dirt.

Lizzie stood in silence beside them, stunned, and unable to stop watching. It was not as though she didn't understand how chickens got to her grocery store's refrigerated displays. But it was one thing to see a sign proclaiming, *Fresh, Never Frozen*, at her pristine store in Eden Prairie, and quite another to witness the bloody price chickens paid to be fresh or frozen.

The rest of the steps in the process seemed to Lizzie easier to tolerate, as if each one brought the chicken closer to what she was familiar with from her own kitchen. Dipping the bird into boiling water to loosen the feathers surprised her, but after the second dip, she and Afiya took great glee in racing to peel the plumage. Later, when the wing tips were removed, and the feet, and the neck, Lizzie felt her stomach start to settle. The chicken finally looked the way she expected it to look. None of the rest of the preparation bothered her at all: not the removal of the guts, not the setting aside of the livers, not the additional knife work, none of it. It was just the immediacy of that first step, the suddenness of the cut, the blood and the death, that gave her pause, and made her briefly consider the values of being a vegetarian.

Afiya was right. The *samosas* were fabulous. Lizzie didn't want to ruin her own enjoyment by inquiring too closely about those ingredients. Deciding that ignorance was bliss, she happily accepted a second serving when it was offered. Despite the unseen mishap in the kitchen, Afiya's chai was sweet and refreshing. Lizzie sat relaxed and watched the steam rise above the *matoke* pot. Her nose picked up the aroma of the simmering chicken. Muted noises from the neighbors, preparing their own dinners, floated over the walls, along with the tantalizing murmur of their voices. Lizzie admired the colors of the sun as it set behind the clouds. Something deep in her body began to respond to the laid back tempos of Kampala. Time here seemed to travel at a slower rate, and it was clear that suppers were seldom hurried.

Somewhere between the savory bites of her second *samosa*, Lizzie remembered a nagging concern. "Nana, how will we get my malaria medicine?"

Mrs. Birungi smiled calmly. "Don't worry. Pastor has a friend – a western doctor. Friend to the school. He will know."

"Is he American?"

"No. Scottish, I think. Doctor MacLaird." She laughed. "His accent is much different from yours!"

Lizzie smirked. "I bet that makes him a lot harder to understand, huh?"

Afiya perked up, still chewing but anxious to join in. "No. He is *so* much easier!"

Nana scowled at her daughter, and Afiya cringed. "Ah...I mean...Sorry, *Jjajja*."

Lizzie took a quick sip of chai to cover the awkwardness. "Nothing to be sorry for, dear. It's all right." Inside, she rebuked herself for being such an ugly American. As if you don't have an accent! Stupid *muzungu*! Get a clue!

Mrs. Birungi tried to recover the conversation. "Tomorrow, you and I will visit the foreign clinic and hope Doctor Mac is in. MSF doctors spend much time working way out in the country."

Lizzie squinted an eye. "*Emesseff?* What's that?"

"Sorry. It is not a word, just letters – MSF. I think they are French. *Medicines-Sans-Frontiers*, or something – I do not know French. We just say the letters, MSF. Americans call them *doctors-without-borders*."

"Oh. I think I heard about them in the news. Wasn't there a… hospital bombed by mistake somewhere…or something?

"I don't know."

"They aren't part of a mission group, are they?"

Nana chuckled. "No, far from it. Doctor MacLaird does not believe in God at all. He says, God is out-of-date, like a tail on a person."

Afiya looked startled. "*Kki?*"

Birungi glanced fondly at her and replied in Luganda. "*I was just checking if you were still listening.*"

Afiya frowned. "*Do people have tails?*"

"*No.*"

"*Did they ever?*"

"*No. Monkeys have tails, not people.*"

Afiya nodded, satisfied, and finished off the final *samosa*.

Nana looked over at Lizzie. "Did you need a translation?"

"No. I'm pretty sure I got it."

Lizzie set down her tea cup with a soft clink. They all sat for a while in silent companionship. The cricket chorus threatened to upstage the frogs.

Nana continued the earlier train of thought. "MSF came here because of AIDS and the HIV. Now they help in many other ways.

They know how to get safe medicines. They are good. Pastor helped them in the past. They help us now. That is the God we share."

Lizzie nodded, wondering what on earth this Doctor MacLaird was going to be like.

Birungi settled her cup and saucer with finality and rose to her feet. "And now we check the *matoke*. If it's soft enough, we eat." She moved toward the charcoal stoves. "Afiya, get me a pan of water."

Mrs. Birungi spread a fresh banana leaf out on the ground. She cupped her hands in the pan of cold water that Afiya brought and then quickly removed the inverted pot from the *matoke*. Dipping her hands back in the water again, she swiftly lifted out the steaming sack and set it on the new banana leaf. Lizzie wondered what Ugandan cooks had against hot pads or basic cooking utensils, but wisely chose not to comment. She watched with fascination as Nana used her bare hands to rapidly pound down, squish and squeeze the frightfully steaming sack. She alternated each rapid action on the sack with a quick swish in the cold water to avoid steam burns: swish, squish, repeat; swish, squish, repeat.

Pleased with the final feel, Birungi declared the *matoke* ready, and placed the sack in a serving bowl. Afiya sliced off the top and spread apart the sodden leaf to present Lizzie with her first glimpse inside. The steaming mound of *matoke* was a pleasing yellow color, almost lemon in hue. Thanks to Nana's capable fingers, it had an apparent consistency of creamy mashed potatoes.

Every plate received a generous dollop of *matoke*, a heap of the lovely chicken stew, and two different sauces for mixing. They carried their plates inside to a small dining table that Afiya had carefully laid with silverware and cloth napkins. Since the power hadn't come back on, there were two low burning lanterns nearby, lending the dim room a soft glow. Lizzie noticed the absence of glasses or water on the table. Fearing to offend, she declined to ask about it. She could only hope the dinner wouldn't betray her.

To her palate, *matoke* had all the subtle and surprising flavors of library paste, but that didn't prevent her from *oohing* and *ahhing* through forkfuls of the sludge. Nana glowed, feeling vindicated. Lizzie laughed internally at her charade while she papered an agreeably serene look across her face as she ate. *Matoke* must be an acquired lack of taste, she grinned to herself. Still, it made a decorative appearance on the plate and, so far, it hadn't caused even a ripple of rebellion in her stomach. Thankfully, the chicken stew was truly delicious, if she could only erase the image of how fresh it actually was.

Nana filled a fork with *matoke*, scooped a bit of stew along with it, and dipped both into one of the sauces before she slipped it into her mouth. Her eyes closed and she moaned softly as she gently chewed and swallowed. She took a breath and slowly let it out. "We can live another day."

Lizzie watched curiously from across the table. "What?"

Afiya, sitting to Lizzie's right, smiled and kept on eating. She had heard her mother say this at nearly every meal of her young life.

Nana continued. "It is something we say in my family." She lifted another forkful. "My *Jjajja* taught us that every day is a new struggle to survive. But if we have food in our mouth today, we know we can live at least one more day."

Lizzie pondered that as she felt her mind explore new paths. "Everything is so different here. I'm ashamed that I've never thought of something like that in my whole life."

Nana shook her head. "Never regret a blessing." Her face took on a faraway look. "When I was a child, much younger than Afiya, I had to foot to school with my older brother, to be safe. It was a time of troubles. Many mornings we stepped around dead bodies."

Lizzie put her fork down, her face filling with sympathy.

"We would grab handfuls of bullet shells from the ground to trade at market. I remember hearing the jingle of loose brass in my book bag. And every day we were afraid."

"I am so sorry, Nana."

"No. It is behind me now. I just want you to understand that for people my age, it is not just a thought."

Lizzie watched her, knowing that silence was the only reply.

Nana stirred her fork around in her plate and then stopped. "When I married my husband, he asked me what would make me happy. I thought a long time and then I told him, 'Sugar for my tea.' Do you understand?"

Lizzie leaned a little forward. One of her hands automatically rose up to support her chin. "I think so. I'm beginning to." She thought again of Jonathan's decade long battle for his mind, and her own hidden life trying to protect him. For some reason, Dembe came to mind. She saw him patiently watching over her in the alley. The lost boys danced once more around the trash bin fire, and she almost longed to join them. Even when the taxi driver's face rose up before her, instead of repulsion, this time she felt a peculiar stirring of compassion.

Her thoughts were interrupted when Nana suddenly got up from her chair. "Oh, Lizzie! I forgot. You want water! Americans always have water with their meals. I am sorry." She rushed back into the storeroom before Lizzie could even reply.

Lizzie turned to Afiya. The girl remained focused on her plate, thoroughly enjoying her food. She didn't use silverware; she ate with her right hand.

Afiya looked up when she felt Lizzie's gaze. "Good food, is it not?"

Lizzie forced a nod. "Very good."

Nana returned with a tall glass and a sealed plastic bottle of water. "Lizzie, please observe." She grinned playfully as she showed off the bottle. "You can see the cap is still on and sealed. And look, when I squeeze it, no water sprays out from any extra holes in the sides. I just want you to feel sure that taking a water here is safe."

Lizzie snorted at the joke. "Yeah, yeah, one can never be too careful. I get it. Thanks."

Afiya looked at both of them, confused. "Is that what really happened?"

Lizzie smiled at her. "No one told you?"

She shook her head, *no.*

Nana noticed her daughter's hand in her food. "Afiya! We have a guest...*from America!*"

Afiya's eyes grew large and her hand froze, stew still dripping from some of her fingers. "Sorry. I forgot...but, mother, you know it just tastes better without the fork."

Lizzie stared. "Really?" She frowned at Nana. "Do you usually eat with your hands? I didn't know that."

Nana returned to her chair, looking a bit flustered. "Yes and no, Lizzie. When we are alone, we often eat with our right hand. When we have guests, we tend to use silverware, since we know most foreigners aren't...ah...comfortable."

"Please," Lizzie replied. "I don't want to be treated as a guest. I want to be a family friend. Nothing special for me. Okay?"

Nana pursed her lips, and then quietly complied. "Okay."

Lizzie batted her eyelashes. "Besides, we chopped the head off a chicken together, didn't we? If that's not family, I don't know what is!"

Afiya burst into laughter. Nana shook her head. "Lizzie, you say the strangest things!"

The girl happily went back to eating, using her thumb and the first two fingers of her right hand.

Lizzie watched for a moment and winced. "But it's okay if I continue to use silverware, right? I mean, you won't be offended, will you?"

"No. Not at all." Nana smiled. "You should make yourself feel at home, too." She carefully put down her fork, and she used her hand to skillfully sweep up her next mouthful, all the while relishing Lizzie's squeamish reaction.

SEVENTEEN
Something Old, Something New

Afiya stood in the dark outside the open storeroom door and held the kerosene lantern high in the air. It cast a wide circle of illumination over the cold charcoal stoves and the dirty pots. A halo of bugs flitted around her light and batted themselves against the lantern glass with buzzes and clicks. Nana and Lizzie worked quickly to bring everything back into the storeroom. They set the stoves on the concrete floor near the door, the pots they piled on the counters beside the dirty dishes. The food went into special containers, and they stacked the chairs in the center of the room. As they hurried in and out of the doorway, they both swatted at the flies and mosquitoes that pursued them.

Nana chuckled as she worked. "You see, this is why all Ugandans have malaria, Lizzie. We are always running around outside at night with our hands full."

"That's not a happy thought, Nana. Ouch!" Lizzie awkwardly cocked her head toward her shoulder. She tried to squish a biting insect she couldn't reach because her hands were full.

"We do dishes in the morning, outside. Tonight, we lock everything up to make it harder for thieves and dogs to make trouble."

Lizzie nodded as she noisily set her load of pans down on the counter. She could hear a light rain starting to fall outside.

Nana extended her hand toward her daughter. "Child, give me the lantern. I'll finish up here. You go to the front, bring in the porch chairs, and then lock the door."

"Yes, mother." Afiya handed over the lantern and left.

Nana set the lamp on the floor and locked the storeroom door from the inside. The drumming rain grew more insistent. She leaned back against a counter and sighed. "Just in time. Thanks, Lizzie, for your help."

"Of course."

Nana took up the lantern and turned to leave. She paused when Lizzie spoke. "Can I ask you something, now that Afiya is gone?"

Nana nodded.

"It's about money – *my* money. I need to get more. I want to be able to pay you for staying here, and for food. And I'm sure I—"

"Oh, Lizzie. That's not necessary. We want you to—"

"No. It's not just that. And we can argue about it some other time. My point is, I have money in my account back home, but I don't know how to get it here. Do I use a bank? Western Union? What?"

Mrs. Birungi set the lantern onto an open space on the counter and folded her arms. "Is there someone at home who can use your account?"

"Yes, my son, David. He can write checks and transfer money for me. I set it up before I left." Lizzie looked glum. "I never expected to be penniless quite so soon!"

"I think I may know a way."

Lizzie's face brightened. "Oh, Nana, you are a wonder!"

She waved her hand. "It is not me. Some donors send money to Pastor this way. That is the only reason I know about it."

"But, is it safe? David won't do anything unless it's safe."

"Yes. A new way to send money. It only works if you are sending from the U.S. to Uganda. You don't need a bank, just a smartphone."

"But I don't have a phone, remember?"

"I meant *my* phone. I already have the app. It is called *Sendwave*. Your David will need to load the app on his phone and then fill out all the information the first time."

"How does it work? I know he's gonna ask me."

"He uses *Sendwave* to withdraw money from your account. *Sendwave* sends my phone a text that says how much was sent, along with a confirmation number."

"Okay, but how do I get the cash?"

"Do you remember all those yellow shops along the road with the MTN signs on them?"

"*Emchien*? What does that mean?"

"Letters again, Lizzie. Not a word – MTN."

"Oh, yes – small, bright yellow shops without windows. I saw them all over the place. I thought the letters were short for *mountain*. No wonder I was confused."

"The cash is there. We can go to any one of them. We just give the agent our phone number, confirm our ID, give the confirmation number, and they hand over the shillings. Simple."

Lizzie thought about the process for a time and then frowned. "Wait. You mean those agents are sitting inside those little yellow shacks with piles of cash?"

Birungi made a comical face. "Yes. Not the safest job in Kampala. The workers are usually nervous. There are many robberies. But, do not worry, we will go in the day, when there are many people."

Lizzie considered the information and then nodded decisively. "I need to call David. I just won't tell him about that last part."

They heard Afiya calling to them from the front room. Nana grabbed the lantern and led the way. "Remember, we are eight hours ahead. Right now it is very early where David is."

Lizzie followed close behind. "That's right. Okay. Maybe we can send him a text later to call at a certain time."

Birungi nodded over her shoulder. "Good idea."

As they passed by the dining room and entered the tiny living room, they met an anxious Afiya. She held a small package. "This was inside the house, by the door. It is for you, *Jjajja*."

"For me? How do you know?"

The girl gently placed the small box on the coffee table. Rectangular in shape, and neatly wrapped in newspaper, the package had a notecard attached to the top with Lizzie's name carefully printed in block letters across it – ELIZABETH WARTON.

Nana placed her lantern on a stand and then sat in a chair beside the low table. "Did you see anyone near the house?"

Afiya shook her head. Outside, the heavy rain beat steadily against their metal roof. "I only found it when I closed the door."

Lizzie knelt next to the table and touched the box. "So, it might have been left a long time ago?"

Afiya nodded.

Lizzie slid her fingers along the sides. "It's not wet." She fiddled with a short cord at one end. "What do you suppose this is?" The cord came from inside the box and terminated in a circular pull-tab, salvaged from a soft-drink can.

Birungi slowly smiled and placed her thick brown hands on her knees. "I have seen things like this before. I believe you are meant to pull the cord."

Lizzie was bemused. "Really?"

"Yes. I am pretty sure."

Afiya's face lit up with expectation. "Do it, *Jjaja*!"

Lizzie put her finger in the tab, and held the package down at one end while she pulled the cord at the other. There was a low *click* followed by a series of tiny *ticks*. Lizzie quickly pulled her hands away, not sure what to expect. Each of the four sides of the package snapped open in sequence, from left to right. There was a short pause followed by a new *click*. The lid of the box hinged up on one of its narrow sides, pushed by a spring, until it was fully vertical. The contents of the package were revealed. There, within a protective container, nestled in soft cotton, sat Lizzie's original glasses, now fully repaired.

Afiya clapped her hands in delight at the workings of the mechanism.

Lizzie was speechless, her mind circling. Suddenly, she jumped to her feet and ran to yank open the front door, stepping immediately outside. Rain poured down in sheets just beyond the lip of the roof that shielded the porch. Walking all the way to the very edge, she vainly scanned the grounds near the house, hoping to catch a glimpse of a slender figure. She called out into the noisy night. "Dembe! Dembe!" She received no answer, saw no movement in the rain. Nothing and no one there.

Behind her and looking concerned, Nana and Afiya stood just inside the doorway.

⋘

Lizzie carefully turned the shiny glasses over in her hands, amazed by the many subtle repairs and improvements she discovered. The work appeared so exquisitely executed, she had a hard time deciding if what she held was now elevated to art or simply a creative patch up. The separated nose bridge had been somehow reattached, but since the entire arched piece was now tightly wrapped in a fine filament of wire, from rim to rim, she was unsure how it had been accomplished. Above the bridge, the frames sported a new top bar that also connected the two eye wires together and provided extra support. She smiled to herself; the repaired glasses were stronger now than when they were new. The material used for the top bar matched the rest of the glasses – how that was possible, Lizzie couldn't imagine. The original frames were constructed of a new, lightweight hybrid metal, unique to expensive eyewear. At the end points, where the top bar met the rims, they were wrapped in the same filament of wire as the bridge, creating a pleasing uniformity in appearance. No one looking at the result would suspect a repair.

Tipping the glasses forward, she checked the hinges and saw that the tiny screws were tight and now covered with a clear, protective coating. When she placed her nose near the screws and sniffed, she picked up the faint scent of nail polish. Tiny grey rings, perhaps orthodontic rubber bands, enclosed the hinges, providing extra flexibility while holding them firmly in place.

Lizzie opened and closed the temples and found their movements silky smooth. Flipping the glasses upside down, and keeping the temples fully extended, she placed them on the coffee table and bent low to look. They lay utterly flat and seemed perfectly square. She ran her inquisitive fingers along the temples, from the tips to the end pieces, painstakingly feeling for any indications of the bent places that she was sure had to be there. She could find no traces. Impossible! Reconstructing her arrival night, she knew these glasses had been dropped, bent, stepped on, rolled over, shoved into the mud, broken in half and stuffed into a vest pocket; and yet, here they were: whole, clean, level and straight.

Nana and Afiya sat nearby, content to wait.

Lizzie finally took off her backup glasses, and put on the pair that Dembe had restored. The fit was perfect, and they felt wonderful on her face. She slowly stood and looked around the room, enjoying the experience. She turned to them. "Can you believe this? How do I look in my *new* glasses?"

Nana smiled. "Just lovely."

Afiya seemed close to tears. "Oh, *Jjajja!*"

Lizzie nodded back at the girl. "I know. I'm trying to imagine how I should feel, too. If you hadn't accidentally found my glasses at Owino, this would be the first time I could see again. The very first time!"

Her eyes glistened as she swallowed back a lump in her throat. "Who is this boy, really, Nana? And why is he back on the street?"

Mrs. Birungi folded her hands in her lap and sat very still. When she began speaking, her voice was soft. "Dembe was a brilliant student. All his teachers said so. They also reported that he was undisciplined, easily bored, and full of mischief – but so smart! I am ashamed to say that he was caned more often than he was praised. Still, everyone admired the toys he would make and the clever machines, like this box, from cast-off pieces that no one wanted. His mind saw possibilities in everything. He could look at contraptions like clocks, or pencil sharpeners, flashlights or door locks, and know how they worked, how to fix them, how to make them better. When he sat for the national exam his first time, he scored the highest in our school, fifth highest for his age in Uganda."

Afiya looked at her mother in shock and automatically lapsed back into Luganda. *"I never knew that."*

Her mother cast her a brief, cross look. *"You weren't supposed to know that. And if you're smart, you still don't know it."*

Burning from the unanticipated reprimand, Afiya blinked a few times and fell silent.

Lizzie sat down in a chair directly across from Nana. She leaned forward, her arms on her knees, hands tightly intertwined. "Nana, I need you to tell me the truth about what Dembe did at your school."

Nana's face betrayed an inner conflict. "I understand, Lizzie. Believe me, I do. But I promised not to say."

Lizzie's eyes never wavered. "That may be, but you still must. You must tell me."

Nana looked away, her resignation obvious. "I know. I will. But not here." She glanced at her daughter. "And not *now*."

Afiya looked away, her eyes darting around the room, not knowing where to settle.

Nana continued, "Tomorrow, when we are done with Doctor MacLaird, we will stop at the school and I will show you."

"Show me?"

"Yes."

Lizzie bowed her head in agreement.

Nana stood abruptly. "Afiya, we both need to go to bed. You have school in the morning, and a day to make up for since you skipped classes today. And tomorrow, I have dishes to wash and taxis to catch."

Afiya rose without a sound and followed her mother out of the room. Lizzie heard Nana's melodious voice from the hall. "Good night, Lizzie. Turn the lantern off when you go to bed."

"I will." Lizzie lifted her head up. "Good night, Nana. Good night, Afiya."

She sank back in her chair and stared up at the ceiling, listening to the raindrops as they loudly probed for ways to get inside. Her own roof at home was shingled and insulated, and it didn't allow for such a distinctive tapping. For the first time that she could remember, she wondered what it was really like to sleep on the walkways and in the alleys, without a roof, in a rainstorm.

EIGHTEEN

Doctors without Borders

A long line of patients stood outside the MSF clinic when Lizzie and Nana stepped out of their packed taxi van. The cloud of orange dust raised by the tires caught up with the vehicle and enveloped it. Lizzie calmly waved her hands back and forth to clear the air, then followed Nana past the row of waiting people. There seemed to be mainly mothers and children queued up, some babies strapped onto backs, but mostly large women with skinny toddlers clinging to their legs. She noticed only a smattering of old men and young adults. The unmistakable smells of rotting garbage and sewage drifted in on a warm breeze blowing from the nearby Namuwongo slums.

Lizzie cast her gaze in that direction. She saw a sea of metal roofs stained in orange rust and packed so tightly together, she could not discern individual dwellings or the walkways and roads between them. It reminded her of Owino market. She found it so ironic that the striking beauty of such a morning sky would be spread out above the depressing expanse of squalid grey shacks gathered beneath it. She spotted a few distant children chasing each other and heard the faint sounds of their voices, and even laughter.

The clinic management had thoughtfully erected canopies on poles for those in line – a protection from sun and rain. Lizzie watched young Ugandans, men and women, wearing white vests imprinted with the orange and white MSF logo. Circulating through the line with clipboards, they would stop and ask questions. They handed out sealed bottles of water, and earnestly talked with each patient, taking careful notes. This usually resulted in providing people with a laminated card bearing a large black number.

The tiny clinic was set in an open lot with room for parking and easy taxi access. Currently, there were only two dusty cars parked off to the side, but a full rack of worn bikes leaned against each other on the porch. Just below the lot, Lizzie's eyes were drawn to a few large storks taking fastidious steps among piles of shredded debris. Their long, shockingly white legs stood out against their coal black bodies. A narrow band of white feathers ringed the base of the birds' ghastly pink necks like a cravat. Lizzie couldn't help but imagine bald undertakers in formal clothes meandering among the dead.

"Nana, shouldn't we get in line?"

Mrs. Birungi walked by the patients. "We are not here for treatment. We are simply asking a question."

"But, I don't want these people to think—"

Nana gave her a look. "This is not the library. You are in *my* world now."

Lizzie swallowed further argument, muttering, "Okay."

Nana continued to walk steadily toward the clinic, scanning the MSF workers with every step. She suddenly hurried over to a tall black woman clad in one of the vests. They spoke in Luganda and broke into grins, hugging each other. After a lively exchange, with lots of hand motions and laughter, Nana vigorously waved Lizzie over.

"Come, come, Lizzie! Meet my good friend, Mwajje Rachel. Rachel, this is Elizabeth Warton, our new school librarian."

Rachel extended a friendly hand that dwarfed Lizzie's. "A pleasure, Miss Elizabeth."

"Nice to meet you, too, Rachel." She shot a brief look at Nana. "But I'm not a real librarian, yet. We still don't have any books, and the library isn't even built."

Rachel laughed loudly. "Minor inconveniences! Trust me, you get used to things like that. It is Africa, you know." She laughed again, her oversized earrings sparkling in the sunlight.

Lizzie smiled at Rachel's sharp sense of humor and decided that she liked her. She liked her short hairstyle. She liked her silver cross on a fine chain around her neck; and she especially liked the size of her hips.

Nana put her hand on Rachel's thick upper arm and gave it a fond squeeze. "Rachel and I attended secondary together." They both giggled loudly. "And misbehaved together."

Rachel waved her free arm in a chopping motion. "We got caned together is what she means!" The tall woman rocked her upper torso as she laughed. "Remember the time you threw mud?"

Nana put on an exaggerated grimace. "Me? We both had mud on our hands, and on our uniforms. Besides, it was a long time ago, and that teacher is dead."

"True. I forgive you anyway!"

Nana playfully slapped her friend's shoulder. "Thanks!" She turned to Lizzie, excited. "We are in luck. Rachel says that Doctor MacLaird is back, and we can see him."

Rachel shook her head in mock concern. "I warn you, he is not in the best of moods, and…" She let her eyes grow big. "…he is always looking for someone to do surgery on."

Lizzie felt uneasy and turned to Nana for an explanation, but she had already waved goodbye to Rachel and was headed for the clinic's entrance.

Rachel leaned over to Lizzie. "I'm kidding. Doctor Mac is a bit worn at the edges, is all. Just back from South Sudan, so…" She shook her head. "Go on, Miss Elizabeth. Once Nana is on a hunt, she waits for no one."

Lizzie dashed off. Nana had just vanished into a crowd of staff and patients clustered outside the front door.

The inside of the clinic was simple, white and clean. Privacy curtains and low wooden dividers separated the examining rooms from the halls. A large dispensary table, piled with neat stacks of health literature, dominated the busy main area. Multiple MSF pharmacists and assistants, some Ugandan and some foreign, manned the busy table. They matched the patients' laminated numbers to the clipboard notes submitted by the outdoor workers. Behind the table staff, shipping boxes of drugs and vaccines stood stacked in orderly rows. Patients who simply needed prescriptions filled were provided the medicines, free of charge, and given instructions right at the table. Those who came for treatments were guided to other areas within the small building. Those patients who needed shots, or throat and nose swabs, or cultures run on sputum, stepped to the side to have the procedures done in little half enclosures beside the table. Despite the noisy crowd, the MSF staff worked efficiently, and even cheerfully, to meet the changing needs as they appeared.

Lizzie looked back and forth, searching for Nana. She noticed a young patient on a gurney, moaning in pain. A concerned woman held his hand while MSF nurses wheeled him into a curtained enclosure. Lizzie heard her name called and spotted Nana's head as she leaned out from a distant door, with her hand waving.

When she entered the room, Lizzie found a cramped office with a small desk and chair. The walls were plain, no window, and barely enough space left over for a waste basket and two plastic visitors' chairs. Nana overfilled one, and she motioned Lizzie to take the other.

Perched on the edge of the desk was a blue-eyed man of medium height. He wore an open collared black shirt emblazoned with white palm leafs. His mouth slowly curved into a half smile. "So, you'll no doubt be the infamous losin' Lizzie that Nana's been tellin' me about."

"Losing Lizzie?"

"Aye. The one who loses her Uncle Sam's cash and all of her malaria pills on her first night out! Shameful! Musta been quite a party! And you, knocked out on drugs."

Lizzie stood awkwardly between the chairs, unable to think of a single comeback, unable to think at all. "Nana?"

Doctor MacLaird slid off the desk and warmly shook her limp hand. "Oh, relax there, Missy. I'm just yankin' on your leg a bit. Don't let it get to you. I'm Calum MacLaird, a medical miracle worker and chief bottle washer, at your service, ma'am." He bowed slightly while clicking his heels, and then grandly waved her to the other plastic chair.

Recovering her composure, Lizzie primly seated herself. "I hope I am pleased to meet you, Doctor. My name is Elizabeth Warton, but you may continue to call me Lizzie, if you wish. And, just so you know, I have heard a lot of odd reports about you, too!"

MacLaird smiled wider, showing deep dimples hidden beneath his salt and pepper stubble. "Ah, that's the way! I'm liking you already." His weary eyes gleamed with mischief. "It seems to me that American women should be classified as their own separate species. What do you say?"

Lizzie calmly folded her hands in her lap. "I thought we already were, Doctor MacLaird. Don't they teach you anything current at those medical schools in Scotland?"

Nana put a sudden hand over her mouth to stifle a laugh.

MacLaird shook his head in glee and held his palms up in mock surrender. "Nicely done, me dear Lizzie! I'm soundly put in my place, with no doubt about it."

"I'm happy to hear it," Lizzie commented quietly.

"Have no fear, I never stay there." MacLaird folded his arms. "So now, on to your purpose to be visitin' this poor Scotsman. Nana sketched your dilemma, but I need a bit more…clarity." He fixed Lizzie with an exaggerated scowl. "Am I to understand you're hopin' for a drug deal?"

Lizzie shot Nana a questioning look. "No. I just need to be

sure my malaria pills are real. She said you could direct us to a secure supplier."

"Did she now? *Secure supplier*, how artfully put. That sounds so like the crafty Mrs. Birungi's usual approach."

Nana made a half-hearted snort of protest.

Lizzie couldn't quite follow the obscure conversation. "What are you saying?"

"Just that the beautiful Birungi is the black magic behind Kajumba. Or dinna ye know that?"

"What?"

Nana flashed a baleful glance at the doctor.

MacLaird waved both hands up like a guilty soccer player, feigning innocence. "Sorry! Totally offside. My apologies, Nana, for overstatement. Okay?"

He focused back on Lizzie. "What I meant to say is that the good Mrs. Birungi knows that guilt can move mountains of delays. It always has."

"Faith moves mountains," Lizzie corrected sarcastically.

"Maybe where you come from, but where I toil, Miss Lizzie, guilt works a damn sight quicker 'n faith ever does."

"I'm still not following."

"Not to worry. Which regimen were you on?"

"What? You mean which pill?"

"Aye."

"Doxycycline."

"100 mg?"

"Yes."

"Did you start before you left home?"

"Yes, two days before."

"Of course, ye did." He smirked. "Rule follower." He winked at Nana. "It's still in her system. She's safe, if anyone ever is, for now." He squinted suspiciously at Lizzie. "Still usin' bug spray in the day? Nets at night?"

"Yes." Her tone sharpened, her eyes narrowed.

"That's fine, fine. Not that anythin's a hundred percent, though."

"What?"

He ignored her question. "How much longer are ye with us here in this…this charmin' little bit a' the globe?"

Lizzie was getting irked. "My visa is good for another three months, but…"

MacLaird cut her off. "Got it! Got the drug – doxy. Got the quantity – a hundred and twenty. Now, I just need the reason."

Lizzie snapped at him, "Do you enjoy talking to yourself in code?"

The doctor paused and pretended to weigh things, tapping his lips with a finger. "Never thought of it quite that way." He sounded flippant. "Aye, I guess I do. I do like codes. But I don't much like rules – most rules, anyway."

He rearranged himself on the desk, wiggling his hips until he was comfortable. "Here's me own personal quandary, dearie. MSF targets people overlooked by everyone else. It's called, *neglected populations*, in our puffy little PR pieces. Nice ring to it, don't you think? It doesn't usually include old, white suburban women, ye see, unless we can think of anoth—"

Lizzie jumped in. "Look, I can have money sent to me. I can pay you, or make a *contribution* if…" Her mouth curled as if she'd bitten into something sour. "…if that's where you were going."

"Aye, right." He rolled his eyes and made a silly face. "Yer off yer head if you think that would actually help. No, that's not at all where I was goin'." He became suddenly thoughtful. "Wait! Drugged, robbed, and left in an alley; I may be able to use that. What's the name a' that boy who saved her, Nana?"

"Dembe."

"Right. Dembe." He tasted the name. "Dembe. Did I meet him at some time? Maybe at your school? TB tests, or somethin'? Name's familiar."

Nana nodded. "Possibly. He is slender. About fifteen. He makes clever toys and mechanisms out of scraps."

MacLaird clapped his hands. "That's it! I do remember now. Clever boy. A tinkerer. Always had other boys around him."

"Yes."

The doctor sucked in some air and slowly let it whistle out between his lips, evaluating something. "Hang on. What was *he* doin' in an alley in the middle a' the night? Nana, isn't he still boardin'?"

She sighed. "No. He was expelled."

MacLaird waited for her to say more. They looked at each other, warily. It was clear that he was willing to wait as long as it took.

Nana continued. "He was expelled by Pastor, along with… other boys."

"Ah! Not for grades then, I'd wager?"

"No."

MacLaird rolled his tongue around in his mouth before drawing a conclusion. "Got crossways with old Kajumba, huh? Not good. Nothin' like a poor sinner hittin' the buzz saw of a black preacher."

Nana shook her head, offended. "That's unfair, Doctor! And this has nothing to do with Lizzie's pills!"

MacLaird's voice remained perfectly level. "That's where you're wrong. You see, it may be part of my solution. Where does Dembe live now?"

Lizzie was peeved and tired of all the questions. "He lives on the street! He's a street boy! Satisfied? What possible difference does that make for my malaria pills?"

Doctor MacLaird wiggled his hand back and forth, ringing an invisible bell. "Ding! Ding! Ding! *Street boys!* Bingo! As you delightful Americans like to shout. Those are the magic words! They open the drug doors!"

Lizzie looked at Birungi with her mouth open. Nana gaped back, equally befuddled.

The doctor hopped down off his desk. "*Street boys* are listed as a neglected population. Pure dead brilliant! That's how I can give you the pills."

Lizzie was exasperated. "But the pills are for *me*, not *him*!"

"That, Miss Lizzie, is known as a detail – a minor detail. I'm sure Dembe would want you to have 'em. And, besides, he's a local, he'd never take malaria pills, anyway."

MacLaird stretched across the desk to pull free a pad of paper. He quickly scratched out a prescription, ripped off the sheet, and hurried from the room. "Be right back."

He stopped at the door and turned around. "Oh, forgive me. Did either of you care for tea?" He hesitated, waiting for a reaction.

Lizzie was too stunned to say a thing.

MacLaird looked at her and tapped the side of his head. "Of course, stupid of me, you're American, so… ahh…we have Nescafe, although I'd na' recommend it."

❧

The speeding taxi van struck a series of potholes and belatedly slowed down. Inside, bounced around on the hard bench seat, Lizzie grunted in pain. She popped a malaria pill out from a blister card into her hand and quickly tossed it in her mouth. Trying to time her movements to the road conditions, she washed down the pill with a swig from an MSF water bottle.

"He's insufferable, Nana! I can't stand him!"

"Yes, yes, I know. But we do have your pills now, don't we?"

Lizzie angrily shoved the water bottle deep into her bag. "But I feel dirty. Like I stole someone else's medicine."

"That's because you are an American. You can afford to feel that way."

Lizzie glowered at her. "You sound like him now."

Nana patiently held her gaze as she replied. "Here is how I see it. You came to help us, and we stole your malaria pills. Doctor MacLaird has found a way to give them back. That is all."

Lizzie's anger lost its edge as she concentrated on the passing scenery outside the taxi. Cramped shops floated by the glass. She was drawn to a crooked sign for *Kibul Butchers of Beef.* Behind open shutters, she fleetingly glimpsed skinned carcasses hanging by their hoofs. The flesh gleamed in streaks of white, yellow, red and grey. A tired man in a bloody apron leaned against the door frame while a calico cat sniffed the puddle at his feet. Next door, as the taxi turned, she noticed a man stepping through a set of blue and white checked curtains. In the brief sway as the cloth settled, she caught the backs of seated customers crowded inside, and the whirl of ceiling fans. An oddly lettered placard above the shop read: *Friendly Eating Place.*

Birungi twisted in her seat. "I know you are angry, Lizzie, but you are not at home now. Everything moves differently here. Uganda works like an open market. All of us are bartering all the time. And only Jesus is perfect."

Lizzie listened, but she said nothing. She let her eyes follow a young woman in braids walking with a bouncy step beside the road. She wore a pink sweater over a long blue dress. Her shapely feet were bare and one hand swung the typical black plastic bag of purchases. In the other hand, she carried an open Fanta soft drink bottle. Casually balanced atop her head rode a surprisingly huge bag of charcoal. Her shiny face glowed. Her mouth held a wide smile. Lizzie spotted the telltale lines of earbud wires snaking from her hidden ears to someplace under the sweater.

Turning back to Nana, Lizzie grinned disarmingly. "Maybe not so different, after all. I'm learning, Nana. Honestly, I'm trying to learn more every day. I'm not angry. Not really. But that crazy MacLaird was a hard one for me."

She nodded slowly. "He has seen too much. But trust me, he is a good man and a good doctor. He was in South Sudan last week. Do you know Sudan, Lizzie?"

"No. Just on the map. It borders you on the north."

"It is two countries now. And there is civil war in the south."
Birungi glanced carefully around the taxi at the other riders. She
licked her lips and lowered her voice. "Rebels fight the government troops and each other. Tribes fight tribes. Clan against clan.
Religions fight religions. Nothing makes sense there now. It is all
stealing and killing. Doctor MacLaird was sent to their clinic in
Leer – a small town there – to do emergency surgeries. MSF takes
no sides; everyone knows this, but rebels attacked the clinic anyway.
They stole their medicines. They burned the buildings and the
records. Doctor Mac lost both patients. He fled with a few staff
into the swamps, and another died there. That is what I heard. They
want him to rest. He refuses."

Lizzie's eyes widened in shock. "The poor man!"

Nana's eyes were kind. "I know he is proud and acts like one
of our thorn bushes." She searched to find the best way to explain.
"His kindness hides behind his large mouth, Lizzie. His mouth is all
he has to protect himself. It is how he keeps going."

The taxi van abruptly swerved to avoid another hole in the road,
and Lizzie automatically grabbed the back of the seat in front of her.
Her body swayed with the vehicle, but her mind imagined a swamp
in Sudan and the popping sounds of gunfire. She realized she had
no idea what actual gunfire sounded like. Shifting uneasily in her
seat, she felt the cold clutch of guilt for having judged the man.

NINETEEN

A Question of Copper

The maintenance worker at the Wobulezi school was old and, as far as Lizzie could tell, spoke little English. Nana said his name was Kirumira Joseph, and that he had been with the school from the start. His neatly patched pants were secured by a worn leather strap pulled tight and knotted. A bundle of keys held together by a thick shoestring hung at his waist. He nervously accompanied them to the lowest level in one of the school buildings, his keys making a soft *clink* with every other step. Above them, Lizzie heard the muted sing-song repetitions of English phrases from one of the classrooms. First, the teacher would speak the words, and then the entire class would repeat them in unison. Other distant sounds of school activities filtered down to them, but it seemed clear, for now, that their level was deserted.

Mrs. Birungi asked something in Luganda and Joseph motioned with his arm to a wide door ahead of them. He held it open, and they passed through into a long, communal bathroom. Along one side of the large room was a row of western style toilet stalls and a line of sinks with cloth towels on hooks. On the other side stood a series of simple changing rooms with curtained doorways.

Joseph selected a key from his bundle and stepped to a tall access door at the end of the room and unlocked it. Turning back, he asked a terse question of Mrs. Birungi. A tense back and forth ensued. Giving in, Joseph reluctantly opened the door to a dark room and stepped back so the women could enter first. Nana led. Lizzie nervously followed close behind her.

Standing inside the room, Lizzie sensed Nana waving her hand in the air, searching for a pull string. She heard a quick pull and release. A bare bulb snapped to life over her head. The illuminated room was narrow and drab. Since it ran behind the sinks and stalls, it was as deep as the outer room, and its distant reaches were still in semi-darkness, despite the swinging bulb. Two additional pull lights dangled from the open ceiling in the distance. Nana methodically walked the entire length of the room, pulling each string.

Lizzie looked around, as much concerned about bugs and spiders as she was interested in the room itself. The floor and walls were simple, unfinished concrete. The side that faced the bathroom was crisscrossed with complex levels of white PVC pipes. She saw feeder lines and drainage pipes, elbows and supports, joints and couplings, all serving the toilets and sinks on the other side of the wall. Even though Lizzie couldn't understand the intricacies of the pipe layout, she was struck by the neatness and craftsmanship of it all. Plumbing had never been something she thought much about; that was Jonathan's domain, at least before his sickness. It's not that he had been all that handy. Far from it. Most of those genes had gone to his brothers, but Jonathan excelled at hiring competent people, and he thoroughly admired a job well done. Lizzie thought he might have enjoyed looking at these pipes. She also noticed a set of circular drains in the center of the bone dry floor. Clearly, nothing leaked here, so Lizzie considered that a plus.

Mrs. Birungi's heels echoed on the concrete floor as she walked back to Lizzie. "There are many plumbing rooms like this one in both school buildings and the dormitory. Some of the pipework is more complex, and many of the areas are more difficult to reach."

Lizzie nodded as Nana paused in front of her. The nearest light bulb hung above and to the side, casting her face into sharp, black, angled shadows. Lizzie felt she had drifted into a spy movie.

Nana said a few words to Joseph and he quietly pulled closed the access door, staying inside. Now, Lizzie began to feel apprehensive.

Nana glanced toward the wall of white pipes and sighed. "One of our oldest donors was from Knoxville, in your state called Tennessee. His name was Bertram Seterdahl. He was a plumber, who started a plumbing supply company and became wealthy. When Pastor visited his Baptist church, many years ago, on a missions' Sunday, Mr. Seterdahl was moved to help us. Over the years, he became a close friend. His help built both school buildings. And he loved to hear about our students. Just like Pastor, Mr. Seterdahl believed education was the key to their future, and he was pleased to be the blessing that made it real for them. When he died, Pastor flew to Knoxville to officiate at his funeral. His widow helped complete our dormitory, in her husband's memory. She even partly funded your library, Lizzie."

Lizzie blinked and said nothing, wondering where this was going.

"And in all the years of their generosity, even up to now, the Seterdahls only placed one condition on their gifts. Copper pipes." Nana took a breath. "Copper pipes had to be used for any plumbing. You see, Mr. Seterdahl trusted copper pipes. Copper was the only thing he recommended when he was a plumber. It was a source of pride. He never changed. He believed copper was the best piping that money could buy, and he insisted on only the best for Pastor's students. We were faithful to his wishes, even though it cost so much more to do so. No tour here was complete without telling the story of our copper pipes and our beloved donors, the Seterdahls. Our copper was a source of pride for us, too."

Feeling self-conscious, Lizzie slowly turned toward the wall of alabaster pipes, letting her eyes carefully roam across the sea of PVC. Copper? She struggled to understand how any of this confusing story related to Dembe's expulsion.

Nana interrupted her thoughts. "Obviously, our tours are shorter now."

"But, Nana, what happened to your copper?"

"Dembe happened."

There was a still moment as Lizzie's mind chewed on that bald statement. "What? He did this?"

"All of it. In all the buildings."

"How?"

"That is an interesting question. But look at this." Nana moved closer to the pipework and studied the orderly arrangement. She lightly placed a hand on one of the pipes. "It is hard not to admire this work. How could a boy learn so much by just looking?" Her voice carried a wistful edge. "We have never had a plumbing problem at the school – not before Dembe, and not after."

She turned away from the pipes and back to Lizzie. "I cannot tell you how much pain this brought. In his heart, I think Pastor lost his old friend a second time. I understand that. But when I come down here and look, I also see something else. That boy does fine work, even when he steals."

Lizzie was dumbfounded. She pictured Dembe secretly working in this lonely concrete room in the middle of the night, his tools spread out around him. What was in it for him? Why did he do it?

She heard Joseph speak something complicated in Luganda to Mrs. Birungi. She answered him, and then turned back to Lizzie. "As far as we can understand, they worked at this project for many months."

"They?"

"Yes. Dembe and the other boys from Safe Haven, Musaazi and Ogwambi, who attended school here with him. They were the workers; he was the boss. They would do anything for him."

"But how could they get away with it? Surely, someone must have seen something?"

Nana smiled sadly. "Dembe and his boys volunteered for every job imaginable around the school for a year. Pastor was so pleased with them. We all were. They were such a help and an example. For months, in the heat and the rain, when they were not in class, they were seen trimming bushes, washing windows, scrubbing floors, taking out rubbish, always busy – and all the time, they were smuggling in PVC pipe and carrying away our copper."

Behind Lizzie, Joseph said something low and soft. She turned his way as Nana translated. "He says he still misses their help, even though they tricked him and got him in trouble. They were good boys, he says, even if what they did was bad."

Letting her eyes roam across the room, Lizzie gauged the sheer quantity of the pipes. "What did Dembe do with all the copper?"

"Sold it, we think. Easy to do. Pipe companies, scrap dealers; they are all hungry for it. Copper is rare here. Children strip the wires out of parked cars. Gangs steal power lines off the poles – it is one of the reasons for our blackouts."

Lizzie was stunned. "How did you find out?"

"By accident. Nobody checked on the pipes. There was never a reason to check. Oh, Joseph said he peeked in the rooms, once in a while, with a torch, but he only looked at the floor around the drains. There was never a leak. Never a reason to look farther."

Joseph bowed his head and groaned softly. He seemed unhappy about what he knew was coming. Lizzie watched him. Evidently, he understood more English than he let on.

"Then one weekend, Pastor held a seminar here for local ministers. They were discussing donors, and Pastor told them the Seterdahl story. When the meeting was over, one of the younger ministers asked to see some of the actual pipes. He was so excited. We brought him to a room like this one, and proudly pulled on the lights – but there wasn't any copper. It was all gone."

Nana's eyes glistened as she relived that initial shock.

"I hope to never see Pastor Kajumba like that again. He was lost. For the next hour that night, he rushed through his buildings checking pipe rooms, opening access panels, inspecting wherever he could. The story was the same everywhere he looked. All the copper had been replaced."

Nana looked away, focused on the past. "At first, we thought poor Joseph must have done it. Who else? We never suspected our own students. Who would imagine that? Pastor convinced the young minister to keep our secret. We investigated quietly, not wanting anyone to find out. Those were such terrible days! After we fired Joseph, Dembe must have realized we knew about the pipes. He came to us and confessed. Pastor didn't believe him; he thought he was lying to save Joseph. He was sure no boy could do what Dembe claimed to have done. But, in the end, the truth was the truth.

"Dembe refused to say where the copper went or why he did it. He claimed no one helped him. The other boys admitted their roles on their own, faithful to Dembe, not to their own welfare. And there was no forgiveness in Pastor. There was only wrath." She looked directly into Lizzie's eyes. "And, at the time, I agreed with him."

Lizzie's lips formed a tight line. The muscles in her shoulders clenched.

Mrs. Birungi stood still. Her voice softened. "We wanted nothing more to do with Safe Haven. We would accept no more students from them. Of course, we had to explain, but Jedediah and Margaret understood; they live by donors, too. They agreed to keep our secret. We never spoke again, until the day they called us with the startling news of you. Going to their house was the first time we were face-to-face since we expelled their boys."

Lizzie nodded her understanding. "Meg told me there was something dark between you and them, but she never said what. She kept your secret."

"And now you understand?"

"Yes."

Sadness crossed Nana's face. "And I have broken my solemn promise to Pastor Kajumba. We now have a secret within a secret, you and me."

"I'm sorry."

Nana was about to say more when her phone chimed with an incoming call. She pulled it out and checked the screen. Her eyes narrowed. She pushed the *accept* icon. "Hello?" She listened briefly, then said, "*Wangi.*"

Lizzie could hear the faint threads of a voice on the phone.

Nana nodded, "*Ye, ali wanno.*" She glanced at Lizzie. "*Okitegeza?*"

Lizzie didn't understand the conversation. Why is she looking at me? she wondered.

Nana took a step closer to her. "*Kaale. Lindako, kangede munoone.*" She placed the phone against her leg to muffle the microphone. "It is for you, Lizzie."

"Me? Who could be calling me?"

Her mouth wrinkled. "Your *muyaye.*"

Lizzie experienced a momentary lapse, then sucked in a quick breath as she understood. Slowly letting the air out, she straightened her posture, put a smile on her face, and carefully took the phone. One hand unconsciously fluffed her hair as she spoke. "Hello, Mr. Salongo, how nice of you to call."

"Ah, my Lizzie," said the shopkeeper. "How good to talk with you again. Please call me Wasswa. I have news about your books."

TWENTY
Library Fees

Lizzie and Nana walked a path beside the road near the school. The bright sun was high overhead and it was past time for lunch, even though Lizzie's battered body remained unconvinced. The only thing her lagging mind seemed to crave right now was sleep. Oblivious, Nana focused on food and assured Lizzie she knew a safe place to eat nearby.

They passed rows of tiny street shops with their wares spilling out next to the pathway. The smells of dust, diesel and vegetables teased their noses. Lizzie gave a wide berth to a lean bike mechanic crouched in the dirt, guiding a shrieking grinder across the edge of a metal frame. Cascading waves of dazzling sparks danced on the ground, bouncing in every direction. Out of habit, Lizzie's mouth opened to offer safety complaints and judgments, but just as swiftly, she recalled where she was and clamped her lips shut again. The open air bike shop displayed a crowd of rusty frames and mounds of old tires in front of a windowless shack. She noticed another worker casually shielding his face with a broken welder's mask as he tig-welded a plate to a used frame. Lizzie whipped her head away, fearing for her eyes. She caught a glimpse of Nana's back in the loose crowd, striding ahead without hesitation or concern. Lizzie increased her pace.

People were walking everywhere she looked. Mothers carried their slinged babies on their lower backs, leaning forward with their arms behind and hands under the infant. Men idly wandered around with their arms folded over their heads, like wings at rest. Young boys in shorts or worn jeans pushed each other and showed off their faded American sport shirts: LA Lakers, Denver Broncos, and the Yankees. Here and there appeared the sudden blare of women in bright colors: red, yellow, orange; and always children played underfoot, hitting each other, laughing and crying – quick smiles, white teeth, big eyes.

"Here it is." Nana pointed ahead.

Lizzie saw a shop with red and white vertical blinds across its opening. Two scratched plastic tables with mismatched chairs sat out in front under a floppy tarp.

Nana ducked inside, flicking aside the blinds with a practiced wave of her hand. Before following, Lizzie paused long enough to study the fat fonts on the sign above: *Pork Palace.*

Inside the dark and noisy room, Lizzie's eyes took time to dilate. She slowly discerned many tables of people in a tight space. Most of their eyes were now brightly staring back at the only *muzungu* in the room. Embarrassed, Lizzie turned away, but the pleasant aroma of roasting pork had already caused her stomach to rethink its confusion. Lunch sounded more appealing by the second.

At the back of the shop, Mrs. Birungi stood talking Luganda in an open doorway. When Lizzie joined her, she saw that the door led outside where two large black women worked beside a pair of smoking charcoal stoves. A few young girls slid quickly in and out, delivering paper plates of pork on slices of crusty bread. Nana stepped through the opening to get out of the way and moved closer to the cooks. Lizzie slipped through the door to stand beside her. Several children played games on the yellowed grass under everyone's feet. It made Lizzie nervous to see how close the wiggling youngsters were to the sizzling stoves, but no one else seemed to pay any mind. A sturdy table held a shoulder of steaming roasted pork. One of the women rapidly carved from it, wielding a wide, wickedly sharp blade, while chatting and laughing with Mrs. Birungi.

The conversation at an end, Nana flipped open a nearby cooler and grabbed two plastic bottles of water. She called out an airy comment in Luganda to the cooks, and they responded with nods and laughs before she waved at Lizzie. "Come. We will sit out front and talk. They will bring." Nana immediately vanished back inside.

Lizzie started to follow her but was waylaid by a word from the lady at the carving table. "Wait."

Lizzie turned.

The woman flashed her knife in a swirl, a small cutting of pork appeared, balanced on the tip of her blade. Her damp black skin gleamed in the sun, her hair pulled tight with a dark cloth knotted at the top. She smiled with an open mouth. "Small eat."

Lizzie opened her hand. With a sudden flick of the knife, the woman dropped the succulent morsel onto her palm. Lizzie popped it into her mouth. Her tongue reveled in the moist, spicy meat. As she chewed, without even thinking, she moaned in pleasure. The cook nodded in satisfaction, her bright teeth gleaming.

The other woman joined her and studied Lizzie. "Like?"

Lizzie looked at their round, sweaty faces and nodded.

Nana suddenly reappeared in the doorway from the shop and feigned irritation. She waggled her finger at the laughing cooks, shouting and pretending to rebuke them. As she gathered Lizzie by the arm and urged her to the door, she explained, "I told them to stop bewitching you with their sneaky tastings or you will never leave."

"Thank you for saving me."

Nana grinned at her as they passed back into the shop. "And what do you think of the pork?"

Lizzie licked her palm and grinned back. "We can live another day."

Mrs. Birungi tipped back her head and took a long drink from her water bottle. She sighed as she twisted the cap back on it, and frowned at Lizzie. "Look at me! I am becoming just like you, drinking water with food." She shook her head in mock horror. "Filling up food space with water. What a waste! You are a bad influence on me."

Lizzie pushed her empty plate away and wiped her lips with a paper napkin. A slight breeze rattled the faded tarp overhead that gave shade to their table. "Be careful who your friends are? Is that what you mean?"

"Exactly. Be careful."

Lizzie studied Nana's posture and the way her smooth arms wrapped around each other at the edge of the table. "You're worried about Wasswa, aren't you? But you don't want to say it."

She slowly nodded. "I am. Lizzie, do you really trust him?"

"Yes. In this, I do."

"Maybe he is trying to get money back from you for what he lost at Owino."

"Maybe he is."

One of the serving girls swung by the table and gathered up their discarded plates and plastic ware, flashing a brief smile at Lizzie.

Nana waited until the server moved out of ear range. Even then, she lowered her voice. "700 U.S. dollars is a lot of money."

Lizzie rocked her head side to side like an Indian. "But much less than before. Much less than those customs thieves claimed."

Nana growled in grudging agreement. "Okay. Much less than that."

"And it's not really 700. For customs, it's only 200. The 500 is a rental fee from the shipping company for their container. Wasswa says that's not negotiable. They're not Ugandans, and I don't blame them. It's been stuck in customs for months, and they want their container back. But Wasswa talked customs out of all their *charges*. We're just tipping them the 200 for their *assistance*."

Nana made a buzzing noise in her throat. "Words. Just words."

"Words that save money and can free the books."

She shook her head. "It is still a bribe, no matter what you call it."

"But you can still report to Pastor that the *school* paid no bribes, or tips, or whatever words you want to use." She twisted her lips in a tease. "It was God's librarian who freed the books, not you."

"I do not trust this." Nana snorted. "Something will change."

"No. I think you shouldn't look a gift horse in the mouth. I trust him."

Nana stopped talking and frowned. "A gift horse?"

"Sorry. Just an old expression."

She rolled her shoulders and stared expectantly at Lizzie, waiting for the explanation. Lizzie closed one eye, thought for a while, and then gave it a shot. "It means…well, if someone gives you something – I mean, something big, like a horse – you shouldn't inspect it, you should just accept it."

Mrs. Birungi blinked. "In the mouth? Why in the mouth?"

"Ahh, I think you can tell the age and, maybe, I don't know, the health of a horse by looking at its teeth." Her words held little conviction. She skated on thin ice, and she knew it. Oh, no – another metaphor she wouldn't want to explain! "So, if a man gives you a horse for free, and you check its teeth, it means you don't trust him. It's bad manners. You see? It's insulting."

Nana pursed her lips. "This is not for free. You must pay 700 U.S. dollars. That is not a gift."

"Well, in a manner of speaking, it is. We didn't have a chance before. Now, we do."

"I do not trust Wasswa."

"Nana, I don't completely trust him, either. But let's pretend we do. Okay?"

She said nothing.

Lizzie went on, "It's the only way I know to get the books."

Nana made a worried face. "What will Pastor say?"

"Well, if we hurry, we can have the books in the library before Pastor's back from his trip."

"He is back in three days."

"I know. You told me."

"Can we do this in three days?"

"I hope so. The first step is to get money."

"So, we need to set up a call to your son. We can text him and suggest a…"

"Wait. What's the time difference between here and Minnesota?"

Nana considered briefly. "Eight hours."

"Right…" Lizzie calculated in her head. "Okay. Perfect. Forget texting. Let's call David right now."

Nana seemed a little rattled. "Now?" She glanced around at the many passersby. "Right here at the table?"

"Why not? He won't know where we are."

"Later would be better. You could call from my office at the school."

"No. This is fine." Lizzie was already digging in her pocket for the slip of paper that held David's number. "The sooner, the better, right?"

Nana sat back in her chair, clearly unsettled, and pulled out her phone. "Okay." While Lizzie slid the paper across the tabletop, Nana activated her phone. She paused. "You are sure it will be okay? Do you know what to say?"

Lizzie scoffed, "To my own son? Of course. Oh, you mean about that *Sendwave* app?"

She nodded at her as she dialed.

Lizzie shook her head. "I'm not worried at all, Nana. You're going to do all the explaining when we get to that."

Mrs. Birungi finished dialing, but she hadn't pushed the phone icon to actually make the call yet. "Me?"

"Who else?" Lizzie smiled blandly. "I'll explain to him how much money we need, and you'll tell him how to get it here. We're partners, remember? Secrets within secrets?"

Birungi sniffed and sat very still, her frozen finger poised above her phone.

Lizzie tapped her nails against the plastic tabletop. "C'mon, make the call. He'll be fine. Don't worry."

Mrs. Birungi grimaced ever so slightly as she touched the icon and heard the digital chitter of numbers dialing. "You are sure he won't be upset at the time?"

Lizzie shook her head. Big deal, she thought, it's nine at night there. She took a hurried swig of water from her bottle and cleared her throat. She pictured David sitting in his family room – Tomlin would already be in bed. He was probably watching television, or dozing on the couch in front of the fireplace. She hummed out loud to make sure her voice was working. Answer the phone, David! And please be in a good mood.

"It's ringing," Birungi announced as she handed over the phone.

Lizzie listened to a few more rings, a click, and then a voice that was so groggy, she wasn't sure it was her son.

"Hello?"

"David?"

He sounded irritated and guarded. "Yes. Who is this? Why are you calling now?"

"David! It's your mother."

"What? My mother? Mom! Is that you?"

"Yes!"

David's voice suddenly rose an octave and sped up. "Are you kidding? Mom! Are you okay? We've been out of our minds here! For God's sake, Mom! Why didn't you call?"

"I am. Now."

"But it's five in the morning! What happened? Where are you?"

"Five in the morning?" Lizzie flashed an accusing look at Mrs. Birungi.

Nana nodded at her and whispered, "Eight hours." She pointed to the left with a finger. "They are eight hours behind us." She pointed with a different finger to the right. "Not eight hours ahead."

Lizzie growled at her. On the phone she heard David explain to his sleepy wife that his mother was on the phone. Lizzie tried to regain his attention. "David? I'm sorry about the time, but…"

Her son suddenly returned to the phone, his words washing over hers like an overfilled sink. "This number doesn't even come up as your phone! We've been calling and calling. Do you know your number won't ring? It just goes to voicemail and—"

"My phone was broken. That's why you couldn't get through, and I couldn't call out until now."

"Broken? How did it get broken?"

"Long story. Not important anymore."

"What?"

"Nothing. Just an accident."

"An accident? Are you okay? What kind of accident? Everybody's upset here. We thought that—"

"I'm fine, David! The *phone* had an accident, not me. I'm just fine. I'm sorry. Tell everyone that things are great here."

David couldn't seem to listen. Every time Lizzie took a breath, he plunged on. "I tried the embassy. That was useless! I Googled *Kampala*. Do you know you didn't leave us any numbers to call?"

"David—"

"I mean a few, maybe, but no list of contacts. And that pastor-what's-his-name doesn't ever pick up, and his voicemail says it's full, and—"

"David!"

"Yes."

"Stop talking."

"But Mom—"

"I'm here now. You reached me. I'm fine. Really. Take a breath. Okay?"

"But Mom I—"

"Listen." Lizzie modulated her voice so the conversation would slow down. "I'm sitting outside in the sunshine. It's the middle of the day here. And it's 80 degrees out."

"What? Really?" David's voice instantly mellowed into more normal tones. Lizzie knew her son couldn't resist shiny objects. "80?" he asked longingly.

"Yes. And it's so beautiful. We just finished a lovely lunch at a sidewalk café." Nana gave her an odd expression. Lizzie brushed off her look with a hand.

"Lunch? Outside?" David sounded wistful. "That's so strange. It's super cold here. And it's—"

"Yes. It's morning. Really, really early in the morning. I know, dear, and I'm very sorry about that. But David, it's so good to hear your voice. I'm glad we finally connected."

"Me, too. You sound so clear. Like you're right here in town, instead of…the other side of the world."

"Glad to hear it. Now, I need your help." Across the table from her, Nana grimaced and sighed. Lizzie shushed her. "You might want to turn on a light and get a pencil and paper, dear. Okay?"

"What kind of help?"

"The kind only you can do. I'll explain everything."

"But Mom—"

"Just listen now. Okay, David?"

❧

Returning from lunch, Nana and Lizzie walked through the pedestrian gate into the school grounds. A sleepy guard, sitting against the wall in a broken plastic chair, nodded cheerfully to them as they passed. Afternoon classes were in session, and the voices of the teachers and students floated faintly across the quad like the random buzzing of bees.

Nana guided Lizzie toward the main school offices and then had her wait in the hall while she checked inside. Lizzie contentedly leaned against the wall and closed her eyes, sleep stealing into her shoulders. She half dreamed of homemade pumpkin pie in her kitchen when she heard her tea kettle whistle from the stovetop. She realized abruptly that Nana had her head out the office door, hissing to get her attention.

"The power is on. The computers are running. I must catch up on my work, Lizzie, while I can."

Lizzie masked her fatigue with a quick smile. "No problem." She stood up straight. "Why don't I...I'll go check on the library. How about that? Are they working today?"

Nana nodded. "Every day! Pastor told them to hurry. He wanted it ready for your books, remember?"

"What I remember is that he wasn't listening to me."

She grinned. "That, too. But he did set a fire under the contractor, believe me."

"What did he say?"

"He told them he expected the men to work like Americans."

"What does that mean?"

Nana wiggled her brows. "Not like Africans."

Lizzie frowned, but refused to play Nana's question game. "And?"

Nana gave in. "And...it means, fast. Long days. Short breaks. Do everything right because the books are coming very soon."

"Really?"

"Really."

Lizzie seemed surprised. "So, Pastor Kajumba actually had faith in me before I did?"

Nana thought about that. "No. I think it was more an act of

hope than faith. Desperate hope." She let a chuckle sneak into her voice. "And it was more in God than in you."

Lizzie sighed. "Thanks a lot for the humble pie, Nana. And no, I'm not going to explain that."

Nana nodded. "No big deal. It is food. I understand about food."

Lizzie started for the library. "I'm just not used to being an answer to someone else's prayer."

Nana rolled her shoulders. "You get used to it around here. I have work. I will find you when I am done."

"Okay."

TWENTY-ONE

Work like Americans

As Lizzie approached the unfinished library, the first thing she noticed was that all the doors were hung. The rasp of saws and the clack of tools grew louder as she pushed open the front door and entered the noisy main room.

Two workers stood at the top of tall, rickety scaffolds, loudly arguing with a man peeking in from an opening in the roof. They couldn't seem to agree on the best way to fasten the final corrugated panel. Below them, three men on their knees were laying tile on the concrete floor, working from the back wall toward the bank of windows. Rows of wooden bookshelves stood snugly together against a far wall. A pair of sawhorses near the door supported a warped piece of plywood littered with blueprints, drawings, pencils, and measuring tape.

A bony-shouldered black man with tight, snowy curls on his head looked up as she entered. His chin was covered in a grizzled stubble and the leathery skin around his eyes wrinkled into familiar lines as he smiled at her. "Come to check our work, lady?"

Lizzie, caught by surprise, paused to look at him. "What? No.

I'm sure I wouldn't know the first thing about it. I just...I just wanted to see the progress."

The older man nodded and stepped closer to her.

Lizzie hesitated. "That's okay, isn't it?"

"Of course. You are the librarian. You can come when you want."

"How do you know that's who I am? Do you...?" Lizzie looked at his patient face and then reconsidered her words. "Never mind." She pointed at her own face. "I know. I know. *Muzungu*. Who else would I be, right?"

He canted his head in polite agreement.

Lizzie extended her hand. "Okay. My name is Lizzie Warton. And I'm the new librarian here – for now."

The Ugandan wiped his palm on his tan pants and then shook. "Musoke Barnabas. These are my men." He waved a long-fingered hand at the other people in the room, all of whom had ceased work to watch the interaction.

Lizzie put on her business friendly look. "Pleased to meet you. How's the work going?"

"It is moving along well." He glanced around at the now silent room. "Or it was, until we started talking." His eyes flashed in mischief. "Can you excuse me for a moment, Mrs. Warton?"

Lizzie nodded.

Barnabas turned away. His shoulders rose, his hands suddenly fisted against his hips, and he erupted in a spate of harsh Luganda verbiage that shook the library with sound. He rotated his head so that all the workers got an equal dose of his commanding voice. Everyone jumped back to work. Even the noise of sawing from the other room quickly started up again.

Barnabas looked back at her. "Sorry. That sounds better now, does it not?"

"Yes. I didn't mean to be in the way."

"You are not in the way. You are the reason we work."

Lizzie smirked. "What did you say to them just now?"

He pressed his lips together and rubbed at his chin stubble. "Well, basically, I reminded them that Africa is outside, and America is in here. And if they did not want to be sent back to Africa without pay, they best get back to work in here."

"I see."

"That is not an exact translation, lady."

"I understand."

"Okay, then."

"I'm told the Lunganda language can be quite colorful."

"*Colorful.* Nice. That is a good word."

Lizzie stared at the busy riveters on the scaffolds. "So, you must be the one that Pastor Kajumba encouraged to speed things up."

Barnabas grinned and rubbed his mouth with the back of his hand. "Yes, that is me. Kajumba can be colorful, too."

"Seriously?"

"Oh, yes." One of his eyes squinted for a moment. "He was not always a pastor. I have known him a long time."

"What was he before?"

"Every man has many *befores*." He gently touched the outside of her arm. "Come. I will walk you around so you can see our... progress."

Turning, Lizzie walked beside him as he began a tour.

They sat on plastic chairs in an out-of-the-way corner and shared cups of chai from a dented thermos. Once she sat and held the cup, Lizzie found she could barely keep her head up.

Barnabas had been a charming guide, and she had marveled at how much had been accomplished in such a short time. All the bookcases, desks, tables and chairs were assembled and stained and only waited for the tile to be finished before they would be installed. Lizzie had been most adamant to see the bathrooms and to view the new copper pipes gleaming behind the unfinished walls. She knew Barnabas had regarded her queerly over this, but she didn't care, and she couldn't explain. She found him to be equally guarded about the past lives of Pastor Kajumba. He only mentioned something about the pastor's large hands and the scars on his knuckles, and how they spoke for themselves. Lizzie pondered that as she fought to stay awake.

"Is the chai to your liking?" Barnabas asked, trying to help keep her awake.

She sipped and stretched her neck, rallying from the fatigue. "I like it very much. I love the tea here. But I'm surprised, Barnabas, that you offered no escort with it." Her tired eyes said that she was joking.

Barnabas bowed slightly. "You are becoming Ugandan. You know about escorts."

"I try to pay attention – especially when it involves eating."

He smiled in a funny way. "Actually, I do have an escort, but I decided it was best not to offer it."

"Why? What is it?"

"*Nsenene.* My wife prepared some last night, fresh. They were wonderful. I brought what we had left for the men."

"Oh, that's what we call, *leftovers.*"

"Leftovers. Yes, that is what they are."

"No need to feel bad. I eat leftovers all the time. I'm sure they're fine. What is *en-sen ´-nen-nee?*"

"*Nsenene.* Yes." He produced a clear plastic bag bulging with yellowish-brown, stubby, pencil shaped objects, glistening in the sunlight from the windows. "You can only get these in November and December, during our rainy season. You are lucky to be here now."

"Oh." Lizzie's voice had lost a considerable amount of its animation. Was she imagining it, or did those small objects in the bag have eyes?

He lifted one out and bit it in half with a cheerful crunch. She could hear his teeth grinding. Definitely eyes, black, shiny eyes! He smiled contentedly as he tossed the other half into his mouth. "So tasty! Would you try? My wife fries them with a little oil, some onions and pepper. Delicious!" He held the bag out, the top spread temptingly open, the inside gleaming with a thin film of grease.

Lizzie looked and considered, but her hands remained safely locked around her cup. "I don't think so."

Barnabas realized her discomfort. "I am sorry. I did not mean to upset you."

"No. You didn't. Go ahead. Enjoy your escort. I'm just not…" She swallowed nervously. "I'm not hungry, is all."

He nodded as he hurriedly stuffed the bag out of sight and grabbed his thermos. "Care for more tea?"

"Yes, please." She extended her cup, a feeling of drowsiness tangling with her thoughts. "What is *nsenene* anyway?"

He filled her cup with the steaming brew. "I would rather not say, lady. I'm sure Mrs. Birungi can explain better than me."

Lizzie took a sip of tea and realized the cup seemed too heavy to hold, so she set it down. She knew Barnabas was watching her, but he seemed content to sit and act attentive. She couldn't think of any more questions. Her mind felt thick and slow, despite the caffeine in the tea. It was ridiculous that her body found the cheap plastic chair to be comfortable. She knew she was crossing into sleep and felt that she should be angry with herself, or at least embarrassed, but her last thought was mild surprise that she no longer cared.

She dreamed of an expanse of green and yellow grasses, some quite tall, swirling in patterns from a gusty wind. Warm raindrops pattered her head and shoulders. She watched black children jumping and laughing in a line, moving through the blades of grass, driving an undulating wave of winged grasshoppers ahead of them. The frightened insects leaped together in quick, buzzing flights to and fro, just above and between the tender blades. Men with fine meshed nets held high and taut between each other met the pencil shaped fugitives as they soared to escape the children. The black-eyed hoppers were quickly snared, rolled up in the netting, and dragged in bundles from the field. The hiss of the squirming nets rubbing against the trampled grass made a repetitive sound in Lizzie's mind: *nsenene, nsenene, nsenene.*

∿

"Lizzie, wake up. We need to go home," said Mrs. Birungi. The heavy shadows in the library stretched long and wide behind her.

Lizzie found that she was still in the chair but now there was a soft, folded cloth under her head. The room was quiet. The workers had gone. She slowly reassembled her consciousness and understood her location. Puzzled, she stared at Mrs. Birungi. "I thought you had work to do."

Nana made a noise with her lips. "I did. I finished it."

"Already?"

"Already! I worked five hours! School is done. Everyone has gone home."

Lizzie sat up straight. "Five hours! I slept for five hours?"

She nodded. "Mr. Mosoke stopped by before he left. He was concerned for you."

Lizzie tentatively stretched her arms while remaining seated. "I'm so ashamed. I fell asleep right in front of him. Great first impression."

"Why? It does not matter what he thinks. Your body is on another clock. You have been through a lot. You should sleep. We need you rested for tomorrow."

She squinted. "What's tomorrow? Have I forgotten something else?"

"Wasswa called again. We meet the customs agents tomorrow afternoon."

Startled, Lizzie stood up. "But we still need to get the money David sent." She had moved too fast and the prickle of dizziness made her stagger slightly. Nana instinctively clasped her arm to steady her. Lizzie persisted. "Are MTN shops open at night?"

Birungi moved her toward the door. "We are sleeping tonight, not gathering money."

"But we have to pay the—"

"We will get the shillings in the morning." Nana sounded firm. "There will be enough time."

"But..." Lizzie's body surged back to life and her steps grew stronger.

"Enough!" Nana increased her pace, cutting off further discussion. "Hurry up, Lizzie, Afiya is waiting. I am not supposed to say, but she has a surprise for you for supper – and we are already late."

Lizzie's face filled with doubt. "Oh, no. It's not...grasshoppers, is it?"

"Grasshoppers? What are you talking about?"

"*Nsenene*."

"*Nsenene?*"

"Yes."

"The grasshoppers that you eat?"

"Yes. No, not me. That *you* eat."

Nana laughed. "Your mind can be so odd, Lizzie. I really wonder about you. No, it is not grasshoppers. We would never make you eat grasshoppers. She is cooking beans and rice. Her first time by herself. Promise me you will like it, even if you don't."

It took a moment for Lizzie to make sure she understood. "Oh. Beans and rice. That's good. I can like that, no matter what."

"And be surprised."

"Right. Okay. I'll be surprised."

Shaking her head, Nana led her out through the new library doors and into the fading light of early evening.

❧

Late that night, Lizzie's eyes remained open in her dark room. Outside her window, rain whispered against the roofs. A cool breeze brushed her shoulders as she lay on her back in the bed, wide awake.

There's no way I can sleep now, she told herself. I just slept for hours in front of a complete stranger and his entire crew. My body's so messed up, I don't know if I'll ever be normal again.

It was the last fully conscious thought she had before she registered the grating screeches of a rooster next door, and the subdued morning noises of Nana and Afiya. Clearly, a new day was already upon her.

✦

To: davidwarton27x@centurylink.net; joanjohnson@yahoo.com; ceceliawarton99@hotmail.com
From: nankundabirungi@wobulezischool.com
Subj: I'm Fine!!

So sorry!! And I had such plans to stay in touch! My phone broke in Amsterdam (long story).
Lots of surprises here make it hard to call or send messages. Looks like this e-mail method may be the best. It was Mrs. Birungi's idea. (She's the school administrator, and I'm staying at her house.) Here's how it works. I type a message, usually in the evening, and give it to her on a thumb drive. She puts it into an e-mail and sends it to you from her computer at school (when the electricity works).
Okay, here's what's up so far. I talked to David on Mrs. Birungi's phone (needed some cash sent – another long story). Sorry I made you worry! I'm fine! Lots to adjust to here. People are kind (mostly). It's hot during the day and rains most nights. I miss flush toilets and hot showers (not to mention roofs!) and dependable electricity.
I enjoy the food (mostly). Remind me to tell you about my chicken stew (really fresh!) and something called matowkay (sp?). Oh, and they eat grasshoppers here! No, I'm not kidding!
Traffic is horrible and the roads have big holes. Taxi vans are crowded. I went to a huge open market called Owino. Wow! What

a noisy and smelly experience that was! Oh, by the way, everything I packed is working out great.

Guess what? Many women here are shaped a lot like me! I've even gotten some "compliments" about my looks. Imagine that!

I met a doctor from Scotland who volunteers here. I think he helps out at the school sometimes. He has an accent and seems to be quite eccentric.

Tell Will and Sandy that our students wear uniforms and most have super short haircuts. Even the girls! It's hard to tell them apart sometimes.

The library job is turning out to be a lot more exciting than I expected. If my poor body can just get over the time change, things will get better. Right now, I fall asleep in the middle of conversations (embarrassing), and I'm wide awake when it's dark outside. I feel like I'm having a real adventure.

 Don't worry about me. Miss you all.

Please give special hugs to Tomlin, Sandy and Will for me!!

Love,

Grandma XXOO

(Use Mrs. Birungi's e-mail address if you want to write me back)

TWENTY-TWO

Transfer of Funds

The taxi van swerved around a rough patch of road in heavy traffic. The driver tapped the brakes to avoid colliding with a *boda-boda*. Inside the crowded vehicle, Nana and Lizzie swayed together in the middle seat, and then jerked forward with the sudden braking.

Lizzie frowned at the folded bag Nana clutched. "What do we need that for? It's not a hold-up. I brought my purse."

"Hold-up?"

"A robbery. I mean, we're not stealing piles of money, you know. It's not like we're Bonnie and Clyde. It's only 700 dollars."

The taxi van pulled over and stopped. The conductor slid the door open so a few passengers could squeeze out. Birungi stared blankly at Lizzie. "Who is Bonnie and the Clyde?"

"Uh…bank robbers. Famous bank robbers."

The taxi's engine rattled as it pulled back into traffic. Nana made a face. "But we are not going to a bank."

"I know that." Lizzie looked exasperated. "It's nothing. I just—"

"Which one of us is the Clyde?"

"Never mind."

"Clyde is a *man's* name, is it not?"

"Forget it. I just wondered about your bag is all."

Nana put on her factual teacher's voice. "Do you know what Uganda's largest paper note is for shillings?"

"No."

"50,000."

"One bill? 50,000 shillings? How much is that worth in dollars?"

Nana did a quick computation in her head. "Right now? Maybe…15 dollars."

"What? 15! That's all?"

She nodded. "That's the problem. We have five other notes that are smaller, not to mention all the nearly worthless coins."

"That's crazy! 700 dollars in shillings is gonna make a pile of… Oh, I get it."

Nana smiled smugly and flipped the top of her bag back and forth. "Right."

"You never told me about that."

"You never asked."

The taxi van let them off at a roundabout that featured many shops, large and small, a busy open market, a few two-story buildings with offices below and apartments above, and a sizeable yellow MTN shack with metal walls.

Nana activated her phone as she walked. She brought up the confirmation text from *Sendwave* with David's money transfer information. Taking a breath and squaring her shoulders, she stepped up to the closed metal window and tapped against it with her nail. Lizzie nervously looked around at the milling crowd.

A harsh click rasped from inside the shack and then the window slid aside to reveal the face of a suspicious young man, who looked at Nana. He had a wrinkled scar high on his cheek that extended all the way into his ear. A single gold front tooth gleamed when he spoke. His Luganda was gruff.

"*Yes? What do you want, lady?*"

Lizzie could see inside the cramped shack and noted a couple of computer screens, a bare bulb dangling on a cord, a small TV showing a soccer game, and a couple of metal lock boxes bolted to the back wall. Two additional Ugandan men turned from the television to watch the transaction at the window.

Nana held up her phone. *"I received a confirmation text of a money transfer from the United States."*

"Show me the text."

She angled her phone so he could read it. He jotted down the confirmation number and handed that to the smaller of the other men, who entered it into his computer.

The man with the scar glanced over at Lizzie and then back at Nana. *"So, who's the muzungu over there?"*

"A friend."

"But you're the only one getting the money, right?"

"Right."

He paused, made a disapproving noise in his throat, and then continued. *"What's your phone number? And do you have identification?"*

Nana handed him a business card along with her National ID Card. The man scrutinized the ID photo and compared it carefully to her face. Behind him, the third man, considerably larger than the other two, exited through a hidden back door and came around outside to stand beside Birungi, with his muscular arms folded. His eyes moved across the passing shoppers, searching for threats.

The man at the window passed back Birungi's ID. He seemed much friendlier now. *"We found the transaction and confirmed it. Everything's good. You understand, we have to be careful."*

She nodded. *"Of course."*

His eyelid fluttered briefly in a nervous tick. *"But 700 US! That's gonna take us a few minutes to do the conversion and count out the shillings."*

"I understand."

"*We'll try and keep to larger bills, but really, lady, it'll still be a lotta shillings.*"

Nana handed the bag to him. "*Maybe this will help?*"

He nodded. "*Yes. Okay. Thanks.*" The metal panel snarled in protest as he slid it shut again.

Nana breathed out a sigh of relief. She tipped her head toward Lizzie. "They are gathering the money. It should not be long now."

Lizzie smiled. "Good."

She leaned back and relaxed in the warm sun while she waited. Her eyes roved languidly over the activities in the roundabout. She noticed a shoe and sandal repair vendor whose tiny shop perched precariously on poles over the flood canal. His toothy smile was wide as he pedaled his manual sewing machine while his customers waited. On the pathway behind him, two tall, thin men walked by, their eyes searching faces instead of shopping. They were darker skinned than the rest of the pedestrians. Something about their behavior struck Lizzie as odd. She pointed them out to Nana, who suggested they were probably Maasai cattle herders from the country, or maybe Sudanese. When Lizzie looked back, they were gone.

Her attention went to a women's clothing shop that displayed a line of headless mannequins beside the walkway. The enterprising vendor had also strung a wire between posts on which he had suspended an array of female forms, each wearing a different style of tights. Lizzie was thinking it looked a lot like a butcher shop when she noticed a young boy dash out from behind a wall. Dressed in loose clothing, he acted frantic. In his haste, he tumbled into the dirt, raising puffs of orange dust. Jumping back up, he careened through the mannequins, windmilling his arms to knock them aside, and rushed toward the MTN shack.

Suddenly, chasing him, a group of ragged street boys appeared, yelling in Luganda. By this time, the shop vendor charged out to protect his merchandise, adding to the commotion. Some of the street boys bumped the female forms on the wire, causing them to spin; others trampled the fallen mannequins as they raced by. The shopkeeper grabbed at the boys but only became tangled in his own legs. Cursing, he tumbled helplessly to the ground.

The young boy in loose clothing raced by the MTN shack, dodging the strong man and brushing between Nana and Lizzie. He grabbed the metal corner of the shack to change directions, but he crashed headlong into a clump of unaware shoppers in the open market. Customers catapulted into tomatoes and peppers. The frightened boy somehow kept his feet. He leaped a mound of banana leaves and headed for the street.

The boys in pursuit ran full speed after him, but they split up into twos and threes, like a pack of wolves trying to cut off escape routes.

Lizzie heard honking and spotted the fleeing boy once more. He squeezed between speeding lines of taxis and motorbikes, vanishing on the other side of the road.

One of the pursuers, obviously the leader, shouted directions and issued orders. Lizzie watched, stunned. She recognized the face, the movement of the arms, the sound of the voice. Dembe! He carried something in one hand that reflected the sun, his facial expression intense.

Lizzie exclaimed, "It's Dembe, Nana! Look!"

Just taking the bag of shillings from the MTN clerk, Nana turned. She saw Dembe, too.

Without hesitation, Lizzie ran, shouting his name. She heard her own angry inner voice, questioning her, but she ignored it. No time to think things through. She was determined not to lose this boy again.

Dembe heard her voice. When he saw her charging toward him, he stopped. "Mrs. Warton? You can't be here!" His face held fear.

Lizzie grabbed his shoulders. "Dembe! I've been looking all over for you. I know about the copper pipes. I know what you—"

"No!" He firmly pushed her backwards. "Get away from here!"

Lizzie was aware of something in Dembe's hand. It felt crinkly, like foil. It was getting crushed against her shoulder. "What? No. Listen to me. I can help. I—"

Dembe turned her. He swiftly pushed her back toward the MTN shack. "Not now! There is a bomb!"

Lizzie was amazed at his strength. She felt powerless. He rushed her across the dirt and pressed her down against the base of the yellow metal wall. Her mind finally registered his words. "A bomb? What do you mean?"

Dembe grabbed Nana and pulled her down beside Lizzie. "That running boy has a bomb-vest under his clothes. Rebels from Sudan tricked him. I was trying to help, but he panicked."

Two of Dembe's street boys rushed up. They shouted something, pointing across the street.

Dembe nodded and then flashed a look at the women scrunched against the wall. "I have to go. You *must* stay here!"

Nana scowled and snapped a question in Luganda.

Dembe angrily fired back. He shook the wrinkled aluminum foil at her in explanation as he got up. He turned, intending to resume the chase, when the ground itself rose up and slapped him off his feet.

The sudden concussive overpressure from the bomb blast slammed into Lizzie like a giant punch to the back of her head. Her inner ears shrieked in agony. Needles plunged deep inside. Teeth clenched. Eyes jammed shut. Her body curled around itself, instinctively burrowing into the dirt. Somewhere inside her head, she cowered, utterly alone, and bereft of any sense of time. Her shaken mind dumbly marveled at the oddity of silence in the middle of an explosion. Every single muscle in her body squeezed painfully tight, staying tight while she waited. What am I supposed to do now? What happens next? What am I waiting for?

Timidly, she peeked out from beneath dust-laden eyelids. The wall of the MTN shack had shielded them from the vicious metal debris that peppered the ground beyond where they lay. The clean space of dirt around them sketched a mirror image of the building they had huddled against.

Lizzie's ears crackled and squeaked. She sat up, dazed. The dusty bodies of Nana and Dembe began to stir. Nana propped herself up on her elbows. Her lips moved as she looked around. No sound reached Lizzie's ears.

Dembe shook himself like a dog, creating a halo of dust. He scuttled rapidly over to the women. His hands gently shook each of their shoulders in turn. He looked into their eyes. His lips moved again and again. Lizzie only heard hissing and a fractured voice at a great distance. She understood none of it.

The two street boys nearby climbed unsteadily to their feet. One dug in his ears with his fingers, vainly trying to unlock his hearing. The other looked wildly around, bleeding from multiple cuts on his arm. He sank back to his knees, lost and afraid.

Lizzie sluggishly checked her hands and arms for cuts. She bent her head and squinted as pressures deep in her ears bubbled. Then, with a painful ringing, parts of Lizzie's muffled hearing abruptly cracked opened. The sudden onslaught of sound felt so shocking, she covered her ears with dirty hands even as she staggered to the edge of the building to view the chaos.

Cries of agony filled the air. Fiery explosions erupted, triggered from the leaking gas tanks of riddled cars and downed motorbikes. The open market, just behind the MTN shack, was in shambles. Car alarms bleated, competing with the pleas for help. Small fires burned unheeded on both sides of the road. Lizzie reeled in the maelstrom and turned away, unable to cope with the tragedy.

"Mrs. Warton? Mrs. Warton! Can you hear me?"

Black smoke swirled around her face, blotting out the sun. Lizzie held onto that voice. She forced her mind to focus on the words. The air cleared for an instant. There he stood, right in front of her. Dembe. Lizzie looked into his eyes and nodded that she could hear him. She grabbed his shoulder so she wouldn't lose him. Nana's face appeared close beside his. For a moment, the two of them occupied her entire world, and she welcomed it – she knew who they were, and she knew they were alive.

"Lizzie! We have to get away from here!" It was Nana, her black hair jumbled, her eyes red with the dust. "There may be more bombs!"

"More? But..." Lizzie felt anxious, confused, indecisive. "But people are hurt. We have to... Shouldn't we help?"

"You need to leave," said Dembe. "Go while you can."

Lizzie coughed and held a hand over her mouth. "What?" The oily smoke closed around them again.

Nana shouted and pulled at her. "We must get away! We can do nothing here." She coughed, as well.

"But they need help until the... Won't ambulances come? Fire trucks?"

Dembe spoke rapidly, cutting her off. "No! You don't understand. The army will come first. Looking for enemies. Only later will help be allowed."

Nana nodded her agreement while wiping her eyes. "Nothing we can do!"

The thickening smoke waffled and momentarily thinned. Dembe gently moved Lizzie toward Nana. "I have to get my boys out. Run! Now! Before the trucks get here."

Nana pulled Lizzie's hand. "Follow behind me!"

Clear of the smoke, they hurried down the dirt paths beside clotted roads. Trying to look presentable, they kept slapping at their clothes to drive out the dust. Around them, crowds of people streamed from nearby shops and markets, staring fearfully at the billowing cloud of dark smoke a short distance away. A few suspicious faces eyed them as they rushed by. Everyone had heard the explosion. Nervous crowds gathered in the road, voices rising with questions.

Lizzie paled. She stopped in her tracks. "Wait! Nana! The money! What about the money?"

Spinning around, Nana shook the dusty money bag at her. "I have it! Keep going!"

Low flying helicopters roared over their heads and streaked toward the distant pillar of smoke. Lizzie glanced up in time to see them pass over. Painted in the army's tan camouflage, the equipment looked old and the engines made an incredible howl. She counted at least three of them circling in the smoke, like dragonflies above a campfire, before she looked away.

Nana left the path, and she led Lizzie between shacks and across a vacant lot. At one point, she ducked under a broken fence, skirted a field that had been allowed to go wild, and reconnected with an alternate paved road. Standing at an intersection, she argued briefly with a taxi van conductor over the fare and then motioned Lizzie on board. The half full van accelerated unevenly into traffic, belching its typical snake of exhaust. The driver headed away from the bomb scene.

Breathing hard and sitting side-by-side in the seat, Nana and Lizzie took a moment to stare at each other with red eyes. They reeked of smoke and sweat and looked a fright.

Lizzie dug into her pockets and came up with crumpled tissues that she put to work wiping Nana's smudged face. "Where're we going?"

Birungi rubbed at Lizzie's cheek using a semi-clean portion of her own sleeve. "Home. Start over."

Lizzie closed her eyes as Birungi brushed dirt from her eyebrows and lids. "What happened back there?"

Birungi shook her head. "Sudanese rebels making terror. Who knows? Angry about our border policies."

"No. I mean with Dembe."

She looked angry but controlled her voice. "Stupid boy! He thought he could stop a bomb!"

"How? What did he say to you?"

"He said the bomb-vest was hooked to a phone. If he wrapped it in foil, it would not be able to receive calls."

"Does that work? Is that even possible?"

"How do I know? I know nothing about bombs!" She looked away, overcome with delayed emotion and then looked back. Her eyes streamed tears from the grime in them. "But if Dembe says it is so, then I believe him."

Lizzie slumped in the stiff seat. Without warning, her body began to shake. She groaned. Nana quickly wrapped both arms around her and held on tight.

"You are safe now, Lizzie. Safe! It is just the shock. You will be fine. Let it happen. The shaking will pass soon, do not worry. Just hold on to me."

Lizzie's voice shuddered as she attempted to talk. "How can you be so sure?"

"Because I have been through this before."

TWENTY-THREE

Bribes for Books

The shillings were stacked in tied bundles on the coffee table in Mrs. Birungi's small front room. Marked with cards, the smaller stack said, *customs* and the larger one said, *container.*

"We have an hour," Nana called out. Now dressed in a two-button, pinstriped pantsuit with low heeled shoes and her hair tightly coiled, she pressed a damp cloth tightly against her stinging eyes to cool the pain. "Lizzie? Do you hear? We need to leave."

"I know." Lizzie entered quickly from the back of the house, wearing a clean skirt and blouse. She ran her fingers through her damp hair and scrunched it here and there with little effect. "I'm giving up on my hair. This'll just have to do."

Birungi lowered the cloth and checked her over, nodding. "Fine." She began methodically emptying her purse of all but essentials.

Lizzie sank tiredly into a chair. "I can't believe how much soap and how many buckets of rinse water I used. I thought I'd never get clean. I just left my filthy clothes in a pile."

"Do not worry."

Lizzie watched Nana cram the larger stack of bills into her purse. "I don't know if I can do this. I can't stop shaking."

Birungi snapped closed her purse and looked at her. "You can do it. I know you can."

"But I keep seeing the fire and the bodies and—"

"Do not think about it now. Let the pictures float through your mind without stopping. There will be time later. Not now."

"But, Nana, they were calling for help. We should have tried to—"

She sharply cut her off. "No! We did what we had to do. Now, we must meet Wasswa outside the warehouse. Come."

Lizzie slowly stood. Birungi handed her the smaller stack of paper money. "Take this. Hurry. We do not want to be late."

Lizzie awkwardly stuffed the wedge of shillings into her bag and seemed unsteady on her feet. Birungi watched carefully and then stepped close to her. She placed her soft black hands on either side of Lizzie's pale face; with her thumbs, she gently smoothed the skin beneath Lizzie's eyes, just under her glasses.

"You are a good person, Lizzie Warton. Do not forget that. Keep looking forward, not backward. Can you do that?"

Lizzie stared into Nana's brown eyes and borrowed some strength from them. "Yes."

Birungi lifted her hands gently away. "Good."

The two women turned to scan the room, gathered their purses, smoothed each other's collars, and headed out the door.

❦

Lurching along in traffic, their taxi van bubbled over with loud and animated conversations in Luganda from the other passengers. Lizzie glanced furtively at Nana for an explanation. Her lips formed the word *bomb* before she looked away. Of course! The attack would be the talk of the day. Why was she surprised? Lizzie felt her body start to tremble again, but she fought it off by staring forward and breathing slowly through her nose. Her eyes tracked an empty armored personnel carrier as it rumbled by, going the other way. It was followed closely by a black Humvee.

Ahead of them, a tall policewoman dressed in a snowy white uniform stood in the center of the busy intersection. She waved at their taxi van to make its turn. Lizzie observed pairs of armed soldiers in green camouflage patrolling at the edges of the road. This was new, she thought. The young men appeared watchful, each one kept both hands poised on their weapons.

The roadways in the Nakawa Industrial Area were choked with randomly parked trucks on each shoulder. Some of the dusty cabs held sleeping drivers inside; most sat empty. Many of the larger trucks had shipping containers from Maersk, Emirates, CMA-CGM and Gateway clamped to their flat trailers. Most of the rest were just empty frames waiting for a load. A few engine hoods were up. Lizzie saw the bent backs of mechanics, their bodies half inside the motors. Between the sloppily parked vehicles, she noticed brown and white goats grazing in the tall grass. A stoop-shouldered man with a stick moved among them, a blanket looped over his shoulder. Skipping around the goat man, a joyful young girl sang a song.

Their taxi driver spotted an opening between trucks at the next intersection and swooped in to the curb to let them out. Gingerly stepping down onto the dirt-impregnated asphalt of the road, Lizzie nervously looked around. She couldn't help herself. Her eyes darted and jumped at any quick movement or loud sound.

The smell of diesel and dust was ever-present. In front of her, a narrow brick walkway ran below a concrete wall covered with faded notices and billboards. Rusty angled pipes were set at intervals on the top of the wall with tightly strung lines of barbed wire running between them. To Lizzie, it looked like a prison wall. Beside her, a soldier with an orange beret stood facing the street, carefully scrutinizing the pedestrians and vehicles as they passed by. His rifle pointed down, but his finger was beside the trigger. Oddly, she noticed his black, fingerless shooting glove sported a yellow batman logo. I'm definitely too old for this, she thought.

Standing a short distance away, she picked out Wasswa and his brother, Rokani. They leaned against a parked car on the main road, watching traffic. By the time Nana squeezed out of the taxi van, the two men were already striding toward them with smiles on their faces.

"Lizzie! Mrs. Birungi! It is so nice to see you again. This way, please. All is prepared." Wasswa motioned with his open hand, pointing farther down the wall toward the main gate of the bonded warehouse area.

Wasswa seemed upbeat. His gait flowed loose and breezy as he walked beside them. "The agents are ready for us. All the documents are drawn up for signing. We just have to sit down, drink chai, smile and nod." He eyed Mrs. Birungi and rubbed his fingers together, indicating cash. "You know how it is. We must do what is expected."

Nana flashed a displeased face, but nodded.

Lizzie balked. "Chai? What? With these people? While they steal my money?"

Wasswa's eyes bulged in shock. He looked quickly around. Beside the entrance to the customs compound, a guard stepped out from a security room set into the wall itself. He wore a blue uniform with pink epaulettes on his shoulders. A large plastic ID hung from a strap around his neck. Seeing Wasswa with the group, he smiled and nodded for them to proceed.

The truck-sized double gate was slightly ajar at the center so pedestrians could pass through. Crossing the wide driveway, Lizzie felt the afternoon sun reflecting off the brick pavement in waves of heat. Her ears were ringing again. As they approached the gate, she had to concentrate on her shoes to keep from stumbling. All she wanted was to get this over with and sit in her room with the curtains pulled and a cool cloth over her face.

She growled at Wasswa, "Why do I have to pretend to be nice to these people?"

Shaking his head, Wasswa sent a pained expression back at Rokani. Nana hissed a warning at her. "Lizzie! Hush! Think of the books."

As they cleared the gate, they found a group of three male customs officials waiting for them in the cool shade beneath a tarp. One wore a suit, the other two wore identical white shirts with black tabs clipped to the shoulders, blue ties and black pants. All had red IDs dangling from neck straps. The men smiled a greeting and moved forward to shake hands. Wasswa did the introductions, and breathed a sigh of relief when Lizzie made it through the exchange-of-names ritual without a hitch.

Around them, rows of warehouses extended off to the distance. The featureless structures were painted grey with blue trim pieces at the corners. Lizzie stared up at razor wire coils fastened along the edges of the roofs to prevent climbers from breaking in. Circling the buildings, huge metal shipping containers were set out in haphazard lines, stacked four and even five high, making long colorful walls, much taller than the concrete barrier that protected them. In fact, in some places, the empty containers stood almost as high as the warehouses themselves.

"Lizzie?"

When she heard Wasswa's uneasy voice, she turned and saw that the group was being shepherded toward a low brick office building, presumably to smile and drink chai and trade shillings for signatures. She started in that direction, allowing herself to follow along, but then she resisted. "No! I don't want chai. Not today!" Her voice sounded louder than she had expected.

Everyone stopped. The customs agents turned troubled faces toward Wasswa. He rolled his shoulders, at a loss for words. Birungi's face was neutral, eyes curious.

Lizzie read their reactions and expected to be embarrassed, but instead found that she actually didn't care what they thought. She didn't care what was expected, what would make things smoother, or easier, or whatever it was that their culture demanded. Not after the morning she'd had. "Gentlemen, I'm sorry, but I want to see the container first. I want to place my hands on the books. I've no more time to waste. And whatever it is that we need to do after that, we can do there. Okay? Wasswa, would you...explain?"

Wasswa was caught without a plan. He began blathering in Luganda, trying to spin things and make the best of a degrading situation, but he was waved to silence by the man in the suit.

"Excuse me, Mrs. Warton." His English was only slightly accented. "We understand your words well enough without Mr. Salongo's assistance. Regrettably, your books have been impounded here for a long time, but surely, a few moments for tea is not too much to ask as we make things right."

Lizzie's nose flared at his tone. "Make things right?" Her mouth formed a crooked smile. "Look, it's been a long day, and I apologize if I'm insensitive right now. Just take me to the container."

The man stood for a moment and stared. Finally, shaking his head in disdain, he led off, walking stiffly toward the warehouses. "Of course, lady. Let me guide you." He huffed as he walked, "I should have known. You Americans are always in such a hurry – even the women, apparently."

Lizzie kept pace with him, her natural stubbornness rising up. "And you Ugandans are always so full of...surprises – even the men."

The man broke stride but couldn't think of a comeback, or chose not to try, and decided just to lead on. Lizzie matched him step for step, her earlier weakness forgotten. The rest of the group straggled in a loose line behind them.

✧

"Open it," Lizzie said calmly.

The forty-foot long yellow container sat by itself just inside the open doors of one of the warehouses. Easily twice as tall as Lizzie, the ribbed metal box was raised off the ground by thick blocks of wood. Its latched doors at the end were hinged on each side and split in the middle. Pairs of vertical lock rods extended top to bottom on each door, and each lock rod had horizontal handles at chest height. A lockbox on the right-hand door overlapped the other door and carried a customs' impound notice taped across its face.

The man in the suit nodded to one of his other agents. Searching for the correct key, the agent stepped up to the lockbox, reached inside it from below, and released an unseen padlock. Obviously familiar with the process, he quickly lifted the door handles on the right-hand door, swiveled them in tandem, forcing the cams out of their keepers, and pulled open the door. A *snicking* noise sounded as the heavy door swung out, since both doors had thick rubber gaskets running along their edges to keep the contents dry. Using the same procedure, he swung the left door all the way open until it, too, rested against the container's outside wall.

Lizzie looked into the deep interior. Sunlight from the open warehouse filled the front of the container with a glowing slant of light. Dust motes swirled in the air, raised by the swinging of the doors. She watched the tiny specks slowly turning in the sunbeams and remembered that morning in the hospice room when she was alone with Jonathan. It seemed so long ago and so far away, and yet, somehow, it was inescapably connected to now. She could sense an unimpeded flow of purpose, from that moment to this one, and she basked in the strength of that assurance.

"May I go inside?" She glanced at the man in the suit.

"Why not, lady?" he replied tiredly. "They are your books."

She put a hand out to Wasswa. He helped her to step up over the lip and stand inside. Big ghostly shapes filled the interior, pushed together, shoulder-to-shoulder, as far as the light could penetrate. They were tall stacks of book boxes, bundled and shrink wrapped on wooden pallets. The stack nearest to her had been partially cut open and a few of the boxes lifted out for inspection. Two of those boxes were sitting at her feet, their sealing tape cut, and the flaps loose.

She crouched and slid her hand inside, feeling the familiar shapes packed tightly, side-by-side. Her nose picked up the faint but wonderful sweetness of print stock paper that she had always associated with libraries. Grabbing one at random, she brought it into the light and recognized its worn cover. Her smile was shaken by the stream of memories the book unleashed into her mind. She felt such a rush of the past into the present, she almost cried out. It wasn't just the story within the treasured book itself. It was the memories tangled with it: who she was when she first read it; whom she read it aloud to later; how she had re-discovered its comforting presence during the lost years of Jonathan's illness; and who she was now as the old book made its fresh appearance in this land of lions and Ebola. She smiled inside her heart. Such a deceptively simple book to shoulder such a weight of shared histories – *The Long Winter* by Laura Ingalls Wilder.

She lifted the flap on the box and replaced the softback book, pleasantly noticing that other members of the series appeared to be inside. What would Pastor Kajumba's students make of that awful winter in South Dakota? A blizzard? Here? Then, she realized that the unfamiliarity of winter wouldn't matter. They would understand the hunger and the fight for survival. They would love the book in their own way.

It suddenly struck Lizzie how selfish and short-sighted these agents were. How could they not understand that this shipment was different? Not to be trifled with? An anger welled up inside of her that she hadn't felt in a long time – maybe never. How dare they? She stood up and faced the group.

The agent with the suit fluttered his eyebrows in irritation. "So? Satisfied now?"

Lizzie stepped to the front edge of the shipping container and looked down at him. "Do you have any real appreciation of what's in here?"

The man cocked his head. He looked for support from the other agents.

Lizzie answered for him. "I know, books. Right? Isn't that what you think? But it's not books! In here is a gift of knowledge from schools in America to a school here in Uganda. Those schools paid every expense. The teachers and students and parents volunteered their time, packed boxes, got UPS to donate transportation, paid all the bills in advance, to make it this far. And then what happened?"

The two agents in white shirts began to squirm. Obviously, their English comprehension was good enough to make them feel uncomfortable. The man in the suit opened his mouth to answer. Lizzie didn't give him a chance.

"But these Ugandan students aren't *your* children, right? Not from *your* family. Probably not even from *your* precious tribe. And besides, this is how things work. Isn't it? It's expected. What do you call it? A tip? Some grease? A kindness? I don't know how to say it in Luganda. In the end, it doesn't matter what name it's given. In any language, you know what it is."

She focused her gaze on the main agent. "And so, you thought you'd just delay things until we paid up. Huh? You made up your lists of fees. You stuck your impound paper on the door. You changed the locks. And all the time, you knew there was nothing wrong. Nothing owed. Nothing to be computed, since there was nothing bought and nothing sold – except for the three of you!"

Lizzie's hands shook. She felt her heart pounding in her chest. Her better senses were desperately waving red flags. She couldn't believe what she was saying. Her words had just rolled out, almost on their own, and she knew she couldn't take them back, even if she wanted to. A stiff-necked part of her whispered that she didn't want to take anything back! In fact, she had more to say! And despite her fears, she just let it fly.

"I was almost killed this morning because of you! A bomb went off in a market. I'm sure you've heard about it. It was terrible…just… terrible! I was right there! And Mrs. Birungi was there, too. We were at an MTN shack getting your money! It's a miracle we survived. A street boy saved us. A street boy! Not my family. Not my tribe. Not even my skin color! He saved our lives, and yet he never asked me for…for anything. Not a thing. Not a single blessed thing."

Taking a breath, she knew that she was done. She opened her purse and brandished the thick wad of shillings in the air. "Here is your cash, gentlemen."

She raised her other hand out to Wasswa, who helped her to step back down to the ground. Her legs trembled. Her back and hips reminded her of the day's abuse they'd suffered. Handing her bundle of cash to Wasswa, she explained, "Mr. Salongo will handle everything."

She motioned to Nana, who quickly produced the other stack of shillings. She passed that on to Wasswa, as well.

"And there's the container rental fee. Whatever paperwork we need, in order to *make things right*, please give to Wasswa." She sniffed and cleared her throat. "We're done now."

Without another look at the customs agents, Lizzie walked briskly out the sun-filled warehouse doors, followed by Mrs. Birungi. Rokani rushed out in their wake and offered to accompany them to Wasswa's car.

Back in the warehouse, the agents hurriedly huddled around Wasswa. Even though they spoke quietly in Luganda, there was no mistaking the intensity of their discussion.

※

Lizzie sat with her eyes closed in the backseat of Wasswa's parked car, but her mind was awake. "Rokani?"

"Yes, lady." Wasswa's younger brother turned and looked at her from the passenger's side of the front seat.

Lizzie's eyes remained shut. "Do you and your brother have a truck?"

"We have two trucks, lady. A big one with a tarp and a small one."

Lizzie opened her eyes and made an effort to smile at him, despite how her body felt. "Can you help us move the books?"

Rokani looked uneasy at the suggestion. "How soon?"

"Right away."

He swallowed nervously. "We are using the trucks all the time but..." His tone conveyed little hope. "But I can talk to Wasswa."

"And if I promised to pay?"

Rokani's eyebrows lifted ever so slightly. "Then, maybe we could...adjust our schedule."

"Good enough. Can we talk tomorrow?"

Birungi, sitting next to Lizzie, touched her arm. "Lizzie, tomorrow is Sunday. We should not move the books on a Sunday."

Lizzie sighed. "Sorry. I've completely lost track of my days. Rokani, can we talk on Monday?"

"Yes, Monday."

"Okay. Thank you."

Rokani nodded quickly, happy to have the conversation over.

Nana's expression clouded over. "And what if we do not get the books?"

"We will."

"How do you know?"

"I don't, but I'm hopeful." She made a face. "Desperately hopeful."

Birungi took in a deep breath and sat back. Lizzie closed her eyes again. Her head throbbed in the heat and her ears were back to ringing. If she could only get to her room soon. Where was Wasswa?

She heard the driver's side door rattle. Opening one eye, she watched the sweating merchant climb in carrying a rectangular carton with a lid. He shut his door and twisted around in the seat. "I have all the signed paperwork here."

Lizzie nodded. She opened the other eye and could clearly see in his face that there was something more that he wasn't saying. She was too tired to play games. "What else?"

Wasswa lifted the lid and tipped the carton in her direction, so she could see inside. "The money. They don't want the money."

Nana slid forward with big eyes and stared into the carton. "*All* the money? Even the rental fee?"

Wasswa handed the carton to Birungi and then turned to face forward again. He shot a nervous look at Rokani before answering. "There was no rental fee. You saw. They have stacks of empty containers. They already returned one to the shipper."

Nana and Lizzie gaped at each other.

If Lizzie had had more energy, she would have cheered. As it was, her eyes grew glassy and tears welled up. "We did it, Nana. No bribes."

Nana smiled so wide, Lizzie could see her gums. "And I was so afraid when you were talking. I saw no hope. To talk in that way! To men! I was sure we had lost the books."

"Me too. I didn't know what I was doing. I couldn't stop. I was just so angry – and words kept coming out."

"They were good words, Lizzie. Good words."

"I can't even remember what I said."

Both Wasswa and Rokani had turned in their seats to listen to the women. Wasswa looked confused. "You mean this was not a plan? The two of you? This was not a…trick?"

Lizzie sat up, offended. "No! Of course not! What do you mean?"

Wasswa hurriedly looked away. "Nothing."

Lizzie's face grew suspicious. "Wasswa?"

"Yes, lady."

"Didn't you tell me the container fee wasn't negotiable? That customs had nothing to do with it? That the shipper was charging rent because of the long delay?"

"Yes, lady."

Lizzie's voice grew very quiet. "And you knew that was a lie when you told me, didn't you?"

Wasswa stared stoically forward, his voice flat. "Yes."

Lizzie pulled herself up a little bit. "And what was your share to be?"

"My share?"

Her voice snapped at him with an edge. "Don't play with me. What percentage of the money taken from these stupid women was to be yours?"

Wasswa rubbed his nose and watched a pedestrian walk by the car. "A quarter."

The car's interior suddenly felt pressurized, as if the air pushed against their ears. Nana grumbled something ugly in Luganda. Wasswa sounded peeved as he replied. He started the engine.

Lizzie looked at Birungi. "What?"

"We have a saying. 'The lines of the zebra do not rub off.'"

Lizzie raised her eyebrows a little. "And what did he say?"

"He said he is not a zebra. And zebras pay no bills."

Lizzie tipped her head and nodded, acknowledging his point. "In America we say, 'You can't teach an old dog new tricks.'"

Nana giggled, putting her hand over her mouth. The pressure in the car dissipated a bit. "Oh, that is so true! Afiya will laugh. She loves sayings."

Wasswa gunned the car as he jerked into the moving traffic. "I am not a dog, either!"

Lizzie poked his seat. "And you're a lot younger than I am, too."

Wasswa glanced into his rearview mirror and met Lizzie's eyes. There was a moment of truce, and then he looked away to change lanes.

TWENTY-FOUR

Church is Church

Lizzie slept like the dead. No dreams disturbed her, just a blessed nothingness until the neighboring rooster screamed his welcome to the morning. Her bones and joints objected to every movement she made when she had first climbed through the mosquito netting and out of her bed. But the more she moved, the more their complaints diminished. Now, there were just a few whispered yips when she changed positions.

It was such a recurring relief to have her own clothes again. She felt like thanking each item as she held it up, selecting what to wear. She had settled on a blue and beige floral print skirt that seemed sufficiently dressy for church, and a cream top, long and loose enough to obscure her lack of a waistline. Sitting in her single chair, she propped her compact mirror up on the tiny table and spread out a few supplies from her recovered makeup bag. She applied a tinted moisturizer under her eyes and her cheeks.

Behind her, Nana peeked in through the open door. "How was the night?"

Lizzie smoothed the makeup over her skin. "Come in, Nana.

My night was good; it's my morning that was tough. My bones feel old and crabby."

Nana swept through the doorway, wearing a vibrant green dress swirled with gold. The colors so enhanced her warm brown skin, she appeared radiant in the morning light. Her hair was pulled back from her high cheekbones, and coiled atop her head in a crowning circlet of braids.

Lizzie caught her breath. "Kill me now. There's no way I'm walking into church next to you!"

Relishing the praise, Nana noticed Lizzie's tiny compact. "You know, I have a large mirror in my room you can use."

"No. This is fine. Believe me, the less I can see, the better."

Nana frowned and then chuckled as she sat on the edge of Lizzie's bed. "You always surprise me."

"I'll take that as a good thing."

"Yes. It is good. You are good for me."

Lizzie flicked her eyes toward Nana. "Thank you." She began to fill in her eyebrows with a brow pencil. "Anything I need to know about church?"

"About church? What do you mean?"

"Things I should or shouldn't say? Or do? I don't know. What should I expect?"

"Church is church. Just be yourself. You are *muzungu*. They will be pleased that you are there. What is your church like?"

Lizzie curtailed her efforts to improve her looks and thought about the question. She put her pencil away and closed up her small makeup case. "Predictable," she finally said. "That's what my church is – predictable. That's what Jonathan liked about all our churches, back when he still had likes."

She grew quiet and her gaze turned inward. She remembered Jonathan secretly teasing toddlers in the row ahead of him. He would get them to laugh, or scream, and embarrass their shocked parents. Then to escape discovery, he would feign a sudden rapt attention on the preacher. She smiled sadly. "Mostly predictable."

Birungi observed her play of emotion. "It is not easy to be widows."

"No. But you have to understand that my husband was ill for many years. At the end, his mind was…" She tipped her head slightly. "He was not the man I married."

"I am sorry."

"Don't be. We had many good years, and a family. He wasn't perfect, but he was kind – he came from a kind family." She took a breath. "I have no complaints. How about your husband?"

Birungi looked away. Her eyes wandered toward the window and the sunlight outside. "He was a good man. We cared for each other. He was unusual. He encouraged me to finish my schooling." Nana's melodious voice thickened. "And when I talked, he listened to me."

Lizzie folded her hands in her lap. "Nana, I didn't mean to pry. You don't have to tell me anything."

Nana sniffed quietly as she turned back. "No. It is fine. I want to tell you." She sat very still. When her voice returned, it was controlled. "There was an accident on the road. Treatment was delayed because of money. The hospital made mistakes; and then he was gone."

Lizzie moved to sit next to her on the bed. She wrapped her hands around Nana's. "That must have been so hard."

She nodded without looking at Lizzie. "My mother and my *Jjajja* taught me that a widow has no time to cry. The laws of our country say one thing, but the laws of our culture say something quite different. Our country says inheritance goes from husband to wife to children. Our culture says the husband's family controls everything."

She looked at Lizzie, her large eyes shining as she continued. "Mother said that if my husband died, I would need to lock the cabinets and the doors, find the paperwork for the house, the land,

and for anything of value, because his family would be coming to take them away."

Lizzie's mind faltered as she tried to understand. "Oh, Nana! But, surely your husband's family…did they?"

Birungi slowly nodded. "It was just as my mother said it would be, but they were too late. I had gone straight to the courts from the hospital. I made sure that Afiya and I were secure, even before I announced burial plans." She used her fingers to dab cautiously at her eyes, trying to preserve her mascara. "I did not cry until weeks later – and then, sometimes even now."

Lizzie squeezed her friend's hand. "But if the law is on your side, can't women fight in court?"

Nana stared at her, smiling patiently. "Yes. If you have the money, and if you have the time. Here, our lawyers stretch out cases, and judges can be bought." She looked away again, staring at the window. "A widow with children may end up begging on the street while her husband's family swallows everything."

Lizzie's shoulders slumped and her hands slid back into her lap. "How can I be as old as I am and still so naïve? I didn't know. In our country, it is not like that."

"Your country has no tribes. No clans."

"No. Not really."

"Sometimes, even here, it is not this way. But for me, there was envy because of my schooling. I moved fast. I kept this house and our things. I still have my position at the school, thanks to Pastor. I survived. Other women are not so lucky."

Lizzie sat up straighter and looked at Nana with new eyes. "It wasn't luck, dear. You had a plan and the courage to carry it out. I'm sure your husband would be proud of you. I know I am."

From somewhere in the house, a raucous hip-hop ringtone erupted. Startled, they both jerked their heads toward the open door. As the unpleasant sound repeated, Nana rolled her eyes and snorted. "Afiya has been playing again with my rings!"

The phone kept going off. Nana shouted out the door, *"Afiya! Kwata esimu!"*

The ringing stopped abruptly. She stood and put out a hand to help Lizzie to her feet. "Sorry if I talked too much. You are a good listener."

Lizzie smoothed the folds of her skirt. "Widows have to stick together."

Afiya appeared in the doorway, dressed in a colorful skirt and top, holding out the cell phone. She spoke in Luganda. "Mother, it's for you. It's that lady from Safe Haven."

Lizzie thought she might have heard the words "safe haven," but she couldn't be sure.

Birungi took the phone and pressed it against her chest. They continued in Luganda. "You mean, Mrs. Mayombwe?"

Afiya nodded. "I think so. She said Meg Mayombwe."

Birungi tipped her head. "Why would she be calling?"

"I don't know."

Birungi glanced sharply at Afiya. "No. I wasn't asking you! I was just thinking out loud."

"Oh. Okay." The young girl turned to leave.

"Daughter! Wait!"

She turned back and stood looking up at her mother.

"When I am off this phone, you will change that horrible ringtone back to my setting, and not change it again!"

"But it's so boring."

"Afiya!"

The girl immediately lowered her face and her tone. "Yes, mother."

Nana turned away from her daughter and cleared her throat before lifting the phone to her ear. "Hello?" she asked warmly in English.

᪥

Compared to what she was accustomed to, this church service felt more foreign to Lizzie than any other of her experiences thus far in Uganda. She felt embarrassed. Was her faith so rigidly rooted in her own style that she really couldn't enter in? Or was she right to remain cautious and wrap herself in hesitancy? How does a person decide things like that? Experience warned her that comfort wasn't a reliable measure.

Tightly packed with grinning people, the assembly swayed in perfect rhythm to the surprising notes rolling out from a battered keyboard. The music leader stood on a raised platform at the front. Other musicians and singers clustered around him, all clearly enjoying their role in leading worship. The thin walls vibrated to the stirring beats thumped out of hide-covered drums. The air was thick with heat generated by the moving bodies. Every member of the congregation, with the exception of Lizzie, waved outstretched hands to the ceiling, straining on tiptoes to reach ever higher. Hips and shoulders rocked to the music. Every throat belted out the words to the hymn, the women singing high, the men singing low, stuffing the space with harmonized sound. It was overwhelming.

Lizzie's heart and mind cringed with automatic, nearly involuntary fears. Get me out of here, out of here, out of here! Her back was stiff. Her shoulders hunched protectively. Still, she could sense another part of her, cautiously stretching out and sipping at the edges of the spiritual waters roaring through the room. What did she fear? That she would be swept away? That she would lose herself? That she would no longer be in control?

Standing on either side of her, Nana and Afiya seemed oblivious to her struggle. They were just another part of the joyful crowd, effortlessly joining in the shared celebration with their Christian brothers and sisters. Lizzie wished she could disappear. Her fingers anxiously rubbed against each other. Her eyes darted around. Nearby, she noticed people dancing in the aisle. Not far away, an older man sat in one of the folding chairs and wept. The hymn rolled on and on, verse after unending verse, and the many voices continued to revel in it.

Was this the same God that she knew? The same quiet One who spoke to her in the silence of the sunsets? The same One whose voice whispered through the leaves of the twin maples at her home church's parking lot? If He wasn't, she feared that her God was much smaller than this One; and if He was the same God, then she realized that there were far more harnesses to let loose inside herself than she had ever dreamed of.

She slowly raised her hands until they were level with her shoulders, but she could force them no higher. What on earth was she going to do when they got to the heart of the service? This was only the third song! Church is church! Lizzie shuddered and braced herself to weather the storm.

Afiya softly brushed at her elbow and whispered in Lizzie's ear. "It's all right, *Jjajja*. You can sit if you want. No one will notice."

During the taking of the offering, a small group of secondary school girls performed a special song in English. Lizzie was captivated by the simple beauty of the voices and the sweet innocence in their faces. One in particular caused a resonance in her heart. Hers was the voice that stood out, the one rising above the others as she sang a solo in the center of the piece. Something about the timbre of her voice and the sweetness of her accent broke Lizzie's heart. As the sparsely filled collection baskets made the rounds, Lizzie listened to that voice and felt at peace. For the moment, no internal conflicts prevented her from letting the music enter her spirit and lift it up. When the final notes were sung, she stared hard at the young soloist and tried to memorize her features. She very much wanted to thank the singer later, if she had the chance.

Nana had explained to Lizzie that Ugandan church services were always conducted in two languages. English was regarded as the more prestigious of the two. It was, after all, the language of commerce and college, and in a country of multiple languages and countless dialects, it was the more universally understood and, therefore, the one more fitting for the things of God.

In practice, this meant there were always two people on the platform, each dressed in similar clothes, each clutching a microphone. The preacher, who spoke first, and in English, was immediately followed by the interpreter, who spoke in Luganda. It seemed to Lizzie to be an odd, sing-song battle as a few impassioned sentences at a time were tossed back and forth between them, with short pauses in between. It reminded her of a loud visit to the United Nations except, in this case, she could swear the young, dynamic translator was doing everything in his power to upstage the preacher. Left and right across the platform they went, the preacher making a strong point and then pausing, the translator coming right on his heels, making the same point more strongly. The preacher would make a joke. The translator would tell it better, or at least get a bigger laugh. Lizzie was mesmerized by the process and wondered who was winning the game.

The minister's name was Evangelist Peter, and he was a favorite replacement when Pastor Kajumba was away. Short and stocky, he had a wide, friendly face and a glistening, bald head. Dressed in a tight suit and bright tie, he was blessed with a voice both liquid and strong. An animated speaker, he kept his handheld mic tight to his mouth and refused to be confined to the podium, using the entire platform as he spoke. The interpreter, by contrast, was rail thin, with tight black hair and a goatee. Probably of college age, he seemed to vibrate with a barely coiled energy, even when he stood still.

Surreptitiously checking to her right, Lizzie felt confident, after a while, that Nana didn't much approve of the young man. But when she looked to her left, she noticed Afiya followed every wave of his hand, and fairly glowed when he spoke.

Apparently, Lizzie had let her attention to the content of the service lapse, because she was shocked to hear Evangelist Peter's rich voice mention her own name in a sentence that was amplified throughout the room!

"At great personal sacrifice, Mrs. Elizabeth Warton has recently joined our school family. She travelled all the way from the Eden Prairie of the United States to become our first director for the new library!"

Trapped in her folding chair in the middle of the row, Lizzie sat rigidly and held her breath. She willed the blood to stop pumping into her face. Already mortified, she braced herself to endure the translator's extravagant version in Luganda of what was already an exaggeration. She shot nails from her eyes into Nana at close range. Her friend simply smiled beatifically back as the interpreter did his thing. When the young man's voice and arms and hands had finally subsided, much to Lizzie's horror, Evangelist Peter's voice continued.

"As our sister, Nankunda Birungi, has reported, like Moses from the Bible, Mrs. Warton broke through the obstacles fashioned by the enemy and set our books free to fill the shelves for our students."

Lizzie's eyes locked onto the packed dirt floor beneath her feet. She wondered how fast she could tunnel under its surface. A tiny ant hurried by her shoe, intent on some task, oblivious to the greater world above him. For just an instant, she envied him.

A smattering of applause greeted Evangelist Peter's words. Once the translator completed his version, the entire congregation erupted in clapping, along with shouts of "*Ameena!*" and "Praise God!"

Lizzie practiced breathing techniques she hadn't employed since giving birth to Cecelia. As she prayed fervently for the end of the world, a small hand slipped under her elbow and gently tugged. She heard Afiya's eager voice near her ear, "*Jjajja*, you must stand. They want you to go to the front."

Lizzie turned her head and looked past Afiya toward the aisle. A kindly usher nodded at her, his hand extended. Somehow, Lizzie slid past people's knees on her way out of the row before she fully realized she had stood up. Moving in a compliant daze, she reached the front, unassisted, and mounted the two steps to join Evangelist Peter on the platform. He greeted her with a warm smile. Together, they faced the crowd. The interpreter hovered nearby but all Lizzie comprehended was how painfully self-conscious she felt.

Evangelist Peter casually waved for quiet. "Thank you. I am sure Sister Elizabeth appreciates your welcome, even if this much attention is probably outside her comfort zone. Right, sister?"

Lizzie gave him a big nod but then remembered she had to suffer through the translator's vigorous version of the same remarks, and felt stupid standing there, waiting to nod again. Hoping she was done now, Lizzie took a step away, but Evangelist Peter had other ideas.

"I want our sister to share some of her thoughts about what God is doing in her life, and in our school. Sister Elizabeth?"

He placed the mic firmly in her hands and stepped back while the Luganda speaker repeated his words. Finishing with a flourish, the translator moved right beside her, with an avid smile, ready to interpret her every word.

The microphone felt unexpectedly heavy in her hands, its metal surface slippery beneath her fingers. Unfamiliar with public speaking, Lizzie struggled to string together a few thoughts that might assemble into sentences, but failed. She remembered feeling this same way at the end of Jonathan's wake, when she stood to say a few words. On that day, she knew what she wanted to say; she had even practiced, but somehow the eyes of everyone looking up, and the kind expectancy in their faces, had driven away all her words. She had stood there like a fly on sticky paper, holding the mic and feeling inadequate. Her daughters had rescued her then, but no one could save her now.

She lifted the mic to her mouth, the way she had watched Evangelist Peter do. She spoke slowly. "Just before he died, my husband asked me to do something big. Something only I wanted to do. And coming here is what I chose." She paused.

The translator tried to jump in.

She instantly cleared her throat and waved a reproachful finger his way. "Not yet," she said.

He swallowed his words, looking decidedly unsettled.

Scanning the faces in the near rows, she caught Nana's eye and continued. "I want you to know that everything you have heard, so far, is an exaggeration." She nodded back at the stalled translator. "Now you can go ahead."

He pondered for a moment and then launched into a complex series of Luganda sentences, accompanied by large hand movements.

When he finished, Lizzie smirked and held her mic away from her mouth. "Did you actually say what I said?"

Like a child with something to hide, he whispered back, "Yes, lady." But then he scrunched his lips. "Maybe a little better."

Shaking her head, she haltingly went on. "I can't speak for God. All I know is that as long as I'm still breathing, He must have some work left for me to do. And what I've learned is to put one foot in front of the other, and keep walking."

She made a face at the young man. He commenced his translation like a colt let out of the barn. Lizzie used the time to hand the mic back to Evangelist Peter, indicating that she was done.

Peter nodded to her and waited for the Luganda to finish. Then, instead of speaking, he closed his eyes and bowed his head, letting the church grow still around him. Soon there were only a few scattered coughs, a child's brief question, and finally, nothing. Lizzie heard the breeze passing through the trees outside the windows, and the distant hum of traffic.

A deep sigh came from Evangelist Peter, followed by a groan as he brought the mic back up. "I am humbled. Truly. Our sister has said more in two sentences than I have managed in an hour."

Lizzie glanced at him in astonishment while the young man translated his words.

Peter moved to the edge of the platform and waved a large hand in an arc. "I want to open the altar. I want our Sister Elizabeth to pray for you. If you are facing obstacles, if you wonder what God wants you to do, if you just need reassurance, please come up now. Come and we will pray."

Lizzie's mind flickered. Wait! What? She had thought she was free. She had already pictured herself seated back on her folding chair, hidden from view. What does he mean, pray? Now? Me? Out loud? We don't do that at my church!

As the translator's voice crackled through the speakers, Lizzie saw rows begin to empty and people streaming toward the platform, fanning out for prayer. She rushed up to Evangelist Peter with a thousand questions poised on her lips. He simply placed a hand on her back and guided her down the steps and over to the first person on the far right side.

"Start here, sister, and move left. I will go to the other end."

With a quick turn, he vanished, leaving the young interpreter standing next to her. She faced the first person – a young woman with her hands held up and her eyes closed – without a clue in her head as to what to do. She had never in sixty-nine years of living felt more unworthy. Who am I? What do I know?

She placed a trembling hand on the woman's shoulder, not knowing how else to begin, and felt the living warmth beneath her palm. Squeezing her eyes shut, she desperately looked for a glimmer of direction, but saw only darkness.

When she opened them again, Nana stood beside her. "It is going to be okay, Lizzie. I know the routine. Do not worry, we do this all the time."

The translator tried to protest being upstaged. Nana dismissed him with a few flicks of her hand.

Halfway through the first wave of prayer seekers, Lizzie began to breathe normally again. With Nana's help, she developed a simple method that worked for her. Even though still uncomfortable, she had to admit that praying out loud for people was actually – well, almost, exhilarating. The experience was all new to her but she no longer feared it. After all, it was God's job, not hers, to come through for them.

Moving on to her next person, she recognized the sweet face of the young soloist. She smiled at the girl and turned to Nana. "Ask her name."

The girl answered before Birungi could speak. "Mirembe. My name is Mirembe."

Lizzie repeated it. "*Mir-em´-bee*? Did I say it right?"

The girl nodded.

Lizzie took her hands. "Mirembe, I want to tell you how much I loved your singing. It was like being in heaven. Really."

The girl dropped her head in shyness. "Thank you, lady."

"You're welcome. Now, what do you want prayer for, sweetheart?"

Looking up again, Mirembe took a shuddering breath and struggled to speak. "My life is lie. But I have no choice. Truth will make worse. Pray so I can do what you do, keep walking. Pray for my brother so he be safe."

Lizzie squeezed her hands. "I'm so sorry. Can you help me understand better? How can I help? How is your brother in danger?"

The girl shook her head, refusing to say more.

Nana gently probed in Luganda. After a few questions and answers she turned a troubled face to Lizzie and shook her head. "Nothing different. She has said what she can say. Many girls in our country must keep secrets. Just pray as she asked."

Lizzie did. She couldn't recall what words she used, but she remembered the girl's arms around her waist and the way she had melted against her chest before slipping away.

The rest of the service was a blur of faces and voices until Nana led her to rejoin Afiya near the church's outside door. Lizzie felt drained but at peace with herself. The sanctuary was nearly empty by then, and she patiently allowed Birungi to fuss with her hair and face.

"Don't worry how I look, Nana. I'm sure the boys at Safe Haven won't notice, anyway."

"First impressions are important. No matter who it is."

"Fine." She frowned. "You're the expert."

Afiya burst into giggles. "I never know what to expect from you, *Jjajja*."

"You and me both, kiddo."

"Kiddo?"

"It's slang...it's, ah, a funny word that means a young person. It's like the word 'kid' but you add an 'o' to make it sound funny. Kiddo. You see?"

Afiya nodded uncertainly. "Kiddo...kiddo. I like it."

Nana shaped Lizzie's hair with a few final taps and pats. "Well, that is the best I can do, *kiddo*. Let's go out and meet Jedediah. I am sure he is wondering where we are."

TWENTY-FIVE

Lunch at the Boys' House

The main road was jammed and traffic crawled. All their windows were down since the car's AC unit hadn't run in a decade, but there wasn't the breath of a breeze, anyway. What a city, Lizzie thought. Even on a Sunday afternoon, no one can go anywhere fast.

Jedediah casually announced he knew a quicker way and abruptly turned, without signaling. The car bounced onto a narrow, water-rutted side road, weaving between parked pickups, *cha'pati* vendors and a garishly painted cell phone shack.

Rocked against each other in the cramped backseat, Mrs. Birungi and Afiya carried on their light conversation as if nothing unusual was happening. Lizzie, in the front passenger side, stared forward in cold terror. Her hands gripped the vinyl seat cushion beneath her with all the strength in her fingers.

Jedediah cheerfully beeped the horn and swerved just in time to avoid perilously overloaded bicycles and careless pedestrians. Lizzie spied glimpses of other lives within the walled backyards that blinked by inches away from her side window. She caught fleeting images of tiny gardens, piles of broken bricks, running chickens and bleating goats.

By the time the little car bumped back onto another asphalt

road and shouldered its way into another traffic stream, Lizzie's mouth was bone dry. Her eyes ached from staring without blinking.

Jedediah glanced at her. "Not much farther. You okay?"

"Yes." Her voice sounded as tight as a violin string. "Fine."

He braked and veered to avoid a taxi. "Meg was so pleased you could join us." He gunned the accelerator again. "And the boys enjoy visitors."

"That's nice." She cleared her throat and attempted to swallow. "What's...what's for lunch?"

"Oh, you never know," he replied affably. "Something good, I'm sure. Here we are."

Lizzie saw a walled house with an old green car gate across a cracked driveway. The rusty gate opened as they turned in, and she thought she heard singing in accented English. The two boys handling the gates pulled them wide. She saw the rest of the boys gathered in front of their porch, singing and dancing to hand drums.

"I'm so excited, on top of the mountain,

I feel joy down in my heart,

That's why I'm singing and dancing.

You are welcome,

We love you, visitors.

You are welcome,

We love you, visitors."

The boys, of varying ages and dressed in a variety of outfits, smiled brightly. They were really getting into the dancing. Everyone made synchronized hand motions that accompanied the lyrics. Outbursts of laughter revealed that not everyone had practiced.

As Lizzie, Nana and Afiya climbed out of the car, the volume increased. With a big grin, one of the older boys stepped forward to sing alone.

"My name is Matthew,

I feel joy down in my heart,

That's why I'm singing and dancing.

You are welcome,

I love you, visitors.

You are welcome,

I love you, visitors."

The whole group picked up the song again from the beginning as Matthew stepped back.

"I'm so excited, on top of the mountain…"

Lizzie noticed that Nana and Afiya automatically moved to the drumbeats with a natural grace, centered in their hips and knees, she couldn't hope to imitate. She tapped a foot and softly clapped her hands to the drums, doing her best to join in.

Nana leaned close to her. "This is very African, even though the words are in English. It is a welcome song. Every part of our life has a song and a dance." She nudged against Lizzie's hip. "Try to let go, Lizzie. Let go."

Lizzie did try. Standing there in the sun, next to the car, with the drums pounding, she tried to let go of her worries about decorum, or age, or white, or black, or gender. She began to surrender to the rhythms of the moment. She kept her eyes on the happy faces of these boys welcoming her to their home. Their *home*! These were street boys, homeless boys, lost boys, until they'd found their way here. Most had no home at all, until this one. How lavish of them to share something that precious with her, she thought. That's when her wide hips began to move and respond to the drums, as if they'd known what to do all along but had just been waiting until now.

A small boy, encouraged by Auntie Meg, stepped proudly forward and took the next solo verse. His high-pitched voice was jumpy and filled with the heady glee of being the center of attention.

"My name is Anthony,

I feel joy down in my heart,

That's why I'm singing and dancing.

You are welcome,

I...I..."

His small voice faltered, lost in the verse. The group instantly swept in to bail him out, effortlessly completing his words.

"I love you, visitors.

You are welcome,

I love you, visitors."

The boy looked embarrassed but he grinned along with the rest of the boys as he stepped back to his place.

Everyone belted out the main chorus again.

"I'm so excited, on top of the mountain..."

❧

Before the meal was served, Uncle Kabuye Phillips, the house father, gave Lizzie a private tour of their brick and mud home. He highlighted the many improvements they had built themselves and pointed out the rows of bunkbeds that a U.S. church had donated. At the foot of each bed sat a simple box with a clasp and a lock. These held each boy's personal treasures and school books – only the boy who used that bed had the key. Uncle Kabuye explained that everyone worked together at Safe Haven, sharing chores, learning to be a family, but the boys were used to the street, and stealing was a hard habit to break. Life was better here, he told her, but here they also had school to attend, and responsibilities. Sometimes that was too much for them.

"Once their bellies are full, life can grow boring. The street sings to them again." Standing in one of the bedrooms, Uncle Kabuye placed a flat hand on an upper bunk, smoothing the covers. "They miss the petrol. They remember the freedom."

Lizzie didn't understand. "Petrol?"

"In your country, you say *huffing*. Here we say *okunussa*. Breathing petrol fumes, or glue, or other things makes you high. Makes you forget hunger. Forget everything. Most street boys are *omuyagga* – *huffers*."

Lizzie remembered Dembe's bottle and the smell of gasoline. "But they were never free on the street."

"No. But when you are no longer hungry, the past feels like freedom."

"Have you lost many?"

"Some. And some we have sent back."

"Then, what?"

"Once they return to the street, we do not take them back."

"Never?" The word came out higher than she meant it to be.

He smiled and softened his voice. "*Almost* never. Our boys have to know that we are serious here. Life is serious."

"But they're children! It's not their fault."

Uncle Kabuye, short in stature and compact, looked at her with dark, expressive eyes. "Every boy is different. You are *Jjajja*; you know this." He patted her arm. "We save as many as we can, but if they refuse to change…" He turned his hands palm up and empty.

Lizzie gazed beyond him at an angled sunbeam streaming through a window between the bunks. "Did you know Dembe?"

Uncle Kabuye sighed. His hands ceased their movements. "Of course. We all knew Dembe."

Settling onto the edge of a lower bunk, she looked firmly up at the house father. "He's important to me. I want to know what happened."

"There are many boys, Mrs. Warton. He is just one more."

"I know. But he's the one who saved me. He's *my* boy – the one *I'm* supposed to save."

The house father's expression was hard to read. "Aunt Meg warned me that you might ask about him."

"What did she say?"

Uncle Kabuye looked uncomfortable. "That I could do as I wished."

"Which means?"

"I can tell you the truth, or tell you nothing."

Lizzie pondered this before replying, "What do you wish to do?"

❧

Finished with her meal, Lizzie sat flanked by the three youngest Safe Haven boys, the same ones she had met at Meg's house on her first morning – Gwandoya, Mukiibi and Waloga. Uncle Kabuye interpreted an amusing conversation between the small boys and her. They sat outside, in the courtyard, at a table made from planks of plywood held up by sawhorses. Since there was a limited number of plastic chairs, many of the boys had casually tucked blocks of wood or boxes under themselves at other makeshift tables. Lacking even that, a number of boys had spread out in laughing clumps along the porch steps, balancing the plastic plates on their laps. A long-haired dog of mixed bloodlines made his nosey rounds among the eaters, dispersing smiles and licks for handouts.

The food was simple. Meg had guided her gang of boy cooks to prepare grilled chicken, cassava root, rice and beans, *matoke* and *cha 'pati*. The meal was served as a casual buffet, with guests going first, since the chicken was in shorter supply.

Later, Lizzie found Meg outside at the back of the house. She was overseeing the talkative cleanup crews washing plastic ware in bins of water. Extra jerry cans sat nearby. In Lizzie's experience, boys and bins of water were always a volatile combination.

As soon as Meg spotted her, she quickly gathered Lizzie's arm into both of hers and cheerfully pulled her away from the splash zone. "Guests aren't allowed back here, Lizzie."

"Oh? I didn't see a sign."

Meg grinned as she strolled beside her. "It's understood." She grabbed a tall stick leaning against the wall. "No one should watch how sausage is made and no one should see how Ugandan boys do dishes."

They laughed together like old friends. Meg guided her along the border wall, tapping the stick against the ground. They bent their heads to pass beneath the lower branches of a stunning tree covered in orange trumpet-shaped flowers. Meg paused to look at the foliage above her before she rested her back against the grainy grey bark of the trunk. "This is one of my *give-me-a-break* places when I'm at the boys' house." Smiling, she slowly breathed in and sighed.

Lizzie stared up into the graceful limbs of the tree, slowly rotating her view as she studied the clustered blossoms at the end of every branch. She fingered the green oval leaves just above her, enjoying the shade. "It's nice here. What kind of tree is this?"

"They call it an African Tulip Tree." Meg laughed. "The most important thing about it is that everyone knows to leave me alone when I'm here."

Lizzie chuckled. "Perfect." She was enjoying the breeze when she noticed two small buckets sitting on the ground on either side of the trunk. A waxy solid filled each one. "What's in the buckets?"

Meg looked down. "Oh. Paraffin. Snakes don't like the smell. Keeps them out of the tree."

"What?"

Meg smiled at Lizzie's wide eyes. "Don't panic. I've not seen one up there, yet."

Lizzie rapidly searched the thick branches above her. When her head brushed a leaf, she jerked back. Nervous now, she turned in a tight circle, studying the uneven ground near her feet. "Is that what the stick's for?"

Meg nodded calmly. "Relax. We have a whole house full of boys. They love killing snakes." She grinned playfully. "It's what boys are for."

Lizzie glared at her. She felt goose bumps creeping across her shoulders and down her arms. She couldn't help but clench her toes inside her shoes. "This isn't funny, Meg."

Meg managed a penitent expression. "I didn't mean to make a joke of it. We're fine. Trust me."

Lizzie made a valiant effort to breathe normally. "Sorry. Of course there's snakes here, it's…it's tropical. I…I just forgot, is all."

Meg stood up from the trunk and shook her head. "Okay, then! Let's shake this off and start over, shall we?"

Lizzie braced herself. "Yes. Let's."

"I take it that Uncle Kabuye gave you the grand tour?"

"Yes. He was quite thorough."

"Uh-huh. What did he tell you?"

"Everything." Lizzie caught Meg's eyes. "You knew I'd ask."

Meg nodded. "What do you think now?"

"Something doesn't make sense."

"What do you mean?"

Lizzie folded her arms. "I know about the copper pipes, Meg."

Meg's voice was carefully neutral. "Oh."

"Yes. That secret has been expanded by one. But it puzzles me. You have this brilliant boy, doing well in school, who can fix any-thing, but won't stop stealing. Why?"

"Maybe there's not a why."

Unfolding her arms, Lizzie snapped off a leaf in irritation. "I know enough about boys to know there's a piece missing." It was only after the leaf was in her hand that she remembered about snakes and furtively checked the nearby branches.

"American boys."

"What?"

"You know about American boys."

Lizzie twirled the tree leaf in her hand, turning it from the dark green top side to the pale green bottom side, back and forth. "No. I mean *any* boys. Any good boys."

"Are you still sure Dembe's one of those?"

Lizzie let the leaf drop to the ground. "Aren't you?"

Meg didn't answer. Instead, Lizzie watched her stare off at the boys running around the house. Clearly, the dish washing was finished. The colorful plates and cups were drying in the sun. Meg's eyes shifted toward the front of the house, where Lizzie could see Jedediah talking with Nana and Afiya. It seemed a number of interested boys hovered there. After a bit, Meg turned back and brought her eyes to Lizzie.

"Kabuye told you about the thefts from the boys' footlockers? And the backpacks? And from the house?"

"Yes."

"I was the one who believed Dembe then. And he told you about Dembe even stealing *my* phone?"

"Yes."

"I believed him then, too. He talked me into letting him help look for it! But in the end, he was lying – about everything. Just like at the school." She lowered her eyes. "He steals and lies and can't stop. And that's the end of it." She looked up again. "I still care about him, but I can't have him back here anymore."

Lizzie took her glasses off and handed them to Meg. "Look at these."

Perplexed, Meg took them. "They were the first thing I noticed when you arrived. Mrs. Birungi told us the story of Owino

Market. Amazing!" She looked up. "Didn't I say you were made for this place?"

Lizzie's face remained unchanged. "These didn't come from Owino. They're the same broken pair I was looking for here."

"These?" Meg looked more closely at the beautiful frames. "These are the ones you lost?"

"They were never lost. They were...*borrowed*. Dembe repaired them and secretly returned them to me."

Meg gently handed the eyewear back and shook her head. "He can't help himself. He has to fix things. That's all it means. You're chasing shadows."

"Maybe you're right. But I want to talk to Musaazi."

"About the glasses?"

Lizzie nodded. "He's been avoiding me."

"Oh. So that's why he was so helpful in the kitchen, and volunteered for trash detail. I wondered."

"Right. Boys."

"What do you hope to learn? Musaazi's a tough nut to crack."

"Maybe nothing. But I have to try." Her lips formed a firm line. "I won't give up."

Meg snorted. "That was funny – that look! The more I know you, the more I think of my mother." Her eyes floated up into the tree above her. "We used to go round and round on things, but there was no changing her mind either. Once she had the bit in her mouth, that woman was gonna keep pullin', no matter what." She shot Lizzie a crooked smile. "I love stubborn women."

Lizzie blinked and cocked her head. "I don't know whether to feel pleased or convicted."

"Yeah. Bein' stubborn isn't exactly on the list of virtues, that's for sure. But you know what? I have an idea."

Lizzie waited.

Meg carefully reached up into the center of a flower cluster and pulled free a couple of the long, claw-like buds. She rolled them around in her hand, as if to weigh them. "I'm thinking I should send Ogwambi along with Musaazi to talk to you."

"Who is Ogwambi?"

"The third member of the copper pipe heist." She made a sour expression. "Since you know the story, you know that all three of our *clever* students were expelled: first Dembe, then Musaazi, and Ogwambi's number three."

"Now I recall the name. Mrs. Birungi told me. Why would he be any help?"

"Because you're not the only one who knows about boys. Ogwambi looks tough, but he's not; he's kind. Wants to please. From the country. And he's a talker. He's Musaazi's friend, but not as... smooth. And nowhere near as good at keeping secrets. But very good at killing snakes." She smirked. "And did I mention, stubborn?"

She selected one of the flower buds and held it between her thumb and first finger. "Watch."

Meg squeezed the back of the brown bud. In a sudden hiss of released pressure, a tight stream of clear nectar shot from the tip and sailed away in an arc, watering the grass ten feet away.

Lizzie puffed out a sudden breath. "It's like a squirt gun!"

"Exactly. The boys periodically raid my tree and have nectar squirt fights. It's wild. And you'd never expect it by just looking at the buds. Ogwambi may be just the leak you're looking for. If you put him under the right pressure, who knows what'll come out of him?"

◈

"What do you think of my glasses, Musaazi?"

He glanced fleetingly at her. "They are nice, lady."

The two boys and Lizzie were gathered beside a sturdy young tree, near the clotheslines. Its slender trunk was scuffed from play, the lower limbs stripped bare of leaves. A worn out car tire hung on a broken branch. Old logs had been left beneath the tree, forming a rough triangle. Lizzie sat on one log and Musaazi and Ogwambi straddled an adjacent one.

"You know these are the very same glasses you took from my vest, right?"

Musaazi's face gave nothing away even as he hunched his shoulders and nodded.

"And I know why you lied about it," she continued. "And how you got my passport and the cash. By the way, I never told anyone about the hands at my window."

Ogwambi followed the exchange with growing anxiety. Lizzie noted that one of his eyes didn't track with the other but had a tendency to turn in toward his nose. His wide face was marred by a pair of bumpy scars curving across the length of his left cheek. Without Meg's comments, she might have been put off by him.

Lizzie patiently waited and watched without saying anything further.

Ogwambi began to fidget. He spoke quickly in Luganda to Musaazi. "What? You stole the *muzungu's* glasses?"

Musaazi looked sharply at him. "No!"

"But she said you lied and…"

"They were broken. I didn't steal. Dembe wanted to fix them." Musaazi was exasperated. "You don't need to know about any of this!"

"Then why did Auntie Meg send me here?"

"Who knows? Stay out of it! Stop talking!"

When there was a pause in the bickering, Lizzie chimed in. "Boys, I asked to meet with you because I was told you were Dembe's friends."

Ogwambi looked insulted. "We *are* his friends. His best friends!"

Musaazi scowled and barked in Luganda. "Keep your mouth closed!"

Ogwambi's chin set. He prepared to reply with something harsh.

Lizzie cut him off. "Look, I know you both helped Dembe steal the copper pipes. Okay?"

They stared at her. She had their undivided attention now.

"Yes, I know all about it. I stood in one of the pipe rooms there. I even touched the PVC that Dembe put in their place. You sold Pastor Kajumba's pipes."

Ogwambi's face hardened. His calloused hands fluttered in agitation. She saw old scarring up and down the backs of his fingers. "We didn't do it for the money," he blurted out.

Musaazi hissed at him. Ogwambi closed his mouth but glowered. Musaazi faced Lizzie and sighed. "What do you want from us?"

"I want to know why. Why did Dembe start stealing at school? Why did he keep stealing here at Safe Haven? If it wasn't for the money, then why?"

Musaazi shook his head. "We cannot tell you."

Lizzie tried a different tack. "So, you know why, but you won't say?"

Musaazi fell silent. Ogwambi struggled to keep quiet but just couldn't. "We swore we would never say."

Musaazi growled at him.

Lizzie tried to soothe over the moment, hoping to wheedle more information. "I'm not trying to trick you. I only want to help Dembe. Can't you understand that?"

Musaazi slid forward on the log, his face conflicted, his eyes focused on Lizzie's feet. "When we were on the street, lady, Dembe took care of us. He was *makanika* – a fixer of things. Shopkeepers would pay. We were brothers. We protected each other. When we came to Safe Haven, our family got bigger. Last year, Uncle Jed found that my *Jjajja* still lived. He took me there. She had thought she was the last, and that I was long dead. Now, she has died."

His eyes moved up to meet hers with an unwavering look. "Here is all the family I have. And Dembe is first, over all. You say you care. But lady, you are *muzungu*. Here for a moment and then gone. Can you understand?"

To Lizzie, his words struck her like physical blows. She felt such a personal connection with Dembe, she had forgotten the vast separation that actually lay between them. Of course, they wouldn't confide in her. How could they? She was just a stupid old privileged white woman, and she would soon vanish from their lives like the morning mist.

Ogwambi suddenly spoke to Musaazi in a rush of Luganda. "But can't we tell her something? Something that doesn't break our promise?"

"We can't. It's all part of what we swore not to say."

"We can say the name of the school. We can say her name. Those aren't actually a part of our promise."

"It's too dangerous. Don't even think about it."

"The *Jjajja* wants to help. Maybe she can."

Musaazi looked hard at Ogwambi. "She's not *jjajja*. She's *muzungu*."

"Boys?" Lizzie's voice sounded calm, even though her heart felt leaden in her chest. "I'm right here. And I don't speak your language. Tell me what you're saying."

Musaazi dug his thumbnail into the old log, picking off tiny pieces of bark. "I am sorry, lady. We cannot say to you what Dembe told us not to say."

Lizzie decided she only had one card left. "But what if he's in danger? What, then?"

Ogwambi reacted first. "What kind of danger?"

Musaazi remained controlled. "The street is always dangerous, lady."

Lizzie lowered her voice and leaned closer to them. "I will tell you a secret no one knows – not Auntie Meg, not Uncle Jed, not... not even your government. Can I trust you?"

They both nodded.

At least I have their ears, she told herself. "Do you know about the bomb that went off in the market yesterday?"

Ogwambi replied with interest. "Yes, everyone knows. It was on the news. Six dead. Many more injured."

Musaazi added, "*New Vision* had photos on the front page. We all read it before church."

Lizzie pushed on. "What did they say?"

"Some terrorist from South Sudan blew himself up," Musaazi replied. "They want our army to stay away from their border."

Ogwambi looked at Lizzie suspiciously. "Why, lady? What do you know?"

"I was there," she answered. "I saw the bomber running. He wasn't from Sudan. He was just a street boy, younger than you." They listened closely. Lizzie paused for a second to build tension. "And Dembe was also there. He told me the boy was tricked by rebels from Sudan."

Both boys hung on her every word.

"Dembe thought he knew a way to stop the bomb, but someone set it off before he could help."

Musaazi took a moment to consider. "How did *you* survive?"

"Dembe saved me." Lizzie thrust her hands toward the dirt. "He shoved me behind a building before the bomb went off. Later, I saw the fires and the injured."

"Was he okay?" asked Ogwambi.

Lizzie nodded. "I think so. He told me to run away before the army came. He went to find the other boys. I don't know anything after that."

Musaazi turned to Ogwambi and spat something urgent in Luganda. Ogwambi agreed and rattled back a few words.

Musaazi looked at Lizzie. "Is this the danger you mean?"

"Yes. Help me find a way to bring him back. He saved my life, twice. I know you see me as a *muzungu* and a woman, but I owe him a debt, the same as you do. To me, he's my own family."

Both boys looked at her with sober faces. No one was ready to speak.

A sudden commotion of voices interrupted them. Lizzie and the boys looked up. The laughing and talking grew louder as an excited group of boys, followed by Mrs. Birungi, Afiya and Uncle Jed, came around the house and encircled their tree. Everyone talked at once. Boys quickly grabbed places on the logs and sat down. A few immediately climbed into the tree, sitting astride the tire.

Spotting Lizzie, Nana waved at everyone to quiet down. "Lizzie! There you are! We were looking for you. I have such exciting news!"

Lizzie found it hard to shift emotional gears so abruptly. Part of her was frustrated to be stopped just when she thought she was getting somewhere. But another part looked around at the gleeful faces and wondered what this news could be. She put on a smile and extended her hands in an open question. "So, tell me, Nana. What news?"

Birungi circled the log and took one of Lizzie's hands. "First, I told them all the story of your victory at customs."

"Why do you keep doing this to me?"

"People should know. It gives them hope."

Lizzie shook her hand free and covered her face. "Stop! I'm sure you exaggerated again." She looked up. "I told you I barely remember what I said."

Nana ignored her. "Please listen. Tomorrow, when Wasswa brings his trucks..."

Lizzie scoffed, "*If* he brings his trucks."

"He has to. You told him."

"No. I asked Rokani to ask him. That's all. You were there."

Nana just shook her head, the way she might to discourage a pesky fly. "Fine, I will call them. But, when they show up, Uncle Jed has agreed to let the older Safe Haven boys be our workers, to load and unload the books!"

"What?"

"Yes! It can be a great work project for them. We need the help. Did you think you and I were going to lift the boxes? And I can pay them from our money."

"Pay them?" Lizzie hated repeating things. She sounded like a brainless echo, but she couldn't help herself.

Nana frowned at her. "I was sure it would be okay. After all, you are paying Wasswa for the trucks."

"Yes...but..." Her mind struggled to keep up. "Aren't you being awfully free with *my* money?"

Nana sat beside her on the log and lowered her voice. "It is not, actually, your money anymore."

"How do you figure?"

She smiled sweetly. "Well, it *was* your money when you gave it to Wasswa at the warehouse. But when God gave it back to us, I think it became *our* money."

Lizzie's mouth dropped open. Her mind slowly chewed through the logic. She closed her mouth, shook her head, and gave Nana a begrudging smile. "Just who is the *muyaye* now?"

⌁

To: davidwarton27x@centurylink.net; joanjohnson@yahoo.com; ceceliawarton99@hotmail.com
From: nankundabirungi@wobulezischool.com
Subj: Time is flying

I know it's been awhile. Things are just so hectic here, it's hard to find time. The good news is my body finally knows what time it is! Miss all of you!

Thanks for your e-mails. I'm glad Will and Sandy are doing so well in school. Yes, I think piano lessons are a great idea. The sooner the better — as long as they want to.

I got the cash! It's already come in handy. Thanks David!

There were some problems recently but we worked them all out. I don't know if I told you that those books donated by the Austin, TX schools were stuck in some local government customs baloney. Not anymore!!

Oh, you'll probably want to know that I went to church here. Boy, it's a LOT different than I'm used to. I even had to say a few words, since I was a visitor. (Ugh!) It's strange but they preach in English and then instantly interpret into Luganda (that's one of their main languages). When I said my words there was an interpreter for me too! (It felt like the UN, or something.) Their services are a lot longer and more energetic than ours are, but it all worked out for the best.

After church we had lunch at a home for street boys (I'll explain about them when I'm home). They sang and danced a welcome song when we arrived. It was so unexpected! You know me, I got all emotional. The food was interesting – the boys helped to cook it.

Tell the grandkids there's a tree here with buds that you can squeeze and shoot liquid from, like a squirt gun. Really. I shot one. It went a long ways.

So much more to tell you, but I have to sleep now.

Love you all,
Grandma XXOO

TWENTY-SIX

A Load of Books

The Mitsubishi truck roared up to the front of the school library, a tattered tarp flapping over the bed, and then slid to a long shuddering stop. Orange road dust that had been patiently chasing behind the wheels suddenly caught up, swallowing the cab whole. Wasswa jumped down to the ground, slamming the door behind him.

With a careful smile pasted across her lips, Lizzie watched the performance from the front step of the library. She searched behind the truck for a smaller pickup she expected to be following. After a moment, she was rewarded with the sparkle of the sun off a windshield as a white pickup entered the school road. Turning back, she observed Wasswa's puffy, red-eyed face. He looked as if he'd gotten little sleep lately.

The shopkeeper bellowed as he walked up to her. "How did you ever talk my worthless brother into letting you use our trucks to move your books?"

Lizzie remained unruffled. "I didn't. Your brother simply said he would talk to you." Dressed in work clothes – pants, tie-shoes and a short sleeved shirt – Lizzie looked beyond the fuming man to evaluate his truck. The twenty foot bed was open on top, but three foot high, solid metal panels lined the sides. Slots in the side panels supported a heavy metal frame of poles and crosspieces that completely enclosed the cargo area. If needed, a canvas tarp could be pulled over it and cinched to the frame. She noted the poorly lashed and frayed tarp sagging at the front of the frame and clucked to herself. Good thing it's not raining.

"He did!" Wasswa wanted to regain her attention. "He talked to me. But you left me no choice. How could I refuse?"

Lizzie walked out toward the road. "Whatever do you mean?"

Wasswa kept right beside her, his feet kicking peevishly at the dirt, his hands swirling. "You know exactly what I mean." He shook his head at the sky. "I will never again call myself a *muyaye*! Really! I had no idea what that word meant until I met you!"

The white Isuzu pickup pulled up behind the big truck and came to a slow, nearly dustless stop. Lizzie saw Rokani's weary face peer out at her. He raised two limp fingers off the wheel in greeting. Otherwise, he didn't move.

Lizzie circled Wasswa's truck and made a face. "What's that smell?" She peeked through cracks in the side slats into the cargo area. "And why is all that filthy straw in there?"

Wasswa put hands on his hips and scowled. "Don't start on me! We transport things. Many things. A truck carries what you put in it. You wanted a truck. This is a truck. You get what you pay for."

"I thought you were a clothing vendor. This smells like animals! My books can't be placed in here!"

Wasswa was about to launch into another tirade when a car horn beeped rapidly. They both looked up. Jedediah's small vehicle swung into a leveled area beside the library. His open windows were crammed with smiling faces. Right behind him, a taxi van followed with more boys excitedly waving their brown arms out the dirty windows.

Wasswa shook his head. "What is all this now? More of your tricks?"

Lizzie nodded fondly at the boys. "No. Actually this was Mrs. Birungi's idea. These are your workers, my dear Mr. Salongo." She smiled serenely at him. "Unless you and your *worthless* brother insist on doing all the lifting by yourselves."

Wasswa quietly walked back toward the cab of his truck with his head down while Lizzie cheerfully welcomed Jedediah and his Safe Haven boys.

⋘

The *Super Jet Car Wash* sign split in half when its car gate was opened and, as far as Lizzie could tell, that was the only part of the operation that was, even remotely, super. She decided that all you needed to create a car wash business in Uganda was an empty lot, a couple of water storage tanks on stilts, lots of leaky hoses and an army of young men slinging buckets and rags. Oh, and a few gas-powered portable pumps to propel hand sprayers didn't hurt, she noted, plus they added to the general wet mayhem of the place.

The Safe Haven boys were ecstatic over the potentials for water and soap. Lizzie was already wet, and Wasswa stolidly refused to leave his cab. The sudden snarl of pumps and the roar of the water jets caused Lizzie to duck her head, but not before the overspray covered her glasses in droplets. Busy workers funneled the straw and debris out of the truck with wide swaths of water from the high powered nozzles. Everything loose inside the cargo space flew out the back and onto the crumbling asphalt of the car wash lot. Lizzie hurriedly retreated beyond the spray, wiping her glasses with the front corner of her shirt. Nearby, she heard something make a metallic clink against the ground and then rattle along, pushed by the water. One of the younger boys heard it, too, and quickly felt along the cracks with his nimble fingers. Finding something, he wiped it against his leg, and then ran up to Lizzie to show her. It was a flat piece of metal, bent over itself into a U-shaped clip. At the open end of the "U" she saw holes. When she tipped the flat sides in the sun, there appeared to be the worn indentations of numbers or lettering, which she couldn't decipher, even squinting through the bottom sections of her trifocals. She handed it back and asked the boy what he thought it was.

He shook his head. "Maybe something to do with animals." He waved an arm at Ogwambi. "He knows. He is country."

Ogwambi was dripping wet and throwing a rag at someone when the young boy finally got his attention. He held up the clip. Lizzie watched Ogwambi slide it over his ear and make a squeezing gesture with his other hand. He suddenly shook his large head and made snorting noises at the younger boy, chasing him back to Lizzie. They both laughed.

"It's a tag." Ogwambi dropped the clip back into her hand. "A pig tag. Farmers fix it to a pig ear with a...a..."

"A rivet?"

He thought about the word and then nodded. "Okay. Maybe. Metal. Small rivet."

Lizzie stared at the shiny tag in her hand and pictured it riveted to her ear. Ouch!

"A pig? Really?"

Ogwambi motioned at the truck with his head. "Someone was hauling pigs. No wonder it stinks. I only like to eat pigs."

Jed called Ogwambi to help wash the pickup, and he hurried off. Lizzie slipped the tag into a pocket and hoped her books didn't end up smelling like pigs.

❧

The wind ruffled Lizzie's hair and she laughed aloud at the sheer joy of it. For once, the hard dirt road ahead was clear of cars. They barreled along, up and down a set of hills. From her new vantage point, standing on the bed and peering over the top of the truck cab, the land around her looked picturesque. She gazed to her right and drank in the soft hills with dark green foliage rolling to a cloud-ringed blue sky. Between the trees, orange tiled roofs and brown walls dotted the hillsides. Tracking the view as the truck hurtled down the road, she thought the hills almost looked the way she imagined Tuscany's hills to look – or at least the way Ruthie described them after her friend's wine tour to Italy. What would Ruthie say now, if she could see her? Lizzie braced her legs as the fast-moving truck shook. She'd probably snort some wine up her nose in shock, Lizzie thought.

The truck swerved to minimize a bump and all the boys swayed in sync with her. Inside, she squealed with glee. Look at me! I'm sixty-nine and I'm riding in the back of a speeding truck, hanging onto metal poles! She loved it. What had taken her so long? She always wanted to do it, but she feared worrying her parents, or teachers, or somebody. Later, she feared what Jonathan would think, and then she worried that it might be illegal anyway. But not here! Not now!

When she scrambled into the back with the boys after the car wash, Wasswa had looked at her with horror through the cab's small rear window. She had wiggled her fingers back at him in reply, then ignored him. Jedediah, who rode behind in the pickup with Rokani, had simply smiled knowingly and given her an appreciative wave.

Now, the truck slowed abruptly as it crested a hill. Part of the reason for the scarcity of traffic became clear. Ahead, in the gentle dip between hills, lines of cars and taxi vans were tightly parked on both sides of the road, all the way up to the next crest, and beyond. Some of the Jeeps had pulled deep into the tall grass to park, leaving room for others. An army of *boda-bodas* and bikes leaned against the trunks of trees. The road was left with only a torturously tight single lane in the middle for through traffic.

As Wasswa slowed and eased his way, driving in the center and watching his side mirrors, Lizzie began to hear drums and singing. Looking off to the left, she saw the tops of large white tents and the heads of a multitude of people. Crowds of Ugandans, dressed in their best clothes, filled up all the spaces between the trees and the houses. They utterly overwhelmed the open area beneath the tents. As the truck crawled by, Lizzie spotted colorful *Gomesi* and formal dresses in the gathering, along with fancy hats and feathers, suit-coats and bright shirts. Guests spilled out to the edges of the road, more people continually arriving. The fragrance of roasting pork and beef wafted over the truck, along with other aromas that Lizzie's nose couldn't identify. She carefully shifted to that side of the truck, moving hand-over-hand along the pipes like a nervous child on a playground apparatus.

The boys made room for her, and she asked about the activity. "Is this a wedding?"

Musaazi shook his head. "Introduction ceremony. Weddings are smaller."

Lizzie looked back, puzzled. "Really? Bigger than a wedding?"

All the boys nodded enthusiastically, some hanging carelessly over the side rail.

Musaazi continued, "This is first time families meet. Groom must give good gifts. There is big banquet with free food and free drink. Everyone comes. They eat and play and see the couple."

Ogwambi closed his eyes and inhaled the delicious smells. "Weddings are nothing like this."

The rest of the trip proved far less eventful. Soon, they turned into the industrial area, the paved road filled with trucks and traffic, as well as the ongoing presence of the military. Lizzie recognized the bonded warehouse as they pulled into the driveway. The same guard with pink epaulettes waved them through and yanked the gates wide, obviously alerted to their arrival. Lizzie thought she caught a glimpse of one of the customs agents in the shadows, walking away, but she couldn't be sure. She was glad Wasswa remembered the way to the right building since the details of that incident had grown dim in her mind. She only realized they had backed up to the opened shipping container when the truck stopped and the boys streamed over the back. Calmly crossing the bed, she waited until Wasswa dropped the tailgate before crouching and extending her hand to let him help her down to the ground.

⤚

The industrial shrink wrap around the book boxes popped open as Wasswa slid his keen knife halfway down the front. Peeling back the layers of clinging plastic, this time he slit the thick covering all the way to the wooden palette at the base, making a harsh hissing sound. Around him, revealed within the dim light, additional palettes of sealed boxes filled the container. He sheathed his knife with a practiced move and slid the top box off a stack. Turning, he handed it to a Safe Haven boy. "Be careful," he whispered. "It's filled with gold."

The boy smiled and took a few steps to hand it off to another young worker. "Diamonds. Watch out."

The line of boys snaked out from the shipping container and over to the back of the truck. There, balanced on piled palettes, boys hefted the boxes up to squatting youngsters inside the truck. These handed them off to others until they reached Rokani, who carefully stacked them on the cargo bed. The truck was already more than half filled.

Jedediah and Lizzie stood off to the side in shade from the warehouse wall, watching the progress. The boys laughed even though their skin shone with sweat. Lizzie heard Wasswa's voice singing in Luganda from inside the container unit.

Jedediah grinned. "Your man, Wasswa, is very good with the boys."

Lizzie raised her eyebrows. "I don't know if he's *my man*, but he finds ways to get things done. What's he singing?"

"Just a silly old song about a rich man. We all sing it sometimes."

"What did he say to the boys at the beginning? When he gathered them around him?"

"He explained what he wanted them to do. And then he made up a story. He said the shipping container was a treasure hut from old King Kato Kintu, and they were stealing his riches. So, they needed to work quickly and quietly."

"*Kae-toe' Chin-too*? Is he a real person?"

"Oh, yes. Long ago. First king of the Buganda. The royal tombs are still here in the city." He pointed off toward a nearby hill. "The palace is a museum."

Lizzie shook her head. "I see. So, Wasswa has them pretending to be a gang of thieves?"

"Something like that."

"Probably not far from the truth."

"In a way, I guess." Jedediah made a face. "He may have too much in common with them."

She sighed. "You think?"

⤙

On the way back, she rode beside Wasswa, bouncing up and down in the cab. He kept his eyes fixed on the road ahead, but he seemed to be in a good mood as he hummed to himself. Lizzie decided that less was more, and didn't attempt any conversation. The truck groaned and squeaked under the load, but they made good progress. As they pulled onto the school road, she braved the silence with a question. "How many more loads will it take?"

He answered quickly, as if he had already worked it out and didn't have to think. "Two more, lady. One full. One, maybe half."

She nodded. "How much should I pay you?"

Now, he looked at her. His eyes twitched. His lips turned up slightly. "I must talk to Rokani. We will see."

Lizzie just nodded.

The truck pulled up to the library and stopped. The boys piled out of the back. Inside the cab, Wasswa turned off the engine and pulled out the key. "I like the boys. Good workers."

Lizzie caught his eye. "They seem to like you, too."

Wasswa moved his shoulders back theatrically as he opened the door. "What is not to like?"

~∽~

In the main room of the library, the already impressive pile of books grew quickly as Lizzie directed the fast-moving line of boys where to stack more. Box after box came in the door. They were placed in an array of neat stacks, four high, by the wall of windows. Lizzie was careful to leave walking space between the rows.

Across the room, Barnabas, the building contractor, and one of his workers bolted down the final bookcase in a long line of bookcases. Next to them, study desks were already in place. New chairs and tables had been pushed against a far wall to make room for Lizzie's boxes. The room looked more like a library now than at any time previously.

Jedediah came in with a box and placed it on the floor near the windows. He waited until there was an opening in Lizzie's directions to the boys before he spoke. "The trucks are empty. We stacked a pile on the ground. Ogwambi volunteered to move them inside while we go back for another load. Okay?"

Lizzie brushed a wisp of hair off her sweaty forehead and looked puzzled. "Ogwambi?"

"Yeah. He wanted to do it. He's strong."

Just then, Ogwambi carried in another box. Lizzie studied the odd look on his face before answering Jedediah. "Sounds like a plan."

Jedediah left and Ogwambi set the box down on top of another one. When he turned to head back for more, Lizzie's voice stopped him. "Ogwambi? What's going on?"

He didn't look back. "Nothing, lady."

Outside, they heard the trucks start up and the voices of the boys as they clambered into the backs. Engines whined and the tires turned against sliding gravel. The sounds receded into the distance. Ogwambi hadn't moved; he waited for Lizzie to speak again.

When she did, her voice was quiet. "Have you decided to help me then?"

"In my own way, lady." As if released from a spell, Ogwambi continued out the door to retrieve more boxes. Lizzie watched him, wondering what he meant, trying not to hope too much.

Barnabas passed by carrying his toolbox. "Well, Mrs. Warton, I guess Pastor was right, after all."

"What?" Lizzie had forgotten he was there. Behind him, she saw his worker leave the room. "Right about what?"

"About hurrying. We just finished the shelves and here you are with the books."

"Oh. Yes. Here I am." Her mind was elsewhere.

"Anything you need?"

She glanced about herself and took in all the stacks of sealed boxes. "Can't think of anything. Thanks."

He smiled at her. "How do you plan to open the boxes?"

Lizzie stared down at the strapping tape sealing the seams of every one of her boxes. "Oh…"

Barnabas already had his toolbox open and was digging inside. "Here." He plunked two box cutters down on top of a nearby box.

She looked up, sheepishly. "Thanks. What would we do without such a practical man?"

Barnabas latched his toolbox and started off. "I don't know. Maybe you could remind Pastor of that when it comes time to pay the rest of my bills."

The contractor left through the front door, passing Ogwambi as he returned with a new box. Lizzie adjusted the blade on one of the box cutters and ran it down the center seam of a box, easily slitting the tape. Opening the flaps, she cocked her head to read the spine titles. Ogwambi watched with interest. She noticed him. "You can start a new row over there." She pointed. "And, once you have all the boxes inside, you can help me open these up so we can see what surprises we have."

᠅

Lizzie smiled as she leafed through an elementary school reader. The wall of windows beside her glowed with heat as well as light from the relentless sun. She was sitting on a short stack of boxes. Around her, many of the box flaps were folded back and sampled books lay in little piles.

Ogwambi was at the edge of the windows, sorting through some young-adult novels and comparing their covers. One in particular seemed to have captured his attention. It showed the long shadow of a dog falling across sparkling snow. "Is *The Call of the Wild* good?"

Lizzie shut her book and took a breath, trying to recall a story she hadn't thought of in more than fifty years. "Yes. It's good. The dog tells his own story."

Ogwambi slowly flipped through the pages of Jack London's famous novel. "Is it happy or sad?"

"I don't know." In her mind, seemingly disconnected memories flitted by in a rush: wearing shorts, being wrapped in a familiar couch, feeling helpless to stop reading pages in order to save a dog. "Good things happen and bad things happen – but his life keeps going." She rolled her shoulders. "I think it's bigger than happy or sad."

Ogwambi closed the book and set it on top of the box. "Okay."

They both heard the click of the front doors and looked over, expecting the boys with the next load of books. They saw Mrs. Birungi instead, followed by Pastor Kajumba.

Nana squealed her delight. "Oh, Lizzie! The books are here! They are here!"

She rushed over to Lizzie who quickly rose, all smiles, and caught her hands in her own, sharing the excitement. "Yes! And this is only the first load! They went back for more."

"We did it! We really did it!"

Pastor Kajumba beamed. "Thank God! And thank you, Lizzie." He joined the women and clasped Lizzie's hand. "I am so proud. And Mrs. Birungi assured me that we did it all without bribes. What a miracle!"

Lizzie cast a side glance at Nana who shot a wink and the glimmer of a grin back at her. Lizzie looked up at Pastor. "Yes, well, I'm just happy you made it back in time to witness delivery."

He released her hand. "I was afraid I would miss it. I was delayed. My conference ran into some…" His face showed the concern of revealing too much. "…some delays."

Nana tried to smooth things over. "The Association of Private African Schools is facing many donation challenges right now and… not everyone agrees with the new directions." She smiled weakly.

Lizzie understood enough not to ask any more questions about Pastor's trip to Nairobi. Stepping toward the books, she excitedly waved her hands. "You need to see these. I couldn't resist opening a few just to peek. It's like Christmas."

Pastor Kajumba turned with a smile on his face. "I totally understand, I…" His eyes fell on Ogwambi, silently sitting among the boxes. As recognition set in, Kajumba blinked and then his entire countenance altered. Every muscle tensed. His voice snapped out, short and sharp. "Ogwambi! What are you doing on my school grounds? You don't belong here!"

The boy looked stunned. Not a word came out of his mouth. In fact, his lips didn't even attempt to form a word.

Lizzie's mind felt jumbled. She rushed to intervene, placing herself between Ogwambi and Kajumba. "I'm sorry. I should have warned you. He's…he's helping to carry boxes. He's…"

"It's not your fault." Kajumba's voice sounded strained. "There is no way you could know."

"Know what?" Lizzie remembered to play the secrets game.

"That this boy was expelled. He is not allowed back at my school."

"But I…I thought…"

"He knows the rules!" Kajumba stared angrily at Ogwambi. "He and the others!" Without a pause, he shouted in Luganda. "Go! Now! Get off my property!"

Ogwambi stood, his legs uncertain, his face clouded with shame.

Nana stepped into the fray. "No! Stop! This wasn't Lizzie's idea. It was mine."

Kajumba turned on her. "You? How could you? You know better!"

The pastor towered over her, but Nana stood her ground. "I hired him as a *worker* – not a *student*. He has needs beyond school. Besides, I thought it was time that—"

"Time!" Kajumba pounced on the word. "You thought it was time! What? That enough time has passed? That time would erase what they did to me?"

"No. Let me explain."

"Not here. This is not the *time* nor the place."

Nana didn't flinch. "Where, then? When?"

Kajumba shook his head in exasperation at her. He switched to Luganda. "Stop this! I can't believe you!"

Her voice sounded firm as she switched, too. "No. I won't back down. I won't stay quiet."

"What is wrong with you, woman?" His voice was imperious, cold.

Feeling flustered, Birungi switched languages back again. "Say that in English. Say it so Lizzie can hear."

Kajumba looked at Lizzie and regained control of his voice. He took a few breaths through his nose. Then, in a far less severe tone, he repeated his question in English. "What is wrong with you? That is what I said."

Birungi took a breath. "It is not me who is wrong, Pastor."

Kajumba checked around the room, noting where Lizzie and

Ogwambi stood. His voice dropped to an angry whisper for Nana's ears. "I will not discuss this in front of them! Come outside." He immediately turned toward the door.

Lizzie moved after him. "I'm coming, too."

Kajumba whirled, his face tight. "No! You will stay right where you are! There are things that you cannot know."

Lizzie kept her eyes steady on his and her voice level. "If it's those copper pipes, I already know. And I *am* coming."

Kajumba appeared struck mute for a moment. He fixed Nana with a searing look of betrayal before disappearing out the door.

⬧

The sun rode high in a cloudless sky and the heat beat down on the three of them. There was no shade in front of the new library building, and they sought none. Pastor Kajumba faced away from the two women, his arms wrapped around himself, lost in his own troubled thoughts.

What have I done? Lizzie asked herself. Me and my big mouth! She looked timidly at Nana, expecting reproach. Instead she received a lifted palm, signaling, *wait.*

So, they waited. The grinding rasp of cicadas floated to them from the tall trees. Young voices reciting lessons carried from the open windows of distant classrooms. The heat continued to beat down.

"I am sorry."

Pastor Kajumba's voice sounded rich and kind again. He hadn't turned around yet. He still looked away from them, facing the horizon. Sweat drops beaded his head, flies buzzed around him, but he remained still. "Just now, I asked God what he wanted me to do next."

He turned to them, letting his arms go slack. "And there was a churning inside me, like water poured on a fire. Then a deep conviction came from the ashes, to apologize." The lines in his face had relaxed. "And it was right. I need to apologize to you, Mrs. Birungi. And to you, Mrs. Warton. Forgive me."

Nana breathed a sigh of relief. "Of course, Pastor. Of course, we do. You are tired. You were caught by surprise. It could happen to any of us. Only Jesus is perfect."

He smiled sadly, ignoring her ready excuses. "The pipes are pride, aren't they? My pride. My shameful pride…"

The rumbling of Wasswa's trucks returning with more books caused them to look up. Some of the boys rode high atop the stacks, like young cowboys, waving their arms and whooping. Just behind the big truck, Rokani's overloaded pickup beeped its horn. More riders waved wildly from behind his cab.

Kajumba lifted his hand in an unruffled acknowledgement of the exuberant boys. "We will talk more another time. I see you hired a whole tribe of workers, aye, Mrs. Birungi?"

"Yes, Pastor. I am afraid I did."

Wiping his forehead with a snowy handkerchief, he started for the road. "Well, ladies, the least we can do is go greet them."

TWENTY-SEVEN
Following Clues

By the time the three arrived at the parked trucks, the boys had already dropped the tailgates and were busy handing down boxes.

Wasswa descended from his cab and flicked the dust coated door shut behind him. Spotting Lizzie, he sauntered forward with a grin. "We loaded more than last time, Lizzie. Only one palette is left. Rokani can get that with just the pickup."

Lizzie patted his arm. "I am so pleased! You've done good work for us today." Wasswa bowed slightly, his cheeks dimpling with the praise. Lizzie introduced him to Kajumba. "Pastor, this is Wasswa Salongo, our import helper and the owner of quality clothing shops, who has generously let us hire his trucks. Wasswa, this is Pastor Agaba-Benjamin Kajumba, the head of our school."

Kajumba gave Wasswa a firm handshake. "Mr. Salongo. Thanks for your help. This is a great day for our school." He tilted his head toward Lizzie. "Is this the same one from Owino Market that Mrs. Birungi told me about?"

Lizzie looked a bit worried. "Well, I'm not sure what story Nana may have told you happened in Owino, but—"

Her words were cut off by the sudden noisy arrival of a small military convoy. It swiftly passed behind Wasswa's trucks in a clatter of engine noise and raised dust. The boys put down their boxes to watch, concern rising in their faces. It was a wonder that no one heard the vehicles approach, since their engines were loud, but everyone had been hard at work. One of the boys next to Jedediah instinctively turned to flee, but Uncle Jed grabbed his arm and pulled him close.

As she followed the convoy's quick passing, Lizzie felt trepidation crawling up from her toes. She couldn't decide if it was warranted.

The first truck was large, sand colored, with slat sides and an open top of pipework meant to support a tarp. Sitting inside, somber faced soldiers dressed in camouflage, eyed her group from beneath tightly strapped helmets. Over their uniforms they wore bulging vests with multiple pockets. Every one gripped a strapped rifle tight to his chest while holding onto a pipe or the top of the side slats.

Next in line, a wide, flat-sided vehicle, painted in green camouflage, rode low to the ground on oversized tires. Lizzie thought she remembered her son David telling her that the U.S. Army called these Humvees.

After the Humvee, a white Toyota pickup with a four door cab and a bristle of antennas passed. All the extra black metal on it surprised her. A heavy grid stretched across the windshield and thick pipes boxed in the grill. Additional racks were attached to the roof and the back of the truck. The whole thing looked scary to her.

A dark blue car with a reinforced bumper followed the pickup, the word *police* stenciled in white caps along its side. Lizzie caught a glimpse of female officers jammed into the backseat.

At the rear, a drab green pickup trailed the convoy, maintaining some space between itself and the rest. The compact truck carried four helmeted soldiers in the back, riding in cramped seat racks, guns in their laps, eyes scanning their surroundings.

The moment the lead transport stopped, its tailgate crashed open. The soldiers swarmed out. Lizzie heard the menacing sounds of boots running on gravel, the clink of gunmetal against steel, the jingle of harnesses and a few quick words in Luganda. Swiftly deploying in an arc, they secured the outer area of the library and then stood still. They held their rifles up and close, their eyes steady and directed at the civilians in front of them. Lizzie waited nervously for what came next.

All the doors of the Humvee clicked open at once. More armed soldiers emerged. She saw one wore vertical red tabs on his collar. Since the rest seemed to defer to him, Lizzie concluded he must be in charge.

From the white pickup, two men in different uniforms and helmets stepped out and moved smoothly over to the command group. They both looked scruffy, wore sunglasses and had facial hair. She was surprised to see that one was white. She wondered why their weapons were different and who they might be, until she spotted small American flag patches on the upper sleeves of their grey and white speckled uniforms.

The man with the red collar tabs spoke Luganda in a loud voice. Lizzie looked around, but no one moved. What had he said? The officer stared at Lizzie and then repeated his words in English with a thick accent. "Everyone. Remain where you are. You are in no danger. Please, do not make any sudden moves. All right?"

He made a little wave with one hand. The soldiers beside him walked briskly toward the boys near the truck and toward the men around Pastor Kajumba. Lizzie noted that the police had joined the command group, two female officers among them.

"For your own safety and our safety, these officers will search you," the man continued. "If you have anything sharp, or any weapons, please put them on the ground now."

Wasswa immediately dropped his knife on the loose dirt at his feet, as did Rokani. Soldiers began to pat down the boys and the men. The female police officers approached Mrs. Birungi and Lizzie.

"Stay relaxed. Legs loose. Arms away from your sides. This will only take a moment."

The black member of the American soldiers quietly conversed with the commander in Luganda. Nodding, the leader motioned to a few of his men, who immediately moved toward the library.

"Is there anyone inside that building?" the commander asked in Luganda. "We need to secure it."

Kajumba lifted a hand to get his attention. "There is one boy in there. We left him standing in the main room. He poses no danger to you."

Lizzie nervously watched the soldiers approach the main door. She hadn't understood the exchange but hoped Kajumba had told them about Ogwambi. While a policewoman patted her for weapons, Lizzie observed how the soldiers worked together at the door, one covering for the other as they slipped inside. In no time, she saw Ogwambi walk out followed by the soldiers. He went to stand by Uncle Jed. One of the soldiers tossed two box cutters to the ground and signaled that all was clear.

The commander stood still and waited. His eyes moved carefully left to right. He took his time. Satisfied, he licked his lips and grunted. "Okay. Thank you." Unsnapping his helmet, he handed it off to a soldier beside him. His head was completely bald and shone in the sun. He secured his rifle and lifted the strap over his head, handing that off, as well. Finally, he unhooked the bulky vest and slid out his arms, letting another soldier carry it away. From somewhere behind his back, the officer retrieved a dark green beret and slipped it on. A yellow and red insignia was prominent on the front, but Lizzie didn't know what it meant.

The man took a few steps forward. "I am Captain Godrey Muhoozi of the UPDF. I apologize for the extra caution but, as you know, there was a bombing in a market two days ago. Right now, we are looking for a woman named Nankunda Birungi. Can any of you help us locate her?"

Filled with dread, Lizzie snapped a fearful look over at Nana. She wore a dark expression as she replied, "I am Nankunda Birungi."

The officer appraised her. "Ah. Thank you. Please understand, Mrs. Birungi, we are simply following clues." He put his hands behind his back and paced. "Records from the MTN Company show you had a transaction near the bomb location just before it detonated. One of their agents says he talked to you. We want to know why you were there and what you may have seen."

Ignoring the fear pressing her chest, Lizzie raised her voice before he could go on. "She was only there because of me! I saw the bomber! I'm the one you should talk to."

Capt. Muhoozi stared at her, confused. "Saw the bomber? Who are you?"

"My name is Elizabeth Warton." She felt so anxious, her voice sounded paper thin. Forcing down a few swallows, she tried again. "I'm helping with the school library here."

The black American soldier stepped up to the Captain's side and spoke quietly in Luganda. Muhoozi replied curtly, and then fell silent.

Turning toward Lizzie, the American removed his helmet and tucked it under an arm. He stepped toward her. "Excuse me, ma'am. Are you, by any chance, a United States citizen?" The young man's voice sounded mellow and, to Lizzie's ears, as Midwest American as apple pie and ice-cream.

Lizzie was flustered, "Umm…" She wasn't sure of anything at the moment. "Ah, yes. Yes, I am. I'm from Minnesota. Eden Prairie, actually…" She rolled her eyes, "Not that that matters…"

The mid-30's soldier smiled brightly. "EP? No kiddin'? I've been there. I'm from Chicago, but I have friends who moved to Chaska. Do you know where that is?"

"I sure do! What a small world." The tension started to drain from her limbs. "Do your friends know the Schmieg family in—?"

The soldier held up a hand to stop her. "Ma'am. Not now. But just so we're clear. You won't be talking to any UPDF troops. You're an American citizen, so we're gonna find a nice quiet place, and you'll only be talkin' to me. Okay?"

∽

His name was Abel Elwelu. He was a Marine sergeant in Special Operations – an intelligence specialist assigned to work alongside the Uganda Peoples Defense Force. He had unstacked a couple of chairs near the back wall of the library and positioned them face to face. Lizzie found it easy to talk with the young man.

An attentive listener, Sgt. Elwelu would occasionally jot a few comments into his pocket-sized spiral notebook. Otherwise, he just let her talk. Lizzie had spun her whole tale out in front of him, from Amsterdam to the delivery of the donated books. She made it clear how important Dembe was to her, and how impossible he was to find.

"Mrs. Warton, you say the explosion knocked you out?"

"I think so. It felt like a punch, and then I was face down. I didn't know how I got there."

"Hearing problems?"

"At the time. But it all came back."

"Ringing in your ears? Dizziness?"

"That's all gone now. The building shielded us. I'm okay."

"Any breathing issues? Sleep problems?"

"Is this a doctor visit, Sergeant?"

"No. But you should make one. You were lucky, but things can develop later on…"

"I know I was lucky." She felt distressed. "I saw some of the others."

"Ma'am, you had a concussion. I'd like to connect you with our medical people. You know, have 'em check you out."

"No. I'm fine. I was shaky for a day or so, but I'm okay now. If I need help, I'll go to the MSF clinic."

"You know them then?"

"Uh-huh, I met Dr. MacLaird."

The sergeant snickered. "That crazy Scotsman? You met old Calum MacLaird? I'm so sorry, ma'am. He's a trip, ain't he? Likes to visit us when he can. Calls us his Happy Hour, 'cause we have drinks available."

"I can only imagine."

Sgt. Elwelu stuffed his tiny notebook into a pocket, indicating that the interview was at an end, and stretched his arms. "Mrs. Warton, you've had more adventures here in a few weeks as a librarian than I've had in three months as a Marine. Maybe I'm in the wrong job."

Lizzie grinned at him. "You can call me Lizzie, sergeant."

"No, ma'am. I can't. This needs to stay official."

"Okay. Can I ask how you speak the language so well?"

"Yes, ma'am. Pretty simple. Both parents are Ugandan, and we live in Chicago. I was born there. We spoke both English and Luganda at home."

"Lucky you."

He smirked. "Yep. That's why I got assigned here."

"How much trouble are we in, really?"

"Who?"

"Mrs. Birungi and me?"

"Far as I can figure, you're in no trouble at all. We're happy for the info."

"But we did leave the bomb scene. I mean, we ran away. That wasn't right."

He tapped a few fingers against his knee. "Well, ma'am, this isn't the U.S., and based on what I've seen around here, that was probably the right choice. Even though it keeps feelin' wrong."

⤚

When Sgt. Elwelu and Lizzie came out of the library, the troops were already mounted up in the transport and waiting. Capt. Muhoozi chatted with Pastor Kajumba by his Humvee while Mrs. Birungi stood quietly beside them. Over by the road, the boys unloaded book boxes. She noticed that Wasswa was in a spirited conversation with a circle of police next to his truck cab. Something about that situation struck her as troubling.

"Sergeant, can you do me a favor?"

"If I can, sure."

"Check on the problem our truck driver seems to be having with the police."

He glanced that way and nodded. "Can do."

"His name is Wasswa. He's been a great help to us. Wouldn't want him to get into any trouble here, you know?"

"I'm on it, ma'am."

While Sgt. Elwelu headed off, Lizzie drifted over to where Nana stood listening to the conversation between the captain and Kajumba. Once she was close enough, Lizzie spoke in a low tone to Nana. "You okay?"

She made eye contact. "Fine. Everything is fine."

Lizzie watched the men's conversation for a while. It was all in Luganda. Muhoozi laughed, enjoying himself, using his hands to tell a lively story. Kajumba barely nodded, and he appeared uncomfortable.

"What're they talking about?"

"The captain recognized Pastor from a long time ago. Way before he was…a pastor."

Lizzie wrinkled her eyebrows. "Oh. And what was he back then? Or is that another secret?"

"It is not a secret but…no one talks about it." Nana looked her full in the eyes. "A fighter. In the ring. We say *omukubi webikondde*. It means 'the one who punches with fists.'"

"A boxer? A prizefighter?"

"Yes. A boxer. It is very popular here."

Lizzie's eyes widened. "Pastor?"

"Yes. The captain remembers winning a large bet with good odds. Pastor would rather not remember. It was very long ago. Much has changed."

Lizzie gazed with new eyes at the large preacher with his scarred fingers. "Nothing here is as it seems," she said softly.

"What?"

"Something Jedediah told me. Not important."

Lizzie looked up as Sgt. Elwelu returned. "All set, ma'am. Police thought somebody'd seen his truck before. Somethin' suspicious. You know cops. They said fine, they'd let it go this time."

She looked off at Wasswa standing alone by his cab. Their eyes met and she gave him a knowing half smile. He tipped his head to her and walked toward the boys to help unload.

"Thank you, sergeant."

"No problem, ma'am."

⌘

The entire main room of the library was filled with stacks of boxes, four high, in lines that marched from the windows almost all the way across the room to the rows of empty bookcases. Lizzie stood in the middle of it all with a book in her hand and considered the overwhelming task ahead. Unpacking was only the beginning. She had spent so much time focused on freeing the books from the warehouse, she had forgotten what their arrival would demand from her library. How should she organize them? How should the books be shelved? No easy answers.

Each book already carried spine tags with the Dewey Decimal Classifications from their previous lives at various school libraries. Most even had barcodes, for goodness' sakes! When she flipped open the covers, the facing page was stamped or had a sticker proclaiming *Property of Austin Independent School District*. But none of that would be helpful for Ugandan primary and secondary students for whom English was a second language. Whatever system she settled on needed to be simple and sensible. Then it struck her – the most important part. Her system must be easy to maintain and to apply because she wouldn't always be here.

One of the boys came in with a box. Lizzie showed him where to place it. Wasswa followed with another box. "This is the end, Lizzie. The last box. Rokani already made his run. This is it."

Lizzie put down her book and grinned at him. "Oh, Wasswa, we did it! I almost can't believe it."

"Yes."

She hurriedly threaded her way out from the stacked books and awkwardly stood in front of him. For just a fraction of a second, she almost put her arms around him and gave him a hug. Instead, she clumsily brushed her hands against each other. "So, we need to find Mrs. Birungi. She has the cash. Did you decide what we owe you?"

Wasswa looked at her uneasily and didn't reply.

Lizzie cocked her head. "What? Isn't that what we said?"

"Yes, but…there is no charge, lady."

Lizzie gave him a look. He just stood there and said nothing more. She thought about the police and Sgt. Elwelu's intervention. "Oh. I see. You owe me again, huh?"

He looked away.

"Well, can we at least pay you for the fuel?"

"No, lady. Nothing."

Wasswa and Rokani's trucks growled away down the school's dusty road as Lizzie watched. She observed that clouds were starting to roll in from the edges of the sky, gathering for the evening rainfall. When she turned away, she saw Nana hand Jedediah a thick envelope of cash to pay for the boys' day of work. Pastor Kajumba stood silently apart. Lizzie saw that he watched everything, and she noticed a kind of quietness in his features.

With a great deal of commotion and groans, as many boys as could possibly fit, squeezed into Jedediah's car. It made Lizzie think of the clowns at the circus during her childhood. After Uncle Jed drove off in a flurry of waves, the remaining boys gathered into a group and walked toward the paved road. Musaazi took the lead, skipping ahead and brandishing some of Uncle Jed's cash in the air like little fluttering flags. Once they made it out to the road, they planned to catch the attention of a taxi van to get home.

Nana grabbed Lizzie's arm, pulling her along to walk with the boys. "Lizzie, come. This is something you need to learn. This is called a Ugandan goodbye."

"What is it?"

"You give them a *push*."

"A push?"

"Yes. What we are doing right now – a push. You walk with them for a while, and you keep talking and visiting. You might even carry something for them. And then you walk some more, and some more, before you finally let them go."

"Oh."

"We always do it. It shows we wish they could stay."

So, they walked with the boys. And Mrs. Birungi kidded them mercilessly in Luganda. Jokes went back and forth, laughter followed. Lizzie enjoyed herself, even though she didn't know the language, and despite the flying insects that pestered them. She saw Ogwambi flash a grin her way, and then she felt a jolt – *Ogwambi*!

Letting go of Birungi's arm, she slid over next to Ogwambi and walked beside him for a time before speaking. "Ogwambi, did I see you and Pastor talking to each other again?"

The boy looked at her oddly. "He said he was sorry he yelled at me. He said he was…wrong."

"I'm glad."

They walked a bit farther. Lizzie spoke again. "I thought you said you were going to help me – in your own way. Remember?"

Ogwambi's eyebrows went up and a scampish smile teased at the corners of his mouth. "I did."

"You did?"

He nodded.

Lizzie was at a loss. "How?"

"The dog book."

"What…" Understanding slowly blossomed in Lizzie's mind. She gave him a quick squeeze on the shoulder. "Thank you!"

Hurrying back to Nana, she took her arm. "Have we gone far enough? I mean, for a Ugandan goodbye?"

Nana looked at her strangely. "I guess. Yes. Why the rush?"

"Come back to the library and see."

They waved goodbye to the boys and hurried back, Lizzie leading the way.

⁓

The library room was just the way she'd left it. Lizzie looked to where she had last seen Ogwambi. She could picture him again, on the edge of the windows, among the books.

Nana followed her into the room and then stopped, shaking her head. "What are we looking for?"

Lizzie moved between the stacks, "I'm not sure exactly."

Positioned to be noticed, she spotted Jack London's book leaning against the glass, the cover facing her. When she picked it up she realized how worn it was, how many fingers had touched it over the years. She let the novel fall open in her hands. A folded note was tucked inside. She pulled it free and balanced it on her palm. She could see that there was printing on the outside. It was crabbed and uneven but perfectly legible: *Writing is not saying.* When she unfolded the note, she discovered two additional lines in the same crooked scrawl: *Nansana Boarding School* and *Mirembe.*

Nana quietly joined her. "What is it?"

Lizzie's mouth formed a line. "An answer for the pipes."

TWENTY-EIGHT

Boarding Student

Mrs. Birungi's office was small, but still roomy enough for Lizzie to squeeze behind Nana and peek at her computer screen. Luckily, today seemed to be a good power day, so the internet was up and holding steady. They wanted to get an earlier start, but Mrs. Birungi had had morning meetings with Pastor Kajumba and a few of the teachers. Lizzie couldn't help but feel they had lost a precious couple of hours before the two of them could focus on Ogwambi's clues.

Lizzie studied the slowly loading website for Nansana Private School in Muyenga. All the perfect photos showed happy students wearing colorful uniforms, some raising hands in bright classrooms, others carrying new books as they strolled to class. She lifted her eyes to glance out Mrs. Birungi's office window and saw their own students rushing by. She felt the sharp prick of self-doubt. *Why must I stick my nose into everything? Why can't I let Dembe be? He doesn't want my help.* But then she recalled that terrible moment at Meg's house, the feel of his face against her side. Her arm tingled again from his cheek brushing in a silent goodbye as Jedediah sent him back to the streets.

Nana rolled the wheel on her mouse. The screen scrolled up to a pleasant photo of one of the school directors. "This is Susan Bossa. She is in charge of the boarding students. I met her at a conference. Our mothers knew each other."

Lizzie's focus returned to the present. "Okay."

Nana's eyes shifted toward her open door, checking for ears. Lizzie moved around the desk and softly nudged the door closer to the jamb. Nana lowered her voice. "I talked to her this morning, unofficially. Mirembe is a common name. Susan has three boarders called Mirembe. Two are quite young and from known families. The third is thirteen, and her background is vague – parents dead or absent. An uncle pays her fees."

Lizzie perched on the visitor's chair in front of the desk, listening closely.

"Money has not been a problem, until this term. They are near the end and the uncle still owes part. Susan is not sure what to do since the girl has been such a good student, and..." Her lips turned up at the corners. "...she has the sweetest singing voice."

"No."

"That is what she said."

Lizzie sucked in a small breath. "You don't really think... do you?"

"Our little Mirembe? From church?" Nana leaned forward in her chair, making it squeak. "My mind says it is unlikely, but my heart hopes what it hopes."

❧

Whining like giant wasps, a pack of *boda-bodas* careened around their speeding taxi van. Lizzie struggled to hear Nana's last comment. She thought she had said that Mrs. Bossa would bring Mirembe to her office, and then something about lunchtime. Close enough! Lizzie nodded and shouted over the traffic noise, "Good!"

The van was overcrowded. It could hold twelve but Lizzie knew there were extras on board this time. The day was hot. Fumes flooded through the dirty windows to mingle with the all-too-human smells inside. Lizzie's eyes watered. She tried to take shallow breaths, and only through her mouth. She frowned at herself. *I can't believe I'm breathing like a dog!*

"Nana, did you know Pastor Kajumba apologized to Ogwambi last night?"

"Yes." She smiled. "Pastor told me himself this morning…after he apologized to me, again."

Lizzie just shook her head, pleased.

Nana continued. "He is also considering a call to Mrs. Seterdahl."

"What? The donor's widow?"

She nodded. "He feels he was wrong to hide the truth from her about what happened to their gifts."

Lizzie looked shocked. "Is that a good idea? I'm afraid I'm just making a big mess of everything around here."

A large shadow passed over the taxi. A pale green tank truck lumbered by, barely inches from the window. The heavy lozenge shaped tank carried the printed letters H_2O in blue on the side, and the word *Water* on the back. Blaring his horn, the truck driver edged into their lane. Their van slowed suddenly, forced to veer and give way.

After the taxi steadied again, Nana placed her hand over Lizzie's. "You are good for us. You make us change."

Lizzie wasn't so sure, but she liked having her hand held, anyway.

At intersections, she noticed that the military presence was still clearly in evidence. It made her nervous. A few times, she thought she glimpsed Sgt. Elwelu's white pickup in the distance, or passing by. On the other hand, there were many cars and pickups driving around everywhere, and most of them were white.

Later, the taxi van swung over to the side of the road beside an open market. The conductor let off a mother and daughter, freeing up some room inside. As the taxi merged into traffic again, Lizzie breathed easier. "Do you think Pastor will actually call the donor?"

Nana brushed at her skirt. "Not right away. Something else has come up."

"What now?"

"One of his church members has a problem. He leads a group which raises pigs. You know, using micro loans from western people?"

At the word *pigs*, Lizzie's attention ratcheted up. She hurriedly nodded at Nana as if she understood. She feared what would follow.

"Well, this man banded together with other farmers. They have been quite successful, up to now."

"What happened?"

"Over the weekend, many of their pigs disappeared."

"Disappeared?"

"Stolen. Right from their pens. One of the farmers may have seen a pickup from far away, following a bigger truck."

"Oh." Lizzie's voice sounded odd. She tried again, hoping for empathy. "That's so sad."

"Yes."

"Is there any way to identify the pigs?"

"Not really. Just ear tags." Nana pulled on her own earlobe. "But those are easily removed."

Lizzie winced. She stared out the window, her eyes focused on nothing, while her mind rolled in turmoil. Wasswa!

Nana looked ahead and saw the open gates for Nansana School. She called out in Luganda for the conductor to drop them off.

As the taxi slowed, Lizzie looked up. Cars and taxis were parked along the road ahead, on both sides of the school gate. People passed in and out. A *cha'pati* vendor conducted a brisk business. Someone else sold soft drinks and bottles of water from his overloaded bike. She assumed it must be lunchtime or, perhaps, a scheduled event at the school. As she slid across the bench seat to exit the stopped taxi, something grey and familiar flickered past the windows on the edge of her vision. Chill fingers tickled her neck. Perplexed, she turned back to check, stumbling as she stepped onto the ground. Her body shuddered, despite the heat. An indistinct afterimage tantalized her mind. Had she really just seen a grey baseball cap with a black Nike logo?

She shoved between Mrs. Birungi and the conductor in her rush to circle the taxi. Which way was he headed? Rounding the van, she looked in each direction but saw no one in a Nike cap. What had she actually seen? She wasn't sure. Only the flash of an image, not anything clearly visible. She stepped one way, then the other, looking and looking. She saw clumps of men, some with hats. Cars and taxis drove away, some white. But nothing leaped to her eyes as clearly him or clearly his taxi.

Nana hastened to her side, sensing the fear. "Are you feeling sick? Do you shake again from the bomb?"

Lizzie gave up her search. She shook her head. "It's not that. It's...it's like somebody just walked across my grave."

"What?"

"I thought I saw...his hat. That taxi driver's hat. The one from the airport who drugged me."

"His hat?"

"It was on his head. I thought he walked by the taxi just now. Outside the window."

"Did he?" Nana glanced around with concern.

"I'm not sure. I don't know what I saw. If I saw...anything."

"Why would he be here?"

"I don't know. Maybe he's not."

She gently touched Lizzie's arm. "What was...the grave?"

"Nothing. Just a bad feeling. It's nothing."

"You are all right?"

Lizzie shook out her arms and forced herself to stand a little taller. "Yes. I'm fine now. Really."

"Sure?"

"Yes. I'm sure."

"Okay." Nana brushed at her skirt again, secured her purse and led off. "We need to hurry now. Susan is waiting for us."

They briskly followed the pathway onto the school grounds, passing a few slow walkers. Lizzie couldn't help but steal a couple of nervous glances back, but to no avail.

⤚

Director Bossa looked quite different from her website picture. It seemed to Lizzie that the lady had gained significant weight since then, and her hairstyle had changed. Still, her large smile felt genuine and her greeting warm. They met in her cramped reception area, which was hot and congested with staff workers who manually handled paperwork. Explaining that Mirembe was already waiting in her office, Mrs. Bossa launched into rapid-fire Luganda with Mrs. Birungi. Lizzie wasn't sure what Nana said, or how she spun the story of their visit, but soon the director's cheeks softened with understanding. In moments, she nodded along with Nana. Observing the interaction, Lizzie recalled Nana in the markets, working on the vendors. Lizzie got the sense of their agreements even without the specifics of language. Yes, it would be fine to talk with the girl. Yes, of course, they could have privacy. And, yes, someday when I need a favor, you will help me.

With little delay or fanfare, Lizzie followed behind Nana and the director, heading to a closed door. Mrs. Bossa tapped lightly before opening it. She stepped back so they could enter. Nana shared her brightest smile of thanks to the director as she passed. The door softly closed behind them.

Mirembe sat in a wooden chair in front of Mrs. Bossa's neatly arranged desk. She turned around at the sound of the door. Her face betrayed a startled mix of emotions, but it was clear that this was the same girl from the church service.

"I'm sorry if we startled you," Lizzie said gently. "Don't be afraid."

Mirembe looked from Birungi to Lizzie, her lips quivering. Without thinking, she spoke in Luganda. "Why are you here? This is...impossible!"

Nana replied softly, "It'll be fine, child. I think we're part of the answer to your prayer."

Mirembe collapsed into tears. Her head bowed as her hands came up to cover her face. Her shoulders shook.

Lizzie knelt beside her chair and the girl leaned toward her, allowing herself to be folded into Lizzie's strong arms. Nana placed a comforting palm on the girl's shoulder, lightly stroking her upper arm, just the way she would with her daughter, Afiya.

The moment continued for a time. Then Nana's melodious voice spoke again in Luganda. "We need to ask some questions, but I want to do it in English so Mrs. Warton will understand. Can you help me do that?"

Mirembe looked up, brushing away her tears, and nodded. Lizzie helped her to sit up again and slipped a tissue into her hand. Sliding into the other visitor's chair, she kept her eyes on the girl. In the meantime, Nana wheeled Mrs. Bossa's chair around the desk and set it close to the other chairs. Sighing in relief, she sat down.

"Okay," Birungi said, eyeing Lizzie. "The rest of our talk can be in English. Right, Mirembe?"

The girl nodded as she dabbed her eyes.

Lizzie didn't know the best way to begin, so she just cleared her throat and started talking. "I wish I could speak your language. But I have a friend who can. He helped me when I was in trouble. And he made sure I got to a safe place."

Mirembe's tears were done. She listened.

"That's what friends do, don't they?"

"Yes." The girl spoke barely above a whisper.

"He even fixed these glasses." Lizzie smiled and reseated them firmly on her nose. "You should have seen how broken they were. But he mended them. Better than new."

Mirembe breathed quietly through her nose. A sad smile tickled at her mouth.

"This friend saved my life. Twice." Lizzie held the girl's eyes. "I think you know him."

Mirembe's face grew very still.

Lizzie spoke slowly. "His name is Dembe."

The girl's eyes jumped before she could hide her reaction.

Lizzie smiled. "I see you *do* know him. Maybe my friend saved you, too."

Mirembe didn't answer, but she folded her lips inward. Lizzie studied the sweet face: eyes wide and dark, nose broad, lips full – almost puffy. She had it! How simple. How obvious. "Dembe is your brother, isn't he?"

Mirembe froze for an instant, then simply nodded and looked at the floor.

Nana's eyebrows rose. Evidently, that possibility hadn't occurred to her, but her mind rapidly adjusted to it. "Child, does your uncle pay your school fees?"

The girl looked up, relieved to be on solid ground again. "Yes. Mrs. Bossa said he was just here. He paid the last part right before you came."

The uncle was just here? Lizzie felt a sudden queasiness, as if she rode an elevator and it had slowed quicker than her stomach.

Birungi's intuition, after years as an administrator, told her to take a chance. "But it isn't *his* money, is it? He is just here to make things look right." She studied the young face carefully. "Whose money is it?"

Mirembe hesitated. Waves of emotions seemed to roll through her. She looked into the intent faces of the women and wanted to speak the truth, but she held back. In the end, it was simply the kind way that Lizzie tilted her head that broke the girl's resolve.

"From Dembe." Her words rushed out. "The money is from Dembe. Always from Dembe."

"And your uncle only pretends to be responsible?" Birungi asked.

"Yes."

"Because there must always be a grown-up." Not a question.

The girl nodded, worry evident in her eyes.

Lizzie quickly reassured her. "Sweetheart, your secret is safe. We won't tell Mrs. Bossa."

Nana nodded her agreement and patted the girl's hand. "This is a good place. Dembe chose well."

Mirembe took a steadying breath.

Nana looked thoughtful. "But where will you stay during break? You know there are only a few weeks left in the term. Then, what?"

Mirembe shook her head. "We don't know...somewhere..."

"Mirembe, look at me." The girl looked into Nana's large eyes. "Do you still have parents?"

Her expression suddenly forlorn, she spoke slowly. "My father is dead."

"And your mother?"

The girl shrugged. "She has a new husband. A new family."

Lizzie watched the interplay of conflicting feelings on her face. "What happened to your brother?"

"Dembe had to leave."

"Why?"

The girl sat still. Truth was so complicated. "There was anger. And hitting. And loud words." Mirembe struggled to explain better, her hands turning oddly in the air, but she gave up. "He had no food. No bed. And danger."

"What about you?" Nana asked.

The girl spoke quietly, with little color to her words. "I stayed quiet. Mother stayed quiet. But he drinks and... and there is another wife..."

"Your stepfather?"

"Yes."

Lizzie sounded startled. "Another wife? What?"

Nana waved her hand. "It is not uncommon here. Sometimes in secret. Sometimes in public. Sometimes more than one." She rolled her shoulders. "It is Africa."

Lizzie's mouth snapped shut. Nana turned back to Mirembe. "Did your mother know about the other wife?"

"No. Only later."

"And when your stepfather drinks...what happens?"

Mirembe paused again. She looked at the wall. "Mother told me to run away. To hide. To not come back...ever."

Horrified, Lizzie started to speak, but Mirembe wasn't done.

"Mother asked her brother to help, in secret. My uncle. He drives taxi. He let me sleep under his eating table until Dembe could get school money. His wife beat me!"

A careful knock sounded. They looked up as Mrs. Bossa's cheerful face peeked around the slightly opened door. "Sorry. How much longer? I have meetings soon."

Mrs. Birungi donned her pleasant business face. "A few more minutes. Please, Susan? Almost done."

The director glanced at Mirembe. The girl smiled unconvincingly back at her. Mrs. Bossa hesitated, unsure, and then nodded. "Okay. Let me know. And Mirembe? You still have my note for your teachers?"

The girl checked the book bag on the floor next to her chair. "Yes, Mrs. Bossa."

"Fine, then." The door closed.

They looked at each other. For a moment, no one spoke. Then Nana dipped her head as if she had made up her mind about something. "I have a home where you can stay over the break."

Surprised, Mirembe looked up, her eyes watering.

Nana made a half smile. "And I won't beat you."

The girl grinned.

"But don't tell Mrs. Bossa," Birungi continued. "If she asks, just say you're staying with an aunt."

Mirembe nodded, still smiling.

Lizzie switched positions in her chair, looking ill at ease. "Honey, does your mother know about this school and where you're staying?"

Mirembe shook her head. "No."

"Surely, your uncle has told her by now."

"No. He knows she must not know."

Lizzie was troubled by the answer. Beside her, Nana shrugged with resignation. "Lizzie, if the mother knows, her husband can make her tell."

As she decoded the remark, Lizzie shook her head and sighed. "How can we find Dembe? Mirembe, do you know where to look?"

"No. Only uncle knows."

"The uncle with the taxi?"

"Yes."

Lizzie glanced over at Nana and then back at Mirembe. "Can I ask you something about him?"

"Okay."

"Does he ever wear a grey ball cap with a Nike logo?"

"Ball cap?"

"A baseball hat." Lizzie mimicked its shape using her hands about her head.

"Oh. Yes." The girl smiled. "His favorite. He calls it his swoosh hat."

TWENTY-NINE
Uncle Swoosh Hat

Walking toward the school gate, Lizzie and Nana were deep in conversation about what they now knew and what they should do next. Keeping her eyes active, Lizzie noticed that the number of pedestrians around the gates had decreased. The mobile food vendors were closing up their stands.

As the two women left the school grounds, and walked along the busy paved road, Nana shaded her eyes and watched for taxi vans to flag down. Trucks and SUVs and *boda-bodas* flew by, flinging dust into the air. For the moment, no taxi vans appeared in sight. The sun was still hot and high, just beginning its afternoon slide down the sky. It took Nana a few steps to realize that Lizzie no longer walked beside her. When she turned, she saw her friend standing still, a stunned look in her face.

Alarmed, Nana rushed back. "What's happened?"

Lizzie focused just ahead on a white special hire taxi parked with others beside the road. The driver seemed asleep, his windows down, the visor of his grey baseball hat lowered over his eyes. "It's him!" she said in a fierce whisper. "The one who drugged me."

Nana let her eyes drift to where Lizzie cautiously indicated. The two women stood close together, wondering what to do. Nana slid casually in front of Lizzie, blocking the view to the driver, and put her hands firmly on her friend's shoulders. "How are you doing? Is this too much for you?"

Lizzie stared back. Defiance replaced the fear in her eyes. "I'm more angry than afraid. Part of me just wants to punch him right in the face while he's sleeping!"

Nana sighed, amused. "Yes, but we are women. What is the next best thing to do?" She couldn't read Lizzie's face, so she continued. "You know, we can always walk back in the other direction – and live another day."

Shaking her head, Lizzie glanced at the unsuspecting driver, snoozing in the sun. "No. I can't do that. He knows how to find Dembe. And he knows where Mirembe's mother lives."

Birungi frowned. "Yes."

"And I need that information."

"But, Lizzie, how do you—?"

Lizzie was already in motion. "Leave that to me – but come along."

They stood quietly outside the taxi's open window, watching the driver. He was placidly breathing in and out, deeply asleep. Lizzie gingerly leaned her head forward to peer inside. Since it was a right-hand-drive car, the ignition was placed directly beside the window, and Lizzie spotted the keys dangling there, like apples ripe for the picking. Smiling to herself, she took a breath, and let her hand gently glide inside. Behind her, Nana's eyes widened, her own hand absently floating in the air. With exceptional delicacy, Lizzie tugged the keys free with a brief click and a tiny jingle. The driver snorted once, but never stirred. Lizzie guided the small ring of keys silently back out the window until she held them securely in front of her. Straightening up, she released the air from her lungs in a slow exhale. The driver's breathing never wavered, the man lost in his dreams.

Keeping the keys in one hand, Lizzie suddenly smacked her

other hand heavily against the car door, right beside his head, while shouting, "Hey!"

Shocked, the driver jolted awake. His body jerked, his eyes went wide and his mouth let out an anguished cry.

Lizzie continued shouting. "Hey! Remember me? The American lady at the airport?"

The unlucky driver was cringing, threatened by the angry face confronting him. His arms flopped about defensively. "*Kiki?* Who? Wha...what lady?"

"The one you tricked! 'You want something to drink?' *That* lady!"

Still rattled, the driver began to put things together. His eyes grew even wider when it dawned on him who stood before him. "You! No! I...this is a dream!"

Lizzie berated him, "It's no dream! I'm back! And police are lookin' for drivers who drug foreigners. They're lookin' for you!"

The fracas drew some of the bystanders near the school gate. Word passed quickly that there was a *muzungu* involved. A small crowd started to form, hoping for a scene. The soft-drink vendor circled back on his bike, anticipating sales.

The driver flashed out a hand to turn on his car. His fingers fumbled at the empty ignition. Bewildered, he desperately searched for the keys: in his lap, on his seat, down on the floor. Frantic, his eyes jumped back to Lizzie, and that's when he saw that she was dangling his keys in the air.

"No, no, no, you can't just drive away!" she taunted him. "Not this time!"

The driver opened his door, intending to grab the keys. Lizzie swiftly tossed them to Nana, who stood farther away.

"Uh-uhh!" Lizzie said, stabbing a finger at him. "Stay in that car! If you get out, we're gonna throw 'em far away!"

As she spoke, she vigorously motioned to Nana. Her friend hesitated, not sure what was expected, but quickly caught on. The usually proper school administrator pantomimed hurling the keys over the road and into thick bushes on the other side. Turning back, she held them up to show that they were still, for the moment, safely in her hand.

Lizzie glared at the man. "And you'll never find 'em. So, if I were you, I'd stay right where you are."

The driver stopped himself. He held fast to his position, with one foot on the road, and his door half open, glowering at Lizzie.

"That's better." She glared at him. "Now, you're not going anywhere until you listen to my proposal."

The man was fully awake, and his eyes darted back and forth. He noted the small crowd gathering. His nose dilated as he struggled to control his frustrations. He focused on Lizzie. "Woman! I have nothing. You are too late! It is gone. The money is gone. Understand? Everything is gone. What do we have to talk about? Give me my keys."

"All in good time." Lizzie modulated her voice. Her tone sounded almost conciliatory. "Let's start by having you lift your foot back into the car and then shut that door. Can you do that for me, please?"

The driver stared with cold eyes, but he slowly pulled his foot back into the taxi. He yanked the door shut with a slam! "Satisfied?"

Lizzie scowled. "Not with the attitude, but so far, so good, I guess." She angled a few steps towards the front of the car so the door would be an impediment if he attempted to leap out. "Now, just to clear things up, I no longer care about what you stole from me. I've gotten most of it back, anyway. That's not what I want to talk to you about."

The driver's forehead wrinkled. His anger drained into confusion. "What, then? There is nothing else."

"In a minute. I want you to understand something first." She glanced back at the bystanders edging ever nearer, and took a few steps closer to the driver, lowering her voice. "Even though I'm just a foolish *muzungu* woman, I know you could be in a lot of trouble over what you did.". She motioned in Birungi's direction. "My friend over there has a brother who's a policeman. You could lose your taxi. Maybe go to jail. At the very least, you'll have to pay a big fat bribe, or maybe more than one, to make it all go away. That's if you even have the cash. Am I right?"

The driver sat still in his seat and silent, but his troubled face told the story.

Lizzie read the signs. "Okay. Good. We agree. You want to avoid problems; I want your information."

"I do not understand." His tone was decidedly less aggressive now. "What information do I have?"

"You're Dembe's uncle, right?"

He made a half-hearted effort to act confused. "Dembe? Who is Dembe?"

"Oh, please!" Lizzie scoffed. "Dembe is Mirembe's brother. You're their mother's brother. Mirembe boards at this school right here. Your name is down as the one responsible for her, but Dembe pays all the bills. And both of you are hiding her from the stepfather. Okay? How am I doing so far, Uncle Swoosh Hat?"

The driver's mouth dropped open during her recitation. It remained open as he looked at her with stunned eyes.

She couldn't resist a final jab. "And it seems to me that you have an awfully mean wife at home, too!"

The driver closed his mouth and swallowed nervously. This time, when his voice emerged, it sounded low, almost respectful. "What can I do for you, lady?"

Lizzie studied him. She made a decision. "Well, for starters, I think we would like a ride to someplace with fewer people. I'm sure you wouldn't mind leaving here."

She waved Birungi over and opened the back door of the taxi. Nana shot doubtful looks her way, but Lizzie ignored her concerns with a shrug as they both climbed in. She took the keys from Nana and gripped them tight before looking back to the driver. "So? Deal?"

He nodded and held out his hand.

"I'd ask you to promise," Lizzie frowned as she gave over the keys. "But who in their right mind would ever believe you?"

The car started up and pulled out. Lizzie glanced out the back window. The onlookers walked away, shaking their heads in disappointment.

෴

The taxi parked off the road in the dappled shade from a tall eucalyptus tree. Grasshoppers buzzed in the thick bushes nearby. The driver sat twisted around in his seat, facing the two women in back. He lifted off his hat and rubbed a hand over his short hair in a practiced movement before pulling it back on. "Why do you care? He is nothing to you."

Lizzie glared at him. "Because Dembe saved my life, no thanks to you."

"Really?" He sounded bemused. "I'm the one who put you in Dembe's alley. I told him to watch over you. I paid him to do it. And I left your passport. Or did your clever little hero tell you something different?"

Lizzie felt momentarily shaken. She instinctively turned to Nana for support, but her friend refused to meet her gaze. Lizzie set her lips in a line. "I don't care about that now. I want to find him. I'm told you know how."

"Lady, he doesn't stay in one place. He moves. Always moves. Street life is tricky."

"I know he moves! But the boys said he could get money on the street, because he was a…*mockie* something. A fixer of things…"

"*Makanika*. Yes. He is a fixer, like his father. That's how I search. I know most of the shopkeepers he does repairs for. Things always break. They pay him. If I follow repairs, sometimes I find Dembe."

"Like his father?" Lizzie scrunched her eyebrows. "Which father?"

"His real father. He had a gift. Dembe has it now. His stepfather is also a fixer, but no gift." The driver shook his head. "My sister was a fool to marry him. But then, she was a fool the first time, too."

"What do you mean?" Lizzie asked.

"Nothing. What is past does not matter now."

They seemed to be deadlocked. Nana fired a few quick questions in Luganda. The driver begrudgingly answered back. Nana spoke a few more times. The driver looked away for a moment before finally nodding. He said something abrupt, and then fell silent.

Nana turned to Lizzie. "She married outside her tribe."

"The first husband?"

"Yes. The first."

Lizzie fluttered her hand at some persistent flying insects circling her head. "Outside? But...he was still Ugandan, wasn't he?"

Nana sighed. "Of course, but many clans still disapprove of marriages between the tribes. Change is slow here."

"So, what happened?"

Birungi considered before answering. "It sounds as if he was a good husband. A good father. Money was tight. But when he died, his family came and took everything. The wife remarried in a hurry, to stay off the streets."

Lizzie growled and tightened her fists. "There are times when I hate this place."

Nana looked away. "I know. But nowhere is perfect."

Lizzie swatted some mosquitoes whining in her ears. She checked her fingers and saw tiny splotches of red. Rubbing them away, she looked at the driver. "That's the other thing I need. The mother's address. I want to talk to her."

The driver grumbled, instantly unhappy. "There are no addresses here. And why? Her life is already hard enough."

Lizzie persisted. "A mother deserves to know that her children are safe – or will be, soon."

"She cannot know details." The driver glared. "She doesn't need to know."

"A mother has rights," Lizzie said.

The driver stared directly at her. "Maybe in your America. Not here."

Lizzie didn't flinch. "Yes. Here. Despite what you think."

Nana placed a pacifying hand on Lizzie's arm while she questioned the driver in rapid Luganda. There was a lot of give-and-take, and Lizzie couldn't decide if the exchange was friendly or ugly, helpful or useless. Once it was over, Birungi nodded at her and smiled. "There is a repair street in Katwe that has shops for all kinds of needs. It is not far from the Kibuya roundabout which has a red and white clock tower in the middle. The stepfather rents a small-appliance fixer shop near the end of the road, with a dwelling behind it. I know the place."

The driver sat stiffly, facing forward, his demeanor clear: he was done talking to either of the two women behind him.

Nana looked at Lizzie. "What is next? The day will soon be over."

Lizzie stared at the back of the driver's head. "Sir?"

The driver didn't turn. His voice sounded robotic. "Yes, lady."

"Can we go now and try to find Dembe?"

Shutting his eyes in irritation, the driver replied, "We can try." He reached out and started the car.

Before they moved, Lizzie said, "Since we're kind of working together now, maybe we should exchange names. Mine is Lizzie Warton. What's yours?"

The driver rotated in his seat to glare wide-eyed at Mrs. Birungi, speaking quickly in Luganda. "Americans are such peculiar people!"

Birungi grinned back. "Tell me about it! You should be with her more often."

He switched his focus to Lizzie and gritted his teeth as he answered, this time in English. "I am Diba. Diba Matsiko."

Lizzie forced an agreeable look. "Okay. Nice to meet you, Mr. Matsiko."

The driver nodded formally before turning back to drive the

car. He waited for a few vehicles to go by, including a white military pickup, before he merged onto the road.

Lizzie sank into the plush seat next to Nana and whispered, "What was that about?"

Her friend sniffed at her and shrugged. "Nothing you don't already know."

This wasn't what Lizzie wanted to hear, but she realized that Nana was now staring out the side window, ignoring her. She stewed for a while and then remembered something.

"Oh, and Mr. Matsiko? It probably should go without saying, but just for the record, all these taxi costs for today have already been paid, okay? You get my meaning, don't you?"

Mr. Matsiko adjusted his visor to block the low angled rays of the bright sun and replied, "I get it, Mrs. Warton." His eyes flitted momentarily in her direction. "I figured that out before we even started."

⁓

Mr. Matsiko left his taxi parked at an angle across a broken sidewalk in a bustling part of the city. Lizzie and Nana, still seated in back, anxiously stared out their open windows. Their eyes and heads constantly moved, checking the crowds. A wide variety of people shared the narrow pathways in front of the cramped shops. Lizzie saw the usual ladies in colorful *Gomesi* dresses, heavy bundles balanced on their heads, a covey of Muslim women covered head-to-toe, and young Ugandans flaunting their western style clothes. Running children moved through the people like bright threads in a waving fabric. Some of the kids were fully dressed, some only in shorts and bare feet; all danced in and around the moving legs.

Lizzie watched their driver exit from one shop, stop to shake his head at them for a moment, and then duck into the next shop. She lifted her eyes above the passersby and noticed a large canvas sign stretched across a rusty roof: *Christ the King Designers Boutique.*

Beneath it were dark hovels with dusty backpacks on display along with colorful shoe wear – mainly women's, from flip-flops to heels – all spread out on old sheets of cardboard.

Suddenly, an unruly bunch of street boys wandered out of an alleyway from behind a mound of trash. Staggering and aimless, they pawed each other, grabbing at an open plastic bottle with liquid sloshing around inside. Each boy would sniff at the open top and then push off the others who demanded their turn.

Lizzie spotted them and immediately slid toward the door to get out. Nana's strong hand held her back. "Too dangerous."

"But they might know something."

Nana motioned with her head to the changing scene outside. Mr. Matsiko had reappeared from the shops and intercepted the clump of boys. He spoke to them, asking questions, handing out cash, and listening. When one of the boys tried to pick his pocket, the taxi driver shoved him back and shouted angrily at the group. The boys moved on, cackling. Mr. Matsiko retreated to his car, wearing a dark scowl. He leaned at their window and shook his head. "Dembe did some repairs this morning, but now no one has seen him. He just disappeared."

Lizzie frowned. "What did the boys say?"

"They know nothing." He hissed air through his teeth. "Useless! High on petrol. They barely remember how to walk."

He got back in the cab and slammed the door. "Maybe Dembe doesn't want you to find him."

Lizzie stared, dumbly. "That's silly. How would he even know we're looking?"

"You would be surprised. He has his ways. They all do."

Across the street, Lizzie noticed two military vehicles pass by, one a white truck. The eyes of the riding soldiers were attentively scanning the crowds, and a few seemed to linger on their taxi. She didn't like the heavy feeling that armed soldiers gave her, even when they were on her side. Trying to clear her head, she turned back to Mr. Matsiko. "Do you know where the boys sleep?"

"No. Never the same. Sometimes they sleep up in the trees on the roundabouts, other times under the bushes by the buildings. They find new places in the alleys. In the parks. You never know."

Nana chimed in. "Tomorrow is another day, Lizzie. I must make sure Afiya got home safely. And we all need to eat and rest."

Lizzie considered protesting but accepted the truth of what she said. "Okay, Nana. You're right. Tell Mr. Matsiko how to take us home."

She explained the directions in quick sentences using Luganda. The taxi set off. Since it was near the end of the workday, traffic was fierce. They crawled along, despite Mr. Matsiko's considerable driving skills.

After a while, Lizzie realized Nana had dozed off, unaccustomed to a taxi with such comfortable seats. When she looked forward, Lizzie caught Mr. Matsiko watching her in his mirror.

"Mrs. Warton, can I ask you a question?"

"Sure. What?"

"After I drop you off, am I done? I gave you what you asked."

Lizzie thought about it and nodded. "Yes, you're done. That was the deal. And...thanks."

The driver was puzzled at that. "Why do you say 'thanks'? You gave me no choice."

She smiled to herself. "I guess that's true...but, maybe because I appreciated it, anyway."

They drove on in silence. Then he added, "I do not usually drug my customers."

"Usually? That's not very comforting."

"I mean, I have not done it since." He swerved to avoid a hole in the road. "And I am sorry about it now." He paused briefly. "It was my idea, not the boy's."

Lizzie leaned her head against her seat rest and pondered his words. "It helps me to hear that."

The driver wore a faraway look. "He is a good boy. Strange, like you are. And stubborn." He sighed quietly. "But a good boy."

She decided to let his words stand and not question them. "Thank you, Mr. Matsiko."

"Welcome, lady."

⁂

To: davidwarton27x@centurylink.net; joanjohnson@yahoo.com; ceceliawarton99@hotmail.com
From: nankundabirungi@wobulezischool.com
Subj: Things are hopping here!

Did you know they have car washes in Kampala? I didn't. They aren't much like ours. I got all wet!

A man with trucks helped us move the books from the customs' warehouse to our new library. So exciting! Don't worry, we had lots of help. I didn't have to lift anything.

I'm almost afraid to tell you that I rode in the back of a big truck with some of the boys who helped us move the books. I loved it! They don't have seatbelt laws here. We were on a dirt road out in the country. So beautiful! I got pretty dusty, though.

Tell Will that I got to see real soldiers and a Humvee (sp?) up close! I even met a special U.S. Marine Sergeant who knows people from Chaska! Crazy, huh?

There are stacks and stacks of books in my library now. I can finally get to work organizing them. (That's what I thought I was going to be doing when I arrived.) It's funny to see all the good old American books in a library in Africa.

Did I mention that a lot of students here are boarding students?

They live right at the schools during the terms. (Their school year is divided into three terms, I think.) Even real young students can be boarders. I can't imagine that working for Will or Sandy...or Tomlin.

It rains most nights. You should hear the racket the frogs and toads make outside my window! I ought to record it. None of you would believe how loud they are. I'd like to put cotton in my ears at night if I had some.

Hugs and kisses to all – XXOO,
Grandma

THIRTY

Looking Deeper

The rain pounding against the metal roof woke her. She sat up within the netting and looked around, disoriented, still caught up in the final threads of a vanished dream. Where was she? Grey light softly filled the room, so it must be morning. The rain seemed so loud. Had Jonathan left the windows open? Her mind blinked for an instant, and then seemed to update. Memories slipped silently back again into their rightful cubbies, as if they'd never left. She was in Africa. This was her room at Mrs. Birungi's house. Today, she would visit Dembe's mother, or attempt to. All the moments were reliably there in her mind now: the plane rides, the man in the tweed suit, Dembe, the books, Owino Market, all of them, secure, accessible, and seemingly unassailable; and yet, they had been missing when she woke up.

Not for the first time, she advised herself to remain calm. It's natural to be confused when you awake in a strange place. Nothing to fret over. Look at all you've been through! It's a wonder you're doing so well. These internal pep talks had been a staple of her inner monologue for as long as she could recall, but after a decade of days watching her husband's long descent down the dark stairway of Alzheimer's, it was hard not to jolt back in fear at every twitch of forgetfulness.

Lizzie pushed through the netting and stepped to the open window. Only the security bars stood between her and the long lines of falling water. She had never liked the rain. Jonathan had been exactly the opposite. He loved to burrow on days like this, and read. Rainy days depressed her. They hid the sun. Oh, she knew the necessities of rainfall and the miracles it did, but if she could, she would fast-forward to the bright moments afterward, when the sun came back and re-established its glory in the freshly washed sky.

She turned away from the window and opened the tiny wardrobe. Uninspired, she stared at her clothes, aware that she should expect to be wet today, no matter what outfit she chose.

Last night, over dinner, Nana had explained that due to their schedules, she had no choice but to meet in the morning with Pastor Kajumba to bring him up-to-date on all that they'd learned. She felt cautiously confident that with his current attitude, Pastor would consider reinstating the three boys.

Since she would be unavailable, Nana had asked Jedediah to pick up Lizzie, and escort her to the location in Katwe where Dembe's mother lived.

"That is, if you still think you should go," she had said.

"Yes."

"Okay, then. He will be here in the morning, shine or rain."

Lizzie dug through the extra pockets in her suitcase and eventually came up with her compact umbrella. She remembered packing the perfect rain poncho for days like this but, somehow, it was not returned with the rest of her clothes from Owino Market. Unsnapping the strap that secured the umbrella, she pulled out the telescoping shaft and thumbed the button. Released, the coiled spring snapped everything open with a sliding metallic *zing*.

"Oops!" She stared into the arched and taut waterproof covering with a wistful smile. "Well, I'm glad you still work, but I wish

I hadn't opened you inside the house. I think that's supposed to be bad luck."

✦

The rainstorm continued unabated. Lizzie scampered over deep puddles and circled Jedediah's idling car to reach the front passenger door. Struggling to get in, she tipped her umbrella and shivered when streams of rainwater unexpectedly ran inside her collar. She squealed in shock and hunched her shoulders. Forcing her wide frame into the car, she attempted to close her umbrella and slam the door with something akin to synchronization.

Triumphant at last, she shoved her deflated umbrella to the floor with a snort and turned her eyes on a grinning Jedediah. "Was that entertaining enough for you? Or what?"

"Yes, truly." He seemed only slightly abashed, but was quick to defend himself. "And before you ask, I would have jumped out and helped, but I have no umbrella. Besides, if I take my foot off the gas pedal, this car dies. It never idles on its own when the rains come. Sorry."

Lizzie cinched her seatbelt. "Not a problem. Every woman understands that for men the car always comes first." She smiled sweetly. "I'm just happy you showed up at all."

Jed laughed as he pulled out, straining to see through the flailing wipers. "Lizzie, Lizzie, you are something!"

"Am I?"

"Yes, you are." He wedged the little car into the line of traffic. "You are something special. I admit when we first met, I didn't know what to think of you."

Lizzie cringed as she recalled those first moments. "I wasn't at my best, I—"

Jed held a hand up. "No. Let me finish. I need to say this." The car plowed through a huge puddle, sending up high splashes on each side. "I misjudged you. Meg had a sense about you, but I had none. I decided you were just another *muzungu* grandma with a soft heart. I am sorry, Lizzie. You are no such thing."

Lizzie sat spellbound. This was unexpected. "And what am I?"

Jed adjusted the speed of the worn wipers, vainly trying to keep the flooded windshield clear. "A force to be reckoned with. A *jjajja* with a quick mind and a strong heart. Mrs. Birungi told us last night what you discovered about Dembe." He shook his head. "With all my experience, I still had it wrong. You just knew. You had everything right. And you never gave up." He tipped his head to make sure he caught her eyes. "Thank God for you, Lizzie."

She felt her face flush. Moving her eyes away from his, she concentrated on the drops hitting the windshield. She counted the repetitive swipes of the wipers and let them calm her. "You're a very unusual man, Jed."

His face brightened with a teasing look. "You mean for a *Ugandan* man?"

"No. For a man. Any man."

Jed sobered, since he knew she was serious. "Thank you." But then he winked, and added, "*Jjajja.*"

More than forty minutes later, Jed swung the car around the Kibuye roundabout. Lizzie stared through the downpour at the ornate red-and-white clock tower in the center, which featured many extra spires and frills. Lizzie thought it looked like a cartoon cake.

Jed spun off the roundabout onto one of the lesser paved roads, and they soon entered an area with repair shops on both sides. The heavy rain made the signs above the doors hard to read, so Jed slowed down more and more, ignoring the angry honks as other drivers zipped around him. They passed car and truck garages, tire sellers, motorbike shops, large appliance repair, rebuilt generator vendors, and then a swath of small repair shops of all types. The road meandered up and down and around, and some of the last shops' doors were actually lower than the surface of the road. Jed spotted a somewhat level place on a bend and pulled over into the squishy maroon mud.

He pointed across the street to a narrow storefront with a blue tarp stretched over the entrance. "That should be it. At least, I think so, according to what Mrs. Birungi said."

Lizzie squinted in the rain, trying to get a sense of the place, but she really couldn't see much. It looked shabby and dim. She thought she saw movement in the windows, but then doubted herself. When the tarp flapped for a moment, she was able to read the sign: *Otema Best Repair*.

"Okay…"

Jed turned off the car. The sound of the beating rain seemed to surge without the engine noise to mute it. "You have the umbrella. Keep yourself dry. Don't worry about me, I'm used to this."

Lizzie nodded vacantly.

Jed hesitated. "Look. No one says you have to do this. And I don't know how it will go. Probably not well." He waited for a response.

She nodded with a resigned look.

He asked, "Do you have a plan?"

"No. Just a desire and a hunch." She shrugged. "That's all."

"Well, since it's you, Lizzie, that's enough for me." He cracked open his door and the rain seemed to sizzle around his feet. "What do we have to lose?"

❧

The large man was lifting the center of his sagging tarp with a pole to spill out the collected water when he noticed their approach. Lizzie felt his eyes immediately swing to her, following her steps, noting the sway of her hips; it made her skin crawl.

The rain began to lessen in intensity. As they came closer, Lizzie picked up more details. The man carried a heavy gut in a flaccid body. His movements were plodding, and he rocked when he took his steps. His hair was tight to his head, and a poorly trimmed moustache bristled beneath his nose. Small black eyes set deeply in a fleshy face.

He called out to them in thickly accented English. "*Muzungu* lady! You come for repair? Yes?"

The shop had a step-down entrance into a small open area just in front of its narrow door. This was what the tarp was meant to shield. They paused at the entry steps, and Jed looked down at the man. "May we enter?"

The man leaned his pole against the wall and waved with cupped hands. "Come. Come. Out of the rain."

They stepped down and passed under the protection of the leaky tarp. Lizzie closed her umbrella, aware of the man's eyes tracking her. The rain made continuous popping noises against the tarp.

Jedediah smiled disarmingly and lifted his sodden shirt away from his skin. "Thanks. Good to be out of the rain."

The man nodded. "Can I help? This is my repair shop." His voice sounded thick, his words slurring. He studied each of them in turn with some suspicion. "You carry nothing to fix."

"No. Nothing for repair." Jedediah held the man's eyes. "We were told that you, or your wife, may know of a boy named Dembe."

The man's entire bearing shifted. His expression turned vile and his voice crackled with fury. "Dembe! That thief! That demon who ate my food and stole my best tools! Do you have him? Do you know where he is?"

The raw anger surging from him drove Lizzie back a step. Even with Jed standing beside her, she felt fear tightening in cold coils around her heart. She saw a door open behind the man. A pregnant woman stepped halfway out from the dim shop and spoke to him in Luganda, using soft tones.

"What're you talking about? Who are these people?"

The man angrily snapped at her. "Get out of here, woman! It's no concern of yours!"

She persisted, eyes darting. She raised her voice slightly. "I thought I heard Dembe's name."

He barked at her again, waving a hand. "It's nothing! Go away!"

The woman studied Jedediah and Lizzie. She came all the way out of the door. Her eyes settled on Lizzie, and she asked in clear English, "Who are you?"

The man tried to block the woman's view and shoved her back with a thick hand. His Luganda words cracked like a whip. "Get out! Get out of my shop! Leave!" Flecks of spit peppered his lips and his mustache. "This is my business!"

"But it's raining."

"So what? Go! Now! Or you'll be sorry!" He lifted his arm as if to strike her, and she hastily retreated back inside the shop.

Lizzie caught the woman's eyes staring at her from behind the glass. The woman pointed up the road, nodded once, and then swiftly faded away into the dark interior.

Jed leaned closer to Lizzie and touched her upper arm. "We should go. Nothing good will come of this."

Shaken by the situation, Lizzie managed to nod and turn away.

The heavy man swept up the pole he had used to poke the tarp and slapped it across the steps leading out, impeding their path. "Wait! You did not say where Dembe is!" His voice sounded harsh, but more controlled. His eyes glistened. "I want him. I have rights. I am his father. And he owes me."

Jed stepped in front of Lizzie and faced the man. "We don't know where he is. And he owes you nothing!"

The sound of the rain increased suddenly with a fresh downpour. Lizzie looked with loathing at the wretched man and his dark shop. She thought of Dembe guiding her through the slums on her first night, and said, "You're not his father. You never will be."

The man spat on the ground. "I know what I am. I know my rights. You best be careful, woman!"

Jed had had enough. He took a step toward the man and

snarled in Luganda. "Move the pole, or I'll break it over your head – fat man!"

There was a dangerous moment, made more intense by the pounding of the rain, and then the pole lifted out of their way. They plunged back into the deluge, Lizzie popping her umbrella up. They hurried back across the road.

The man shouted after them in Luganda. "Do not come back unless you have what I want! That little devil owes me!"

As they reached the car, Jed opened Lizzie's door and flashed a grin. "Well, that went well."

Lizzie shut her umbrella as she climbed in. "Thanks for coming along. I never realized how valiant you could be."

"Oh, you have no idea." He closed her door and pranced through the thick mud to his door. "No idea!"

Jed backed the car up and was maneuvering in the mud to turn around when Lizzie touched his shoulder. "No. Don't go back the way we came."

"What?"

"Let's go on farther."

"Seriously?"

"Yes. I have a hunch."

"Another hunch?" He sighed, but dutifully spun the wheel the other way, and straightened the car. "Okay. It may be shorter going on anyway." Jed checked the traffic and pulled out, continuing down the road.

In a short distance, they came upon an open market, resplendent in tarps and makeshift coverings of all colors. In the dripping dryness beneath, smoke wafted up from blackened pots. Green mounds of *matoke* and the angled displays of vegetables beckoned. Despite the wet day, there seemed to be a good assortment of customers milling about the stands.

Lizzie's eyes were searching. "Go slower."

Jed glanced at her, "Why? Are we grocery shopping?"

She pointed ahead. "There she is. Pull over. Quickly."

The woman from the repair shop stood at the corner of a rain tarp, holding a plastic dishpan over her head, her back to the busy market. She stepped swiftly toward the car and slipped into the backseat. Keeping her head down, she spoke softly. "Drive on. I will tell you where to stop."

Jed glanced at Lizzie in amazement before putting the car back in gear.

The road soon switched from pavement to gravel. After that, the woman had them park behind a cluster of trees.

Jed switched off the engine and turned around. Already studying the woman, Lizzie listened to the rain beat on the roof and waited. The woman looked at them both, her face worn and tired, but her eyes bright.

"When did you see my Dembe?"

Lizzie said, "A few days ago."

"Is he well?"

"I don't know. He lives on the street. We can't find him."

A distressed look passed across the woman's face. Her words flowed slowly. "My brother said he was expelled from a school. But I thought he still lived in a home for...boys..."

Jedediah completed her thought. "Street boys. Yes. My wife and I run a boys' home. But I sent him away months ago, for stealing."

The woman shook her head, puzzled. "Dembe was never a thief."

Lizzie scowled, remembering the shopkeeper. "That's not what your husband thinks."

The woman's voice came sudden and sharp. "That one is an empty bowl! He claims everything is his when he drinks." She took a breath and slowed down. "Dembe took his own father's tools – his by right. This husband married me for the tools and our repair customers. He was jealous of my first husband, and hungry for me."

Lizzie watched the woman's face, weighing the emotions there, and aware of how much her eyes reminded her of the boy. "Your son does repairs for cash. And he steals for Mirembe, to pay her school fees and keep her safe. That's why he was expelled. Why he's on the street."

The woman held a hand in front of her face. "Do not tell too much. If he beats me, I cannot say what I do not know."

Lizzie had been all set to give more details, but she stopped herself. "Okay."

The rain began to ease. Everything outside the car grew brighter. Lizzie thought the nearby trees appeared more distinct and she could see farther into the distance. Looking back at the woman, she wondered what to say. Instead, the woman asked a question.

"Does my brother still help Dembe?"

"Help?" Lizzie scoffed. "Your brother talks. Your son works and pays. Dembe is the one protecting your daughter."

The woman managed a small proud smile. "He was always his father's son."

"What do you mean?"

The woman leaned her head against the edge of the front seat. "They were so close. Maybe closer than me. They shared the fixer's gift." Her eyes were looking away, staring back in time. "I loved his father. He was not from my tribe, but we married anyway. And his family hated me. He promised to be my tribe, but the mosquitoes took him away."

Lizzie glanced at Jedediah and then back. "You mean, malaria?"

The woman nodded, still caught up in the past. "It got into his brain. We had no money for hospital. At the end, he had bad dreams, and fevers, and much shaking. Dembe did our customers' repairs all day and talked with his father at night."

The woman's voice stopped and she sat silently for a moment before going on. "It was a hard death."

"I'm sorry. I had no—"

The woman talked over her, unwilling to be interrupted or slowed. "And when my husband was gone, his family took everything away. They cared nothing about the children or me. I hid his tools. I took what I could. I was afraid. I married to save us from the street."

Lizzie remembered Nana's story of her own husband's death. Her heart felt tight. Her mind was incensed. She struggled to keep her voice neutral, for the woman's sake, even though she wanted to pound the seat and scream at the injustice. "But things got worse, after that?"

"How could I know he was a drunk and...mean?" The woman's voice rose. "That he would use his fists?" Clearly, these thoughts ate at her. "How could I know he would hate my son for his gift, and want my daughter...for her beauty?" Her voice fell to a whisper. "Who could know he had another wife?" She scrunched lower in the seat and put her damp hands on top of her head.

"What will you do now?" Lizzie asked.

The woman took slow breaths and looked toward the floor. "What else can a woman do here? I have nothing to trade. I am too old to beg and not young enough to trap a better man. I will live on, where I am."

The bleakness at the core of her answer chilled Lizzie. It wasn't at all what she expected. When she replied, her voice gave away her attitude. "But what about your kids? You can't just let them—"

The woman sat straight up in the backseat, eyes flaring, hands clenched. "Do not judge me, *muzungu*! I have lost everything, but I am still here! I know my son lives. I know he takes care of his sister. It is all I can do."

Lizzie's hands squeezed the headrest on top of her seat. "No. I don't judge you." Her voice was filled with sorrow. "I'm sorry. Neither of us chose where we were born, dear. We're just women."

Their eyes searched within each other's for a way to link, for a place to reach peace with the other, for a bridge to span the differences of time and birth and geography. Their genders were calling, each to each, to rise beyond their current situations to their shared sisterhood. The fragile moment passed, unfulfilled.

The woman placed her hand on the door handle. "I have been gone too long."

"Wait." Lizzie rooted in her belongings on the floor and came back with a small stack of shilling notes. "Take these."

The woman shifted away from her, affronted. "Am I a beggar? I do not want your money, *muzungu*! Or your pity!"

Lizzie's own eyes grew stern. She refused to be dissuaded. "You misjudge *me*!"

The woman stared back angrily, air hissing through her nose, but she remained seated, waiting.

Lizzie explained in a calm but firm tone. "I am giving you a story to keep you safe." She pointed the bills at her. "You tell him you found this money floating in the ditch. You went to the market and bought his favorite foods to make up for his bad day. Okay? His belly is one of his great weaknesses, isn't it? I'm sure there're more."

The woman's irritation cooled. She nodded at Lizzie, her arm instinctively curving around the baby she carried. Lizzie extended the cash. The woman accepted it and stuffed the bills deep within the folds of her clothes, before opening the car door.

Jedediah spoke in a rush of Luganda. "You don't have to get out here. We can drive you closer. It's no trouble."

She slid out of the seat and lifted the dishpan to block the light rain. "No," she replied in Luganda. "My feet still work." She stepped out and then turned back to glance one last time at Lizzie, speaking this time in English. "Thank you for your news."

They watched her walk along the road, heading for the market. Her small figure soon grew blurry and then vanished into the falling rain.

Jedediah looked sobered by the encounter. "Lizzie, there are times when I am ashamed of my nation."

Lizzie settled heavily into her seat. "Me, too. Just not at the moment."

He started the car and made a circle so they could head back out the way they came. "How did you know she would be waiting?"

Lizzie snapped on her seatbelt. "I told you. A hunch. It's a woman's thing, you know? Hard to explain."

Jedediah checked her matter-of-fact face, and then looked back to his driving. "Right. Well, whatever it is, I sure don't have it."

⤚⤙

The rain slacked off as Jedediah drove through the open gates of the Wobulezi School. He and Lizzie both motioned at the cheerful guard, still leaning back in his plastic chair, this time under a large faded umbrella.

Jed looked at Lizzie. "Where do I drop you off? Library or main building?"

Lizzie gazed out the window at the high sun trying to pierce the piled rainclouds. Its beams seemed like slender fingers of brightness poking through the holes. "I guess the main building. I'm not sure where her meeting is, but at least I know where her office is."

"Okay." He pulled over to the edge of the gravel road and stopped by the busy main building. Lizzie opened the door, gathered her things, triggered the umbrella and smoothly slid out.

Jed called after her, "Lizzie?" She crouched down and looked at him. "I will talk to the house father and the boys. See if any of them have ideas where to find Dembe."

She nodded. "Thanks."

Jed grinned in reply.

Lizzie stuck her palm out and looked up. The rain had stopped. She collapsed the umbrella while holding open the door. "And thanks again for being my knight in shining armor."

Jed's face clouded. "A what?"

"Um…ask Meg about it when you see her. I guess it's a *muzungu* thing."

She shut the door and could see Jed laughing as he drove away. At least there's no dust when it rains, she thought. Ahead of her, the school's courtyard filled with laughing students recently freed from their classrooms. Must be lunch break, she told herself. Plodding tiredly forward, her shoes made squishing sounds in the red mud as she set out to find Nana.

THIRTY-ONE

On The Run

As she opened the door to the main building, Lizzie heard a familiar voice calling from the courtyard behind her, "*Jjajja! Jjajja!*"

Turning, she saw Afiya charging toward her with a bright smile and an air of intrigue. Some of her school friends trailed behind her, suddenly shy in front of the older white woman.

Afiya was nearly breathless. "Is it not exciting? Like a storybook!" The girl could barely stand still.

Lizzie let go of the door and looked around. "What? Is what… not exciting?"

"The Safe Haven boys. They're here! Ogwambi and Musaazi! You know, the ones who were expelled." She moved in closer and altered her voice to sound mysterious. "We are not to know – but we do! Their classmates spotted them. Mrs. Mayombwe is here, too. You know, the one they call Auntie Meg."

Her friends overcame their bashfulness and circled like moths, anxious to listen. Afiya rushed her words in her eagerness to share the rumors. "They say Pastor Kajumba might let them come back. Some say *yes*, some say *no*. We are all talking about it. But nobody has seen Dembe. Is he here, too? Is he coming back? Do you know?"

Lizzie felt trapped and overwhelmed. "I…I don't know anything. This is all news to me. I just got here."

Afiya cocked her head and studied Lizzie more critically. "Where have you been? Your clothes are all wet."

Aware of the attentive eyes and ears of Afiya's followers, Lizzie answered, "Ahh, I've been out in the rain…"

Afiya's face slumped. "But…okay." She brightened. "Do you want me to show you where mother's meeting is?"

Lizzie stepped out of the constricting circle of Afiya's friends and pulled open the building's door. "No thank you. I think I'll just wait outside your mother's office." She went in.

Afiya hurried after her. Her friends stopped at the door, apparently not bold enough to enter without permission.

Lizzie saw that Nana's office door was open but the room empty, so she sat in one of the plastic chairs outside to wait. Afiya soon stood beside her.

"*Jjajja*, will you tell me if you know something? I mean, as soon as you know it?"

Lizzie recognized the insatiable gossip drive of a thirteen-year-old girl and shook her head. "Afiya, this is not a story. Okay? I don't think it's right for me to be your—"

Mrs. Birungi and Pastor Kajumba arrived in a rush from another part of the building. Lizzie saw Meg, Ogwambi and Musaazi hurrying behind them. She stood.

Nana looked anxious, her hand still holding a cell phone. She seemed startled to see Lizzie. "Oh, Lizzie! I'm so glad you are here. I don't know what to say. I – something terrible has happened!" She suddenly noticed her daughter. "Afiya! What are you doing? Go back to class. Now!"

Afiya ducked her head and immediately withdrew a short distance down the hall, but she didn't leave.

Nana turned to Lizzie. "I just took a frantic call from Mrs.

Bossa. Mirembe is missing! All her clothes and books are gone. Friends saw her leave school with a boy early this morning."

Lizzie had trouble following. "What? Mirembe's running away? Is that what—"

"No." Pastor Kajumba held up a hand. "That is not exactly what Mrs. Bossa said."

"But it is what she thinks!" Birungi's face was firm. "I know her, Pastor."

"You may be right." Kajumba's voice remained level. "But I suggest we go there and see for ourselves, and talk to the friends before we decide what to do."

Lizzie glanced at Meg and the boys, feigning ignorance. "Nana, what's all this?"

"Well, I…I told you Pastor Kajumba and I had a…a meeting…"

Kajumba interrupted. "It is my doing, Lizzie. I thought it was time that I do more than apologize for what I did. There is blame on both sides and maybe room for mercy. Meg and the boys were kind enough to come in and talk."

Nana hurried into her office while the pastor spoke. She rushed back out slinging her purse across a shoulder. "But none of that matters right now."

As if hearing a cue, Kajumba nodded and hurried off. "I will bring the car to the front." He glanced back as he left. "You are welcome to come along, Lizzie."

The women looked at each other in the lull following his departure. No one was quite sure what to say. Finally, Meg spoke up. "Is it Dembe? Are we sure he's the boy?"

Nana frowned. "Who else could it be?"

"But why now?" Meg asked. "Just when things are changing."

Lizzie sighed. "Because the grownups have gotten too close, that's why. He can't trust us to protect his sister." Her voice hardened. "And I don't blame him."

"What?" Nana looked at her.

"I've met the stepfather." Her tone conveyed her disgust.

Both Nana and Meg had questions but Nana forestalled any further talk. "We have to go. Lizzie, are you coming?"

Lizzie opened her mouth to answer, when she noticed a small movement behind Meg. Ogwambi shook his head. Once he had her attention, he added a small negative wave to his signs. Lizzie frowned, confused.

Nana and Meg headed down the hallway. Nana abruptly stopped. "Lizzie?"

Lizzie hesitated and then held her arms out from her sides, awkwardly. "I'm...completely soaked from the rain. All the way to the skin. I need to change...but I don't want to slow you down."

Nana looked unsure. Meg faced Lizzie. "The boys have to get home, too. I'm sure they can take a taxi with you and get you safely to Mrs. Birungi's house on their way."

Meg dug in her purse for money. Lizzie saw her. "I have cash, Meg. Don't worry about it."

Nana still looked doubtful. "Okay, but...how will we stay in touch?"

Afiya's voice came from around the corner. "I can help, Mother." She stepped into the hall and instantly switched to Luganda as she made her case. "If you give me your phone, I'll stay right beside *Jjajja*. That way Pastor or Mrs. Mayombwe can call us at any time, or I can call them. And I can also guide the taxi. Please!"

Nana listened but remained unmoved. "I told you to get to class."

Afiya stood her ground. "Mother, I need to help in someway. You're not the only person who cares about Dembe and *Jjajja*."

Nana seemed torn. Lizzie seized the opportunity. "I don't know what you said just now, but I promise I won't let her out of my sight."

Making a decision, Nana reluctantly handed her phone to Afiya, who grinned from ear-to-ear. Birungi frowned at Lizzie. "I wish I could tell you that your promise eases my mind, but it doesn't. Still,

I don't know what else to do." She turned and hurried down the hall toward the outer door, Meg right behind.

Once the hall cleared, Lizzie advanced on Ogwambi and fixed him with a look. "Okay, young man, you better explain to me why I did what I just did!"

Ogwambi bunched his shoulders, uncomfortable with the pressure. "They waste time, lady. Dembe is moving his sister to a new school."

Musaazi nodded. "He will find someplace far away and start over. It is what he told us he would do, if he had to."

Lizzie studied them both. "Can you find him in time?"

Ogwambi made a face. "Maybe. He is tricky. But we have boys to ask and places to look."

Musaazi scowled. "But we must go fast. No time for questions."

Lizzie unceremoniously dumped her umbrella and anything extra into the chair while securing her purse. "Okay, buster! I'm ready. Let's go."

The boys moved speedily down the hall, Lizzie barely keeping up. Afiya paced along by Lizzie's side, pecking at the cell phone.

Lizzie snapped a look at her. "Are you snitching to your mom?"

"No!" Her eyes wavered. "What is *snitching*?"

"Using the phone to tell her what we're doing."

Afiya pinched her brows together. "No! Changing settings."

"I really shouldn't let you come with us, you know."

Afiya shot her an incredulous look. "I told Mother I would stay right beside you, remember?" She pocketed the phone.

"I never heard you say that."

"Oh." Afiya gave it a quick thought. "That was in Luganda."

"Then it doesn't count."

"But I did say it!" Afiya made a face. "Wait! *You* promised not to let me out of your sight. And that was in English! How about that?"

Lizzie snorted in frustration.

They filed rapidly through the outer doors and headed for the paved road. The hot sun dried the ground and sucked the wetness into the air. Lizzie heard the sounds of traffic in the distance.

Afiya looked at her. "Buster?"

"What?" Lizzie could feel the sweat as she struggled to keep up with the boys.

"You said, 'okay, buster.' What is *buster*?"

Lizzie just rolled her eyes and increased her walking speed. Afiya easily matched her. "Is it a bad word?"

✧

Standing outside the school gate, Lizzie scanned the busy highway for taxi vans to hail. She noticed a military Humvee pass by that looked familiar, but no taxis. Behind her, Ogwambi called out, "Lady, what are you doing?"

Puzzled, she turned with a frown. "Don't we need to wave for a taxi? That's what Mrs. Birungi does."

"No lady. No taxi. Too slow. Too many stops."

It was then that she noticed the activity behind Ogwambi. Musaazi was over by the edge of the gate loudly haggling with a line of motorcycle-taxi drivers. He was checking their bikes, squeezing their cushioned seats, running his hands over the treads on their tires, all the time talking and pointing, then shaking his head and turning to start over with another driver.

Lizzie's heart and stomach dropped instantly into her shoes. Her mind stuttered and flailed. Dear God in heaven! Not a *boda-boda*! I can't! I've never! I…I…

The wind snapped her hair against her glasses, forcing her to squint. She felt powerless to brush it away. Both of her hands were dedicated to a death grip on Ogwambi. He sat in between her and the driver. They leaned to the right and shot through an opening between two lanes of cars. They leaned back to the left as they gained some open space. She heard the whine and grumble of the other bike, carrying

Musaazi and Afiya. It swung in right behind her. Lizzie was too stiff with fear to turn her head. The padded bumper at the back end of the long cushion pushed hard against her rump, keeping her pinned tightly in her precarious perch. Her knees gripped the bike from either side like a bear trap. The taut muscles of her inner thighs trembled, threatening cramps. Her shoes were jammed onto welded studs just above the hot muffler on one side and the whirring chain on the other. The soles of her feet danced with every vibration from the motor or bump from the roadway. Whatever hearing she had left was swallowed up by the snarling engine and the roaring wind. She would have screamed in terror, but she was too busy trying to breathe. Yet, except for the non-stop threat of death and dismemberment, she had never felt so alive. And, if she dared to confess to herself a secret, she was starting to enjoy the rush!

Enveloped in the moment, Lizzie timidly swiveled her head and let her eyes take in everything. She couldn't remember ever having such a visual feast assail her mind: shooting past trucks and buses, their humming tires at eye-level; splitting lanes with speeding cars close enough to touch; pushing through angry pedestrians in the crosswalks; tipping and zipping through roundabouts, caution tossed to the wind.

A sudden hip-hop ringtone forced her attention over to the red *boda-boda* tearing along next to her. She noticed Musaazi leaned forward, talking into his driver's ear. Behind him, Afiya rode side-saddle, relaxed, with one hand casually draped over the grab bar at the back. Her other hand held the ringing cell phone to her face, straining to read the name. Her thumb swiped the screen and the ringtone cut off. Afiya put the phone to her ear and started talking as casually as if seated in her living room.

Aghast, Lizzie couldn't stop herself from shouting. "Afiya! Hold on! Are you crazy? Put that phone down!"

The young girl shook her head and said something into the phone. Ending the call, she graced Lizzie with a blank look before yelling at her. "Sorry, *Jjajja*! I could not hear you!" She stowed the phone in a pocket. "That was Mother. She wanted to know if we were home yet."

Lizzie's stomach sank. She yelled back. "What…what did you tell her?"

Afiya smirked. "I said we were in traffic. That it was hard to hear because of *boda-bodas*. And I would call when we reached home." She smiled innocently across the gap between the bikes, a devilish gleam in her eyes. "All true, *Jjajja*!"

⁓

The *boda-bodas* stood up on their kickstands in the hard-packed dirt. The drivers had parked by a sea of idle motorcycle-taxis in a busy intersection. The boys had vanished into the alleys between the buildings.

Lizzie leaned against her bike, annoyed at the grainy orange mud spattered on her clothes from puddles and potholes. She felt the eyes of other drivers move her way and heard comments. No longer surprised, she had come to accept that she was a kind of minor celebrity. A *muzungu* woman riding a *boda-boda*. Of course, that would be a novelty. But one with big hips and covered in mud? How could they resist? Sighing, she scanned the last place she had seen Ogwambi and Musaazi, silently pleading with them to hurry it up.

At the sound of snoring, Lizzie turned and saw the other driver stretched out across the top of his machine, helmet wedged between the handlebars as a pillow. She happened to look up just as a white Toyota pickup with extra antennas passed by. Frowning, she tried to peer inside the dark windows, but a high piled vegetable truck blocked her view. And then the pickup was gone. Was that Sgt. Elwelu? Alerted now, she paid closer attention. She picked out a few soldiers standing at strategic places, attentively watching the crowd. In the distance, she thought she saw another military vehicle cross the road.

"Here they come, *Jjajja!*" Afiya eagerly pointed toward some distant shops.

Racing around a metal shack and ducking full clotheslines, the boys dashed back to them. Lizzie read concern in their expressions, but excitement as well.

Musaazi promptly poked the sleeping driver and fussed at him in Luganda. The driver snorted in shock and loudly complained, but he still rolled to his feet and strapped on his helmet.

Ogwambi motioned hurriedly at the other driver and then looked at Lizzie. "They were here. Some boys saw them both."

Their driver pushed the bike forward off its kickstand and climbed on, supporting it with both legs. He waited for them to board.

Ogwambi swung up behind him. "Dembe took his tools. No one knows for sure where he went. But one says he heard *bus*. Another thinks Mirembe said, 'Why Entebbe?'"

Lizzie awkwardly clambered into her back position and clutched Ogwambi's waist. "What's it mean?"

The driver turned the key. The bike fired up. He revved the gas a few times before walking it forward to the other bike.

Ogwambi turned his head halfway back towards Lizzie. She leaned close to hear him above the noise. "He is leaving Kampala. Maybe to find a school in Entebbe."

Musaazi and Afiya were settled into their slots when their driver started his bike. Lizzie shouted to be heard above the two engines. "Where are we going now?

Musaazi leaned away from talking to his driver and hollered back. "Pioneer Easy bus station. Orange buses! Best chance! Must hurry!"

Lizzie nodded. Before she could ask anything further, the bikes roared off together, bouncing over broken curbs. All she could do was hold on tight and hope for the best.

⤳

Lizzie's driver swerved in front of the flat, glassed in nose of a large orange bus trying to exit the Pioneer Easy bus lot. That earned him a loud bray of the horn from the peeved driver. Their *boda-boda* proceeded down the left side of the bus. Behind them, Musaazi's bike swerved to the right side of the bus.

"Look in the windows!" Musaazi called out.

Lizzie swallowed her fear at the nearness of the moving metal and focused on the curious black faces staring back at her through the windows. She saw neither Dembe nor Mirembe.

Caught in the wash of noxious diesel fumes as the bus departed, Musaazi waved at both drivers to pull over at the edge of the lot near a set of trees. He hopped off and hurried up to Lizzie. "Lady, we foot from here. Okay?" He put his hand out. "Sorry. I need to pay the rest of money."

"Oh, right." Lizzie dug in her purse and handed him a wad of shilling notes. Beside her, Afiya's cell phone blared hip-hop music. The girl slipped off the bike and stepped away, ducking her head as she answered to minimize the noise.

Musaazi swiftly paid the *boda-boda* drivers and handed the remaining bills back to Lizzie. Ogwambi joined them. The boys huddled. Lizzie heard short spurts of Luganda fly back and forth. Ogwambi rushed off, speed walking between buses.

Musaazi explained. "He asks which ones go to Entebbe and when." He squinted at the crowds milling around. "Keep looking, lady."

Lizzie turned her tired eyes to the huge bus lot. Moving groups of people walked everywhere, some preparing to leave, others having just arrived. Piles of worn bags littered the crumbled asphalt. Children and adults sat near their possessions, or leaned against them, or slept on them. Old cardboard boxes bulged with personal belongings.

On the periphery of the station, small food vendors plied their craft. She saw *cha'pati* stands with lines of customers, and boys weaving through the travelers hawking pieces of roasted chicken skewered on sticks. Carts and over loaded bicycles displayed cold drinks and offered biscuits. She watched a loaded bus toot its horn and majestically move people aside like a ship's prow dividing seawater.

Lizzie felt the prickling of despair. Maybe they were already too late. How would they ever spot Dembe in this busy place? She felt a small hand on her arm and looked down into the wide-eyed face of Afiya. The girl nervously held out the phone.

"For you, *Jjajja*." Lizzie cocked her head, Afiya replied, "Mother."

Experiencing a sudden wash of dread, Lizzie took the phone and carefully spoke into it. "Hello?"

She heard Mrs. Birungi's voice sizzle from the earpiece. "Where are you? Tell me the truth! I am in no mood for stories!'"

"Nana, I—"

Birungi cut her off. "Don't *Nana* me! Just tell me where you are!"

Lizzie was cowed. "At a bus station." She saw Afiya nervously watching her. Lizzie turned away.

"Which one?"

"Umm...orange buses. Pioneer something—"

"Pioneer Easy?"

"Yes. That's it." Lizzie tried again, saying, "The boys think Dembe is—"

Birungi cut her off again. "I know that station. Stay there! Do not move!"

"Please!" Lizzie was determined. "I know we let you down. But the boys are sure Dembe's fleeing to Entebbe. I should have... Nana?" She listened, but heard nothing. "Are you still there? Nana?" Lizzie stared at the *hang-up* icon. She felt the same queasy weight settle in her intestines that she had felt as a teen caught red-handed skipping school.

Afiya took back the phone and shook her head, letting out a long sigh.

Lizzie glanced up as Ogwambi reappeared with news. The next bus to Entebbe would leave in thirty minutes.

"But what if he's headed somewhere else?" Lizzie asked. "Then what?"

The boys looked at each other and shrugged. Ogwambi suggested they split up and meet back at the trees in twenty minutes if they didn't spot anyone. Lizzie and Afiya set off together. Musaazi joined Ogwambi.

THIRTY-TWO

The Boy on the Bus

Lizzie trailed her hand along the warm metal skin of a parked bus as she walked toward the back wheel. They had looked everywhere, and twenty minutes were nearly up. The windows above her were void of faces and she knew she was out of ideas. She could feel the humidity in the air with each breath and a growing hopelessness with every step. Passing the muddy treads on the huge rear tire, she rounded the bumper to scan ahead. Beside her, Afiya kept dutifully checking faces, allowing her eyes to flit across the restless press of travelers nearby.

Lizzie stood motionless, unaware her feet had stopped. Her wary eyes were locked onto a pair of familiar figures, and the marrow in her bones cooled to ice. She remembered them. Lean and darker skinned than others, taller than average, always on the look-out. Yes. Definitely the same ones. She recalled picking them out in the market near the MTN shack. What had Nana said they were? Maasai or from Sudan – just before the bomb! Sudan!

She grabbed Afiya's arm and pulled the girl close, whispering. "Do you see those tall men ahead?"

Startled, Afiya looked and nodded.

Lizzie pressed, "What's your guess? Sudanese?"

Afiya stared at her strangely and then studied the men from behind. "I don't know. Maybe. Not Ugandan. Why?"

"I'm positive I saw them just before the bomb in the market."

The girl quickly swung her eyes back. She stared closely. "You think they might be the rebels who—"

Lizzie spoke in a rush. "I don't know what I think. They scare me! That's what I know."

Afiya's eyes widened. She whispered, "Should we follow them, *Jjajja*?"

Without answering, Lizzie entered the crowd, tracking in the two men's wake. Afiya jumped to catch up. As they closed the distance, Lizzie began to note details. Their shirts were shabby and permeated with dirt, the elbows frayed and unrepaired. They wore nearly identical tan backpacks in far better shape than their clothes. She could see the smooth edge of a cell phone in one of the pack's exterior mesh pockets. The men were in the crowd, but Lizzie felt certain from the way they moved and swiveled their heads, they were not really part of the crowd. She was sure they had no intention of travelling anywhere. They were stalking.

"*Jjajja*! There is Dembe! Up ahead! Look!" Afiya's high-pitched voice was so filled with dancing excitement that it cut through the crowd noise. She covered her mouth, suddenly aware of how loud she sounded.

One of the Sudanese turned. His dark eyes swiftly pinpointed Afiya as the source of the squealing voice, but then they passed over her to settle briefly on the *muzungu*. Lizzie caught his eyes. She saw a curious hesitation before he dismissed her and continued on. For Lizzie, his eyes felt like a doll's eyes, black, shiny and utterly empty.

Ahead, beside a bus with an open door, Lizzie spotted Dembe. He argued with Ogwambi and Musaazi. Mirembe stood next to him, guarding heavy bags and wearing an old backpack.

Lizzie felt torn. She had thought everything hinged on finding

Dembe – and there he was! She wanted desperately to run to him, but now she was absolutely petrified of losing sight of these men. How could life switch so quickly? She frantically scoured the edges of the crowd, looking for help. Where were soldiers when you needed them?

Afiya hissed at her, frightened. "What do we do?"

Lizzie bit her lip. She felt panic rising in her chest. "I don't know, I don't know, I don't know!" It was difficult to catch her breath. The ends of her fingers felt cold.

She forced herself to step sideways through the crowd, using other bodies to mask her own. She watched the Sudanese men close in on the loading bus near Dembe and Mirembe. Riders began to climb aboard, lugging their awkward packages. Some carried children. One of the tall men joined the queue, standing behind a family. Calmly moving with the line, he smoothly ascended the narrow steps and disappeared into the bus. The other man blended with the mass of waiting people, slowly rotating his head, his eyes on watch.

Lizzie waited until the man's head turned away. Then she pulled on Afiya's hand. "Now! To Dembe!"

Pushing, she slipped through the crowd. Most people easily gave way, once they saw it was a white woman. Lizzie paid little heed to the bodies she moved aside, all of her effort on avoiding the tall man's eyes. She worked her way to Dembe and suddenly grasped him by the shoulders, thrusting her face in front of his.

Dembe looked startled. "*Jjajja*! What?"

Her eyes were wild. "Don't talk! We're in danger!"

"But…Musaazi says that Pastor…"

"Look at me!" She shook him slightly. "It's important! Pretend to be happy!"

Dembe stared in her eyes, confused. "What are you doing?"

"No! Trust me! Smile!"

He smiled, but his eyes remained uneasy. "Okay. I'm smiling. Now, what?"

"Listen to me!" Lizzie's voice was intense. "Bombers are here! The same ones from the market."

Dembe's eyes opened wider and roved behind her. He dropped his voice to match hers. "Here? Where?" His fake smile stayed on his face.

"I saw them. One on the bus. One in the crowd behind me. Don't look!"

Dembe's face didn't move but his eyes locked onto something in the distance. "Too late. Tall. Brown backpack. I see one."

"The other's already on your bus."

Dembe's eyes jumped to the right as he pretended to pat her arm. "He is getting off."

"Stop looking! They'll see."

"No worry. They look at each other."

"Does he have a backpack?"

"No."

Lizzie cringed. "Then he left it on the bus."

Dembe loosened her arms from his shoulders and looked deeply into her eyes. His voice was steady. "We have time. They will wait until the bus is full. Do both backpacks look the same?"

"Yes." Lizzie sounded baffled. "But we don't have time! Don't you get it? We must leave. Now!"

"Did you see a phone on the backpack?"

"Do you hear me? We have to get away!"

"*Jjajja.*" Dembe's voice remained steady but insistent. "Was there a phone?"

Upset, she closed her eyes, visualizing. "Yes. In the front pocket. Why?"

"I can help."

"No. We can call for help."

"We will be too late. Here, pretend I am showing you something."

"Huh?"

Dembe bent over and rummaged in one of the bags next to

Mirembe. Without ever looking at her, he whispered something to his sister. She nodded awkwardly, her expression puzzled. Keeping up the charade, Dembe grinned as he pulled out a stained burlap bag and lifted it for Lizzie to hold open while he dug inside. At hand motions from him, Musaazi, Ogwambi and Afiya stepped closer. Dembe issued short orders in Luganda, barely above a whisper. All the while, he acted as if he was laughing, perhaps telling a funny story. The others registered momentary shock but covered their reaction with ghastly smiles. From the bag, Dembe recovered a thick rectangle of aluminum foil. He began methodically to unfold it.

Lizzie understood his plan. "You can't! Who knows if that even works?"

Dembe was still grinning at her, simulating a deliriously happy departure moment. "I will stop the bomb, and you will call for help." His eyes darted away for an instant, but his head never moved. "They are watching us now. Make sure and wave goodbye as I get on the bus."

"Dembe! No!"

He walked toward the bus, joining a much shortened line, and waved at his friends. "Thanks for seeing me off!" Dembe's eyes bored into Lizzie's. "And *Jjajja*, do not let our...friends get lost in the crowd."

The line moved forward. He zipped up the stairs and vanished into the dark interior. There were only a few left to board after him.

Musaazi and Ogwambi grabbed Mirembe's bags and rapidly shepherded the group away from the bus. Lizzie let her eyes drift over the crowd ahead until she located the Sudanese men moving toward the lot's exits. They slowly walked away, their heads turned to observe the loading bus. Lizzie guided her group in the same direction. She caught her breath when she noticed one of the bombers cradled a phone in his hand, thumb poised over the screen. He tossed a comment to his partner with a laugh. The other simply shook his head and kept walking.

Behind her, Lizzie heard sudden screams. She whipped around and saw the bus rocking.

"*Bomu!*"

Terrified people squeezed out the tight bus doors. Some stumbled on the steps in their push to get away. Men frantically shoved through the bottleneck. Bodies spilled to the pavement. The mobs around the bus scattered like smoke.

"*Bomu! Bomu!*"

Boxes and bags were dropped, stepped on, or tripped over. Luggage abandoned. In the spreading chaos, running people crashed through a soft drink stand, knocking over the vendor and his bike. Panic whirled across the lot, the terrifying word repeated from many throats. "*Bomu! Bomu! Bomu!*"

A rising wave of fleeing bodies pushed towards Lizzie like an ocean swell. Soon, she struggled to keep her feet as the running people swept her closer to the Sudanese men. The bombers fought to stay in place, like angry rocks in a rushing stream. The one with the phone jammed his thumb against the screen, over and over again. His eyes grew frantic. He glared at the bus, face contorted in fury. The other one stood tight to his shoulder, shouting, gesturing. The one ripped the phone away from the other to reset it. Quick fingers tapped keys to redial the call. When they looked up, the bus remained intact.

Intent on the bombers, Lizzie didn't notice Afiya pulling her arm, shouting for attention. Now she turned.

Afiya pointed toward the exits. "It's Mother! Look! And Pastor! And...soldiers!"

Lizzie stared as Nana, Kajumba and Meg ran into the crowd from their car. Nana spotted Afiya's wave and fought against the current of the mob to reach her daughter. Lizzie saw trucks and

Humvees disgorge soldiers in battle gear. The armed men raced to cordon off the bus station.

A white pickup roared up the main driveway and slid to a stop, blocking the exit. Sgt. Elwelu jumped out, helmet on, weapon in hand. His partner rounded the truck to join him. They scanned the fleeing crowd.

How could they be here? Lizzie's mind whirled. How would they know we need help? She began to wildly wave her arms at the soldiers. "Over here! The bombers! The bombers!"

Afiya joined in, jumping to be seen. She pointed at the men nearby. "Bombers! Bombers! Bombers!"

The terrorists spun around, suddenly aware of their own peril. They looked at each other for an instant, then split up. The one without a backpack yanked a pistol from under his clothes. He fired indiscriminately into the crowd, creating havoc. The other slipped off his backpack.

Struck by bullets, a man and a woman flew backwards near Lizzie. Around her, defenseless people ducked and scrambled over each other to get away.

Lizzie clutched Afiya and Mirembe to her, wrapping her arms about their heads. She felt a brush of air as bullets passed by.

Musaazi cut through the crowd. He leaped onto the shooting man's shoulders, bearing him down. Others instinctively jumped back to avoid the fighters. The boy proved no match for the rebel. He clubbed Musaazi with the gun barrel, leaping back to his feet. The pistol swept toward the fallen boy.

Lizzie saw a large scarred hand close on the rebel's arm. In a flurry of devastating blows, Lizzie caught a rare glimpse of the Ugandan boxer who quietly hid within Pastor Kajumba. She did witness, in all its glory, the right cross that crushed the rebel's cheek and dropped him lifeless to the ground.

Then, she fell backwards. The surging crowd washed over her. She lost the girls. Glancing blows struck her head. Lizzie blindly punched out. The mob stepped on her. She scrabbled and pawed at legs, forcing her way up to her knees. Through frenzied limbs, she saw the remaining bomber hurl his backpack!

Time crawled. Parts of her view jumped into crystal clarity, other parts grew blurry. She glimpsed the bomber's fingers as they tightened around a phone. She watched him take a step and leap away. His body appearing to float in the air. The faces of those beside him twisted in fear, hands stretched out in defense, fingers splayed.

The girls! Where were the girls? Afiya's head rose up, turning toward her. Mirembe rolled over, within arm's reach. Lizzie reached out her hand. Fleeing bodies knocked it aside. No! Suddenly, Nana was there, bending down to snatch her daughter. Meg swept her arms around Mirembe, lifting her away.

Lizzie staggered to her feet, stunned but acutely aware of everything. In the blink of an eye, her mind captured a snapshot. She noticed Kajumba carrying Musaazi, blood streaming from the boy's face. She observed soldiers closing in, but knew they would be too late. She saw the bomber hit the ground on his back, aiming his phone like a deadly wand. Her brow furrowed in alarm. Where was Ogwambi?

Hands grabbed her shoulders from behind. A young body swept her in a circle. She felt herself flung over piles of discarded luggage and boxes and bags. As she fell back to earth, she recognized the resolute face floating above her, the kind eyes still unsynchronized, the strong shoulders shielding her. Ogwambi!

A sudden *clap* sounded, as if time itself proclaimed, "Now!"

Everything rushed together, reclaiming all of its horrifying speed.

Her body slammed the asphalt beneath the baggage. Ogwambi sprawled on top of her, body shaking and twisting, left arm caught in shrapnel. Bags and boxes lifted around her, as if gravity had been repealed. Her head felt the blow from the giant's fist. It hurled her into that same silent, dark place she had visited once before.

THIRTY-THREE

New Tribe

This time her sense of smell came back first. She sniffed a pungent, sour odor, mingled with dust and something coppery. She felt herself sneeze. She waited for the second one. When she sneezed again, her eyes blinked open. A man's face hovered above her, partly blocked by his own hand, holding a cloth to her forehead. The scruffy face was familiar. She knew she should have a name in her mind – and then it was there: *Sgt. Elwelu*. His mouth moved as he spoke rapidly to someone nearby. Lizzie only heard the jagged whisperings of sound. A nearly silent helicopter passed by, directly overhead.

Sgt. Elwelu looked down at her and recognized that she was awake. He took away the red-stained cloth and moved his face closer to inspect her forehead. Smiling with reassurance, he asked a question. Lizzie couldn't hear enough to understand. Pointing at her ears, she shook her head. That's when she noticed her right hand was wrapped in a thick bandage. She rotated it in front of her eyes, observing some scarlet seepage below the surface.

Elwelu tapped her gently. When he had her attention again, he touched his own ears, his eyes, and signaled *okay*. Next, he swiveled his wrist up to his face, as if looking at an imaginary watch, and nodded at her. She got it. *"Ears look okay. Takes time."*

Lizzie struggled to sit up. Elwelu signaled his disapproval and kept a firm hand against her shoulder. He pulled together soft fragments from the shredded bags around her head to fashion a makeshift pillow. Lizzie's ears crackled. Her tired mind raised desperate questions she needed to ask.

Sgt. Elwelu disappeared from view. Turning her head to the side, Lizzie watched a pair of soldiers with a stretcher. A lifeless hand dangled over the side, the nails still bright with polish. She turned back as the sergeant lifted her head to help her drink from a plastic bottle. She felt stupid, as if acting the part of an invalid.

Attempting to speak, she suddenly coughed and sputtered the water back up. Her ears squealed, then opened to a sudden sea of sound, along with a knife-edge of agony. Wincing, she heard Elwelu say, "…easy now. Easy does it."

She got her coughing controlled and looked him in the face. "I can hear now, Sergeant." Her words echoed oddly in her skull and the consonants sounded fuzzy. "At least, well enough to talk."

He nodded as he twisted the cap back on the bottle. "That's good. Good."

She stared at him. "When can I get up?"

He smiled. "Soon. But not just yet. Okay?"

"I have questions."

"Shoot."

"Where is Ogwambi?"

"Which one is he?"

"The one who covered me."

He glanced quickly off to the side. "He's…he's right here. Jimbo's still workin' on him."

Lizzie attempted to sit up again, turning in the direction Elwelu had looked. The sergeant gently restrained her and shifted his body to block her view. "No, no, lie still, ma'am. You don't want to…

Jimbo's our best field medic, Mrs. Warton. Don't you worry, he'll get your boy stabilized."

"Stabilized?" Tears flooded her eyes.

"Yes, ma'am. He's pretty much good to go already. We'll be movin' to IHK shortly."

"What's IHK?"

"Sorry. It's a hospital. Good hospital. Dr. Mac's already got a heads-up. He's the best for this sorta thing."

The tears ran down into Lizzie's ears. "What *sorta thing*? What do you mean?"

Elwelu looked away and then back. "His arm took a lotta damage, okay? Maybe some internal stuff, too. But if anyone can patch him back up, it's MacLaird."

"I need to go with him, when he goes." Even though her voice trembled, her volume made it clear this was not a request.

The sergeant nodded. "You got it. We're movin' all the injured in shifts. Most are headed to Mulago, the big government hospital, but we're Ok'd to go to IHK."

"What's the IHK part?"

"International Hospital of Kampala. It's private. Some Irish guy started it. Dr. Mac prefers it there."

"Oh."

"You can have that hand looked at, too. And your concussion."

Lizzie scowled. "I'm sure I'm fine."

Elwelu gave her a look. "Really? You got puncture wounds in your hand. They put old nails and screws in their bombs. You caught a couple."

Lizzie looked soberly at her invisible hand beneath the white covering.

"I cleaned it up with saline and packed it with disinfectant sponges before I wrapped it up. Oughta be hurtin' like a...like a lot about now. Huh?"

"Yes." She gingerly folded her arm against her chest. "Okay, Sergeant, it hurts."

"And this's your second concussion, ma'am. I talked to you after your first one, remember?"

"Of course, I remember!" She sounded defensive.

"Well, that's good then." He smiled. "But they don't even let football players go back in after concussions, so why should we let you?"

"Are you gonna hold up fingers? Have me guess how many?" She knew she was using the bluster to mask her fierce headache and the ringing in her ears.

He shook his head. "No, ma'am. I just want you to lie quiet here for now, stop arguin', and have everything checked when we get there."

Lizzie took a breath. "Yes, Mom."

"Thank you."

"Sergeant, how is it that you and the…the UP-whatever army showed up here?"

"Showed up? Us and the UPDF?"

"Yeah. I mean, just when we needed you. Well, almost."

"Oh, hell, ma'am. You and your Mrs. Birungi were about the only leads we had. Captain Muhoozi's had us following you two all week."

"Following us? Why?"

"He figured you might lead us to that street kid you talked about. Never expected you'd get us the bombers. Dumb luck, I guess. Sure makes the captain look good, though."

Lizzie felt agitated. Her mind was still moving so slowly. "Where's Dembe? The…ah, the street kid?"

"Was he the one on the bus?"

"Yes."

"No scratches on him!" Elwelu laughed. "He was just sittin'

in the middle of that empty bus, still holdin' his tinfoil over that phone. Brave little shit. How'd he figure that out? Saved everyone."

Lizzie felt relief and a tiny glow of pride. "Because he's so smart, Sergeant."

Elwelu raised his eyebrows but didn't reply. Lizzie heard voices nearby and the scrape of boots. She watched the sergeant nod, say a few words in Luganda, and get to his feet.

"Okay, Mrs. Warton, we're movin' to the truck. They got your friend strapped on. I'll help you up, if you promise to take it slow. Otherwise, I'll hafta carry ya."

Lizzie carefully lifted up her good arm and cradled the bad one. "Just give an old lady an arm, Sergeant. I'm still breathin', and I believe my legs still work."

⚜

She stared fixedly at a smudge on the beige wall of the ER cubicle, breathing repetitively in through her nose, out through her mouth. Lizzie purposely didn't watch the Pakistani doctor as he irrigated her puncture wounds with saline solution. She also made a point of not looking while the shiny-haired young resident had debrided her injuries earlier, removing a few stubborn pieces of shrapnel.

She didn't realize Dr. MacLaird had stepped through the curtain and into the room behind her until he spoke.

"Lamaze breathing, Mrs. Warton? Impressive! We have the French to thank for that. Childbirth classes?"

"Yes," Lizzie grunted, still trying to control her breaths. "I'm a little rusty. And you're distracting me, Doctor."

"Ah, sorry. Blame your sergeant. He said we had to chat."

Lizzie glanced down at the resident. "Can we stop for a moment?"

The young doctor sat up straighter on his wheeled stool and nodded. He smiled at Dr. MacLaird. Lizzie saw that MacLaird wore a surgical smock, his hands encased in latex, a pale blue hair net on his head, and a paper mask hanging open near his mouth. The Scotsman bent over Lizzie's hand and studied the damage.

"Hmm. Lovely. Can you move the thumb and first finger?"

"Not without a lotta pain," she grumbled as she wiggled them.

"Good. That's fine," he said, tone bland. "And the rest of the fingers?"

"Yes." She grimaced as she moved them, too.

"Okay. And the wrist?"

Lizzie gently rocked her wrist up and down and then side to side, without too much pain. "Yes."

MacLaird stood back up, his gloved hands held chest high. "So, if we can keep infections at bay, ye might still escape relatively unscathed, aye, Lizzie me girl?"

She eyed him. "From your lips to God's ears."

"Not me," he said, letting a smile creep onto his face. "But nice to see you're still feisty."

"And what about Ogwambi? How is he?"

MacLaird paused. "Is that the young one we're workin' on now?"

She nodded. "You know it is."

He looked away from her. "Well now, that's a different kettle a' fish."

"Can you save his arm?" she asked, giving voice to her biggest fear.

"His arm, now? Is that what you're worried about? Ah, Lizzie, Lizzie. You're jumpin' ahead. We gotta be savin' *him* first – the arm comes later."

"No!" She was shocked. "You mustn't lose him!"

"I know." He raised a hand, almost in defense.

"You can't!"

His voice suddenly sounded gentle. "Aye, but we might. To be honest, dearie."

"No."

"It's not all up to me, ya' know. There's a team of us."

"He has to make it."

MacLaird gave a little sigh. "Well, he's made it through the first go 'round. And they're cleanin' him up for the next. But bomb blasts are sneaky. Ye can't tell what's happened inside by what's showin' outside." He winked at Lizzie. "Still, 'tis early yet – and he's young and strong. That's goin' for him."

Tears freely flowed down her face. Her voice sounded thick. "He threw me out of the way."

MacLaird watched her quietly. "I heard. So, I have a young hero on me hands, then?"

"Yes. You do."

"Okay, then. I'll be headin' back. Surgeries don't do themselves, ya' know."

"Do your best, Dr. Mac, your very best. Please."

He paused at the curtain to the cubicle. "I'll give it my most heroic efforts, Lizzie."

"Thank you. We'll pray."

He gave her an odd smile. "Yeah, and I'm sure that'll help *you*." He turned to leave, then turned back. "Oh, and next time ye get a concussion, stop in and say hello, will ye? Or if the tinnitus continues – that'd be the ringin'. Or if you can't walk straight. Aye? And, in the meantime, my medical advice is to stay away from bombs, at least fer a while."

Then he disappeared. The curtain shook briefly and settled back. Lizzie wiped her eyes with her good hand and looked down at the young Pakistani doctor seated patiently on his stool. "Sorry. Ready to get back to work?" she asked.

❧

Lizzie had a faraway stare in her eyes as she rode in a wheelchair down the gleaming hospital hallway. Her freshly bandaged hand was supported by a simple sling. She had asked the neatly dressed Ugandan orderly if she could walk from the ER, but was told that their rules demanded she ride in a chair – at least as far as the waiting room.

Lizzie was amazed by how much the small private hospital resembled medical facilities she was familiar with in Minnesota. In fact, she thought that if she squinted, and didn't look out the windows, she might believe she was on a patient floor at Fairview Southdale Hospital in Edina, or Methodist in St. Louis Park.

The IHK waiting room was open and bright, a bank of sun-filled windows on one side. Overly cheery walls were painted in eye-popping greens and blues with a wide yellow stripe that ran playfully along near the ceiling. None of that mattered. It was all swallowed up by the squeals of Afiya and Mirembe racing to meet her wheelchair.

"*Jjajja! Jjajja!*"

The ecstatic girls surrounded her with hugs and touches. The others rushed from the chairs to reach her. She saw Meg and Jedediah, Pastor Kajumba and Nana. Her eyes didn't miss the bandages and Band-Aids peeking out from here and there. Kajumba's right hand knuckles were wrapped. Nana's left cheek sported a few butterfly strips. Most of the adults seemed to move cautiously, nursing hidden pains.

Lizzie felt relieved to see them, but her hungry eyes searched for others. Kajumba and Nana stepped back, and she saw Musaazi. His head was swathed in a gauze that covered half his face, but his wide grin remained in plain view. Dembe walked beside his friend, his hand under Musaazi's elbow, helping to steady him as they slowly approached Lizzie. Refusing to wait, she rose out of the chair, crying as she rushed to get to them, her good arm held out wide for an embrace.

Hours later, the waiting room was quiet. The girls had fallen asleep like dominos across the row of armless chairs, Mirembe's head on Afiya's legs, Afiya's head in her mother's lap, and Mrs. Birungi's head angled against the wall behind her chair. Lizzie stood beside one of the tall windows, the side of her head resting on the glass, her forehead showing a small, square dressing. Her eyes appeared to stare into the early evening shadows but she was reliving the talk she'd had with Ogwambi under the tire tree.

Lizzie's clothes were fresh, thanks to Nana's quick thinking. After her treatment in the ER at Mulago Hospital, Nana had called Jedediah and instructed him about which clothes to bring and where to come. Lizzie was mortified when she caught sight of herself in the bathroom mirror at IHK. Nana fussed and clucked over her like a mother hen and used her body to block the reflection while she worked on her hair.

"It's not a style show, Lizzie, it's a hospital," Birungi had said. "When you've been in a bombing, no one expects bling. At least, you are cleaner."

Lizzie knew she was cleaner; not clean, but cleaner. She acknowledged to herself that Nana's kind efforts had helped, but not enough. What would be enough? She didn't know.

The window glass was cool against her cheek. She felt beyond exhausted...and fearful...and numb. But behind it all was the harbinger of bad news about Ogwambi, and the bleak vista of depression waiting, because in the end, she was at fault.

A hand with bandaged knuckles gently touched the glass next to her face. Pastor Kajumba stared out the window toward the hospital's boundary walls and the trees beyond. He just stood with her and said nothing. Lizzie studied the strong lines of his mouth, his cheek, his nose. She admired the fact that he was patient and that he knew not to speak first.

The silence between them carried a soothing weight within it. A peaceful spell that spun a web of relief around her, with no compulsion to break it by talking – and yet she needed to say the words that burned inside her. She knew she must say the words, even though they would shatter this moment. She had to unburden herself to someone.

"It's because I came to Africa," she said softly.

Kajumba didn't turn. "What is?"

"Everything. He's up there fighting for his life because of me. Because I decided I had to come here."

There! She'd said it! And now she felt starkly hollow, like the sound of dry reeds rattling in the fall. She waited for his reaction, but he continued to stare out towards the darkening trees.

"Yes," he said, finally. "That's true."

She didn't move. Was this what she wanted to hear? Her heart waited while her anxious mouth itched to flare back with some darkly clever retort. But instead, she muzzled herself, hoping for something different, something more.

"And why did you come to Africa?" The pastor's voice carried little inflection. A simple question. No hidden meanings.

"You know why," she said. "To free the books. To make a library."

"Yes. The books." He nodded. "If you hadn't come to Africa, we wouldn't have the books, would we?"

Lizzie turned around, facing into the room, the back of her head now resting against the window. "That hardly matters to me now."

She considered the people in the waiting room. Many she knew. Most were sleeping. She noticed Dembe, who sat at the end of the row, Musaazi asleep against his shoulder. A few people she didn't recognize knelt at Dembe's feet, on the tile floor with their heads bowed. One was offering up a cup of water to him. Lizzie thought the whole thing looked strange.

"Pastor, what is that?" She spoke in a low voice. "By Dembe. Who are they? Why are they doing that?"

Kajumba glanced at the scene briefly. "You haven't noticed before?"

"No. Noticed what? What do you mean?"

"They've been coming, off and on, for hours. Those are people from the bus, and families of people from the bus. They know what Dembe did. It is our way to honor someone, to show respect. Even to one so young. He is being called, *omulenzi owo ku baasi*. It means, 'the boy on the bus.'"

"I...I didn't notice. I guess I...I..."

"You were looking somewhere else." His voice remained kind.

Lizzie was lost in her emotions. She could barely watch as the people rose and silently departed. Dembe looked so uncomfortable, so vulnerable and alone, Lizzie turned away, lest he notice she had seen him.

"I wasn't aware." She looked back out the window. "How could I not see?"

Pastor Kajumba joined her at the glass. They both observed the night coming on, the pale half-moon riding low in the sky.

"Lizzie, if you hadn't come to Africa," Kajumba said evenly, "every person on that bus would be dead, and our nation would be in mourning."

Lizzie couldn't move. Her eyes locked on the broken moon, her heart barely beating.

He continued, "And the bombers would be free to strike again. And Dembe would be left on the street." He looked at her. She could feel his eyes, but she couldn't bring herself to turn. His voice wavered ever so slightly. "And I would still be lost in my pride."

Lizzie felt something inside her give way. Some stronghold far down within her cracked. It was like the welcome song at Safe Haven. Somehow, the drums and the voices of those once homeless boys had unlocked a part of her, and it was happening again now. But this time, the entire hidden structure was coming down, the door yawning wide, the contents laid bare. Tears came and the deep groaning over the letting go of years of blame and guilt and obligation for so many things that were never meant for her to carry, reaching back to her childhood, to her marriage, to her children, and sweeping on into the present, to Africa. Pastor Kajumba caught her in his solid arms and let her weeping roll on unchecked, and unashamed and unhurried.

When Lizzie eventually slowed to sniffles and sighs, and started to feel exposed, he said one last thing before he let her stand on her own once again. "I have learned that God does not do one thing at a time. He does many things at one time. He was not sending a librarian to Africa. He knew we needed much more than a librarian. He knew we needed you."

Clouds covered the moon and the night rain softly pattered against the windows as Dr. MacLaird came in with news. Jedediah and Meg were back and everyone, except for the still sleeping girls, gathered around the pale, exhausted surgeon. His eyes included them all as he spoke, but his attention kept returning to Lizzie and Dembe.

"I'm every bit as sorry as can be…and I wish I could tell ye in a kinder way, but we've gone 'n lost the boy's arm, half way to the shoulder. And that's a damn shame!"

Lizzie's eyes welled with tears, but her resigned expression remained steady.

MacLaird's voice grew firmer now, almost stubborn. "But he's keepin' his life, if I have anythin' to say about it. He's one tough laddie. And we're through the worst of it. I'm as sure as the sunrise that he'll make it."

Dembe nodded, sorrowful but relieved. Jedediah and Meg thanked the doctor for his efforts. Pastor Kajumba placed a hand on Lizzie's shoulder, and she sighed with heartache.

Dr. Mac stared at the group and gave a half smile as he continued. "Not that it matters much in the grand scheme, since you all believe he has a life somewhere after this one, but his stayin' right here makes a big difference to me." His body tipped forward from fatigue and his eyes glistened. "I'm not a part of that scheme. This here-and-now stuff is…well, it's all I know about."

Lizzie stepped to him, fondly squeezing his arm. "That's fine, Calum. You just keep him with us, for now. Okay? We'll worry about eternity another day."

He nodded and took a shaky breath as he turned back toward the surgical suite, his covered shoes whispering against the tile floor.

THIRTY-FOUR

Putting Down Roots

For Lizzie, the weeks following the bombing flew by with the blur of a fast train that hurtles through small stations without a stop. Her constants were the persistent tenderness in her injured hand, the returning acuity of her hearing, the daily demands of her fledgling library and repeated visits to Ogwambi.

She still put up with the occasional ringing in her ears and brief moments of vertigo, but these were fading, day by day. Ogwambi was engaged in a far more serious struggle.

The first time she saw him in the recovery room, he was still sedated. She had stared silently from the foot of the bed, too overwhelmed to go closer, or cry, or do anything but stand still. Her eyes traced the IV snaking from his right arm, across the sheets, to the clear bag of fluid hanging on the pole. But they were helplessly drawn back to the domed elastic bandage hiding the residual of his left arm, and to that disturbing empty space below it. There was no stopping her mind from weighing the cost the boy had paid to save her life. It was a shining set of scales that stood in her heart, with the pan on her side hanging high in the air.

During subsequent visits she grew more adept at handling her reactions. Nothing could alter the bright guilt she felt about his sacrifice, but she managed to keep from wearing it on her face. She made sure he only saw smiles.

Thanks to Afiya and her tireless efforts in the library, they made steady progress on the inventory of the books. The young girl had really blossomed. With her mother's help, she had gotten the library declared an official, school-wide project. Together with Lizzie, she organized the many student volunteers into manageable teams, and she helped to schedule their assigned times around their classes.

Among other things, the inventory revealed numbers of duplicate books. It was Mrs. Birungi who suggested that one of those extra copies should be given to Ogwambi, as a get well gift from the school. Lizzie was more than pleased to wrap the novel in festive paper, and she even fashioned a passable bow from old ribbons. She surprised him with it on her very next visit. Sitting beside his bed as he tore away the paper, she drank in his pleasure as the familiar title was revealed: *The Call of the Wild*. Lizzie remained quiet as he examined the inscription inside the front cover. *To Ogwambi, whose bravery and quick action saved our school librarian.* It was signed and dated in his typical bold style by Pastor Kajumba.

Although Jack London's prose was difficult at first for Ogwambi, the story of the stolen dog fighting to survive in the Yukon captured his imagination and transported him far from his pain-filled bed. Lizzie would sometimes read aloud to him, as did Dembe and Musaazi, who often came with her. The boys were all mystified by the idea of a dog team pulling a heavy sled over a frozen lake. Lizzie assured them such lakes were real. She claimed that she herself had walked upon ice-stilled waters in Minnesota. She'd even seen people drive trucks across them! Ogwambi had suddenly laughed aloud, confident *Jjajja* must be kidding. It was his first laugh since the bomb. Lizzie just smiled sweetly and tipped her head, leaving his wrong belief unshaken.

372 | E. A. Fournier

On the way home, she stared out the dirty side windows of the taxi van. Dembe and Musaazi chattered in Luganda beside her. The roads were clotted with cars and trucks, and her clothes stuck to her skin. But her mind was far away. She wondered at the unsuspected immensity of the gift of castoff books from those schools in Texas. They would never know, would they? She was struck by the interconnectedness of all things: from the parents and students who helped pack the books, to UPS who donated services, to the shipping crews, the container company, even to the lying customs agents who delayed the shipment until Lizzie and Wasswa could free it, and on and on until this one book found its way to this one boy without an arm. It forced her to reconsider the power and intricacy of a design that could reach from Jonathan's dying room in Eden Prairie to Ogwambi's hospital room in Kampala.

She blinked, aware of the passing scene of two substantial women wearing black rubber boots and working in a garden. As the taxi drove by, she saw that they were bent over to the ground, in the African way, with their legs straight as they pulled weeds. For an instant, in Lizzie's mind, she was home in her own garden, thinning carrots and feeling certain again of God's unseen hand in all things.

The library was, at long last, starting to look like a library. Lizzie decided that the main goal for the shelving of the books was to make everything inviting for the students. She no longer concerned herself with filing systems and card catalogs. She determined that the library's holdings would be organized by simple subject matters, and then, within the subject matter, alphabetized by authors' last names: simple, understandable, maintainable.

∽

To: davidwarton27x@centurylink.net; joanjohnson@yahoo.com; ceceliawarton99@hotmail.com

From: nankundabirungi@wobulezischool.com
Subj: Lots of surprises

I know I'm a terrible correspondent, but a lot has happened in a short time. I apologize in advance for jumping around on a lot of topics this time. I'll just do my best.

I got caught in a rainstorm. Yes, I had an umbrella with me, but it didn't matter. You should see the traffic in the rain! I have never seen so much mud. It gets into everything! Luckily, I wasn't driving, Jedediah was (he's the husband of the American lady who runs the home for street boys — I'll explain about them when I see you). Anyway, the wipers could hardly keep up and the window kept fogging. We were out to visit the parents of one of the boys (long story). Anyway, I really got wet.

I'm getting more used to roundabouts now, but they still scare me. We don't have many in Mpls and I'm glad. Trust me, they're even worse in the rain, especially since everyone's driving on the wrong side of the road (to me, anyway). Sometimes, I just close my eyes or think of something else.

I don't want to worry you, but there was a terrorist bombing in a bus station here. You may have seen it on the news, I don't know. I'm fine. No problems. But a few of our students happened to be there and got hurt. One was badly injured saving someone. I visit him in the hospital most days. He's a wonderful boy. Say a prayer for him, will you? We're reading "Call of the Wild" to him. He likes it, but he can't believe the parts about lakes freezing over and people walking on the ice! If I was born in Africa, I guess I wouldn't believe it either.

I'm working every day to organize the books. The students are getting excited to have a library. So am I! I have some ladies who help me — it provides a little income for them. Hopefully, they will take over when I leave.

Did I mention there's a rooster in the yard of the house next door?
He wakes me up every morning. Usually before the sun's even up!
I should say he scares me awake, since he's so loud. I used to read
about roosters crowing in the morning and always thought it
sounded charming. I don't think that anymore. I'd like to wring his
neck! He better watch out or I'll make a stew out of him – I know
ALL the steps now!
Wish you could come meet my friends and see my library.

Love to you all,
Grandma XXOO

❦

On the day that Ogwambi was to be moved to the Boys' House, Dr. MacLaird was on hand to reassure Lizzie. He found her in a hospital hallway, and he explained he had given detailed instructions to the House Father, Uncle Kabuye, and that everything would be all right. He even implied he might make a few house calls. In fact, the Scotsman seemed uncharacteristically cheery, and rather devoid of his usual dark quips. He mentioned that he'd been in contact with CoRSU, a private orthopedic rehab hospital newly opened in Kisubi, only thirty minutes from Kampala. Lizzie wasn't sure she followed all that he said, but apparently something new was happening in Uganda with prosthetics. CoRSU had partnered with the University of Toronto and Autodesk, a 3D-design company, to make inexpensive, customized 3D-printed prosthetic limbs for children.

Dr. MacLaird bragged about his "pulling a few strings" and "calling in some chips." When he gathered that Lizzie remained doubtful, he explained.

"Look at it this way," he said in an undertone, pulling Lizzie closer to the wall. "'Tis not every day ye get to help a young hero who saved a VIP white lady from terrorists, aye?" He winked as if they were now in cahoots. "Couldn't hurt their PR campaigns or their presence on YouTube either, d'ya think?"

"Mac, you didn't say that!" Lizzie tried to sound dismayed.

"Oh, but I surely did! Laid it on thick, too. Even dropped the fact that Ogwambi's best friends with *omulenzi owo ku baasi* himself. Shoulda' seen their eyes light up then!"

Lizzie was startled. "You used *the boy on the bus*? Oh, Mac!"

MacLaird remained unrepentant. "Why not? It has a certain cachet, right now. That bumped him to the head of the line. They'll be capturing a 3D image of the lad's residuum as soon as the swelling's down." He cleared his throat with pride. "You're not the only *muzungu* able to drive a bargain!"

She shook her head at him, but with a wide smile. "You're a rascal and incorrigible, but I love you for it." Lizzie gave him a quick hug and then blushed at her own forwardness.

For his part, Dr. MacLaird stood unaccountably silent for a bit before speaking again. "Now, don't ye be tellin' anyone, especially that Nana. It'd ruin me negative image."

⁓

Book checkout and theft were two of Lizzie's ongoing concerns with the library. Checkout was a simple manual system linked to the students' school IDs and a paper tag inside the back cover of each book. The book title and date would be written on a card at the library, and the book's tag would be stamped with the return date based on a two week borrowing limit. It wasn't a perfect system, but it was easy to administer, except that Lizzie was unsure how to penalize students for late books. She couldn't actually fine these students, could she? Afiya proposed the loss of library privileges until late books were returned. The instant horror that appeared in the faces of Afiya's friends at the thought convinced Lizzie to give the idea a try.

Theft was a more thorny issue. Lizzie despaired of coming up with a practical solution until Musaazi casually suggested a more direct approach.

"*Jjajja*, let thieves watch for thieves."

"What?"

"There are Safe Haven boys attending school here again, right?"

"Yes."

"Have Pastor Kajumba make watching the library a school job for us." He grinned impishly and raised his eyebrows. "No one steals better than street boys. Who will dare steal books if we are watching?"

✦

The library was nearly empty of students. It had been a busy day. The end of the term loomed near, and the wide tables in the library's main room had become a favored place to spread out notes and study. Lizzie was pleased with the two ladies she was training to handle checkout and return. In fact, everything was going well, and she, ever so cautiously, inhaled the rare air of contentment, careful not to breathe too deeply. She had learned over a long life not to trust it, but then again, she never wanted to miss it when it showed up – especially on this day.

Lizzie felt so proud of herself for keeping her secret. No one would know or make a fuss. She'd done it! It was her birthday – the big one – seventy. And no one knew. Well, no one *here* knew, she corrected herself. But with the eight hour time difference between Minnesota and Uganda, it was as good as if no one knew. She smiled to herself, content.

The main door made a gentle click as it opened, and she looked up to watch Dembe enter. The boy looked sharp in his school uniform as he walked right up to her desk. The afternoon sun caught him from the side and his skin glowed as if from an inner fire. He leaned toward her and spoke softly. "*Jjajja*, come with me. I want to show you something."

Lizzie hesitated as she felt the pressure of unfinished tasks. "Does it have to be now?"

Dembe stood calmly in front of her and nodded, once. "Yes."

"But who will close up if I leave?"

Dembe smiled at the two ladies at the checkout desk, who were obviously listening. "Your new librarians can do that." He turned. "Yes, ladies? You can close up the library, right?"

They both nodded and smiled shyly.

Lizzie resigned herself to the request and stood. "Okay. But I promised Mrs. Birungi to be at her office by 3:30. She was quite firm."

Dembe turned for the door. "We will be back by then if we leave now."

Lizzie hurried to catch up. "Where are we going?"

"Someplace special." He was already out the door.

She caught up as he crossed the road. "Are we walking there?"

"Yes. Always walking."

They left the immediate neighborhood beside the school. Dembe led her off the main path and onto a side trail. The sun shone bright, the foliage on both sides of Lizzie intensely green.

"Is it far?" she asked.

"A little ways."

"I've heard that before."

Dembe smiled briefly back. "Do not worry. No drunks this time. No crossovers."

They walked along a red dirt ridge, narrow enough that they walked single file, balancing as they went.

Dembe's light voice came to her over his shoulder. "Pastor Kajumba talked to me about the pipes."

"Oh?"

"I need to pay back for what I stole."

Lizzie tried to keep herself calm. "Okay…"

Dembe's voice remained conversational. "Did you meet Kirumira Joseph, the maintenance man?"

"Yes." An image of the quiet worker standing in the pipe room with his shoestring of keys popped into her mind.

"Pastor had Joseph make space for me in his workroom," he said. Lizzie could hear a smile in the boy's tone. "I'm to help repair things that break at the school."

Relieved, she breathed out. "That's perfect."

A thin, indistinct path appeared ahead and snaked off into the tall grasses. Dembe followed it, his shoes leaving little dents in the dirt. Lizzie walked just behind him.

The instant she entered the tunnel of waving elephant grass, something familiar tugged at her. Her feet tarried. She let Dembe go on ahead. The sun felt hot on her shoulders; she could hear the clicks and grinds of insects in the weeds. Looking up at the blue sky through the tops of the grass blades, she remembered!

Dembe glanced back, sensing her hesitation. "Just a little farther. After the grasses."

She stopped where she was and let the orange dust settle onto her shoes. The soft hairs on the back of her neck prickled as they lifted from her skin. She now stood inside the vision she had seen when Pastor Kajumba first preached at her church in Eden Prairie – the vision that she had told to no one but Ruthie. How eerie! An untapped well of amazement began to bubble up from within her. She felt a rush of freshness racing along her limbs and up her spine – the way it felt when she was young and stretched her arms to their limits after a long sleep. Her vision had not been imaginary; it was an actual place upon the earth. Somehow, she had visited here before coming here. How strange and…disturbing it felt. Not disturbing, she scolded herself; comforting, confirming. She looked up and then slowly turned her head left and then right, suddenly aware of the roundness of the planet and the bigness of the universe.

Dembe stopped just beyond the grasses and impatiently waved her on. "Just over here, *Jjajja*."

Lizzie reluctantly propelled herself forward. She stepped out from the tunnel of grasses to a small open space.

Dembe stepped off the path, into the shorter grasses. "I named this my secret place."

She watched him dig in the ground with his hands until he uncovered a metal handle. Carefully sliding his fingers into it, Dembe lifted a lid from a buried container. He set the metal lid to one side, keeping the living sod intact on top of it. His hands reached into the darkness below and brought up a narrow box from within the buried container. Handmade from hardwood, the box was thick, with decorative metal clasps along one side.

"These are my father's best tools," he said proudly. "Joseph is making a locker in the workroom with a key for me. I won't have to hide them anymore."

He unhooked the lid and opened it to reveal a carefully arranged and secured medley of intricate tools. The handles and tips of the many implements glistened in the sun. They were meticulously arranged in layers and rows according to their sizes and applications. None were new, but all exhibited the worn luster of honest usage and fine care.

"My father used these and kept adding to them his whole life. Before he died, he gave them all to me. I wanted you to see them, so you would know I am not a thief."

Lizzie stood in the sunlight and admired the boy holding his tools. "I think I always knew that, Dembe. From the first moment I saw you."

He closed the box and lifted it smoothly from the ground. "Yes. But some people say things."

She nodded. "We visited your mother."

"I know."

"How?"

"I have my ways." Dembe grinned and started back along the path, heading into the grasses again. "We need to go. I promised to get you back by 3:30."

Lizzie followed after him, hurrying to keep pace with his young legs.

⁓

Lizzie stood in front of Nana's office and frowned. The door was shut. A little sign taped to the wood said that the 3:30 meeting had been moved to the conference room. An arrow at the bottom of the penciled words pointed off to the right. Dembe had brought her to the outside doors of the main building, and then left to lock up his tools. Sighing, she followed the hall to the right.

The small meeting room door stood open, and she peeked in to see Mrs. Birungi seated with her cell phone on the table beside her. The phone had wires connected to a small audio speaker. Nana cheerfully beckoned to her. As Lizzie stepped across the threshold, she became aware of people standing against the wall, behind the door. Startled at first, she saw Meg and Jedediah, Afiya, Mirembe, Musaazi and Pastor Kajumba.

Nana simply said, "She is here."

Suddenly, a cluster of intensely familiar voices from home erupted from the loudspeaker. "Surprise! Surprise! Happy Birthday!"

Then, everyone in the room echoed the cheerful cries with their own accented English, "Surprise! Happy Birthday!"

Lizzie was too stunned to do anything but stare around the small room at the Ugandan faces and then at the tabletop speaker where her U.S. family's voices joined with theirs.

Through the cacophony of happy comments, Joanie's voice cut through clear and strong. "And you thought no one would know? Are you kidding, Mom? On your big seven-oh! We are so on to your tricks!"

Lizzie could hardly speak, her smiling face streaming with tears. "I don't know what to say."

David's voice jumped in. "That's good! Mission accomplished!" Everyone laughed on both sides of the world.

Joanie's voice crackled from the speaker. "Mom, I have everyone conferenced in here, including all the grandkids, and even Cecelia."

Lizzie's youngest daughter's voice joined in. "Happy Birthday, Mom! All the way from New York!"

Lizzie's eyes danced with pleasure. "Oh, Cecelia, honey, it's so nice to hear your voice – all your voices!"

"Thank Joanie," Cecelia said. "She's the one who organized it. Even if it is crazy early in the morning here in the big city!"

David chimed in. "Some of us are up this early every morning, you know."

Joanie immediately responded. "David! I warned you..."

David sounded penitent. "Sorry! Sorry! I'll just shut-up now, okay?"

Joanie snorted at him, then continued. "Mom, just so you know, Mrs. Birungi has already introduced us to all your friends, except Dembe. She made it very clear that we can't start without him."

Lizzie turned to the door behind her just as Dembe, grinning ear-to-ear, stepped into the room.

Nana said, "He is here now, Joanie. He just arrived."

Joanie's voice rose, "Okay! Let's go then. I can't keep this herd of cats together much longer. Ready? And..."

The small speaker fuzzed and rattled as a lively, if not melodic, version of the Happy Birthday Song struggled to pour out of it. Everyone in the room joined in by the second verse and both sides of the phone call carried on to the song's messy but hilarious conclusion. Poor Lizzie endured it with both hands on her cheeks, eyes flowing with tears, and her body helplessly caught up in the clutches of nearly unendurable joy.

During the laughter and applause that followed the song, a Ugandan Groundnut Cake appeared. Afiya and Mirembe took charge of cutting and distributing it.

Joanie's voice commanded attention. "Everybody! Quiet, please!"

Lizzie's Ugandan friends circled the table. Most had their cake, or were getting it, and all were focused on the little speaker beside Nana's phone.

"Mom, in lieu of a present on your seventieth birthday, we have an announcement to make." She laughed, uneasily. "Well, actually, it's my own announcement and I – let me think how I want to say this..."

Lizzie made a face at Nana, who rolled her shoulders, looking as baffled as everyone else. Obviously, what was coming wasn't part of any shared plan.

Joanie continued. "Oh, yeah. Before I go on, I want you to know that this time you are the *last* to know!" She paused to let the drama build and then said, "You're going to be a grandmother again!"

"What?" Lizzie's voice was barely above a whisper in the silence after Joanie spoke. "I'm what?" Her voice grew a little louder. "I am?"

Joanie laughed. "Yes! Mike and I are pregnant! A new grandchild! You know, one of those tiny human creatures – a baby! Now, let's hear a better reaction out of you than that last one."

"You are?" This time Lizzie's voice was significantly stronger. Her mother's vocal chords kicked in, and she automatically sailed up the tone register and then back down again, in that wavering squeal of joy women reserved for wedding engagements and birth announcements.

Joanie's voice came back in tear-filled satisfaction. "Yeah! That's the one! That's what I was lookin' for! That's the sound I needed to hear from my Mom!"

⤐

Lizzie lay atop her sheets inside the netting, wide awake in the hot darkness. Homesickness crouched next to her like a living creature, and tangled its long fingers in her heartstrings. She hadn't really thought much about home until now, but after the phone call, she felt the agony of her family's absence like a newly opened wound.

She heard the whispering swish of bare feet on flooring. She turned to watch the soft radiance of a kerosene lantern illuminate Nana in a thin robe as she glided into the room.

"Lizzie? Are you awake?"

"Yes." Lizzie unzipped the netting that hung over the bed. "Don't worry. Come in."

"Sorry. You have another call. He forgot about the time problem."

"Who is it?"

"Your son."

Lizzie felt the icy touch of trouble inside her stomach. Nana passed her the phone through the netting.

"I'll leave the light with you. The power is out."

Nana set the lantern on the floor nearby and quietly left. Lizzie took a breath before lifting the phone to her ear.

"Hello? David?"

His voice was clear. The connection was clean. "Mom? Sorry about the time…"

"That's fine. I wasn't asleep, anyway. What's up?"

"I need to talk to you about…about that announcement. I…I've been thinking about this all day at work, and I…"

"What? Thinking about what?" Lizzie's nervousness made her questions terse.

David was uncomfortable. "Okay. Look, I didn't know Joanie was gonna tell you about the baby. None of us did."

"You're starting to scare me, David. Stop beating around the bush."

David paused and then spoke in a rush. "It's a high risk pregnancy, okay? There's been problems. Joanie and Mike were keepin' it quiet in case she miscarried…but…"

"Oh, no!"

"But now, since they already told the rest of us, I guess she decided you should know, too."

Lizzie stared into the lantern. "Why wouldn't she tell me?" She looked away into the dark corners of the room. "How risky is it?"

"She's...she's like you, Mom. She didn't want to ruin your trip."

Lizzie was firm. "What exactly does the doctor say?"

"I...you know. She has to cut back on everything. No lifting. Extra bedrest. Do as little as possible. He really doesn't even want her to drive, if she can help it."

"Oh, my..."

"Yeah. It's tough. Mike has to keep workin'. I'm...I'm sure they can't afford fulltime help. I mean, we're doin' what we can but... you know..."

Lizzie shook her head as she added to David's list. "And with Sandy and Will to deal with, and school..."

They settled into silence, both of them. Lizzie almost wondered if they'd been cut off, but she could still hear the slight hiss of an open line. When David spoke again, his voice was gentle.

"I think she's scared. I know I would be."

Lizzie slumped forward a little on the bed. Surrounded by the halo of lantern light, the netting made a pattern across her hands and on the walls. She could think of nothing useful to say back to David.

"She needs you, Ma. I know she needs you to come home. But she just couldn't ask."

THIRTY-FIVE
Such Sweet Sorrow

When Lizzie entered the bunkroom at the Boys' House, Ogwambi was seated on his lower bunk, wearing a Yankees' T-shirt and rolled up jeans as he arranged checkers on a board. His stump was covered in a special elastic bandage, like an oversized sock. Lizzie knew it was called a *shrinker*. Across from him, she saw that Musaazi was glumly setting up his own pieces. Dembe stood between them, watching the game, his hands loosely draped over a support for the upper bunk.

Dembe looked up with a bright smile. "Hey, *Jjajja*! Are you here to see the battle of the heroes?"

She smirked. "Did I miss that announcement? Who's winning?"

Dembe winked. "This is game four. Ogwambi has won three in a row."

She raised her eyebrows at Ogwambi. "I didn't realize you were such a powerful player."

Musaazi scowled and grumbled in Luganda. "He has more time to practice."

Ogwambi rolled his eyes. "No one needs to practice to beat you."

Musaazi rubbed a finger along his healing facial scar, putting on a tough look. "We will see what we will see."

Ogwambi chuckled and answered Lizzie in English. "I am not a powerful player."

Behind him, Lizzie noticed three young boys wander in. These were the same three she had met twice before. One of them, Gwandoya, stopped beside Ogwambi and leaned affectionately against the older boy's thick shoulder. The other two, Waloga and Mukiibi, squeezed their small bodies up onto the bed behind Musaazi. All three watched Lizzie with their eyes glittering in the sunlight from a nearby window.

Ogwambi pushed a checker forward one space and shyly glanced up at Lizzie. "Happy Birthday...*Jjajja*."

Lizzie smiled, at the title as much as the greeting. "Thanks. I'm sorry you couldn't make the party. Did they bring you cake?"

Ogwambi nodded happily. "It was sooo good!"

The little boys all nodded and mimicked Ogwambi's deeper voice. "Sooo good!"

Everyone giggled and kept repeating the phrase as Lizzie dragged a white plastic chair over to the bed and sat. Her face slowly sobered and everyone stopped laughing to look at her.

"I wanted to talk to all of you before I decide something. Is that okay?"

The boys waited for her to continue. Lizzie took a breath, but she didn't speak. She wasn't sure how to say what she wanted to say. It had seemed so clear when she had practiced in her room, but now her mouth was suddenly dry and empty of words.

Dembe quietly asked, "Is this about your daughter and the baby?"

Lizzie managed to swallow, and then answered softly, "Yes."

His face took on a look of compassion that belied his years. "Uncle Jed explained the dangers to us. You must go home. Your family needs you. When they call, you must go."

The power of his simple words released a flood of emotion inside her. Pulled equally to stay and to go, she vainly wished she could be in both places at once. Not a new feeling for her, but she had never felt it quite as poignantly as she did now. Her eyes were drawn to Ogwambi as he nodded ever so slightly.

"Go, *Jjajja*. We want you to go."

Lizzie's heart felt thick and tight in her chest. "But…you are family, too…"

Ogwambi tipped up his head to look her full in the eyes. "We know that now."

Lizzie reached out for his good right hand and held it tight. "Thank you."

Dembe added, "But someday, if *we* need to call you, you must come back."

She looked at him and nodded, no longer trusting her voice.

✍

Lizzie stared out the open window of her bedroom, lost in thought. She absently slapped at a mosquito on her neck and then continued looking at the far roofs in the sunlight, and beyond them at the trees. Behind her, spread out on the bed and across the open suitcases, lay her clothes and belts, extra shoes, toiletries, little piles of odd items, and an umbrella.

She turned at a noise and watched Nana come in with a wrapped box.

"I hope you can make room for one last thing."

Lizzie smiled. "Oh, Nana. You shouldn't have. I don't…"

Birungi shushed her as she handed over the box with a casual gesture. "No worries. I have a school chum who is a seamstress. I never pay full price."

Lizzie opened the box and gasped as she lifted out an elegant *Gomesi* with striking orange-red blossoms across it. She held it up against herself and gushed in pleasure.

Nana looked pleased. "The flowers called out to me with your name. I had to get it. They grow on a tree that we call The Flame Tree. Meg has one behind her house."

Lizzie moved her hips, swishing the dress back and forth. "I've seen it. Meg told me all about it. You have no idea how perfect this is!" She reached back into the box and held up a wide, dark green sash. "You'll have to show me how to wear it properly. I hope it's not hard to learn."

"No. Simple."

"It's beautiful, Nana. So beautiful."

Birungi sighed in contentment. "I wanted your family to see what a true Ugandan *Jjajja* looks like." Her tone slowed and became serious. "For that is what you are to me."

Realizing what she had just said, Lizzie put aside the new dress to wrap her friend in a teary hug. "Even when I endangered your daughter's life?"

Nana's eyes were wet as she replied. "Yes, even then." And then she chuckled. "Although there might have been a few moments when I wanted to kill you."

"I'm so glad," Lizzie answered back, wiping at her nose. "I wouldn't have blamed you a bit."

"I know. That's why we are such friends."

They unwrapped from the hug, and Lizzie picked up the dress again. "Can you show me how to wear this now?"

"If you want."

"Let me clear some space." Still holding the dress, Lizzie shoved aside a pile of miscellaneous items on the bed to make room. Something fell off the other side and made a metallic jingle as it struck the floor.

Nana was moving toward the hall. "I have a big mirror in my room. We can practice there."

"Just a minute," Lizzie hurriedly laid her dress in the open space. She had a premonition about what had hit the floor. Hurrying around the bed, she scooped up a U-shaped piece of metal with holes on the ends – the pig tag! Lizzie cried out in a strained voice. "We don't have time to try on the dress now."

Nana turned and took a few steps back into the room, picking up the tension. "Why not?"

"We need to go to Owino."

"Today?"

"Right now."

Nana cocked her head. "Why? What are we shopping for?"

Lizzie grabbed her purse. "Do you remember the pig farmer you told me about? Goes to Pastor's church. The one who lost some pigs?"

Nana put her fists on her hips. "He didn't lose them. They were stolen, but what does that—"

Lizzie stuffed the pig tag into her purse. "Does the farmer have any children in our school?"

"Uhh…" She thought for a moment. "…two boys." Nana stood unmoving, her face puzzled. "They are not our most shining students. Why?"

Lizzie gently took her arm. "Get your purse. We're heading to Owino to get school fees."

⌁

By the time the two women strode down the narrow passageways between stalls in Owino, it was clear to any vendor with eyes that these customers were on a mission and would brook no delays.

Rokani spotted them as they entered Wasswa's shop. Lizzie caught a glimpse of his back as he slipped through curtains to a hidden room. Seconds later, the curtains were swept aside as Wasswa charged out, a smile gleaming across his round face.

"Lizzie! Mrs. Birungi! Welcome back to my shop. Are you here to buy something this time?"

Lizzie stood in an aisle facing him, her face blank. "Not really."

"Too bad." He sounded as if his feelings were hurt. "And I was just thinking about you. A new supply of lovely skirts came in, many in your size."

"Sorry. I won't be here to wear them."

Wasswa's eyes moved from Lizzie to Birungi and back again, his curiosity piqued. "Oh?"

"Yes," Lizzie answered. "I must go home. Family problems."

"No." He let his tone slide downwards. "I am so sorry. Are you here to say goodbye?"

Lizzie's face brightened, slightly. "In a way. I have some...unfinished business."

He made a little nod. "A consignment, perhaps? You have clothes you wish me to sell for you? I—"

"No." Lizzie sounded abrupt. "I need you to make a cash contribution."

Wasswa blinked confusedly before he spoke. "I...I don't understand."

"You will. There is a farmer with two sons at our school who needs someone to – anonymously – pay their school fees for a term."

"Farmer's sons?" He snorted in annoyance. "Why would I be the one to help? Do I know the family?"

"You had a business association with the father."

"I did?" He sounded incredulous. "With a farmer?"

"I'm sure of it, both you and Rokani, from what I can gather."

He made a face at her and spread his hands in doubt. "What possible kind of business was it?"

Lizzie waited for a beat, then said, "Pigs!"

Wasswa's face changed instantly, his eyes contracted, his lips firmed into a hard line. "Says who?"

Lizzie opened her purse and handed him the metal pig tag. He slowly rolled the clip over and over in his hands, the edges clicking against his rings. He tried to scoff, "What's this supposed to be?"

Lizzie gave him a half smile. "You know very well what it is.

There're numbers and letters on it, and it's from the ear of one of the pigs you stole. I found it when we washed your truck out. Remember? Your big white truck that smelled of pigs...from the night before?"

Wasswa stared daggers at her, pretending incomprehension. Then, in a rush, all pretense seemed to drop from his face. He breathed out like a dying balloon. "Why do you keep doing this to me?"

Oddly, Lizzie actually felt a twinge of remorse for the dejected shopkeeper, but a brief look at Nana's expression dissuaded her. "It has nothing whatever to do with me, Mr. Solango," she said. "Honestly."

Wasswa nodded in resignation but then looked up. "Why anonymous? Can't I at least get credit? I need something out of this."

Lizzie looked baffled. "Wasswa, do you really want the farmers to start asking questions about missing pigs?"

He looked crestfallen. "No."

"Besides," she explained, "*not* having a visit from the police is what you're getting out of this donation."

Wasswa stared at Lizzie for a long time before speaking again. "I won't miss you, Mrs. Warton."

Lizzie's face was just a bit sad. "I was afraid of that. Oh, well, I'll miss *you*, though."

He nodded. "I know how the skinned cat feels."

⋘

Lizzie was booked on a KLM night flight. It would head first to Nairobi, and after a layover, fly to Amsterdam, arriving at Schiphol Airport early in the morning. That is, if all went well. She smiled to herself, painfully aware of the unplanned vagaries of travel.

Lizzie watched the wind sweep the light rain across the paved meeting area in front of the Entebbe Airport. Umbrellas sprouted in the crowd like night blossoms. Thin sheets of falling water shimmered in the artificial lights on tall poles and danced in the headlights from taxi vans.

Despite the late hour and the showers, nearly everyone had made it to see her off. She shook her head at the size of her own personal crowd and at how much each member had come to mean to her. It was difficult to hold her emotions at bay. She recalled the crippling fear she felt the first time she walked across this same area when she arrived.

Now, she looked around at her friends. Nana was laughing with her deep voice as she said something funny to Afiya. A grinning Mirembe stood sandwiched between mother and daughter, all three under the same umbrella. Nearby, ignoring the rain, Dembe and Musaazi talked with Pastor Kajumba and his wife. Dembe's arms swirled, his face alight with some new idea.

Meg stood close beside Lizzie, and Jedediah held a large umbrella over both of them. Lizzie could feel the warmth of the short woman's strong arm around her waist. "Jedediah," Lizzie said, looking up. "I thought you told me you didn't have an umbrella."

Jed scrunched his nose. "I don't. This is Meg's."

Lizzie sighed. The glass doors of the terminal were only a few steps behind her, but she understood that once she passed through them, everything would change again. She knew she shouldn't drag this out, but her eyes kept searching the airport arrival road, still hoping against hope.

Dr. MacLaird had warned her earlier in the day that something had gone wrong with the prosthetic. One of the files from Toronto wasn't right, he'd said. The 3D-printing had to be rerun. There were multiple pieces involved, and it just couldn't be helped. Mac had been apologetic. They would try their best to get to Entebbe, but he had told her not to hold her breath.

Lizzie felt Meg's hand gently press against her. "Lizzie, it's time."

She gave one last look at the road. "I know." Straightening, she embraced Meg. "Thanks! You believed in me from the start. Even before I did."

Meg's eyes danced. "I still do. I always will."

The rest of the group saw Lizzie's movement and knew that the time for final goodbyes had arrived. Lizzie moved from one to the other, sharing final thoughts, and hugs, and tears.

She stepped first to Pastor Kajumba and his wife, taking both their hands. "I'm so sorry I have to leave. I feel like there's so much left undone."

Kajumba shook his head. "You did everything God sent you here to do. You're not leaving; he's sending you on another mission."

Lizzie struggled to control her tears. "Thank you. I'll try to remember that."

Kajumba lowered his voice and bent closer to her. "I know you and Nana keep secrets. I want to add one more. I spoke with Mrs. Seterdahl about the pipes. She wasn't upset. In fact, she was quite moved. She's set up a scholarship for deserving students to attend college or technical school, and she wants Dembe to be the first."

Lizzie thought her heart would burst in pride at the news. But before she could respond, Mrs. Kajumba spoke quietly in a voice laced with a touch of humor. "What he didn't tell you is that the award will be called the Copper Pipe Scholarship, to help keep him humble."

Next, she approached Nana and the two girls. Lizzie hugged Afiya and kissed her cheek. While her mouth was close to the girl's ear, Lizzie whispered, "I'm so glad you were the one who answered the phone. You made all this possible."

When she held Mirembe, she told her to keep looking forward, not backward, and to keep singing. And Lizzie promised to pray for her.

With Nana there were only tears. They had shared too much for words. As she wrapped her arms around her, she only managed to say, "Nana," and to kiss her smooth dark cheek before moving on.

When she turned, she found Musaazi standing awkwardly, waiting for her. His curly black hair gleamed, wet in the lights. She placed her hands on his thin shoulders and looked into his eyes. "Thank you for saving my life. And for helping me to save Dembe." She studied his quiet face and then added, "We are family now."

For the first time, she saw him falter, as his eyes began to tear up. He nodded and said, "*Jjajja…*" before he had to look away.

Dembe was last. For a time outside of time, they just looked at each other. His eyes were the same as when she first saw him in the alley – still and dark – but now they were blinking against the gentle rain.

"I'm going now," she said simply. "But we'll see each other again, won't we?"

His puffy lips curled into a smile. "Yes, *Jjajja*. I'm sure of it."

She pulled him to her and softly held his head against her shoulder, threading her fingers into his hair. "Love you, Dembe. I owe you so very much!"

"No," he whispered back. "It was all for free."

She held him away from her so she could sweep the tears from her eyes. She sniffed and shook her head. "You are so smart!"

Dembe gave her a comical look as he shrugged off the compliment.

She was done. Lizzie looked across the faces and gave a little wave that encompassed all of them before turning away. She towed her stacked suitcases behind her and trudged toward the glass doors and the demands of departure. As she reached for the handle, the rain seemed to let up and she could clearly hear Dembe's voice calling out.

"*Jjajja*, wait!"

Glancing over her shoulder, she saw a white pickup with black pipework over the grill and a snarl of antennae on the roof racing toward her. It roared right up onto the curb of the meeting area before skidding to a stop. Nervous security guards moved quickly to block its path until an American soldier in camo slid out from the passenger side, smiling.

The driver's door snapped open and Sgt. Elwelu stood on the running board to wave at her. "We meet again, Mrs. Warton!"

Lizzie abandoned her suitcases and rushed toward the pickup. Its back door opened and Dr. MacLaird stepped out followed by a happy Ogwambi.

"*Jjajja*! We made it!" he cried out. "You haven't left!"

Lizzie paused just in front of the boy and stared. He was wearing a collared shirt with long sleeves and he appeared to have two arms. "Oh, Ogwambi," she said, "Will I break it if I hug you?"

The boy shrugged. "I don't know. I just got it." He held out his right arm. "But this one is still real!"

Lizzie hugged him tightly on the right side as Dr. MacLaird stood nearby. The others gathered around them.

MacLaird rolled his shoulders and waved his hands. "I'm sorry! I knew we were runnin' late, so I called out the army for help."

Lizzie squeezed his arm. "I'm glad you did. You couldn't have cut it much closer."

"You can thank Sgt. Elwelu for that," he replied. "The devil himself couldna' gotten us here any quicker."

Elwelu grinned as Lizzie shook his hand. "Thank you, Sergeant. I hope you don't get in trouble for this stunt."

"Oh, no, ma'am. Don't you worry a bit. *Major* Muhoozi was pleased to help. Catchin' those terrorists is why he got the promotion." He pulled something from inside his shirt. "He sent this for you." He handed her an envelope with government seals.

Lizzie held it, puzzled. "Should I open it now?"

Elwelu laughed. "Yeah. It's only good here. It's a government VIP letter. You won't have any trouble with customs. Pretty much just check your luggage and board the plane. He asked me to tell you thanks, ma'am."

She stood holding the letter and feeling conspicuous. She was never one for the limelight. "Tell the Major that I appreciate it. It'll come in handy since I'm about to be late."

She turned one last time to her friends. She saw Dembe and Musaazi join Ogwambi beside the pickup. It didn't take long before they were poking each other and laughing together. They all grinned at her as the rain really began to pour. She realized there was nothing adequate that she could say. So, she just threw a kiss at them and turned back to the terminal. Jedediah rushed up with the umbrella and escorted her back to the glass door, shielding her from the downpour. She grabbed her luggage and stepped inside.

THIRTY-SIX

Returning to Go

Lizzie dragged her checked bag off the rotating carousel in the restricted Minneapolis/St. Paul International baggage area. Around her, tired travelers gathered their possessions together and assembled their exit paperwork. Lizzie stacked her carry-on bag on top of her checked bag and frowned at the beat up luggage. She knew, despite appearances, that her bags had held up well, all things considered, but if she had to do it over again, she would pick a different color. A picture of her husband floated briefly through her mind. He cleared his throat and nodded knowingly at her, a satisfied twinkle in his eye. Smiling to herself, she stretched and realized that her back didn't ache, at least not in that familiar upper spot at the top of her spine. When had it disappeared? She wasn't sure. She was tired, of course. Who wouldn't be after two days of travel? But her back was fine.

Her worn clothes hung a little looser on her. She had lost twenty pounds, she guessed, and felt more power in her legs. She pulled her bags toward the customs agents, wondering why she was thinking about her weight now. Of course, she had noticed the changes in her body during the time away, but she hadn't cared. It didn't seem important. Other things had demanded her attention. When you're busy, you're busy, she thought. Is it important now? She had fought for so long to lose that extra weight, and when she paid it no mind, it fled. How strange. Should she care? Would Ugandans care? Or would they like her better the old way? She chuckled to herself.

"Anything to declare, ma'am?" The agent's voice sounded pleasant.

"No."

"Where'd you go?"

"Africa. Uganda, actually."

The veteran agent studied her for a moment, evaluating her relaxed demeanor, and then glanced down at her paperwork. "Pretty adventurous for a woman your age, if you don't mind my saying so."

Lizzie cocked an eyebrow in response, but said nothing.

The agent looked up again. "Was this business or pleasure?"

Lizzie hesitated for a moment and then gave him a crooked smile. "Definitely not business."

The agent gave a little grin. They exchanged knowing looks, almost as if they shared a secret, and then he nodded, his face opening up. "Did you have a good time, ma'am?"

Surprised, she stopped to think and pushed her glasses higher on her nose. She realized, belatedly, that they were the pair Dembe had restored. Slipping them off, she looked again at the exquisitely repaired eyewear, rotating them in her hands. She felt bad that she almost took them for granted.

"Yes," she said finally, looking the agent in the eyes. "Yes, I surely did." She put the glasses back on and focused on him. "I had a perfectly wonderful time. Thank you for asking."

The now smiling agent waved her through without any bag checks at all. "Welcome home, ma'am."

Lizzie walked by, towing her suitcases. She added a gentle sway to her hips that she hoped conveyed gratitude to the agent, if he looked.

Ahead of her, to the right, she saw a short escalator that she knew descended directly to the passenger greeting area, and home. To the left, she saw a large elevator for people with luggage and carts. Lizzie stepped left and stopped in front of the metal doors to gather herself, not yet prepared to push the call button. She knew that once she entered the elevator, she would be committed. When the doors opened down below, her excited family would see her, all except Joanie. David would be there with his wife and little Tomlin, Joanie's husband Mike, with Sandy and Will, maybe even Cecelia. Who knows who else might have come to greet her, and ask all the usual questions? She didn't know how to handle this. She knew they would be relieved to have her home, but how could she tell them she had another home now, other family members, and that she already missed them terribly? How could she *not* tell them?

This world of home smelled unfamiliar. Alien. Who was she now? She knew that she was no longer the Mom and Grandma who had left them. And maybe that's good, she told herself, but what if they wanted the old ones back? What then? She thought of her friends…and church. What would she be like at church now?

She could almost hear the jingle of her old life's harness as it tried to slide over her shoulders but she shook herself and it fell away without a sound. No. I am who I am *now* – Lizzie, Mom, Grandma and *Jjajja.* They need to hear me tell the truth. I will start from the beginning and tell it all – tell it all.

A middle-aged couple wheeling an overloaded airport cart swung around her and immediately pushed the call button. Thick metal doors slid smoothly back. They entered, the man struggling with the unbalanced cart until he cleared the door. Turning around, he waited and gave Lizzie an awkward look. "Excuse me? Are you coming?"

Lizzie stared at the open car. There was plenty of room. Was she ready? Would she ever be ready? A helpful memory playfully tickled her mind. What would Jason Bourne do?

"Yes." She looked directly at the man. "Thank you. I'm coming."

She briskly stepped into the elevator, easily rolling her luggage behind her. The man she didn't know smiled oddly at her and pushed the *down* button. As she watched the doors slide shut, Lizzie squared her shoulders, stood a little taller, breathed in deeply, and faced her future.

Author's Note

Few novels leap to the page directly from an author's mind, perfectly written and ready for purchase. This one is no different. Yes, my name is on the cover, but I am humbly aware that it required the hard work of many generous people to produce this final version. Like making a movie or raising a child, a novel is an extended collaborative effort involving many personalities, many moving parts, and a seemingly never-ending firmament of persnickety details. I would like to take a moment here to gratefully recognize some of those people.

I start thanking where I always start, with my wife, Jane. It was her ever present support and cautious coaching that kept me moving forward; it was her untiring corrections that kept me on track.

Since the bulk of this novel takes place in Kampala, a city that I have yet to physically visit, I want to thank my daughter-in-law, Diana Nakakawa Fournier, who grew up there with a delightfully stubborn *jjajja* of her own. She made sure that my Luganda language and names were accurate, that my descriptions of her hometown rang true and that the food in the book tasted right.

Special thanks to the team at Acorn Publishing – Holly Kammier and Jessica Therrien – for guiding this acorn along the dark paths writers must walk to turn a manuscript into a viable book. Holly was one of the first professionals to love my writing. We met at a

Southern California Writers' Conference, and she provided a ray of hope at a critical moment. Whatever positive development that happens next in my writing journey will be, in a large part, thanks to her timely belief in my written words.

I also wish to thank my editor, Laura Taylor. She was a godsend, not just because she was so experienced and book savvy, so careful and motivating, but because she treasured my characters. I think most writers are a timid breed, and insecure, even while proclaiming to be thick-skinned. I was terribly nervous the first time I faced Laura's assessment of my work, but I am so grateful for what she said during that phone conference.

I want to thank the artists at Damonza for their brilliant cover designs and their guidance through the nuances of formatting and fonts, encoding and all those pesky file types.

Finally, I want to say thanks to each member of my small army of beta readers, who faithfully provided input throughout the many critical junctures of this project. They may never know how much I valued what they shared and how much their efforts meant to me.

Writers often default to certain locales where they typically do their writing. It may be an office, the end of a certain table, a corner in a coffee shop, or a library cubby. I have my own personal writing hideaway where I have appeared regularly, day after day, season after season. I want to thank the architect who designed that refuge, and the kind employees who befriended me there. No, I won't be any more specific. After all, I need it to remain *my* quiet place, since I still go there most days to work on my new book.

If you're interested in learning more about me and my novels, please check out my website at *www.eafournier.com*. You can also find me on Twitter at *www.twitter.com/gammera* or visit me on Goodreads at www.goodreads.com/author/show/6967439.E_A_Fournier

In the end, I would be remiss to not acknowledge the real-life people who inspired this novel. Soon after their wedding, David and Aimee

Kyambadde started their work in Africa by helping Kampala's street boys to find a home again. Their fruitful labor in Africa continues still, but their efforts have expanded into many additional areas. No, they aren't the same as my Jedediah and Meg from the book. If anything, I'm sure my characters are pale shadows of their real selves.